The Promises We Made

T.S. CAP

INDIE FORGE PUBLISHING HOUSE

To all the girls who thought that fire inside them dimmed to ashes – it's time to get that spark back. The world deserves to see your light – and you never know, it may just bleed through someone's darkness.

CONTENT WARNING:

This book is a work of fiction that contains very dark themes that may be sensitive or triggering for some readers. Such as domestic violence (discussed and depicted), child abuse (discussed, not depicted), pregnancy and abortion, rape (depicted), explicitly sexual scenes (including but not limited to - blood play, BSM, forced orgasm, knife play, CNC), grooming, murder (depicted), light stalking, PTSD, suicide (discussed, not depicted). This book also ends on a cliff hanger. While this is romance, it is also a *dark* romance. Please consider your mental health before reading.

National Domestic Violence Hotline 800-799-7233

988 Lifeline (Suicide Prevention Hotline) dial 988 - they also have a text option as well as deaf/HOH option

Planned Parenthood Hotline 1-800-230-7526

PLAYLIST

SCAN TO LISTEN TO THE FULL PLAYLIST

Maroon by Taylor Swift
Begin Again (Taylors Version) by Taylor Swift
Complex (demo) by Katie Gregson-MacLeod
Roses by the Chainsmokers
Invisible string by Taylor Swift
Promise me everything will be okay by i don't like mirrors
Peace by Taylor Swift
Augusta by Gracie Abrams
My Boy Only Breaks His Favorite Toys by Taylor Swift
In My Room by Chance Pena
Try by P!nk
The Great War by Taylor Swift
Family Line by Conan Gray

CHAPTER ONE

SUNNY

I SHOULD BE DEAD.

Instead, I sit at the gate, waiting for my flight, picking at my nails that still have his blood in crescent moons underneath. My head throbs behind my eyes and my nose is still sensitive from the impact of his fist from the night prior.

Pulling my hood over my head to try and hide the bruises and scratches on my face, I chew the inside of my tender cheek.

There's nothing yet everything in front of me. I'm free but shackled to an escape. *A plan.*

I stare through the airport window, watching the sun rise and glisten on the ocean's surface I spent my entire life in. I love my parents for creating such a safe space for me, a magical childhood.

I'll miss this place. I'll miss the five-minute walk to the beach, running around barefoot in a bikini all day, working in my parents' garden, and painting in the forest of trees that surrounds the yellow home I grew up in. I'll miss the feel of salty sun kissed skin after a day spent in the ocean.

The last call for my flight sounds, making my heart race as I feel the weight of it all, like an anchor trying to keep me in the only place I've ever known.

Something else, something foreign, is telling me to get on that plane. Tugging me in that direction so profoundly, I have no choice but to listen.

Picking up my backpack, I throw it over my shoulder and remain still, as the war in my heart fights with my mind.

Stay or go.

I hear the call ring out one last time from overhead.

My eyes linger on the sunrise I'm so familiar with. The one I watched with my family almost every morning in our backyard. Tears well up in my eyes at the idea that I may never be able to come back.

It will still be the same sun wherever I go next.

As I turn my back to the rising sun, I fall victim to that tug pulling me from all that I know, as I walk through the gate without looking back.

TYLER

The clock strikes midnight as I sit on my couch in front of the fire with a bourbon in hand. And just like that, I'm twenty-nine years old.

Memories take over me and suddenly I'm twenty years in the past, back to when I was a little boy sitting in a hospital bed, watching the clock strike for my *ninth* birthday.

I sat there, wondering why my father hadn't been arrested—since he was the one that put me there. Even back then, I knew it was the worst it could get, as I sat in that hospital bed while my father pulled strings to wipe out the records.

It was only a short time before our last name was plastered onto the wall of the pediatric wing, in honor of a *generous* donation. One that covered up any evidence I was there, fighting for a life that *he* tried to take from me. I honestly would have let him do it, if it weren't for my sister and mother. Someone had to protect them and that task defaulted to me.

He yelled as he hit me, that *"you cannot save anyone, not even yourself."* Maybe that's why he is the way he is, because no one saved *him*.

I always clung to the hope that he would somehow change. It was the naivety that comes with being a child that made me hopeful the man who sired me would turn for the better. That maybe we could finally be the family I always craved and cried for. Then maybe I wouldn't have to worry about the bruises he'd put on my body. That one day it would finally stop. My birthday gifts would no longer be bruises, but actual presents I could unwrap. Something that was *mine*.

That night was just a reminder that it never would stop, it still hasn't to this day, but at least I knew the worst was over. Because even then, at nine years old, I knew death would be so much easier than that.

I wish I still felt that way, *hopeful*.

Growing up and seeing my parents flaws, I knew they would never change. It's like losing your religion. After that night, I didn't believe in god anymore. Not after he ignored all my unanswered tears and prayers. Not when I begged my mother to leave, but she simply ignored me, despite the fists I took in her place.

My father truly believed it was the only way to make me the man I needed to be. When ultimately, it was preparation for who *he* needed me to be.

You must be calloused, and how can you toughen up without some friction?

No, I don't believe in god anymore. I no longer believe in my father, either. That hope I clung to dissipated along with my soul, my humanity. I buried who I was supposed to be deep in a grave and stopped grieving that version of myself the moment I laid the last of the soil down. It was in that hospital bed I decided I'd be the man I needed to be, the man that he had told me to be.

Not prey, but a *predator*.

Because without my humanity, he could no longer hurt me.

No one could.

Two weeks into my twenty-ninth year, I rub my face as my twin sister talks a million words a minute. We aren't *actually* twins, everyone just calls us that because we're Irish twins, born less than a year apart. Ironically, her being the older of the two of us despite being the immature one.

She lays sprawled on my couch, playing on her phone as words continue to spill from her in an array of color and vulgarity for such an early hour of the morning. Running a hand through my short brown hair, I listen distantly as I lazily pour my coffee in my mug.

I made pour over this morning, hoping it will revive me. It had been a restless night, tossing and turning in my bed after a long night on a hunt. A personal hit of mine for a man who thought it would be a good idea to mess with my sister. He's one out of four I have my eyes on.

One down, three more to go.

Sam puts her phone down. "Anthony should be here soon, too. Then we can all walk to work together," she chimes. "Have you heard from Cole?"

"Sam," I breathe in a yawn while rubbing my eyes with my thumb and forefinger.

It's too early for this.

Grabbing my coffee, I head over to the couches and sit down with her in the living room of my townhome. It doesn't appease my parents, considering it's minimal compared to the penthouse they wanted me to take above our company building.

Space is necessary, especially because this job already consumes a lot of my life. Besides, I enjoy my little townhome. A safe space for my friends, who are more family than my own flesh and blood. *It's my safe space.* Which is far and few in between.

"Tyler," Sam catches my attention.

Her amber eyes narrow on me – a contrast to the green I inherited from our father. Though we both have brown hair, hers is streaked with hot pink, in pigtail buns most days. Our parents never really cared for the animation my sister portrays in her appearance, but I admire it. I love that she stays true to herself when our parents try so hard to suffocate it. She's a rainbow in a world full of gray.

"Yes, Sam?" I take a sip of my coffee, letting its smooth taste revive my tired bones.

Being a hitman for my own company doesn't leave a lot of room for hobbies, but thankfully coffee is one I've been able to keep. Eventually, I'd love to invest in a coffee farm or grower. I order beans from across the globe, which my sister attributes to being a coffee snob.

"Have you heard from Cole?" She asks again.

"You know how he is Sam. He will talk when he wants to talk."

The anniversary of Cole's father's death passed. That isn't necessarily the reason he's been absent the last few days. He is finishing up the business we handled last night while continuing research on the rest of our prey.

Much like myself, he grew up in a rough environment. His father left him and his mother to fend for themselves. So the anniversary is just a reminder of who he could've been if he had had a father figure in his life. Proof that maybe we all aren't so different after all. *We all do what we need to do to survive.*

All it took was a bar fight between the two of us to realize we'd be so much more powerful together. Once we were kicked out of Martha's, we found an old corner liquor store and spent the night on the curb, talking about our pasts and how we may not be so different after all. He needed a job and I needed more people in our company on my side. Through that, an unexpected brotherhood was formed, and the rest is history.

"You look like trash." Sam eyes me, pulling me from the memory.

"Thank you," I say sarcastically.

"Are you okay?"

She's nosy. I love my sister dearly, but she's definitely... *Sam*.

"Just didn't sleep well." I admit.

She just stares at me, her eyes turning to slits. "Is it Shelby?"

"Sam, for the love of God." I run a hand over my tired face.

I don't want to keep talking about that.

"Hey all I'm saying is..."

I cut her off and stand before she opens that can of worms. "I'm going to go get ready."

"Yeah yeah, put a shirt on," She waives a dismissive hand at me.

CHAPTER TWO

SUNNY

After spending the last two weeks in Oregon with my aunt and uncle, I find myself standing outside the bustling Boston airport. The time away was necessary to heal my busted face before making a jump into a travel nursing gig. The contract is longer than I'd like. When my recruiter called me with an offer at a large hospital that pays generously in a big city, I couldn't help but say yes.

I've never been to Boston, or anywhere like it for that matter, but the idea of the city seems…comforting. Hoping I'll somehow get lost in the city, my face morphing into just another one in the crowds, that way he can't find me.

If he's still alive.

I'm as far away from him as I can be without leaving the continent. It's something new and somewhere he will never expect me to go. Somewhere *I* never expected to go.

As soon as I step outside, I'm hit with the frigid morning air, reminding me I am not acclimated to this type of weather at all. I'll have to do some shopping to keep myself from freezing, considering all I have is the backpack over my shoulder.

As the driver takes me through the city, I breathe a little easier while I watch the array of red brick and greenery pass by.

As far as I'm concerned, my parents haven't seen or heard from him since the day I left. No one has. The comfort and fear of it settles deep in me. He can either be long gone or trailing me right now. *Or dead.*

The police don't have any leads, especially since he has no family or friends, either. He has no strings attached except to me. Another reason I stayed for so long – I was his only family.

Despite practically begging on my hands and knees for my parents to not send me off, they knew better than that. Clearly I wasn't in the right mental state to make decisions, which is why ultimately, I listened and ended up leaving them behind, unaware of where he is and when I can come back.

I think back to all the signs I missed that seem so obviously clear now. When the good days happened, they were *so* good. I clung to those days desperately, letting them serve as relief for the hard ones.

It never started that way, and it'd never gotten to the point of physicality until the day I left. That was another justification I used, too.

Swallowing hard, I take in the city before me. At least he gave me the push I needed to finally leave. Because looking back, I know I wouldn't have if we stayed together.

He wouldn't have let me.

I look at the checklist on my phone, noting the busy day I have tomorrow despite my fatigue.

Two weeks is a lot of time to spend in your own mind, so I need to find a distraction where I can. Being in my own mind is too dangerous right now.

TYLER

Our morning ritual stays the same with myself, Sam and

Anthony walking to work together without Cole. As head of security, he has earlier mornings than the rest of us. More often than not, he takes the truck we built together in college to beat rush hour while the rest of us walk to work.

"Let's stop and get some coffee!" Sam skips toward the doors of a little coffee shop owned by an older lady named Betty, to which she named *Betty's Beans*.

It's a place we frequent probably too much, but Betty smiles every time she sees us there. Somehow that little old lady's smile is what keeps bringing me back.

"I made coffee at home. Why didn't you just have some there?" I ask, following my sister inside.

"Tyler, your coffee is good, but you rarely ever make lattes. A girl can only drink black coffee for so long. I want my basic white bitch fufu lattes and Frappuccinos."

Anthony's golden eyes trail her path as he watches in admiration. I know he's in love with her, despite all his efforts to deny it.

He has the best intentions and just like me and Sam, tries his best to not let the thumb of his parents push him down too hard. They're part of the elite in our society as well, creating a pressure on him we all feel.

Sam isn't oblivious to his feelings, but her own towards Cole makes for a good distraction from it. If it's not Cole, then Sam wants fun, not commitment.

Sam doesn't love based on gender. She's a very fluid person and isn't guarded or particular the way I am.

Obviously I've fucked and dated in my twenty-nine years, but as heir to the Caddell Investment Firm, I'm expected to marry based off of my parents choice. I'm not allowed to commit to anyone unless it's to Shelby. I just haven't fucking found it in me to do so yet.

It's a storm looming over my head while I bide my time until the torrential downpour of it all.

I'm basically the foundation of reputation for the future of the company. While I don't care, my father, Mitchell, does. Appeasing him makes my life easier than it does going against him. After all, I'm next in line to take hold of those puppet strings. The world of the rich is a game, and my father is trying to make me the best there is.

He is the puppet master, and they are all his puppets.

"Careful man, if you look too hard you might undress her." I slap Anthony's back as I walk into the coffee shop. "And that's something I don't want to witness." His light brown skin burns with embarrassment at my comment.

We're greeted on a first name basis by the baristas behind the coffee bar. Thankfully the last name has been ditched. Almost anything successful in the city is because of the Caddell name. It makes it easier for people wanting to cling to it for success.

As an investment and wealth firm, we have a string attached to almost any business you can name. It's how we control the world around us. From something as small as investing in restaurants to political campaigns, we've somehow managed to climb to the top over generations of Caddell men.

Sam and Anthony put their orders in while I sit on a couch waiting for them and scroll through my work emails. Every so often I casually glance around the shop. It's a force of habit—needing to always be aware of my surroundings. I may have a powerful name, but that also means powerful enemies, too.

The floor to ceiling windows are open, letting in the cool air that breezes from the waterfront not too far away. Despite the old red brick architecture, it still screams modern day with the ropey green plants and rickety couches people lounge on.

"Would you like anything Tyler?" The barista asks.

I give her a smile. "No thank you."

"He's a coffee snob," Sam scoffs.

I roll my eyes. "Ignore my sister, she *is* a snob."

Sam sticks her tongue out at me and turns back to the barista.

A few tense minutes pass as the barista eyes me and talks with her coworker, giggling with each comment they exchange. Their occasional looks don't go unnoticed where the three of us wait.

"Typical. Tyler gets hit on wherever he goes," Anthony groans.

"Even more typical, Tyler will deny it or deny any passes they make at him and avoid getting a date or laid." Sam pokes.

I flick my eyes to my sister who sits across from me. It's not that I'm not interested in dating again, it's just that I'm enjoying my time alone after everything that happened with Shelby. I didn't love her, but I am exhausted after her. The idea of starting anything back up just seems too draining. Plus, I'm *arranged* to Shelby. I can't be seen with someone who isn't her until I decide what to do with her.

I have my plan, it's just a matter of going about it. I have to be meticulous, precise. Manipulate the situation to seem like it benefits those around me more than myself.

At one point, I was willing to go through with the arrangement. Things have changed, and while I may not have full freedom, I do have power. I'm willing to use it, it's just a matter of *how*.

"Prove me wrong, then," Sam challenges.

My eyes flick back to my phone to go over all the emails I already read, ignoring her.

"See," Sam says with her hands in the air as she leans back into the couch.

Their names are called for their drinks. *Thank god.*

"Thanks!" Sam yells as we walk out.

"Tyler!" The giggly barista calls. She jogs toward me with a bag. "It's on the house." She smiles, her cheeks turning red.

Looking down at her, I take the bag from her. I can't deny that she's cute. Matching chocolate brown hair and eyes. Her smile is kind. *But I am not.*

"Thank you." I peer into the bag, seeing a bagel with cream cheese.

"A hard working man needs to eat."

I rub the back of my neck, say my thank you again and head for the exit. As I walk out of the shop, I notice she wrote her name and phone number on the bag, complemented with a bunch of doodle hearts. *Fucking doodle hearts.*

"My man!" Anthony steals the bag from my hands, examining the name and number on there. "*Cassidy.*"

Walking over to see what all the commotion is about, Sam rolls her eyes and scoffs.

"She was super cute, too. You should definitely follow up with that." Anthony wraps his arm around my shoulders, taking a bite of half of the bagel.

"How about you call her?" I hand him the bag.

He rolls his eyes at me and I laugh, because I know neither of us will call her.

Sam steals the bag from his hand. "Your loss. She's mine now."

SUNNY

Nestled into the plush hotel bed, my tired bones start to relax as I scroll through my email about my contract here.

It's going to be completely different from my small town hospital, but the change feels necessary. I'd been comfortable in that hospital for my two years as a nurse. Prior to that my other years as a CNA.

I was twenty-five when I graduated with my RN, now twenty-seven with a handful of experience. Nothing like what a metro area would provide, but I'm a quick learner. I'm ready for the pace.

As I scroll, I find the email showing my orientation date. My heart drops. It's been moved to *tomorrow. Are you kidding me?*

I sit up and look around, realizing I barely have anything. Not even a place to live. Originally, I had at least an entire week to get myself settled before orientation. Why the hell did they move it?

Swallowing hard, I grab my phone to fulfill the promise of calling my parents. It's still really early in Boston, which means it'll be even earlier in California, but I know they'll already be tending to the garden and the chickens, getting ready for deliveries produced by the garden.

"Hi honey!" My mother chimes. Her big, blue–green eyes are wide with excitement. The eyes I inherited.

Looking at my round-eyed mother on the screen, my heart squeezes in my chest knowing she's so far away. I'm so lucky to have such a good relationship with my parents. Most people aren't as fortunate as I am.

I'm so sorry I had to leave you guys the way I did.

"Hey, mom. I made it safe and sound." I force a smile. I find it hard to do most days, but for them I will.

"She made it, honey!" Mom yells to my dad.

He approaches the screen, the curls of his dirty blonde hair flecked with salt and pepper falling over his forehead, just like the full mustache that sits on his upper lip. A Tom Selleck stash that my father is *very* proud of. His glasses sit on his long, strong nose as he looks at me through them.

"There is our girl," he says with a wide smile.

Feeling tears sting my eyes, I try and swallow down the knot forming in my throat. I have to keep my composure. I can't let them see me break more than I already have. It's torn them apart, I can't be responsible for more bloodshed.

I just miss you both so much already.

"Hey, dad," my voice slightly catches. "Have you...heard anything?"

"No sweetie. The police have been all over it, but it looks like Ryan fled town,"

Or is dead. I swallow hard, trying to ignore that pestering voice. *Murderer.* It whispers. *Stalking you.* I suck in a breath as I double check the lock on the hotel door while all the what-if's fester in my mind.

"But sweetie, there is no way he knows where you are. He probably left town like a little coward because he knew he would go to jail. I don't think we have to worry about him." My father tries to comfort me, seeing my eyes bounce around the room.

I know that isn't true, because of course I have to worry about him. It's why I'm here in Boston in the first place.

Sadness was rarely an emotion I felt. I was always, well, Sunny. But the years of Ryan wore me down, and the day I left was the day that part of me no longer seemed to exist.

Parts of me died because of him.

I know I'll never get those parts of myself back, but sometimes, I find her in my dreams, trying to cling to who I was. Those nights are far worse than my dreams about him, knowing I'll never get her back.

I will never be who I should've been.

"I'm just so sorry," I breathe into a cry.

I'm sorry for a lot of things. In a matter of a few hours, years of mistakes obliterated in my face, taking down everyone around me. But mostly, I'm sorry for having to leave them, their once whole girl now fragments of who she used to be.

"Sweetie," my mom coos. "Don't you ever apologize. This is not your fault at all. Listen, we are safe, he is gone right now. We are okay, you are okay, and we will catch him. That's all that matters."

"And," my father chimes. "You got a badass traveling gig!"

Here I am, twenty-seven years old, crying to my parents about a boy who broke me. Because he isn't a man. A man would never do what he did to me.

"We are just so proud of you, Sunny. You are achieving your dreams. You always wanted to be a travel nurse, and now you're doing it! You are making things happen," my mother says.

God I just adore my parents.

They have given me such a beautiful example of what love should be like. Hopefully one day I'll come to learn what that feels like instead of just what it looks like.

I swipe my runny nose with my sleeve. "I really love you guys."

"We love you too, Sunny girl." My father smiles.

"I know it's only been a few hours, but, how about you tell us about the city, when you start your job, all the things!?" My mother asks.

Smiling at my parents through the phone screen, I tell them all about it as I schedule apartment viewings for that day.

Maybe it will be okay.

TYLER

"Don't forget, we have our dinner with mom and dad tonight," Sam says as I rummage through a stack of paperwork while she lounges on the chair in front of my desk, snacking on carrot sticks.

I clench my jaw at the words. "How could I forget?"

My office is large, with panoramic windows overlooking the city and water, graced with plants from Sam. Stacked with a full bar and couches for clients that she uses more often than not.

"How the hell did *we* end up in this kind of family?" Sam asks, noting my gaze peering around the office.

"I ask myself that every day." The mayor of the city is hosting a campaign at one of the local breweries. As investors to the brewery and the campaign, we are obligated to go. I'm trying to find the contract that has the list of details they want for it.

My father's plan is to move up the political chain, and that's exactly what he's doing. Hence my arranged marriage with the daughter of the current governor. The puppet master doing his best work. It's what investors are notorious for, and how we own politicians.

"I'm betting a coffee tomorrow morning that they'll bring up Shelby tonight. Oh, and that they will try and bring up a good *suitor*," she signs with her hands. "for me to marry."

I set the papers down. "You're on. I'm betting that she will ask me as soon as I walk through the door."

"No. Mom will definitely ease her way into it so that when she does come off as nosy and annoying, she'll try and claim that she wasn't." She plays with a strand of pink hair.

We keep our lives as far as possible from that lifestyle. We were forced to deal with it growing up, but when we both turned eighteen and went to college, we tried to create as much distance between ourselves and our parents. Save for working in the same company. But it's not like we really had a say in the matter.

Caddell is large so we barely see them as it is. The headquarters is in Boston as the heart of the company, beating life into seedy satellite offices across the nation. My father gave the bulk of the work to me here while he travels frequently to manage our other campuses and contracts.

I make my appearance on those trips if he needs me for my *abilities*. While I may be heir to the Caddell fortune, I've become Mitchell's personal cleaner. It's easier to groom your son into doing your dirty work versus having a hitman on payroll and risk everything. Blood runs thick, but certainly not as thick as a payroll.

Thus, resulting in my becoming my fathers personal hitman. He needed someone in the family he could control. His own adjuster to ensure the necessary people are taken out to reach his business and political gains.

Aside from that, we never see them which lead to every other week family dinners. Our mother tries to push for weekly, but that's something we just can't commit to.

We save a weekly dinner slot for the family we made for ourselves. Every week one person from our group hosts a family dinner in their home. It's the one thing that gets me through each week, if I'm being honest. When you come from a broken family, you cling to the one you created yourself.

"Okay, well I should probably get back. Spreadsheets await," she says sarcastically.

Although my sister is wild and rebellious, she's very smart when it comes to numbers. That's why she became the head of the financial department in our company. In addition to our separation anxiety, that's also why she went to Harvard with me.

"I have a meeting I have to get to anyway. Have to finalize for the brewery campaign." I finally find the file.

Sam laughs. "It kills me you do this shit because outside of here, you just would never guess. You'd think you work somewhere more dirty and nitty gritty." With that, she's out the door.

If only you knew, Sam.

I sit in my car, staring at the house I grew up in, but never felt like home. *I hate this place.*

Normally Sam and I drive here together, but she was out tending to her art studio. So, we opted to meet one another here.

So, I wait in the truck because I have a bet waiting, and I know I won't hear the end of it if I go in without her. Things are always easier with Sam by my side.

I reach for the flowers in my passenger seat as she pulls up in her purple jeep wrangler. I may not have much in common with my mother, but that doesn't mean I don't love her. It's my ritual to bring her and Sam flowers each dinner, and each dinner my mother beams at the sight of me and the bouquet before her.

She always switches out the previous dying one with the newest, freshest one. There will come a day when she has to sit and watch the flowers die to ash, knowing she won't get another one. Questions will press her mind, the loudest being *who will protect me now?* even if she doesn't want to admit it.

She's just a product of her generation, her environment, her grooming. Just as we all are. She's the soft spoken, timid, spineless type of delicate woman with no voice. The submissive wife she was groomed to be by her upbringing.

A bang on my window jolts me from my thoughts. Looking over, I see Sam standing there. With her face pressing against the window, her flaring nostrils create perspiration on my truck window as her face squishes against it.

"You coming or what loser?"

SUNNY

I nestle myself into the mattress on the floor of my new apartment with a hot mug of tea in my hands. I'd found the bags of tea shoved into my backpack — a reminder that my parents sent me off with a small part of home.

Despite my weary body, I can't help but think *It was a good day.* I'd just gotten off a video call with my parents, considering they are the only contact in the new phone. Their words of encouragement have my frantic heart only slightly calmed.

I look around the empty studio, save for the string lights I set up, and the few necessary items I picked up. My brand new scrubs sit folded next to my bed with my pre-packed backpack for work.

All I had coming into the city was that backpack I filled before Ryan was able to wake up. If he ever did. His absence when the police arrived tells me he did. Yet that voice still pesters. *Murderer.* Blood loss like that should be considered fatal.

I cashed out my entire savings, which was enough, but not nearly so, that way he couldn't track me via card trail. Over and over my mind plays over each detail, hopeful there is no flaw in my plan.

I try to imagine the day I'll have tomorrow, wondering how the hospital and coworkers will be. I'm in need of the distraction. My paranoid thoughts have me checking the windows and locks numerous times before settling down. Even then, I still glance at them every few minutes.

The exhaustion that weighs on me grants me new hope that I'll be able to sleep through the night. I haven't been able to since the day I left. I can't shake the feeling that he can be around every corner, waiting for his chance to get back at me. If he's alive, he's angry because I did the one thing he was always afraid I'd do.

I left.

Despite the anxiety that seems to be a part of me now, I actually have a small, genuine smile because for a minute, I finally feel a little fragment of myself again.

Like Sunny.

It's a contradicting feeling — being free yet shackled. I glance around the empty apartment. There isn't much here, but if I'm being honest, it's more than I've had in a long time.

TYLER

Sam and I are greeted at the door by our mother's big smile and sparkling amber eyes. "Hello my sweeties!" She chimes with her arms open for a hug.

"Hey mom." Sam gives her a one-handed hug. Waltzing into the house, she beelines for the alcohol cart in the living room.

We always have drinks first in the living room, followed by dinner at seven. Ironic that alcohol still remains in this house when there's a *recovering* alcoholic living in it.

"Hi, mom." I wrap my mother in my arms, kissing her cheek, engulfing her in my broad, tall frame.

"Oh, my Tyler, sweetie. Are you okay? You look tired." She cups my jaw.

"It was just a long day. Doesn't help *someone* woke me up earlier than anticipated." I peer at my sister, who already has a drink in hand.

"I'm not sorry about it." She takes a sip.

"For you." I motion the flowers to my mother.

Her eyes beam as if it's a surprise. Yet my heart blooms a bit in my chest. I spent my entire life trying to keep that smile on her face. I'll take the wins where I can get them.

"Oh, these are just lovely, Tyler. Let me go change them out and then we can sit down and catch up. Come on." She grabs my hand, leading me inside then disappears into the formal dining room.

Sam approaches me with a drink ready. I take a sip, my mouth burning from the alcohol. "Damn, Sam," I choke. It's basically pure vodka.

"Cheers brother." She raises her glass.

"Okay, flowers are set up. Thank you, Tyler. I look forward to them every time." She sits on the couch, clutching a glass of wine.

"No problem, mom." I sit down across from her.

I peer around, unsure of why I do since it hasn't changed from my childhood. Floral rugs, expensive antiques in each corner. Despite the large windows, the house still has an err of darkness by the thick, closed drapes. It's a museum of old art, antique furniture, and my haunted memories.

As I watch my mother on the couch across from me, unbothered by the memories that sit with her, my own thoughts fester. I'd pulled the man she claims to love off her on that very couch.

"Your father won't be joining us. His meeting got delayed so he won't be back until later this evening." Our mothers voice interludes my thoughts, "He said he's so sorry, but he'll for sure be here at the next dinner."

"What a shame," Sam says, sarcasm like venom laced in each word. I try not to smile as I swirl my drink in my hand.

"So, what is new with you two? How is work? Sam, are you still working at that art studio thing?" Diane attempts conversation.

Sam blinks at her. "Yup."

So, it's going to be one of *those* nights.

Sam is colorful compared to our parents who are strictly black and white. Her act of rebellion is running her own little art studio to live out the artistic dream our parents tried to force out of her.

"And Tyler, honey, how are you? How is work? I hope your father isn't pushing you too hard. That man works himself to death." Diane says while taking a sip of her wine.

"Work is just fine, mom. Nothing out of the usual."

"And how is Shelby doing?" My mother pries.

There it is.

I see Sam holding back a smile as I glance at her from the corner of my eye. She scoffs a laugh into her drink, succumbing to the complete humor that is our life.

I sigh. "Oh mom, how many times do I have to tell you, that ship has sailed. For a while now." Well, it hasn't necessarily sailed, but I'm about to fucking sink it.

"I just don't understand, Tyler. She is just such a lovely girl, and comes from a good family. You have known one another since you were babies! You're *arranged.* How will you get your way out of that?" she chimes, thinking she won the battle when she brings up that fact.

I open my mouth to speak but am interrupted by the house maid. "Dinner is ready, Mrs. Caddell."

"Oh, thank god," Sam blurts, pouncing from the couch.

"Thank you, Serena. We will be right in," Our mother says, standing.

As she leads the way to the dining room, I feel Sam tug me back.

"You owe me a coffee, bitch."

The three of us sit at the too big table with the head vacant in my father's absence. Our designated seats haven't changed since we were kids.

As I stare at the empty seat, another memory floods my mind, destroying all the dry corners I've managed since the last invasion.

Just short of seven years old, Sam sat in our fathers chair, twirling around in it while wearing her brand new tutu she received that day. It was innocent, but not for long.

Soon enough, my sweet little sister was sitting on the floor, cradling her arm because he pulled it right out of its socket. I held my crying sister as I attempted to dial for help.

"You want to be a hero?" He'd asked. "I'll make you into a villain."

I can't remember much after that and I'm glad for it. If I'm being honest, I can't even remember how I got to bed that night. The next day I awoke with bruises in all the places no one would see with clothes on. Even in his drunken state, everything he did was with meticulous purpose.

Blinking away the memory, I reach for my drink, making my shirt sleeve move and expose my scars. It catches my mother's attention and her eyes fall to the evidence of what her husband did to me. As if the one running vertically across the right corner of my lips isn't a reminder any time she sees me.

His one slip up he won't let me forget.

"Don't look surprised, mother. You know what he did to me."

Sam chokes on her food, stifling a laugh, or a cry. I'm not sure. Whenever we are here, it can honestly be either.

Rolling up my sleeves to prove my point, I expose the others that lace my forearms. Some old, some new. He may not give me the scars himself anymore, but he's still responsible for them by making me his personal hitman.

"Tyler," Diane grumbles. "You know that he changed. He worked on himself and went to rehab…"

"I don't want to hear the spiel."

It's the same conversation, just different words to describe it, on a different fucking day.

It wasn't too long after his rehab I noticed his drinking again. Mitchell isn't a good person sober, and he's an even worse person drunk. I won't call myself a good man, either. In our world, we are all by products of evil, somehow; whether you're born into it or created by it through circumstance.

By my unlucky stars, I have experienced both.

"Tyler, I know you made so many sacrifices as a child…"

"Mom, just stop!" Sam yells, smacking a hand on the table. "He said cut it out. Stop making him relive things he clearly doesn't want to. Or me for that matter."

I rub a hand up and down my face, knowing she feels guilty. Her little brother had to protect her. But there is no world where I won't act as a shield to the people I love, even if it means permanent scars.

"Well, are you two going to be bringing dates to the hotel opening?" Diane changes the topic to yet another conversation we frequent.

"If I feel like it." Sam sips her drink.

Diane rolls her eyes. "What about you Tyler?" Her tone sounds hopeful, but she already knows my answer.

"Oh, please woman, you already know the answer to that. It's Tyler, when has he ever brought a date to an event? Too much of a statement." Sam laughs as she bites into a piece of roast chicken.

"I'm sure Shelby would be available."

Sam lets out a loud laugh. "HAH. Two coffees, bitch." She points her fork at me.

"That's not how it works, Sam," I mumble into my hands.

"Huh? What?" Our mother blinks, turning her head back and forth between us.

I can't help but laugh in my hands, not sure if it's from the pure comedy or pure hell of this dinner tonight.

CHAPTER THREE

SUNNY

Sweat beads my forehead as I'm jolted by the sound of my alarm. My heart pounds so hard I can feel it in my ears as it slams against my sternum.

Tapping the off button, I suck in a deep breath, trying to gain my composure. I'm disoriented, trying to understand the foreign red brick box I'm sitting in.

The last time I leased an apartment was with Ryan as two giddy kids in love, ready for the next adventure and newfound freedom in our life and as a couple.

The landlord is letting me pay cash with no legal lease. I think she knows I'm running from someone by the hopeful look on my face and the stark pink scar that now sits in the crook of my neck.

I roll myself out of bed, making a mental note to buy a coffee pot today. It's the only way I function for the day, though I'm not proud of my reliance.

I wash my face, brush my teeth, then examine myself in the mirror. Thankfully the bruises and cuts are gone, save for a mark that's there to stay on my neck. The fresh pink skin just barely healed, and is too bright for concealer to cover.

The fluorescent bathroom light does not do me justice. I still bear purplish rings under my eyes from the fitful nights of sleep. Rubbing my darkened eyes, I reorganize my thoughts.

I washed my face, moisturized…mascara, right.

Usually, I don't like to wear much makeup, especially since I spent most of my days outside, in the sun, sweating or in the ocean. Even at work, I'm either being covered in bodily fluids or sweating, wiping my face with my scrub sleeve. So the effort of makeup doesn't feel worth it.

But for today, I throw on that mascara in hopes it will get my life together the way it does my lashes. The mess of blonde curls on my head are barely manageable, but I somehow get them into a halfway decent bun.

A force of habit has me grabbing my stethoscope, ready to put it around my neck when a memory halts me. My breath is stuck in my lungs as a reminder of what it felt like when my own stethoscope was suffocating me surfaces.

I shove it in my pocket and smooth out my scrubs, trying to steady my trembling hands. Despite my attempts to control my ragged breathing, my heart still thumps frantically in my chest. Each beat a litany of small mistakes that got me to this point. All the signs I missed had I not been a girl so in love.

I use a trembling finger to graze the tender scar across my neck.

All because I loved a boy.

TYLER

My morning is spent sparring with Cole after a too long weightlifting session to blow off some steam. Running a hand through my sweaty hair has me shaking off a jab he got at my jaw. He's strong, just as strong as me, which makes sparring a challenge and keeps our skills sharp.

Cole's shoulder length black hair drips with sweat while his hazel eyes fixate on me. "Giving up so soon?" he taunts.

Taking a big swing, my fist lunges for his five o'clock shadow. He ducks, trying to hit me on my bare stomach. My abs contract, preparing to take the brunt of the blow but I'm able to veer back and get him in a choke hold. He fights but I hold firm.

Take that, cocky bastard.

"Okay, okay!" he yells, laughing in my sweaty arm.

"Giving up so soon?" I bite back as I release him.

Chuckling, he looks at his watch. "We should probably head to the office. We went over our time today. We can just shower there."

Nodding my agreement, I pack up my things. "We need to make a quick stop for coffee at Betty's."

"How come?"

"I lost a bet with Sam. I'd rather not have my balls pinned to the wall if I don't hold up to it." I sling my bag over my shoulder.

"You really think Sam will freak over a coffee?"

"Have you met Sam?" I laugh. "Besides, I could use an extra coffee. Sounds good. Something is telling me I'll need it today."

SUNNY

The lack of coffee in my system is already making itself known by a dull ache blooming in my head. I glance at my watch, noting I still have some time for a quick stop before stepping into a day of orientation.

I continue my walk towards Mass Gen, scoping out the next

coffee shop to appear in my trek. Finally, I come across a quaint little place with a fast moving line despite it's booming with people. The homey feel makes me sure the coffee will be worth it.

Within five minutes, I'm facing a cute barista staring at me with big brown eyes. "Welcome to Betty's Beans, what can I get for you?" She smiles brilliantly, an echo of the girl I was just two weeks prior.

"A large black coffee, please." Not just because I don't have the patience to wait for anything more, but because I have to save my pennies. My savings have taken a dip, and I need something for my next location because that's my life now — a girl on the run.

I wait in a corner while reading the directions on how to get to the security office to pick up my badge. This hospital is massive compared to my previous one. The maze I have to navigate through gives me anxiety, but it doesn't take much these days.

As my name is called, I shove my phone in my pocket and grab my coffee from the bar. I take a sip, relishing the taste in hopes it'll simmer down the headache already beating at my temples.

My phone rings, prompting me to shuffle items in my hands as I make my way out of the coffee shop. Just as I'm able to answer, I feel myself colliding with a hard, sweaty figure.

A not so subtle gasp leaves my lips, considering the impact and coffee that spills all over my scrubs. Large hands settle on my shoulders to steady me as I sway.

"Shit," I say, looking up, seeing who just spilled coffee all over me.

A tall body towers over mine, packed with lean muscles, each serving a purpose to build the beautiful man that stands before me. This only fuels my anger, because how can I be upset over *this*?

When I peer up at him, I'm met with shocking emerald eyes and a sweaty hoodie that hangs over short brown hair.

For a brief moment, shock flickers through those beautiful eyes, like I'm an answer to a question that has been lingering. I can't pinpoint what that means or why he feels it.

My very nature has been groomed to read body mannerisms, changes in tone and the way eyes darken or light up. I've been made to analyze every single thing about a person to predict what will happen next, and if it'll hurt or help me. It's my job as a nurse, and it became my life with Ryan, too.

There is something wild behind his green eyes now. A promise of freedom with a threat lurking right behind it. Yet, he looks at *me* as if I'm something exotic or amazing.

A fire I thought was snuffed out kindles inside of me. It's small, but it's aflame and burning. I thought it was nothing but smoke after everything that suffocated it. *Suffocated me.*

A smirk pulls his lips, so feline, so intricate as if each move of his is fluid and filled with purpose. Meticulously planned down to a simple smile that has me wondering why it's appeared.

Keeping my eyes on his, I don't say anything at all while I challenge his stare. He doesn't move out of the way or even take his hands off my shoulders. Not even a damn apology for ruining my scrubs and coffee.

Instead, he says with a voice silk like night, "What filthy words for such a pretty mouth."

TYLER

As soon as she looks up at me with those round blue-green eyes, my heart beats differently because it wants to beat only for *her*. Words can't describe what I see when I see her.

My smile only lights a small fire behind her eyes, one that is begging to become an inferno. Once the shock fades, her anger returns in the form of a scowl that scrunches the constellation of freckles across her nose. The bun of sunshine curls does absolutely nothing to reduce the height difference between us, only making my smile bigger.

That fire only grows behind her eyes, and a part of me wants to edge it on just how big those flames can get.

Clearly unamused by me, she finally looks up while I continue watching her, waiting for her to say something while refusing to remove myself from her. I search her face, waiting for her to say anything because I'm clearly so desperate to hear it.

I finally manage more words, considering my previous comment hasn't elicited any from her. "Are you okay?"

"I'm fine." She blinks, still in shock. But the tone laced between each letter tells me she isn't. In fact, her voice has a *bite*.

Just as quickly as her anger came, it's been replaced by a default of sadness. A quick glance at her watch has her pushing past me without another word.

My eyes search her body, desperate to find a badge to tell me her name, where she works, something to indicate how I can find her again because she is already running from me.

"Please, let me buy you a new coffee at least," I say, observing the coffee stains on her scrubs. "And maybe even reimburse you for the ruined scrubs," I chuckle.

Despite her pause, she still doesn't seem appeased by me. "No, thank you," she says over her shoulder.

I'm trying everything I can to just keep her here a little longer. If curiosity killed the cat, then let me find my grave because I need to know more about this girl. My heart pummels in my chest as I frantically search my own mind for reasons to make her stay. But something tells me old cards won't work on her.

"Or at least new scrubs…" I move in front of her again, blocking her path to the door.

"I've had worse things on me. I really have to go." She gathers herself as she pushes past me, her shoulder hitting my arm as she does.

Fuck, that makes me smile even harder.

"Please, I feel awful. Something tells me I was at the right place at the right time," I plead. Something tells me this isn't an accident.

Just stay a little longer.

"Sure, you tell yourself that, but the coffee stains on my brand-new scrubs on my first day tells me otherwise." She turns around, making me surrender to her escape.

"Well aren't you just a ray of sunshine." I grin, even though she can't hear me.

As I watch her walk away, I feel something in my chest tugging for me to go after her. Yet, I don't.

The only thing that remains of her is the coconut and vanilla scent that has managed to linger in the air.

Not much tends to capture my interest. A life of not reacting, not feeling has consumed me, creating a very goal, predatory mentality, allowing nothing in and nothing out. I'm a glorified hitman, my very purpose is to be calloused in order to get the job done as flawlessly as possible.

But she…she has caused something to invade my darkness and penetrate through these thick black walls. Shine light into me, making my humanity want to resurrect from the grave I buried it in years ago. Thawing what has gone so cold inside me with that little fire kindling inside of her.

And all at once, I am *obsessed*.

Something in me says that her name is the answer to a question I've been seeking my whole life.

And I'm determined to get those answers.

CHAPTER FOUR

SUNNY

WITH A BLINK, TWO WEEKS HAVE COME AND GONE. IN A schedule of routine and trying to figure out a new hospital, time escaped faster than I did that night. Since, I haven't heard anything on Ryan, only feeding into my suspicions on his whereabouts.

The next six months will be with me constantly looking over my shoulder. Maybe even a lifetime. It's practically second nature now.

I just can't shake the feeling.

But if these six months go by as quickly as those two weeks did, hopefully I won't have any problems. It was a risk taking a long contract, but at least it's far enough away. *For now.*

My little apartment is coming together nicely. It may have seemed unnecessary, but I got a little couch for a corner space. I don't know anyone here, so the couch is enough for just me, even as I look at the empty cushions. It'll probably remain that way. *Empty.*

It's slowly becoming a sanctuary for me. Still empty looking, but these touches certainly help make it a home for now. If there's anything I learned about living in a place where I had to constantly walk on eggshells, it's that it's important to make a place of peace.

It may all be pointless, buying things for an apartment that will no longer be mine in a few months. But it's mine for right now, and I'm going to relish that. He never believed I could, and yet here I am.

I can, Ryan.

I smile at the little red brick apartment before me. It's *mine*. All on my own it's mine.

My phone buzzes in my lap, signaling a photo and *Bonnie* across the screen.

"Hi, Sunny girl." My mother beams.

"Hi, mom."

"I see a new piece of furniture." She tries to peer closer as if it'll change her view.

"Oh yeah…" I toy with a loose curl from my bun.

"Seems homey," she says with a tone I don't like. "Big enough for a few extra people."

I roll my eyes. "Just enough for me." I stretch along the small couch.

"What about a painting class? Have you found a studio yet?"

Clearly my mother is pushing me to make a life outside of work and this apartment while I'm trying to keep my space small. No point in planting roots, because pulling them will be a bitch.

"Maybe I'll just get an easel and paint here." I shrug.

My mother has such an artistic soul that rubbed off a little on me. I wouldn't say I'm good, not like my mother anyways. I'm only decent, and I like painting as a mindless task. Mindless is what I need right now. Too much time in my own mind is dangerous.

We'd sit outside in the sun, covered in paint, painting anything our hearts desire. My parents really gave me the most unconventional upbringing, but I loved every minute of it. I was homeschooled up until high school because they felt that was where some major social milestones needed to be made.

That's how I met Ryan.

"Sunny girl, you've got to get out. Make some friends," she encourages. Though she tries to hide it, the look in her eyes shows me how desperately she wants the girl I used to be back.

"What's the point?" I ask. "I'm not staying."

I'm not who I used to be, but eventually I'll get better. I won't be the same. This version of me is going to have cracks, but maybe once I get my light again, it'll be able to bleed through.

"Just live your life, Sunny," she says. "That's all you can do."

There's truth to her words. But the definition of living is different to every person. Mine has changed. It was rewritten the day he ripped out the page of my book that inked the foundation of who I am. Now I have to rewrite it, but my hand is too shaky as it sits on a blank page. Because if I don't write anything at all, no one can take it from me again.

I plaster a weak smile. "I'll try."

We say our goodbyes, and I'm left with the sounds of the bustling city through my open window and my heart beating heavily in my chest.

I clutch a mug of tea and steady my breathing, despite my eyes double checking the lock on the door. *Looking For Alaska* by John Green sits in my lap, so I place my mug of tea on the arm rest and thumb through the pages.

I risked the few seconds I had while Ryan was knocked out to swipe it off the nightstand and head out the door. Call it reckless, but he already took so much, I wouldn't let him try to take that again, too.

I'd never related to Alaska until now, as I sit in the middle of my own labyrinth, unsure of which way to go in order to get out. Maybe somehow, I'll find the clues between the words printed on the pages. Or maybe we just never get out.

The crisp September night air flows through my open window. I'm not used to the cold, but it's a nice change. I've never lived alone until now. So the constant quiet is unfamiliar. Eerie. But somehow exactly what I need, even if it is a little unsettling.

I tell myself that I will get myself back. *I have to.* I have to move forward. Even if it's running from him. It's still forward, nonetheless.

And what if you're running from a ghost?

A part of me died the day I left but another part was created. Gently I'm molding that new, vulnerable part of myself, unsure of what it'll be yet. Desperately trying to gather my broken, jagged pieces, even if I keep getting cut by them.

It's only been a month, but I'm not okay with him taking more of my time than he already did. My mother was onto something, I guess.

Just live your life, Sunny.

TYLER

Sitting in a booth in our favorite bar, I watch my family as they bustle around Martha's. Owned by an ex-biker who'll kick anyone out who causes issues — Cole and I are proof of that.

You wouldn't expect a man who owns millions to be here, but something about the stale beer smell and walls lined with arcade games calls me back every time. I also can't forget the drunk bastards who dance on the rickety dance floor. It's our own personal comedy show when we play at the pool tables.

If I'm being honest, it's a fucking hole in the wall. But it's *our* hole in the wall. I enjoy places like this because I can simply be Tyler. Not Mr. Caddell, not son of Mitchell Caddell, not hitman, not predator. Only Tyler.

Initiation was to prove I'd remain loyal, to ensure my reach is limitless when it came to running and protecting our company. To do anything in my power to protect it and do my jobs without question, without hesitation. Little did I know that initiation began the moment my lungs filled with air as I entered this world.

My family is the anchor that keeps me grounded when I feel like I'm being sent into a dark oblivion. I'm convinced that's another reason my father is the way he is. He let the power and the money take over, and he became more and more hungry for it, never being able to satisfy that need. He didn't have people who loved him. Loyal out of fear, sure. But love? I wonder if he knows what that feels like.

While Cole and I start a game of pool, Sam, Anthony, and Macey chat at the table. This is where we met Macey. While her age difference may not seem so significant, she's still found her role as the little sister, the little fragile bird we all try to protect because she is the only one to not be born into the world we live in.

The lucky one.

It didn't take long to realize she'd been stood up by a date considering her hair and makeup were done up way nicer than what should exist in a bar like this. Shortly after, we welcomed her with open arms and she just simply never left.

After everyone went home, I made sure the man who stood her up knew the right way to treat a woman. You never leave a woman alone at a fucking bar. No matter how bad the date is going, you make sure she gets home safely like a man should.

Needless to say after our little encounter, he got the concept.

I watch as my sister leaps from the table and saunters where Cole and I play pool. Anthony's eyes follow her. I lean on my pool stick as I watch the love triangle unfold in front of me. A man so desperate for a woman eager to be in another man's bed.

It's messy, so fucking messy, but what family isn't?

They've helped me realize that family isn't by blood, but love. They are my true family. There was a hollowness in my chest that I'd spent my life questioning. Something that I wondered would ever feel full. Then I met them.

I keep a tight shield around our family. After Macey, no one has really been able to make their way into our circle. Even with Shelby, I hadn't told her about our dinners until six months prior to our breakup, and I also never invited her.

She was an obligation I put off for too long, and it bit me in the ass. I think a part of her knew that, which is why she did the things she did to me. Her red painted nails were sunk deep into me, leaving an imprint so deep it makes me question whether or not I'll ever be able to escape her. I have a plan, but is it worth it?

That's why I sit in this purgatory. This in between of what to do with Shelby. I have to be strategic in either choice I make. My life is a series of roles necessary for a means to an end. Whatever I do with Shelby is just that, too. If I piss off the wrong people, they will hit me where it hurts.

I look at my family, knowing they'd be the first target.

Sam's dramatic laugh breaks me out of my thoughts, and my eyes focus the moment she places her hand over Cole's callused ones. I don't even have to look to know Anthony is shifting in his seat. I do, and there he is, doing just that as Macey watches with a soft smile. Another perk of my father's grooming. I'm always somehow able to predict the next step.

Twirling my pool stick, my thoughts are brought back to the little fire in the coffee shop. She's consumed most parts of my thoughts and I don't even know her name. I don't know her age. I don't know her job. I don't know her favorite color or food. I don't know the way those pink lips feel or what ignites that fire that sits in those eyes.

I don't know anything except for one thing — I want her. If

Boston doesn't bring her back to me, then I'm just going to have to find her myself.

Another perk of my grooming — *data breach*.

As the clock strikes eleven, the music is bumped louder in que for Tuesday night Karaoke. Because for some reason, Boston is obsessed with it.

Stopping her flirtatious banter with Cole, my sister looks me dead in the eyes as she yells, "let's karaoke!"

Before I know it, I'm being drug to the tiny dance floor and a microphone is being shoved in my hand, making me cringe but still stand my ground, nonetheless.

Only for my family.

CHAPTER FIVE

SUNNY

WALKING ALONG THE HARBOR, I WATCH THE SUNLIGHT GLIMMER on the water. The air feels fresh and crisp as it fills my nose and lungs with the salt water smell. Even the sunshine feels different on my skin than at home, but somehow, it still brings a small comfort, like I'm exactly where I need to be.

As I make my way to my destination, I pass by the little shops that it's nestled between across the harbor. It must look stunning with the moon hanging above it at night. I imagine a lot of the artists getting inspiration watching the sun or night sky above the river.

With a deep inhale, I look at the sign above the door. *Color My Life*. Walking into the little shop, my heart leaps inside my chest at the sight of all the canvases, paint brushes, easels, and paints.

I peer around and see the walls painted in a magenta, the tables already prepped for the class coming, and a small stage where the teacher will guide us.

Today, I opted to take a class instead of the free paint hours. The painting we're doing is of a table with wine glasses overlooking the city. Seems fitting upon my arrival to the city, and maybe I'll even hang it up in my apartment.

I browse the place leisurely, touching the paint brushes with my free hand while the other holds a death grip on the wine bottle I brought.

A loud sound thrums from the low set stage, making me suck in a harsh breath. That's where I see the instructor, setting up on stage and picking up the paint brushes she dropped.

She's *gorgeous*.

Her dark brown hair is streaked in fiery, hot pink pieces, twirled up in a messy bun on top of her head and held together with paint brushes. Her amber eyes sparkle as she sets up the studio, the love for what she does so prevalent.

I smile at her paint covered overalls. I used to have a pair just like them. For now, I have a clean new canvas. Such a rhetoric for my life.

Red lipstick coats her lush lips and the smile never leaves her face as she continues to set up.

You won the genetic lottery.

I always preferred men, but I can respect a gorgeous woman. *And look.* After Ryan, I thought about canceling men out entirely to be honest. *Maybe I'll give it a shot.*

As if she heard my thoughts, she turns around and faces me. A brilliant smile spreads across her face, revealing beautiful straight white teeth. Did I accidentally think out loud? I give a weary smile back.

It's been so long since I've flirted.

"Welcome to Color My Life," The woman purrs. "My name is Sam. What's your name, gorgeous?" She saunters over to me.

Looking around to see if she's talking to anyone else, I straighten my spine when I realize she isn't. She finds her way to me, propping an elbow on the table with her chin in hand.

"My name's Sunny. It's nice to meet you." My cheeks heat, convincing me my freckles will burn off.

I've never done this before. I'm actually flirting with a woman.

"Wow, I love that name! Gorgeous name for a gorgeous girl. Does your name have a backstory?" She bites her pinky. This girl knows *exactly* what she's doing.

I breathe a laugh. "Um, my parents are kind of hippies. I grew up in a very sunny place, that's pretty much the reason. It's boring." I waive a hand of dismissal.

It's a partial truth, but I'm not ready to give the full story.

"Oh honey, there is no way someone like you could be boring. I can feel it," she winks. "Let's see if those curls are as wild as the girl who has them."

My jaw practically hits the floor.

She bites her lip. "You like dick, don't you?"

I bark out a laugh, realizing it's the first time I've laughed since I left home. I didn't realize how *alone* I've been since. The quiet was peaceful until it wasn't, and now it's just *lonely.*

"I have to admit that I have only ever been with men. But you're definitely making me second guess myself." I pathetically flirt back.

It's the best I can give. If I'm being honest, I've only ever been with Ryan. I had a few childhood crushes and boyfriends, but Ryan was my first and only for everything. And I think that's why this has been extra hard. I gave him everything, and when I had nothing left to give, he simply *took* it.

Sam's smile widens. "I have that effect on people. Well, when you decide to cross that bridge, you let me know. Until then, we'll just be best friends."

"That sounds like a good deal to me," I say, a weary smile on my face, because it feels like first grade all over again.

Sam's eyes roll over my body. "Now let's get to painting!" She announces as she claps her hands together.

"But, what about the other people?"

It ended up being only me.

I'm sorry mother, I tried.

Looking down at my overalls and arms, I realize I'm covered in paint, but feeling satisfied with the picture before me. It isn't perfect, but just enough to hang in my little apartment.

Sam approaches me, also covered in paint. "Damn girl, you're really good at this. Do you paint on the regular?"

"Yes, actually. I grew up painting with my mom. I haven't in about a month or so during my transition here, though. So, I figured I'd find a place I can come to regularly now that I'm settled."

"Well, come at your leisure. This is my own art studio. I opened it myself. No charge. Come and go as you wish. Use what you need." She smiles at me, her words genuine.

"I can't. Please, let me pay for my visits and the supplies I use. It's not an issue, really."

She waives a dismissive hand. "Money isn't an issue for me. This is only for sport. Besides, you and I are besties now. Remember?"

I laugh. "Thank you, that truly means so much to me." I fiddle with a paint brush. This little art studio feels safe for me. Probably safer than anywhere else, if I'm being honest.

"So, sexy Sunny, how long have you been in the city for?" Sam grabs another bottle of wine.

"About two weeks, now." I'm still trying to understand how a month has already gone by since Ryan.

"You're a baby to the city!" she chimes. "I grew up here. This city may seem like a daunting beast at first, but I promise, it truly is magical and not nearly as scary as you'd think a big city is. We definitely top New York because here, it's like a family."

"Yeah, it doesn't seem as scary as I thought, especially coming from my small town."

"What brought you here?" she asks, her amber eyes focusing on my lips.

I swallow the knot forming in my throat. Although I already feel like I can tell Sam everything, because that's simply the person she is, I just don't want to reopen the scars that finally started to mend themselves.

So, I give up a partial truth. "I'm a nurse here on a travel assignment."

"Oh god." She fans herself with her hand. "That's fucking hot."

I chuckle. "So this isn't your full-time job?"

She sits down next to me and fills our glasses again with Rosè this time. I smile. *I have a friend to drink wine with.*

I've been isolated for so long. Sure, I talk to coworkers at work, but it's work and that's it. *This* is what friends do. Share a glass of wine, and tell stories.

She's the first friend I've had in a long time.

"No, this is just the thing I actually love to do," she says sarcastically. "My parents own a big ass investing company. They're like the old money bastards." She takes a sip of her wine. "So, after years of hiding my genius ability with numbers, it finally came to light when I took the SATs in high school. God, I can't believe that was like, thirteen years ago? Anyways, regardless of my love for art, I went to college for finance and became the head of the finance department at their firm."

"Wow." I sip my wine. "You're pretty incredible. Smart, gorgeous and artsy."

"Yeah, I know." She places her chin on her hand, her amber eyes beaming with curiosity. "Tell me more about you. I want to know it all."

And I don't know why, but for some reason, I do. I tell her all about what happened with Ryan and why I came here.

Maybe because I just needed to tell *someone*. Get an outsider's view on what happened. Maybe I just needed validation that what I did was the right thing. Even though every day I beat myself up for leaving my home and my family, for leaving him the way he was, not knowing the outcome. How a part of me was lost and died the day I left. What he tried to *take* from me.

Or maybe, I'm just desperate and lonely, or plain crazy for spieling all my dirty laundry to this stranger when I told myself I wouldn't.

But for some ridiculous reason, I just know I can trust Sam. *I trust you more than myself.*

I need someone to hold me accountable. And honestly, I just need someone to make me hold on period. I've spent too long wanting to let go.

So, I swallow the knot in my throat, and tell Sam all about that day, and all the events leading up to it. How it all brought me here, in this magical city, where I sit before a woman who I know will be a friend for a lifetime.

CHAPTER SIX

TYLER

As I sit at my desk, I look out the panoramic windows of my office overlooking the harbor that has the sparkle of the city in its reflection. The finalization of the campaign event for the mayor calls for a late night, all the while finalizing my own little contracts Mitchell won't know about. Small businesses deserve our investment just as much as the big ones.

Tonight, I'm focusing on two—Leo's second restaurant and a florist who wants to open her own shop. Specifically, the florist I've been getting my mother's bouquets from for the last few years.

Originally, I met her on the streets in Boston, selling her bouquets she made at home all by herself. I became a regular and finally talked her into opening her own floral shop. Now, her shop will have its grand opening next week.

She was ecstatic when I told her my one stipulation. *Don't forget me when you become a famous wedding florist.*

Rubbing my tired eyes, I look at my watch and see it's already nine. I've been here since seven-thirty this morning. My father happened to get delayed on his trip again, leaving the work to fall on me to get done for all the other contracts we have in the works.

Escape has always been in the back of my mind, but Mitchell is powerful. While his threats seem like loose words, I'm not ready to test that theory.

I do enjoy the flexibility it gives me in my life, and I can't complain about the money either. It'll never be an issue for any of us.

That's one thing I'll give my sorry bastard father, he makes us work for our money. We're no trust fund babies. Everything we have, we had to earn, and I can appreciate that more than anything.

When my time comes to take over the company, I plan to build a new empire. Our association won't just be with rich bastards who get off on money and power.

We aren't all the same, and I'm going to prove that. The blood in our veins, the name we carry and money in our accounts is what gives us a path in this life. Many think of it as an honor, but I think of it as a curse, yet somehow, here I am at the fucking top.

Mitchell made it clear becoming a part of this life wasn't an option.

For that, I've made sure people understand my blade hurts much worse when the person on the other side of it doesn't care about causing pain. He may be the boss, but I am the one they all *fear*. Which is why the days until I claim this company cannot come sooner.

Once I finish up the bulk of my work, I utilize this spare time to start searching hospital databases nearby for that little fire from the coffee shop.

I start with Mass Gen since it's our biggest hospital, not taking any more than a few minutes before I've hacked into their system. I scour the employees' lists with no clue if she's a nurse, a CNA, an x-ray tech, or hell, even a doctor.

The list of occupations in a hospital goes on, and I know I'll be searching through thousands of names and faces before I find her. So I start with the first list, leisurely scrolling, despite my heart pounding in my chest, desperate to find her.

I lean back in my seat, passing by pictures of employees whose faces don't mean a thing to me. While something in my heart tells me that Boston will bring us back together, I'm unfortunately an impatient man at times, and this is one of them.

I *have* to know her name.

Hearing my phone buzz on my desk, I'm taken out of my hunt and pick it up, finding a text message from Mitchell. I scroll through, finding hundreds from my family chat, most being Sam.

I open the message from my father, seeing it's short, brief and to the point.

> Don't forget the hotel launch next Friday.
> Casual wear. Still business. It's yours to
> handle. Make sure you bring a date. Meaning
> Shelby. Don't fuck it up. Fix what you broke.
> We have a lot of eyes there.

I already know I'll get a message from Shelby this week. I'll do the same thing I always do; I won't respond.

My parents like to believe a man looks more respectable with a good little spineless wife on his arm as an accessory to make me look powerful, but I don't. I won't bring a date, and I sure as shit won't bring Shelby because people will talk. Those eyes my father has also have mouths.

My phone buzzes again as I get another message from my family, saying to meet at Martha's.

Stopping everything I'm doing, I pack up my things so I can go be with them. I'll finish whatever I need to do tomorrow.

I send a message and lock up my office.

> I'm on my way.

SUNNY

The busy day in the hospital has me shocked when I see it's already five. It was a no lunch kind of day, with throbbing feet and an achy back, but I'm truly enjoying the rush of it all.

Finally sitting at the nurse's station, I take a sip of my water, ready to chart. I place my stethoscope on the desk and jolt as my name is called by the charge nurse.

"Sunny!" I hear Tara yell from her place by the ambulance bay. "You're getting another one in A5. Motor Vehicle Accident running from her abusive partner. Twenty-five-year-old female coming by ambulance."

My stomach churns and flips inside out. I just nod, yelling back, "Okay!"

I look at my computer but don't actually see anything as I white knuckle the desk. While the world spins, my heart beats frantically against my sternum.

I left my life and memories in search for a freedom that is only confined to a prison. Yet they still follow me, no matter how fast I run to leave them behind. In the night they present as sinister smiles and my body being defiled. It makes me wonder how such an intense love has turned into pain.

Seeing that girl will be like seeing myself, and I'm not sure I'm ready to revisit that part of me just yet. Because I know despite what he did to her, she'll still have love in her eyes for him, regardless of the hatred that'll slowly take its place.

I don't know if I'm ready for that. My wounds are still bleeding. They haven't even had a chance to close yet. But as the ambulance pulls up and rolls the battered girl on a gurney, I realize I have no choice.

As soon as I see the broken and beaten face on the young girl, I can't stop the images of a hard fist to my face and my stethoscope wrapped around my neck.

I bring a shaky hand to where that reminder of a scar stays on my neck now. He will forever have an imprint on me, no matter how hard I try to scrub myself raw of him.

Grabbing my stethoscope with shaky hands, I place it in my scrub pocket, and enter the room where the girl waits for me.

You are safe with me.

"Good afternoon, my name is Sunny, I'll be your nurse for the next two to three hours. Can you tell me what brought you in today?" I ask, as I gently enter the room and write my name on the board.

It's protocol to make sure the patients know their reasoning for being there, because it helps us assess their mentation.

Though she's curled into herself with her knees drawn up, her grey eyes meet mine. Blood from the cut on her head drips down her face. She looks so small. So scared. And I understand the feeling.

I am so sorry this happened to you.

Her lip quivers. "I, I, I got in an accident." She musters up and swallows hard, meeting my eyes. "He just got very angry. Because I wouldn't take him back." She licks her lips. "He crashed into my car."

I approach the girl, squatting on the floor to get to her eye level. I take her scratched and bloodied hand in my own. My hand looked the same a mere month ago. She's only a few years younger than me.

Parts of me remind me of you.

"Tell me everything," I say with a gentle smile. "You're safe here." I try to remind her and myself.

We are both safe here.

Once I settle and get her stable with a plan of action, I run to the bathroom to release all the contents of my stomach. What little is in there. I heave over and over until I can't anymore. Until my abs and back hurt, and my eyes sting as fresh tears spill down my cheeks. Then I start crying, trying to place a shaky hand over my mouth, muffling the screams that want to escape.

From such a young age we are told that little boys bullying us is justified because it means they like us. In turn as we grow up, we think the man who traps us in a corner and hurts us is somehow madly in love with us. Then they blame *us*. Questions of *why did you stay* or *why didn't you leave sooner* are the first thing to leave their mouths instead of *why did he do this to you?*

The reality of my situation comes crashing down on me. *I'm running*. No matter how good life will get here, I'll always be running until I know Ryan is either dead or behind bars. And right now, I don't know either of those things. Will I ever?

I'm a statistic now. *He* did that to me.

My panic attacks have simmered down and mostly only appear in the middle of the night as dreams of my stethoscope wrapped around my neck, or mental warfare he put me through before it all came down to physicality. His mind games no longer worked, so he decided to use his fists instead. I was screaming but nothing was being heard.

Will I ever be able to move past this?

He is gone. But then that voice whispers, *but what if he finds you?*

There are warrants for his arrest. I filed a restraining order but that's just paper.

I flush the toilet with a kick of my shoe, rinse my mouth out and wash my hands. Looking at myself in the mirror, I see my once sun-kissed skin now flush with anxiety and dread. The purplish rings under my eyes seem more prominent under the fluorescent lights. My lips are chapped and dry from the heaving and lack of water from the day.

How can he still be doing this to me?

I think about the girl sitting in the room here, and how there's no way someone lets something like this happen except for the person who did it to her.

I've officially been in the city for one month.

During that time, I've spent most of it in Sam's paint shop, reading books in the public library, or in my own or Sam's apartment watching trash TV.

We decided to commemorate my monthaversary in the city by ordering take out and downing a bottle of wine while watching the Bachelorette. It's our current weekly ritual on Monday nights. For such a short time, we've somehow grown so close.

Sam plays with her brown and pink streaked hair as she lounges on my couch. The crimped tendrils hang off the arm as she watches the TV upside down. I never thought I'd have anyone but myself sitting on this couch.

It's no longer empty.

"So, we have an event on Friday. I know that's not your scene, but I promise, it's super low key. It's the grand opening of this cute, trendy hotel. It's going to be a little rooftop party. Naturally," She gestures with her wine glass, "my parents want me and Tyler to bring dates. He never does, just so he can make a statement. I tend to bring girls to piss them the fuck off. Will you come and be my date? This is just to get under my parent's skin."

"I will gladly be your date to piss your parents off." I raise my glass.

"Thank god." Sam clinks her glass with mine.

CHAPTER SEVEN

TYLER

I toy with a knife in my hands as I sit in front of a bloodied, terrified man. I always prefer to use a knife. A gun is too easy. A knife is more *precise*.

Fear has his body trembling. My first warning clearly wasn't enough, and that was me being *nice*. It's his own fault that he's landed himself here.

"Listen, man. I'm sorry, okay? I'll do anything to make it up to her." He pleads shakily. It's the same words every time. *I'm sorry. I'll do anything.*

It's the one thing I can applaud Mitchell for. He never once apologized, because he meant everything he was doing, and knew he'd do it again.

My smile only makes him tremble harder, because he knows he isn't going to leave this room alive.

In these moments, I don't have to shut my humanity off to complete my task. The world needs to be rid of people like him — men who *hurt* women. Consider it my penance to balance all the bad that I do.

Cole stands next to me with his arms crossed, his jaw flexing, clearly upset over what he did. If he's so okay to do it to her, someone he claims to love, who else has he done it to or will do it to?

I'm going to watch the blood drain from his body slowly. He's going to feel the pain he caused — and he's never going to cause it again.

"You'll never go near her again." The smile fades from my face.

"You'll never go near another woman again," Cole says, looking up from under his brows.

The man thrashes in his chair, scooting it this way and that way, but never really going anywhere. He's wasting his energy, because he isn't going to be able to run from this. *Run from me.*

"I didn't think it would end up that way! I was just trying to get her attention. I love her!" He yells.

I laugh. "If that's how you love a woman, then I surely can't let you continue." I lean back in my chair, crossing my arms.

"No! No, I swear I'll do better. I'm only human! I made a mistake," he pleas.

"Finish him up." I stand, handing the knife to Cole. Something tells me he needs to be the one to do this.

"No! Please! Please! I'll do better. I'll do anything you want! I can give you any information. Seriously, you name it and I'll do it!" he cries, thrashing more in his chair.

I kneel down to meet his face. "You really think someone like you could give someone like me useful information? Anything I need to find, *I find.* How do you think I found out about you and what you've done?" I give his face a gentle tap and get to my feet. "Meet at the gym upstairs before the opening?" I ask Cole.

"Absolutely." He stares at the sorry bastard tied to the chair.

"Sounds good. I have things I have to do. Have at it." I walk out of the room.

His screams follow me out, and I smile.

SUNNY

Standing on the rooftop on a cool September night, I rub my arms, wishing I brought a coat or scarf. The days have been deceptive by being warm, only to create chilly nights once the sun disappears to give the moon his glow.

The city buildings surround me in a sparkling array of heights and widths, lights and bustling sounds, speaking something magical.

I spent the last few weeks in the commotion of work and haven't truly taken in the magic that surrounds me here, especially from this angle. Boston truly is something else.

This place is magic.

I glance around the hotel's rooftop, looking for the color of Sam among the black suits and cocktail dresses. One person's outfit is a few paychecks of mine *at least*.

Music lightly plays in the background while people stand and talk or lounge in the chairs and couches surrounding the fire pits and pools. Waiters and waitresses dance around the venue, serving drinks and appetizers, making me feel like I don't belong in such a fancy place. It's hard to believe this is considered a small event.

I finally catch Sam mid-stride, hustling around as she greets the guests. All people who I don't know names to or their involvement to make all this happen.

Oddly enough, she's good at this, despite her parents' ideas of her. People like Sam. They feel comfortable with her, and they seem to enjoy their conversation with her. She makes people feel seen.

"My parents aren't here. Those bastards," She scowls as she scans the venue. She snatches a drink from a waiter tray and downs the flute of champagne.

"Nervous?"

"Preparing." She shimmies her shoulders.

I scan the venue too, unsure of what I'm looking for. I know it's something. There's an energy in the air, something that only Boston can claim.

That's when I feel it. *I'm being watched.*

I snap my head and see a tall man wearing a suit that matches his emerald eyes.

No fucking way.

Boston doesn't seem so big after all.

Standing there just a few meters away, he watches me with his head cocked to the side, hands in his pockets and a small smile curved on his full lips. Mirth dances behind those wild eyes, and I'm not sure if I should be flattered or afraid or both.

I grab Sam's arm, stopping her in her tracks. "Sam! That is the guy who spilled coffee all over my scrubs the second day I was here!" I look back at him, not being able to trust what I'm seeing. "Do you know who he is?"

Sam's eyes trace my path of vision, landing on the tall figure now approaching us. This man is all the same but so different from the one I saw in the coffee shop.

As he walks towards us with ease, it's no doubt he's important, considering the people vying for his attention. A simple glance their way exudes an authority that has them essentially bowing down. He serves a purpose, and he knows exactly what it is.

He is no longer just a man in a coffee shop. But I am still just the girl in the coffee shop.

Sam laughs. "Sunny, that's my *brother.*"

"Are you serious?"

"Yes! Was the coffee shop Betty's Beans?" Sam asks, watching her brother saunter towards us while my heart races faster.

"Yes! I wasn't necessarily nice to him," I admit.

"What a small fucking world." She grabs another champagne

as her eyes bounce between the two of us, ignited with anticipation.

His hair isn't the sweaty brown I saw in the coffee shop. Instead, it's groomed back, creating a more angular look to his sharp features. Each step he gets closer my heart bangs against my chest, its echoes bouncing off my ribs and making it hard to breathe.

Slinging an arm around his sister, he eyes me up and down as a smile curves the side of his mouth, bending the scar that slices through it. The only imperfection to appear on his face, and yet it still just somehow adds to him.

"Hello, Sister." He presses a kiss to her head and shifts his gaze back to me. "Why am I not shocked to see you here?"

All at once, my chaotic heart halts.

And I realize, for some reason, I'm somehow not shocked to see him here, either.

"Hello Brother!" Sam chirps a little too enthusiastically.

Her brother's grin widens as he looks at me, making whatever that energy I feel inside me kickstart and hold me hostage. A fire starts to kindle inside me, coursing into my veins and lighting me up.

I take a deep breath in, because this will be the first direct contact I have with a man since Ryan.

"Well, clearly you two have met already at Betty's Beans. But without the mess of splattered coffee and high tensions, let me formally introduce you two. Sunny, this is my not twin, twin brother, but I'm the more attractive of us, Tyler. Tyler, this is Sunny, my newfound best friend of two weeks now."

They look so much alike from the straight nose to the full lips and sharp features. Their smiles even bend the same way.

Both with the same shade of brown hair, save for Sams streaked in pink. Even though her eyes are amber and his are emerald, they both share the same sparkle. Sam's are brilliant, Tyler's are wild.

Reaching out a hand, Tyler looks at me as if he finally got an answer to something I'm not aware of. My eyes fall to the scars peeking from his suit jacket.

"It's nice to formally meet you, Sunny. My sister has kept you quite the secret the last few weeks."

"Um duh, can you blame me? Look at her. She is a master-piece," Sam says.

Tyler's eyes roll over me, as if agreeing with his sister.

My face heats. *Two for two.* I still got it. Somehow, I've managed both twins' attention. It's been so long since I've been able to entertain such a thing, noticing who notices me and not being afraid of it.

I give my hand to him, but instead of shaking it, he brings it to his full lips, kissing the skin on the back of my hand gently. My initial reaction is to pull away, but it's quickly replaced with the warmth of his lips on my chilled skin. The fire that I thought was put out and dwindled to smoke, somehow turns into a small kindle inside me.

And before I can even pull away, he uses my hand to gently and slowly spin me around, giving him a full three-sixty of my outfit. Before I can even comment on the action, he is already speaking.

"*Stunning.*" His eyes fall to my body then flick back up to me. "Well, maybe I can finally pay you back for the scrubs and coffee."

Despite the aura of authority, there's a softness in his eyes when he watches me. Like his human demeanor peaks out from the predator.

Maybe that's the whole point.

"So, how did you and my sister meet, *Sunny*?" Tyler asks,

my name rolling off his tongue as if it were made for that very purpose.

"Sunny is new to the city. She is a travel nurse here on assignment. She came into my paint studio and basically, I tried to hit on her, but you know, she is still deciding whether she plays both fields. I'll change her mind of course, but since we are such besties it can only be a now time thing. So yeah, she is this badass, gorgeous, trauma nurse exploring the best years of her life." Sam speaks for me.

"Wow, Sam," I laugh.

I'm the worst version of myself right now.

"Well, the scrubs make sense then. I hope I didn't leave permanent damage," Tyler says, swiping a drink from a tray.

"Nothing out of the regular ink and bodily fluid stains."

"Tyler, was that the day I won the bet about mom? Where are the parents anyways? I brought Sunny here to shove her in their faces." Sam scans the crowd once more.

"It's all on the heir tonight." Tyler raises his glass. "As for the coffee, yes, I was going there because of our bet. I wasn't going to, if I'm being honest, but I guess something just called me in there that day," he eyes me.

Shameless flirt. Both of them are.

"Ugh, I'm so glad I was the one who didn't get the dick during conception," Sam mumbles.

I bark out a laugh, Tyler along with me.

"You're welcome sister. I'll carry the burden for the both of us," he says. As if, it were an underlying truth to their family. It makes me wonder what went on behind closed doors with the family they seem to loathe.

"All eyes are on you, Tyler. I'm just here to be your moral support," Sam says.

By the way the tone of the party changed as he walked into the place, I know what Sam said is true.

You are a powerful man, Tyler.

And all I see surrounding him is magic.

Wild, dark magic.

Late nights have been far and few between save for the nightmares that plague my mind. Isolation has been my comfort with work as the exception. Needless to say this night, while a breath of fresh air, is also exhausting.

After Tyler went off to do heir type things and Sam escaped into a cleaning closet with a man, I decided it was my cue to leave. I try to get to bed early in hopes to tack more hours onto the few I already get, but it never happens.

I'm still haunted by you.

Shooting my friend a text that I'm heading home, I start for the exit of the rooftop. My apartment isn't too far, maybe only a few miles. My feet may scream from walking it in heels, but I can do it. Or just take my chances and walk the city barefoot. I don't care. My bed is calling my name, even if I won't get the sleep I hope for.

Just a few strides from the exit is when I notice a shadow engulfing my own. I turn around to see emerald eyes staring at me.

My first initial thought of him plays on repeat in my head. *He is the most attractive man I have ever met.* Ryan was handsome, there's no doubt about that, but Tyler, he's *devastating*.

Harsh, yet soft. Broken, yet whole. Confident, yet humble. Warning yet welcoming. A predator but so human. Something about him screams danger, but it only makes you want to fall into him more. He's the *perfect* predator. And someone I should probably avoid.

"Slipping away so soon?" He asks.

"I'm going to miss my bedtime."

His smile widens into a grin as a chuckle leaves his lips. "How are you getting home?"

"I figured I'd just walk." I motion out to the city.

I truly love walking in this city. It's so beautiful, and it gives me time to clear my mind. It hinders me from having to go back to a quiet apartment, stuck in my own thoughts and nightmares.

"I won't have that." He takes a step closer.

I blink a moment of shock and click my tongue. "I don't think anyone asked for your approval."

A smile reappears at the corner of his mouth like he enjoys my bite. "Please," he offers. "It's unsafe for you to walk alone. Let me at least get a car for you."

"I'd rather walk."

"Then let me walk with you."

"You don't have to do that."

He steps towards me, closing in the space between us. "I don't *have* to do anything."

I look up at him, refusing to wave my white flag, despite the fact I gnaw the inside of my cheek.

"Please, Sam would never forgive me for letting you go alone. My balls will be pinned to the wall." He tries to lighten the mood.

I fight the smile pulling my lips. "Well, we can't have that, can we?"

He reaches behind me, opening the door for me to exit and greets the security guard there.

Immediately he's taking his jacket off and placing it over my shoulders. "I noticed you rubbing your arms. It's a bit chilly. I imagine that wasn't your outfit of choice, but Sam is an adamant person."

Sam has a very particular style, so I'm not shocked he picked up on the fact she made me wear this two piece dress that covers most to nothing with its hip thigh slit and spaghetti straps.

"Seems like you guys share that in common. Thank you.

Don't you have to tell anyone that you're leaving?" I ask. He's the one who is supposed to be in charge of this, after all.

"I won't be missed," he whispers and winks. "Shall we?" He motions for the door that exits the building leading to the city.

Within minutes my heels are off my feet, and to my dismay, Tyler swipes them from my hands to carry them on our walk.

"So," I start. "You're the heir to your family's fortune. Sounds medieval."

He smiles with a nod while watching the ground. "If that's what you want to call forced into and legally bound to a company as soon as you came out of the womb. No ifs, ands or buts."

"Isn't there always a choice, though?" I eye him.

A muscle feathers in his jaw as he contemplates his response, looking up to the sky. "I can't tell if this is the easier or hardest choice, to be honest. It's complex in a world like mine."

"I guess you should ask yourself if it's truly what you want to do and if not, why waste your time?"

He laughs, deflecting my comment. "So, you're a nurse? What sparked that?"

I side eye him at his rebound. I'll respect it, though. God knows I want people to when they ask about my past.

"It just brought so much opportunity and I like to help people. I don't have any more of an explanation than that. I just love what I do. The thrill. I can't imagine having to sit at a desk for hours."

"I can appreciate that. That's all you need anyways, right? What kind of nurse are you?" He watches me as we walk.

Tyler is the kind of devastating that shouldn't exist. It's damaging, it's daunting, it's otherworldly. His size alone is something not seen often. A body tall and lean, packed with muscles that his white dress shirt hugs in all the best ways.

For a moment, I wonder if he's cold in the chill of the night, but realize quickly a man his size must radiate enough heat for the both of us. So I inch a little closer.

"I'm a trauma nurse," I reply.

"So, what you're telling me is, you're a badass?" He smiles, inching a bit closer, too.

My heart does something, but I can't quite pinpoint it. Aside from necessary interactions at work, this is the first leisure conversation I've had with a man since Ryan.

"If that's what you want to call it. It doesn't always feel like that." I watch the street ahead.

Ryan never appreciated my job. In fact, when he took over his parents' business, he expected me to quit my job and stay home. For what? I have no clue. It was just another form of control.

"And you travel?" he asks, still keeping his eyes on me, our arms almost touching at this point.

"Yes. This is my first assignment, actually. I've never been to a place like this before." I look up at the city night sky, the buildings around me, the moon and city lights glimmering along the water in the harbor.

Regardless of the hour, it's all still so full of life, even when people are sleeping comfortably in their homes, there's still people wandering the streets. Restaurants, bars, all filled with people smiling, laughing, sharing food and drinks.

"Where are you originally from?" He fires another question.

"So many questions. What's with the third degree?"

He's analyzing me, and rightfully so, considering I've become one of his sister's closest friends. With having so much money comes risk and trust issues on people's intentions. I realize very quickly this isn't curiosity, but interrogation.

"Well, what else are we supposed to do, walk in silence?" He teases.

"I would've been if you didn't insist on coming with me."

He grins, like he enjoys this banter between us. Something Ryan never enjoyed. He said I had a smart mouth.

"I'm from a small town in California on the coast," I finally say. It isn't too much to give, but maybe just enough to suffice his need for information on me. Before I can try and ask him a question, he fires another one.

"Did the town bore you? Is that why you left?"

His eyes are intent on me, unwilling to move, almost desperate to hear my answers. I'm curious why he feels so invested in me. This now feels beyond wanting to protect his sister.

"No. Not at all." I mean it. "I love my hometown and when I feel ready, when I *can*, I'll most likely go back."

Tyler chuckles. "A girl named Sunny from a little beach town in California."

"Yeah, my parents are very unoriginal."

"I like your name," he admits. "*Sunny.*"

Yeah, I kinda like the way it sounds laced with your voice.

We approach my small apartment building nestled in the back streets of Boston. And surprisingly, I wish we had just a little more time.

"Thanks for walking with me." I halt in front of the apartment building.

Tyler hands my shoes back. "Any time. I'm sure I'll be seeing you around again." He takes my hand in his, pressing his warm lips to it. "Goodnight, Sunny." Regardless of his goodbye, he stands like a pillar in the darkness, waiting until I'm inside.

Once I walk in, I peer out the window of the door and see a smile curve the corner of his mouth. He places his hands in his pockets and shakes his head as he turns around, disappearing into the night.

I turn around and press my back to the door, looking up at the stairs leading to my apartment. With a deep inhale, my nose is filled with a faint citrus and salt scent.

He didn't take his jacket back.

TYLER

Such a sad girl for someone named Sunny, and I'm determined to figure out why that is.

Walking back to the hotel to get my truck, her name plays in my mind over and over because I finally have the answer to my greatest question.

Sunny.

Despite her demeanor being the opposite of her name, my obsession has only rooted deeper. But one thing she does have is *fire*. An inferno waiting for her moment. Ready to incinerate you the minute you invade her space. Yet, I can't help but want to sit in her flames, accepting all the raging light and fire she gives me, ready to burn just for her.

God it was so hard to get her to crack a smile, no matter how many I gave her. Even then, she didn't. *Not once.*

I want to take the brokenness out of her eyes, make her whole because of me. Of course, *of course* I understand what it feels like to be partial. I've been feeling like that my whole fucking life. Nothing has ever made me feel complete. Almost, but never quite actually there.

Until her.

A broken man finally finds something that awakens the parts he thought were long dead. A glimpse into what it's like to be whole. A fire that somehow bleeds through what he thought was impenetrable darkness. Yeah, he's going to become obsessed with it. One glimpse at her told me everything I needed to know; that there is something connecting us, even if she doesn't know it yet.

So that's when I pull my phone out and text my sister to invite Sunny to family dinner. I want to know more about her and why her light has been dimmed so much.

That way I can put it in its fucking grave.

CHAPTER EIGHT

SUNNY

Clutching a bottle of wine in one hand, I bring my other shaky one to knock on Sam's door.

After three shifts in a row, I'm the least presentable with bags under my eyes and frizzy curls spilling out of my bun. However, Sam was insistent I come, and from what she's told me, it's an honor to be included in the family circle dinners. Essentially, I wasn't in a position to say no. If I'm being honest, a part of me didn't want to say no anyways.

"You should know by now Sunny that you don't even need to knock!" Sam yells through the door. I'm not greeted by Sam when the door opens. Instead, I'm greeted by a girl with mousy brown hair and big gray eyes.

I refrain from allowing my jaw to drop on the floor at the sight of her. It doesn't take me longer than a second to realize she's the same girl I cared for in the emergency department. That had been weeks ago. I swallow hard, trying to understand a reality where I've collided with three people all connected on such a visceral level in such a big city.

"So, you're Sunny?" She smirks. I can't decide if it's a good or bad thing being known already. "I'm Macey." She holds a hand out, nails painted in blue polish, giving me a flashback to her bloodied hand weeks prior holding mine.

"Yes." I take her hand. I have so many questions for her. She seems *so* okay.

"Sam has a major crush on you, which I'm sure you already knew, but I could see why." Macey moves from the doorway, allowing me inside. She locks the door as soon as she shuts it. "Keep those ratty boys out."

"Fair enough." I do the same thing every night with my own door.

"There's my darling Sunny Sunshine!" Sam practically leaps in my arms.

"Hello to you too, Sam," I chuckle in my friend's neck.

Sam's apartment isn't unfamiliar to me at this point. The loft is covered in a series of pink and purple furniture pieces, and despite the fact she has people coming over, the place is still covered in her own chaotic mess.

Looking at the long table to fit the whole family, I notice it's already set and ready for everyone. There is a place for me, too.

They invited me to family dinners.

Sam goes back to cooking while Macey opens and pours the wine that I brought. I sit on a barstool next to her, grateful I made *some* contribution to the dinner. I have so much to ask her, and I wonder if she's picked up on who I am — though she really shows no semblance of recognizing me.

"So, I've heard the story over and over about how you and Sam met," Macey hands me a glass filled with red wine. "The paint shop. Sam trying to hit on you. Realizing dick is your choice. Does it all seem to add up?" She smiles as she takes a sip.

"Sounds about right."

"Welcome to family dinner. Once you're in, you're in for

life. Which means you can't leave, Sunny," Sam chimes over her shoulder while cooking. The apartment fills with the smell of spices and tomatoes, indicating pasta may be on the menu for dinner tonight.

Chuckling, I take a sip of my wine to bypass the comment.

"Welcome to the family, Sunny. You're going to love it and hate it," Macey says, wrapping an arm around my shoulders.

"It's an honor." I raise my glass. Remorse hits me as soon as I say the words because I *am* leaving in a few months.

"Here, here!" Sam clanks her glass with mine and Macey's.

"So, is Tyler bringing his girlfriend?" I ask, trying to make conversation.

Both Sam and Macey start hysterically laughing. *Noted.* That is an absolute no.

"No." Macey shakes her head, her mousy brown hair shaking with it.

"That bitch can rot in hell," Sam says.

"Although, maybe an arranged marriage is what I need." Macey downs her glass.

"Oh, hush little birdy, you'll find your match!" Sam joins the conversation.

A knock sounds on the front door, followed by incessant jiggling of the knob.

"Hey! Why is it locked?!" I hear a man's voice yell through the door.

"To keep nasty boys like you out!" Sam says, still neglecting to open the door.

"We won't bite!" Another man's voice says, this one lighter, airy.

"Speak for yourself." *Tyler.* His voice is like velvet night. Soft, smooth, like I can trace my finger along it. So easy to pinpoint among others.

"Each one of you is supposed to have a key! If you lose it,

then you're responsible for changing my locks!" Sam yells, stomping towards the door.

As soon as she opens it, three tall men topple inside, all on top of the other as if they were leaning against the door.

"Nice to see you again, Sunny," Tyler purrs, straightening himself. His green eyes watch me as he comes in and rounds the island, making his way through the kitchen.

"Oh, she's a blonde! We needed a blonde, thank god," One of the two men chimes. His eyes match the brilliant smile that pulls his full lips. He is leaner than Tyler and the other man, but by no means any less strong. The warm light of Sam's apartment dances across his brown skin, complimenting his eyes in all the best ways.

"Anthony seriously?" The other man says, bringing my attention to him. He runs a hand through his dark hair, lifting it off his shoulders for a brief moment. He looks like the kind of guy my mother would tell me to stay away from in hopes I won't hop on his motorcycle.

"Hi, I'm Cole. Don't mind my brothers, they can be a bit much sometimes." His hazel eyes gleam with mirth.

"We all have our moments. I'm Sunny." I shake his hand back.

"I know." He grins.

I'm not sure what that means, but I also don't want to find out.

Everyone settles into their roles so easily. Moving around with a fluidity I never had after I moved out of my parents home.

"So, you guys do this every week?" I ask.

Tyler makes his rounds to Sam and Macey, greeting the two with kisses on the cheeks and hugs.

"Sunny." He greets me again, no doubt out of obligation, but refrains from the physical contact he gave his sisters. He has a boyish smile. One I hadn't seen on him before.

"Every single week! The day depends on schedules, events,

holidays. Things like that," Anthony says as he pours himself a drink. "But we spend every holiday together. At least part of it. Then part with the families that don't actually matter."

"Hey, speak for yourself. I actually like my family." Macey finds her place back on a barstool.

They all move in Sam's apartment as if it's their own. I couldn't even act that way in my own apartment with Ryan. Being able to see people do this so comfortably with one another feels so foreign to me.

These people found family, comfort, love, and hope in one another—despite their painful upbringings. It's a relief that it exists. That you can find it after turmoil. These friendships, this love, this life.

It all exists.

"Every week, we alternate who will host it." Tyler lays the dessert out on the kitchen island along with homemade, uncooked pasta noodles. "We do it based on our schedules and who can prepare the food. Sometimes we do potluck style. Sometimes the person cooks. Sam can't bake for her life, so we brought dessert from Mike's Pastry." He motions to the box he places on the island.

I eye the pasta. "I didn't know pasta was considered dessert."

He chuckles, picking up on my sarcasm. "I guess my pasta is just that damn good." He winks and walks to the stove to take over the cooking for Sam.

"How long have you all known one another?" I ask. I want to know all about them, hear all their stories, and learn the dynamics. I know this dinner isn't a trial run for me. No, this is it.

I'm actually a part of something now.

Tyler watches me as he moves around the kitchen, like a predator watching its prey. I'm sure introducing someone new is a scary thing, considering he and Sam love this family beyond measure.

Anthony slings an arm around me and I see a smile play on Tyler's lips. His eyes move back to the stove. *It's safe.*

"I have known these two dipshit siblings since we were in diapers." Anthony points to Sam and Tyler

"True," Sam says, flinging her spatula in the air. "We shit our pants together on the daily."

"Nasty." Macey scrunches her nose.

"Our parents know one another through money and the company. My dad has his own insurance firm. They contracted together before we even existed. My parents learned quickly I was too personable to be captivated in an insurance office. So Tyler's dad put my abilities to good use, and I somehow became a high-end party planner for all their investing journeys," Anthony says satirically.

"Sounds important." I add.

"Tyler and I got into a bar fight." Cole seats himself on Sam's purple couch. He kicks his boots onto her glass coffee table and drinks his beer.

"That's definitely a story I need to hear in detail." I note.

"Another time." Cole waives a hand. "We'll have plenty of chances now."

Against my will, a smile actually pulls my lips. I realize very quickly there is a difference between being wanted and being controlled. These people, they want me.

"Then we have our sweet little baby bird," Anthony chimes, approaching Macey on the barstool, placing his hands on her shoulders.

"Oh god," she huffs into her drink. "Why baby bird of all nicknames?"

"Moral of the story is," Tyler announces. "That family doesn't mean blood. It's love. This family is very strongly knit together, once you're in, it's impossible to get out. So, being welcomed in is a big honor. Welcome to the family Sunny." He raises a glass, his eyes focused on me with a calm threat dancing in them.

You hurt my family, I'll hurt you.

"You missed your chance, Tyler. We already did this," Sam says over her shoulder.

"Sam, don't ruin the moment!" Anthony bites back, raising his glass up. "Cheers bitches!"

"Cheers!" We all clank our glasses together.

That's that. I'm officially part of the family.

CHAPTER NINE

SUNNY

I awake in a bed unfamiliar to my own, sweat plastering my face as I place a hand over my panting chest. My heart thrums wildly, pumping fear through my veins as a threat to my sleep. My hand moves around my neck, trying to shake the feeling of his hands gripping my throat.

It's not real.

I sit up, looking around as realization settles on me. I'm in Tyler's home. A night of too many drinks at family dinner resulted in a slumber party. Apparently not an uncommon theme with this group.

While it's only my third family dinner, I've grown comfortable around them. Outside of that, I easily see them a few more times a week.

Gazing over at Sam and Macey, who are cuddled together, I'm thankful I didn't wake them. Nights are hardest because I'm unable to distract my mind from uncovering the things I hide in the daylight.

A quick glance at the clock on the nightstand tells me it's well after midnight. After trial and error, I learn it's best to get out of bed and make use of my time instead of hashing out in the sheets, tossing and turning, to try and get sleep that won't come.

Quietly, I slip out of the bed and explore the areas of Tyler's townhome. Considering the amount of money they own, I was shocked to see their choices of places to live. Though it makes sense. They don't want money to determine their lives, and I can respect that.

Bookshelves line the hallway, each meticulously placed and categorized. A smile pulls my cracked lips. Tyler is very much a type A personality. I decide to head downstairs for a glass of water and distraction.

When I make it down the open staircase, there he is. He's sitting under the only light on in the living room, which creates an illusion of a spotlight on him, as he holds a book in his hand. The dying fireplace is the only other form of light in the darkness.

With his eyes intent on the words, I see the fatigue shadowed on his face, taunting him to go to sleep. The white t-shirt and gray sweatpants tell me he tried, but failed. Shadows seem to lurk around him no matter what, complementing his sharp features.

Hearing me approach, his head shoots up, his emeralds firing daggers of concern my way as he closes the book shut with a single thud.

I notice the scars lacing his arms, each so different. Threading as white, red, pink lines over the tanned skin. My eyes move to the single scar laced through the right corner of his lips.

Are they haunting your dreams, Tyler?

"Sunny," he says, watching me stand on the last few steps of the staircase, shifting on my feet. "Are you okay?"

"Yeah, I just needed some water." I motion for the kitchen, padding my way over.

"By the look on your face, I don't think that's true." He watches me scour the kitchen for a cup.

If there's anything I learned about Tyler in the last few weeks is that he's a trained observer. He watches and picks up on things when you think no one is.

He lifts himself off the couch and walks over. Opening a cabinet, he pulls a cup out and leans over the island, handing it to me.

"Thank you. Why are you awake?" I ask, filling the cup from the tap.

He runs a hand through his hair and then down his face. "Sleep just seems impossible some nights," he admits.

"Why is that?" I pry, it's *my* turn to ask questions.

The sound of his voice is calming, bringing me back to reality as its velvetiness coats my heart. *I'm so glad you're awake, too.*

"What's with the third degree?" He teases.

I scoff before taking a sip of my water. A comfortable silence settles until he finally asks, "So, why did you come here, Sunny?" His emerald eyes focus on me. The intensity tells me that if I don't tell the truth, he will somehow find out on his own.

I swallow hard, trying to push away the panic wanting to settle in my veins. Tyler tilts his head, observing me as the shadows of the night show off all his best features.

I can't like you, Tyler.

"I already told you." I take another sip of water.

"So, are you going to tell me the truth?"

I feel something inside me. Inside my chest. Something so visceral that I won't be able to stop, no matter the destruction and pain it may cause me.

Seating myself on the couch, I avoid answering him. His eyes track me as he walks over, sitting himself on the opposite end, leaving little room between us. I swallow hard at the small distance between us. Somehow, I want to make it smaller and bigger all at once.

"We all have our traumas, Sunny. And healing is never linear.

I'm a perfect example of that. But just know that you don't have to heal alone. You don't have to *be* alone."

And he's right—healing is not linear. I wish it was, because I had this straight line. This plan that I'm determined to stick to. Yet I keep getting derailed.

"Being alone is the easiest way for no one to get hurt," I say.

A small smile curves on his mouth as he lets out a soft chuckle. "A thought for a thought?" He suggests.

My silence is an indication that I need him to start. Clearly we are two people who have a past. It's why we are here right now. It's why he has scars on his arms and I have one on my neck. They are just a preview to the ones that are inside. We sit here together because anything after midnight is awfully heavy to handle alone.

"I think that a lot of people believe money creates freedom. When in reality it just creates a different kind of prison." He toys with a loose thread on the couch. "My whole life has been planned for me. The story was written before I was born. My wife had already been arranged for me. My career. The children I should have. The place to live. Everything." His voice matches the night. "And that prison was only made worse because of the man my father is. I couldn't get us out, so I had to learn how to live in it."

"I understand that."

"I know." He meets my gaze, his eyes have a softness I've never seen on him before. "My father loves his alcohol more than his family, even if it made him a violent man." He bites the inside of his lip, formulating the words in his mind, contemplating how he'll articulate this. "One day, he came home, drunker than I'd seen him before and he tried to force himself on my mother."

My heart drops. Sam hadn't given much insight on their parents except for the fact they are very old fashioned, cold people. I just didn't think it was to this extent.

"I was eight years old. I was already in bed. Her screams rattled the house. I'll never forget it. It was the kind of scream that begged for help in a moment where no one would come. I didn't think twice before I jumped out of my bed, and I ran downstairs to him pinning her down. I grabbed a kitchen knife and got in between them. I tried to chop his dick off with a kitchen knife." He looks at nothing specifically as he lets out a small chuckle. It isn't humorous. It's the sad reality he had to face.

"He took his rage out on me. I'll spare you the details. But the initial one was snapping my wrist to get the knife out of my hand. That's what this scar is. I had to have surgery on it." He shows the line down his wrist. "I ended up in the hospital that night because of him, spending my ninth birthday there the next day."

"Your birthday…" I whisper.

"But it was me, and not my mom, not Sam, so I could live with that. Of course, with money and the connections my father has, you can make anything go away. So, he did. He made it seem like I was never even admitted in the hospital. The records were gone. The only proof was the scars on my body."

"So that's why your last name is on the pediatric wing? He paid them off." I realize out loud.

He nods. "After that night, something changed in him, in me, in our family dynamic. He learned what he can get away with, and he learned what I could handle. He learned what I was capable of." He swallows hard. "He broke me so badly that nobody else could."

I nod as tears threaten my eyes, because I understand that too. Tyler and I, we may not be so different after all. We share similar pain, in different variations.

"I spent the rest of my years in that house paying for it. Learning how to live in that prison while protecting the two things that mattered most to me." He toys with his hands in his lap. There are scars there too, and I want to lay my hand over his. But I don't.

"He would always get so frustrated with Sam." His brows crease. The only sign of emotion he's shown tonight despite the painful words and memories he is reliving. "I couldn't let her experience what I did. If anyone had to, it'd be me, never them. I just, I couldn't imagine doing that to my family, let alone my children, *your little girl.* Sam says I have a savior complex, and maybe I do. But all I know is it shielded them from him, even if I was the shield myself." He looks at his hands, peeling a callus on his palm.

I place a hand over his festering ones, feeling the calluses and scars because trembling hands need something stable, something secure to hold on to. His hands calm at my touch and his eyes meet mine.

"I've done some bad things, Sunny." A warning, no doubt. "And it makes me wonder if that's how he became the way he did. Because he was forced to do bad things, and in turn, it made him a bad person."

With a sigh, he rubs his face with his free hand but never removes the other from mine. I don't even realize until his thumb is swiping under my eye that I'm crying.

"Don't cry, little fire. *I'm okay.*" His lips twitch to a smile.

I shake my head. "It's not fair we have to learn to survive in order to get through life."

Just because someone does bad things, doesn't make them a bad person. And for some reason, I just know Tyler isn't a bad person, even if he says he has done bad things. Darkness isn't so scary anymore once you've lived in it for awhile.

"I've gotten so used to surviving, Sunny." His smile gets a little bigger. "That sometimes, it almost feels like living."

"How is that fair? How is it fair that some are given such tragic stories while others aren't?"

"I think everyone has their own tragedies." He stares at our interlocked hands, lazily drawing meaningless nothings along the skin of my knuckles and wrist.

"And despite yours, you still aren't him,"

He smiles at our hands and looks up at me. "You don't know me, Sunny. You don't know the things I've done. The thoughts in my head. Who I've been formulated to be by the world I live in. And that I continue to choose to be that person." He breaks our eye contact, bringing his gaze back to our hands.

"I'm running away from someone," I admit.

His eyes move to the scar on my neck, igniting a cold rage behind the green in his eyes. With his free hand, he goes to move the hair from my neck, exposing the scar. A gentle finger traces the tender flesh, making a shiver run up my spine and lace through my bones.

But it doesn't hurt the way I thought it would.

"He did this to you?" He whispers.

I nod, breaking my gaze from his lethal stare as I swallow down the thickness rising in my throat. Silence falls again, indicating the room he is giving me to speak if I choose to.

"We knew of one another growing up, our names and such, but we didn't really get to learn about one another until high school. We were high school sweethearts."

Maybe had I not been so young, I could've gotten out sooner, seen the signs sooner.

"His parents passed away early in our relationship from a car accident. Which felt like another reason to stay with him. It was really hard on him. Devastating. As it should be. My family was his only family."

"It became more of a necessity than a want," he says, the question lingering on the end.

"Yeah," My voice catches. "He was great. We were great. He...he was my first for everything. It was all so perfect until things just started happening." My brows crease as my memory plays over each and every detail I'd missed until it was too late.

"It was subtle. It'd start with small outbursts, leading into bigger ones. Where walls would be punched, doors slammed, things broken or thrown. He'd get angry if we didn't have sex. He'd try to talk me into it, even if I really didn't want it. Finally, I'd just give in because it was easier than dealing with him harassing me the whole time or being in a bad mood because he didn't get what he wanted. I didn't notice the subtle manipulation until it was too late."

He *winces* at my words. This lethal, dangerous predator of a man winces at *my* story. Closing his eyes, he takes in a slow deep breath again. He remains quiet, allowing me to spill secrets I'd kept for over a decade.

"I always justified it because he was never physical with me until the day I left." I rub my face. "I just…I just made stupid fucking excuses all the time. He worked too much. He didn't get enough sleep. Or that I did something wrong. I hate myself for not seeing the signs sooner, or just simply choosing to ignore it altogether and find excuses to validate his behaviors."

Tyler nods, his eyes lost in the darkness of the living room. I see his jaw flex.

"We were together for so long, and I told myself I'd only do this once, so I tried to stay and make it work between us. Then he hit me. He finally had the balls to hit me," I say through clenched teeth. "So, I hit him the fuck back,"

His eyes flick to mine. No other reaction except the glimmer of pride I'm convinced I see and a ghost of a smile on his lips.

I swallow hard and look at our hands. "I paid for that one, too."

My fingers instinctively touch the scar on my neck. It lingers as a daily reminder for me. Much like the scars Tyler has, too.

Maybe we aren't so different.

"I don't know…I don't know where he is. If he's even alive," I croak. "I got a good hit in, which is why I was able to leave. He wasn't there when the police arrived. He could be on the run or he could be dead." I bite my cheek. "But that's fine, because if anyone were to kill him, I hope it'd be me."

I've never admitted that to anyone.

The pain has become bittersweet, because in losing him, I'm hoping to find myself again. The screams that came from my heart have been silenced by my soul—leaving what was left of me. She's in search of something now, I'm just not sure what that is yet.

I don't have to rationalize my feelings with him because he understands what it's like to be abused and want your abuser to understand the depth of the hurt they caused.

"If the time ever comes, you know who to call," he says, looking at me.

I have done bad things, Sunny.

"I was a girl that clung to a boy who refused to become a man." I finally look at him. "Doesn't that make me just as guilty?"

"I think it's a lot more complicated than that."

"My parents, I don't know how they'll ever unsee that version of me. Bloodied, begging. Their home was the first place I went to. He...he killed me. The sunshine I radiated was eclipsed by him with no hint for it to end." I blink back tears. "And yet, when my father had a gun in one hand and a bat in the other to potentially finish the job, I stopped him." My voice catches. "Regardless of what he did to me."

"I still go back to my parents." He shrugs with a shake of his head. "Sunny...you don't have to justify these feelings, or feel guilty about them. Not with me."

"But he said he'd find me," I whisper, staring into the darkness of his living room.

"What?"

I finally meet his emerald eyes. "Ryan said he'd find me."

"No, he won't," he says with finality.

"You don't know that."

"If he is alive, he's on the run too, Sunny."

"Maybe," I sigh. "But how sad do I have to be before it stops hurting?" My voice catches and a tear escapes my pain in a salt tendril down my face.

In one moment we are apart and in the next, his arms are around me. Tyler presses my head to the soft white t-shirt on his chest. Pain manifests in many ways, and unfortunately for me, it's a tear streaked face and bitten down nails.

Vulnerability is a scary thing, yet here we are, two people exposing the most brutally beaten parts of our hearts. I may as well have cracked my chest open and given him my heart, because now we know parts of one another nobody else does. All without a hazed lens of who we were in comparison to who we are now. There's no expectations.

We are simply just Tyler and Sunny.

Safe hasn't been a familiar thing to me in awhile. But sitting right here, I finally feel it with him. Even when he presses his lips into my hair or when he takes in an inhale of me and gives it back. Even when I feel his heartbeat somehow sync with my own. All of these things should scare me, but they simply bring me a familiar comfort I didn't understand I need.

Amidst the tears, I smile.

All of a sudden, I don't feel like the lonely girl anymore.

CHAPTER TEN

TYLER

A FEW DAYS AFTER FAMILY DINNER, I FIND MYSELF SITTING IN MY parents' house for the family dinner I really could care less about.

Ryan.

It echoes in my mind. One name that slipped from her mouth has granted me access to a series of possibilities. That one name is simply all I need.

Straining laughter brings my attention back to the reality in front of me. These family dinners are unfortunately my way of keeping tabs on my mother. Getting eyes on her to ensure she doesn't have any marks or change in her behavior. I may be good at hiding things, but she certainly is better.

While I'd hope Mitchell knew better by now, he's unpredictable in this house. So much time outside of here is spent being precise, meticulous, with every move planned and designed for success.

In here, he's able to bleed into his natural state, staining all of us in his wake. Mitchell is one of the most rationally irrational people I know. Drinking only makes it worse.

Sam sits next to me with a spine of steel and white knuckles around her drink. A total contrast to the mouth full of sass and vulgar gestures she normally has when it's just our mother. Everything about her is unnaturally still, save for the small bounce of her foot as it hangs from her crossed legs.

I keep my calm demeanor, my body lax to show Mitchell he is simply not a threat. He gets off on power and fuels it with fear. The silence is unbearably loud until my mother finally cuts the quiet with her amber eyes longing for interaction.

I'm sorry this is all you get.

"So, Sam, how is that paint shop?" Her eyes are practically pleading the silence away at this point. The frown lines around her mouth and between her dark brows seem to crevice deeper when her husband is around.

I hacked the cameras in their house to keep tabs on her. Notifications pour through if voices get too loud or movement gets too swift. Facial recognition also alerts me as soon as Mitchell comes home for the day. All so I can know when to keep close watch of the footage. He only ever yells—the hitting stopped because he knows the consequences now.

"It's an art studio," Sam corrects her through clenched teeth.

"Right, the art studio. Do you get a lot of business?" Our mother continues, desperate for interaction.

I feel bad for her but I also don't. I tried to give her an out and she wouldn't take it. As a child, I begged her to leave him numerous times and well into adulthood, too. The conversation always stayed the same.

Now I sit here every other week, checking on my frail, soft spoken mother. Hoping when I finally see her, she isn't hiding any physical evidence from me that I wasn't able to see on the cameras.

"It brings enough. I –" Sam is cut off by Mitchell.

"What she means to say is, it pays for the bare minimum to keep it running, because a place like that can't actually be a place of true business and make a profit. Especially when you let people keep coming in for free."

My eyes flick to Mitchell sitting on the couch in front of us with a warning glare. "Watch it."

"Well, since you want to make your presence known Tyler, why don't we talk about you," he bites back.

Here we fucking go again.

Sam snaps her head towards me, her eyes wide as fear starts to glisten in them. I just roll my eyes and give her a reassuring smile.

Growing up, I was afraid of Mitchell. But after he put me in the hospital and I knew the worst was over, something in me shifted. I was no longer afraid. Even now. *Especially* now.

"Mitchell, please," My mother intervenes. "We barely get to have dinner together as it is."

"Quiet woman," he snaps.

"Do not speak to her that way." I clench the now empty glass in my hand.

"Tell me Tyler, what do you know about speaking to women when you can't even keep one long enough to make a wife?"

It's the same conversation about needing a wife on my arm. Children to become shackled as heirs to this life I hope they never have to experience. *It makes you look respectable, Tyler.* But god forbid that person be anyone outside of Shelby. Because big names make big reputations.

"You are the heir to this company! We already had you and Sam by the time we were your age. You need to marry someone of good name and breeding to have a strong front. A solid blood-line with years of success behind it."

By the determination in his voice, I can see he means what he says, and I try not to laugh.

"How can people take you seriously when you are galli-vanting around the city, not bringing a single date to any of your events? You're acting like a bachelor. You left Shelby when everyone was so sure you were going to marry. You pissed off a lot of fucking people. Burned too many damn bridges with that. We all still expect you to follow through with your promise. Your *duty*." He points at me.

"Daddy, that's *not* Tyler. He made it very clear to Shelby his intentions–" Sam tries to chime in before getting cut off once again.

"And you too Sam," he bites back. "You are basically whoring around the city! You guys don't think I have eyes all around, but I do. You of all people should know this Tyler since you have eyes everywhere too. You *are* my eyes. You guys are grown ass adults who come from a good pedigree, and you are creating a disgrace to the Caddell name! You are a damn whore Sam!"

I'm on my feet with a fist balled into his dress shirt before he can take another sip of his drink. The glass falls over and shatters on the ground, but my eyes are set on his greens that match my own.

"I will only say this one more time before I sew those lips shut," I say with lethal calm. "Watch your fucking mouth. I will not think twice before I make you live the nightmares you made me live as a child." I release him, sending him back into the cushions of his chair.

"Mom, leave the house. Go to a friend's home or get a hotel for the night. I won't leave until you do. You need to be away from him while he is drunk like this."

I look at my sister who sits still on the couch, her body frozen in fear as she aimlessly stares where our father sits.

"Let's go, Sam." I reach a hand for her.

"Tyler, please," my mother pleads.

Mitchell gets up from the couch and slams the bottle of bourbon in the fire, making it roar.

"Mom, you heard my words. Please," I urge through clenched teeth. I've been begging her all my life.

Mitchell glares at us with blazing eyes, stalking towards us, slightly swaying. Her contemplation speaks volumes. Allow me to physically handle this or leave to avoid it all. But by the grace of whatever exists, she grabs her coat and keys and rushes to the door.

I shove Mitchell back, and guide Sam out of the house. The harsh cold hits our skin as we walk out the door and get our coats on. Mitchell's yells and slurs are silenced by shutting the door in his face, despite the chaos of them ringing in my head.

I wish this was the last time, but I know it isn't. It never is.

We always come back.

Opening Diane's car door, I kiss her head. "I love you, mom. Text me when you make it. Do not, for the love of god, come back here tonight. Let him sleep it off." I hand her my credit card in case she needs a hotel for the night.

Mitchell has frozen their accounts before, and without his money, she has nothing except me. That's why I always keep an extra card on hand, for her.

Unshed tears gloss her eyes as she looks up at me. "Tyler, I'm so sorry. He hasn't drank like that in a while…"

Holding a hand up, not wanting to hear any more of her excuses, I press another kiss to her cheek. I lean my arms on the open window frame and bend down to tell her one last thing. "The offer still stands. It always does. When you've had enough, you tell me."

As soon as I shut the door of Sam's jeep wrangler, I pinch the brim of my nose and take in a deep inhale. A groan leaves my throat as I rub my face while leaning back into the seat. One single glance at Sam tells me she's just as exhausted as I feel.

"Martha's?" She asks.

"Yes, please," I laugh. It's like she can read my mind.

She smiles at me. "I'll text the family right now." She pulls her phone out, her purple nails tapping the screen speedily.

I hear my own phone alert within a few seconds, getting notifications from my family's chat and everyone agreeing to meet at Martha's. A message from Sunny comes through, bringing just a hint of a smile to my lips.

Getting off work, be there in 30.

I like you, Sunny.

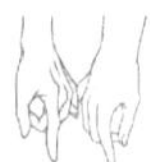

As soon as we get to Martha's, my phone lights up with my mother telling me she's made it to the hotel. I rub my face and check her location anyways. Thankfully, she is where she says she is.

I check my bank account to make sure the purchase of the hotel room is on there for more assurance. To my dismay, it is. Breathing out a shaky breath, I check the cameras in their house for one last reassurance. The feed shows Mitchell sitting by the fire, smoking a cigar, and downing another glass of amber poison. Jumping camera to camera, the house is empty aside from him.

My attention is brought back to reality as Anthony arrives, followed by Cole, then Macey, and then the final piece. I know she's here before I even look up. As soon as I do, Sunny is walking through the door, wearing her scrubs, which seem to be a frequent outfit of hers.

I like you in scrubs, Sunny.

Cole and Sam order drinks with Anthony following after. Macey must be securing a pool table for the night. I sit at our regular booth, itching to look at my phone again. So I glance at it, checking my mother's location to find it's still at the hotel, just like it was five minutes ago. With my eyes set on my phone again, I feel a soft plop right next to me in the booth. Her presence wafts me in a wave of coconut and vanilla.

Sunny.

"You look like you need a drink." She scoots right next to me. My heart starts pounding in my chest at the contact. It's fucking criminal, the way she makes me feel.

Her red nose and rosy cheeks tells me she was outside for far too long. "Did you *walk* here?" I ask.

A series of alternate solutions run through my head. I can order her a car. Hell, I'll *buy* her a fucking car. I'll pick her up. Instead, she chooses to walk and cause every instinct in me to fire off because of it.

She nibbles the inside of her lip, then tongues the spot she bit. "That's none of your concern. It looks like drinks are taken care of." She nods towards the love triangle standing at the bar. "And please, someone has to tell me the story on *that*."

It is my concern when it's you, Sunny.

I sigh and laugh, rubbing my face because this woman will be the death of my peace.

"Well," I start. "I'm sure there is much more to the story. I know Sam has hooked up with both of them. I really don't want to know the details of 'hooked up', but I do know that Anthony has basically been in love with her since we were kids."

Sunny watches the triangle at the bar. "And Cole?" she asks, now looking at me. I like that she cares about my family. *Our family.*

"Cole is like that off limits thing. You know Sam, when you tell her she can't do something, it only makes her want to do it more."

Cole's attention is very tentatively directed to the bar, while Sam's is on Cole, and Anthony's is on Sam. I let out a humorless laugh.

Sunny nods as her eyes flick back and forth between me and the bar. "I can relate to that. Like you have something to prove."

"Is that why you walk alone at night? Because I asked you not to?"

"Makes sense you're next in line to own an investment company, because you sure are pretty fucking invested in me." She arches a brow.

I lick my lips and smile. "A girl with a fire who's not afraid to burn anyone," I lean into her. "Kinda makes my dick hard."

Her mouth falls open and before she can answer, Macey seats herself into the booth next to Sunny. "Hey, Sunny!" She slings an arm around her.

My chuckle doesn't go past her, considering she throws a scowl over her shoulder as she hugs Macey back. I like how comfortable our family is with her, despite how little time they've known her. It takes a lot for a person to make their way here, but it didn't take much with her.

It's easy to love Sunny.

"So, I did some flirting to make sure we have the pool table for the night." Macey smiles victoriously.

"So that explains the disappearance," I say.

I tap my fingers on the table, trying to stop myself from checking Diane's location again and fail miserably. *She's still there*. I look up and see Sunny watching me.

The love triangle comes back with beers for everyone, passing them around. She scoots in closer to me to let everyone else in, and my fucking heart does a somersault inside my chest feeling her so close. Our thighs press up against one another. Her face is so close to mine that I can take in all the small details that make up the girl I'm quickly falling for.

The seventeen freckles that cover her nose, the different curls that cascade around her head. The way her smile is forced and doesn't reach her lips, only fueling my desire to get a genuine one from her.

As the beers are being passed around, she lays a hand over

mine, the one that rests on my phone. "Put it away. Be in the moment," she whispers.

I look at her, bending to her will and immediately put it in my pocket.

I'll do anything for you, Sunny.

SUNNY

All it took was two rounds of beers and time spent with his family for the Tyler I know to reemerge.

I know now why he loves these small moments with his family. Here, with them, he doesn't have to be the protector and problem solver. He can simply just be Tyler.

A smile threatens my lips, because he hasn't touched his phone since I asked him to put it away.

While Macey and Tyler chat, my attention is pulled towards Sam, Anthony and Cole at the pool table. Sam stands with a pool stick parallel to her. Her long brown hair runs down her back as she blinks her sparkling amber eyes at Cole. Despite the fact Anthony is right next to her with an arm wrapped around her and resting on the pool table.

What happened between you two?

Cole doesn't pay mind to either as he shoots his shot on a striped ball and misses. On cue, Sam steps out of Anthony's orbit and flips her hair with a mischievous glint in her eye. She bends over in front of Cole even though his eyes are everywhere else.

"Oh god," I hear Macey groan, watching the love triangle before us. "Let me go intervene." She scoots out of the booth.

Glancing towards Tyler, I see him sitting with his broad shoulders slumped. There's a boyish grin on his face as he rubs his hands on his jean clad thighs. For someone with such a smart mouth earlier, he looks almost…coy now.

"What?" I face him.

The right corner of his lips tug.

I can't like you, Tyler.

"Nothing." He takes another sip of his beer.

"Spit it out, Caddell," I snap back.

"Don't use that name."

"Right." I forgot. He hates using his family name because of the man who sired it to him. I blame that one on the beer.

Here, with his family, he is simply Tyler. A boyish grin, softer features and greens that seem to sparkle. Outside of this, he is Caddell. Sharp features, lethal calm and suits.

I wonder how often he gets to be Tyler, and how often he is punished for it.

"Dance with me." Not a question, but a statement.

"What?" I blink at his outstretched hand. It isn't uncommon for people to dance at Martha's. But we are *not* those people.

He arches a brow. "What?"

"How many beers have you had?" I laugh. Before I can protest, he is pulling me out of the booth and dragging me to the dance floor.

The dress shirt he originally wore is long gone. Now he only wears the black undershirt, exposing all the tragically beautiful scars that lace the muscles of his arms.

One spin has me stumbling on my feet and nose diving into his chest. While I'd normally be embarrassed, the way it makes him laugh has me wanting to do it again and again. It's genuine and light, like stars poking from the darkness that surrounds him.

I like that I make you laugh.

"I wish I could say this is because of the alcohol, but this would happen even if I was sober," I admit. His hand still grips my hip while the other keeps his fingers threaded through mine.

Our laughter subsides, but our gazes hold. While his breathing is so calm, I've almost forgotten how to.

"Sunny..." he whispers.

Then my phone rings.

"Have some decency. She can purr all she wants, but I at least expect dinner first." He smirks.

I slap his chest and he places his hand over mine, keeping it there, feeling his calm heartbeat. I don't pull away, and use my free hand to look at the caller.

"It's my parents," I say, looking back up at him.

Those greens don't leave my face, and I look away because I'm scared about what I see forming in them. What it does to me. How it makes me feel that fire wanting to reignite all over again.

Definitely the alcohol.

"Hey mom," I answer.

"Hey, honey," She greets me. The tone in her voice has a thickness forming in my throat.

"What's wrong?" I plug my other ear to hear her over the music.

Tyler tilts his head, his emerald eyes darken. Once a boyish human, turned into a cold predator. Just like that, he went from Tyler to Caddell in an instant.

"Do you have a free minute to talk? And a safe place to do it?" My father asks.

"Sure." I start walking outside, leaving Tyler alone on the dance floor. "Sorry," I mouth the words to him as I step into the cold October night.

"Okay, I'm in a quiet place now. Are you guys alright?" I scrape my shoe against the faded paint lines that divide the parking spots. I squeeze the phone tighter, trying to calm my trembling hands.

"We have an update on Ryan."

CHAPTER ELEVEN

SUNNY

"Okay," I let out a shaky breath.

"We decided to call you since it's later there and the detectives didn't want to wake you in case you were sleeping. We told them we would update you, we just didn't want to have to wait until tomorrow," My mother says.

"Okay." Because it's the only word I can say.

I'd been living in this in-between for the last two months. Is he dead after crawling his way out of the apartment? Is he alive, hiding in the shadows and already found me, waiting for his moment for revenge? I hate myself for wishing he's dead, but I hate myself even more for wishing he's alive.

"Sunny…Ryan he's…he's alive."

I suck in a sharp breath and squeeze my eyes shut to refrain from letting the pain win again. And yet, it still does, as if the scar on my neck and the cracks of my heart aren't enough of a brand.

No. Now I feel it even deeper. It laces through my bones, writing all the wrongs I have ever done that led up to this point, into my very marrow.

I'll never be able to escape it. I'll never be able to escape *him*. He has left a permanent mark that I'll never be able to undo.

"They found a last known location for him. He wasn't here. He wasn't home," My father says gently.

"Where?"

"He went to Oregon. They think he knows you were there."

I throw a hand over my mouth as a sob escapes my throat. Everything I hoped wouldn't happen is somehow happening. A tear escapes, sliding down my cheek and onto the concrete as evidence of my pain.

"Honey, he will not find you. We won't let him, and the detectives are working hard to find him. They have a lead now, this is a scary thing, but it's good. It's good because now we know where he could be." My mother tries to reassure me.

He is following me.

"He won't be able to find you, Sunny. You are all the way across the country in a place you would never even expect. You do not need to leave. Even the detectives said so. He always knew you have family in Oregon." My father continues, but it does nothing to the panic settling in my chest, awakening from its brief slumber.

"Okay, I love you guys," I rush out and then hang up the call. They've already seen me break enough. Once was already too much. My phone rings again with my fathers name and face on the screen. I stare at it, another tear drop slipping from my eyes and onto the screen.

This is a nightmare coming to me even when I'm not asleep.

"Sunny?"

Tyler.

I jolt, dropping my phone to the ground with a thud. I squat down to pick it up and swipe my nose with the sleeve of my undershirt. Finally turning to look at him, hoping the shadows of the parking lot mask the evidence of my pain.

"I used to be," I croak.

His brows crease and within a second he is closing the space between us. Reaching his arms out, he cradles my face, wiping the tears that unwillingly cascade down it.

"What is it? What happened?"

"*Tyler*," I whisper through a small, pathetic sob. Words are difficult when your voice has been silenced for so long.

"I'm here, baby. What is it? What do you need?" He searches my face.

Another sob claws up my throat, but I get the courage to meet his eyes. "He's alive."

The slow roll of his throat catches my attention, leading me to the beat of his pulse in his neck. Each beat gets faster and faster.

"The detectives found that he *is* or *was* in Oregon. Which is where I was, before coming here. With my aunt and uncle." I clear my throat of the screams that are building up. "So, it's either coincidence because he knew I had family there, or that he truly has found a way to trace my departure."

He nods slowly, his eyes looking elsewhere. Nowhere in this realm, but in his own mind. Finally he brings his gaze back to me. "What do you need from me, Sunny?"

The words are heavy on my tongue. The voice that had been stripped from me clawing at the back of my throat for release. It wants only to yell all the worst things I've kept at bay, because I'm too afraid to admit them.

"I hate myself," I finally breathe. I look at him as tears line my eyes and spill over my cheeks, but I won't run from them anymore. He shakes his head, denying it before anything more can be said.

"Stop," he warns, but his voice catches, too.

"I had a perfect life. And because of my choices, here I am now. I ignored it for so long. I could've left. I could've..."

"You didn't *choose* to be abused," he reminds me.

I know he's right, but the anger remains nonetheless. I have this big, ugly, festering wound of anger, pain and hurt. It used to be filled with sunshine and a fire that refused to succumb to the snuff of anyone else. Now, all that's left are burnt ashes and smoke decaying what's left of me. What if it never heals? What if *I* never heal?

It's this moment I realize I'm hyperventilating with a hand around my throat as I try to step out of his arms. The ground feels like it's caving from my feet while simultaneously spinning.

I am a statistic.

He brings his forehead to mine. "Breathe, Sunny. *Breathe.*"

I follow his commands, closing my eyes and allowing his body to mold to mine as a means to ground me. The tears continue, but I can finally breathe.

"I'm so sorry," I whisper.

"*Don't.* Don't even go there, Sunny." He shakes his head.

"I need to scream," I admit.

"Then scream." He offers his chest as a barrier to muffle my hurt, taking my pain from me and making it his own.

So I scream.

My pain reverberates through his body, and he holds onto me tightly, refusing to let go despite it all. It's unyielding, the way his body clings to mine. No matter the way it continues over and over and over through the echoes of my screams. The way the hurt and pain courses through my veins, as a living thing, now penetrates his skin and becomes a part of him.

Those screams turn into sobs. The anger breaking down my vulnerable heart and manifesting to the pain that has rooted itself so deeply in me. Forcing my body to give way to the abundance of emotions I've finally released. Through it all, Tyler's voice still laces the air, that's filled with my anguish, in a series of soft *it's okay* and *I'm here.*

"I've got you Sunny. I've got you."

And I cry harder, thinking, maybe this is what he needed growing up, too. To just scream all the pain away. For someone to actually listen because that's what he did for me.

He listened.

"Let me find him," he whispers into my hair.

"What?" I look up at him through watery eyes.

He cups my face, gently stroking the tears away. He meets my gaze, those greens a lethal calm.

"Let me find him. If you tell me everything, I can find him and put an end to it all." He continues brushing my tears with his thumbs. "Just give me the word Sunny."

I have done bad things, Sunny.

Shaking my head, more tears well up in my eyes as I try to step back. Bringing him here would make things worse. I want to be as far away from Ryan as possible. Tyler finding him would mean bringing him back into my life.

I may still be shackled, but at least my links are longer. I can live with that.

"No," I whisper.

"Sunny, please. I can put an end to this. Let me and Cole find him. If you can just give me something other than his first name. Give me more." He holds me tighter now, trying to make me look at him.

"*No,*" I sob again. "The detectives said that he is probably just doing what I'm doing—moving on. Moving past this and trying to start a new life."

"You cannot let him walk freely from this. You can't let him get away with it. You and I both know he isn't just trying to move on." His eyes search my face for the answer I refuse to give him.

"He won't stop, Tyler. He won't stop if you bring him here. If you find him. What if the court sides with him because I hit him back and left him for dead?"

"We don't need the court, baby. I can make that go away, too. I can make it as if he never even existed."

I've done bad things, Sunny.

As I look into his eyes, I realize just how much power Tyler holds. Though he won't tell me or give away any details in what he does, it only encourages that curiosity inside me. My mind stuck wondering the lengths he'd go to protect those he cares about.

You've killed people, Tyler.

Mitchell uses him for this very reason. Now I know why Tyler has said his world is one of no law. I will not be like Mitchell—using him for his abilities, for my own benefit.

I just need to stick to the plan. *Stick to the plan.*

Just because Ryan is in Oregon doesn't have to mean anything. We visited there all the time. It's a place he is familiar with, where he can move on, too.

"Promise me, Tyler," I say through more tears and clenched teeth.

His face fractures, knowing what I'm going to make him promise.

"Promise me you won't abuse that power. Just let me stick to my plan. Okay? Let me stick to my plan and live my life." I sniffle. "Promise me you won't go down that dark path. Promise me you won't be like your father abusing the power, the system. Promise me you won't do what I think you want to do," I plead. "Swear it. Swear it on Sam, the family. On us. Our friendship. I'll never forgive you, Tyler. I will never forgive you if you shatter that promise and become who you always feared." I refuse to be a contributing factor to the abuse he's endured. He deserves normalcy. "I don't care if you do it for anything else but not for me. *Not for me.* I won't forgive you. I won't forgive myself."

He stares at me, contemplating, his chest moving slowly up and down. His pulse still bounds in his neck, the only indication of his true thoughts. The only flaw in the lethal calm exterior he presents. His eyes move up and down me, his predatory character breaking as a flash of pain fractures his facade.

He nods. "Okay."

"Promise." I hold my pinky up.

"I promise, Sunny." He hooks his pinky with mine.

CHAPTER TWELVE

SUNNY

THE BACHELORETTE PLAYS ON THE TV WHILE SAM AND I SIT ON the couch with bowls of pasta in our laps—compliments of her brother. Our uncontrollable laughter overcomes what's being said on the screen. A closing shift at the public library explains Macey's absence, but we have a bowl of pasta waiting for her in the microwave.

With how impressed I am at the public library here, Mace promised me a job if the nursing gig changes. The good thing with nursing is I'm too busy keeping my patients alive to spiral down the dark hole that has become my own mind.

"We should apply to be on the bachelor," Sam says while she plays with a pink strand of hair, watching the TV.

"That's not very keep a low profile and run from your abusive ex, of me to do."

She barks out a laugh. "See, this is why we are friends. We can bring humor into our traumas."

That's practically the foundation of our friendship.

I clear my throat. "Speaking of traumas, when the hell are you going to tell me the dynamic between you, Cole, and Anthony?"

I'm hoping it'll be something as comical as a threesome between the three gone wrong. Unfortunately, the look in Sam's eyes tells me it's something much deeper.

She smiles at the screen. "I was waiting for you to ask. I'm surprised it took you this long."

I shrug. "I know what it's like to not want to unleash your traumas. No obligation to tell me if you aren't comfortable. But the obvious is pretty blaring between the three of you."

"Cole and I… we hooked up one night. I could go on about the things Cole has done for me and why I feel the way I do." She toys with a thread on the couch. "While I'm not proud of it, considering I knew Anthony's feelings for me, we slept together too. But that's a story for another time," she sighs. "One night after Martha's, Cole gave me a ride home. Tyler normally would have, but he called it early since he had a big meeting at work the next morning. Anyways, when he got to my place, I asked him to come in and he did." She shrugs. "It was one of the best nights I've ever experienced. It made it even better knowing we both made that decision soberly. Nothing influenced us except for genuine feelings." She smiles. "Or so I thought. It made me fall more in love with him, even though it probably didn't mean the same to him. He acted so odd after that night, and still does to this day. I can't help but wonder if it's because he knew."

"Knew what?" I ask.

"That I got pregnant." She looks at me.

I blink, trying to stifle my reaction.

"Let me just pick your jaw up off the floor," she teases. "One second." She places her glass of wine on the coffee table and runs upstairs.

Sam got pregnant with Cole's baby.

This is a lot more complex than I anticipated. I figured it was a drunken mess of a one-night stand, not this.

I sit anxiously on the couch as I wait for Sam's return. Soon after her departure, she comes back downstairs holding a small pink box. Placing it in her lap, she opens the lid and pulls out a single sonogram. There in the middle is a tiny little baby. *An actual baby.*

"This was her. I was nine weeks."

"She's beautiful."

"Isn't she?" She looks at the picture with admiration that has my eyes glistening. The love and pain in her eyes speaks volumes. I examine the picture, leaving the silence for her to take reins on how she wants the rest of the conversation to go.

"It was a cliché. My period was late. I took a test, and it was clear as day positive. I was waiting to tell Cole because I wanted it to be special. I wanted him to be *excited*." She smiles sadly. "I know he didn't love me the way I love him, but I hoped that maybe this would make him fall in love with me the way I always hoped he would. And I know that's awful to think but regardless, we still love one another, even if just as friends. We still *share* love. That baby would've been loved no matter what. With our family, they wouldn't know anything else, even if their parents weren't together. I was actually excited, but then I started bleeding."

I've held one too many mothers crying in my arms as their baby, slowly and painfully, was taken from their body in a bloody mess. To think Sam had to go through that. *I'm so sorry Sam.*

"Macey took me to the emergency room where I learned I was miscarrying. I already knew before they even confirmed it. I mean, why else would I be bleeding so much? Anyways, she is the only one who knows. I never told Cole because I felt like it would be too painful for him to know. Why tell him anyways since she no longer existed?" Sam traces a finger along the outline of her baby in the sonogram.

"Sam… I'm so sorry." In my experience, I learned there was absolutely nothing more you could say. I never felt I had a maternal instinct and I certainly never pegged Sam to, either. But the way she looks at the picture tells me everything I need to know about the love of a mother.

"It's okay. I sometimes wonder if he knew. Because ever since then, he's been so off towards me. Or maybe it's because he regrets hooking up. Who knows."

"Do you ever think you'll tell him?"

"No. There's no point. This was a year ago, anyway. If I could do it over, I would've told him as soon as I found out. It would've been nice to experience that with him even if it was for a brief moment. I know he would've wanted it. Even if as friends, even if as more, he would've wanted it."

I nod in understanding. "You'd make such a good mom, Sam. I can't wait to see that day come for you."

"Does that mean you're going to stay here?" She raises an eyebrow.

"Slow down there," I laugh.

"Can I use this to guilt trip you now?" She laughs.

I just roll my eyes. "Again, that's not very, stay low key, running from your abusive ex of me, now is it?"

"I'll kick his ass, don't worry." She places the sonogram back into the box where the pregnancy test lays, along with a little onesie inside. My heart cracks.

I wrap my arms around her. "I'm so thankful for you."

"You too, Sunny." She hugs me back.

Tying my hair into a curly mess atop my head, I look in the mirror at a girl who has no clue how to fight. I found my way out of a situation where luck somehow had my hand. Luck won't be my reliance anymore, and skill will be in my back pocket if the situation arises again. Now that I know Ryan is alive, the chances of that are so much greater.

That's why I took up Tyler's offer to train at his gym with him and the guys. It'll be nice knowing I can have some type of leverage if needed.

My phone buzzes on the bathroom counter, drawing my attention from the stranger in the mirror to my screen with Tyler's name on it.

> I'm so sorry, I'll be running a bit late due to work. Cole and Anthony will be there. Cole is on his way to pick you up. You are not walking. Please don't fight me on this, Sunny.

I blink, and before I can type out an argument, a knock on my door halts me.

Gathering my things, I shoot a text to Tyler.

> Fine. But only for tonight. I'm expecting something to make up for your lack of presence.

> And what might that be, little fire?

A smirk pulls my lips.

> I'll come up with something.

> If you can't think of anything, I have a whole list of ways I can make it up to you.

I bite the inside of my cheek.

> A whole list, huh? What might those things be?

> Oh no, I'd rather show you than tell you. Besides, I'd like to see your suggestions first. Mine may be a bit too....much.

My heart beats a little harder in my chest.

> It's a deal. See you soon.

Friends. That's all.

I open the door to find Cole leaning against the frame. "Ready?"

"I have no choice at this point, right?" I shut the door and lock it behind me.

He chuckles, but the smile fades fast. "I hope that it's okay, but Tyler told us your story to prepare us for training you. The fact you knocked him out in one blow is really impressive."

"You think so? I just called it beginner's luck."

"Yeah, you're probably right. I can't wait to see you get your ass kicked." He playfully bumps into me. "You're brave and what you're doing is brave. You put on such a good front, and I want you to know I'm here if you ever need a friend."

"That's why it's called a front, because I'm hiding a lot behind it," I admit.

"We all are, Sunny. Just know you don't have to carry it alone."

"Same to you, Cole." I grab his hand. He slings an arm around my shoulders and plants a kiss on my head. As we approach the truck, he opens the door for me.

"No motorcycle today?" I ask.

"Tyler would have my head if I put you on a motorcycle." He shuts the door.

Of course he would.

"You guys share the truck?"

He leans into the door frame. "Absolutely. We built her together when we were in college." He taps the metal.

"That's incredible. She reminds me of my truck back home," I say, gazing around it. It's a beater for sure, just like how mine was. But it's *their* beater. It means something to them.

"Oh yeah?" He leans against the truck and crosses his arms. "What kind?"

"Just an old teal Chevy nineteen ninety-five truck. It used to be my dad's."

"Why does that not surprise me," he chuckles and closes the door.

Hopping in the driver's seat he says, "Okay, now let's go kick Anthony and Tyler's ass."

I like that idea.

TYLER

I feel guilty not being there at the start of Sunny's first training session. Coming from abuse, my first training session was emotional in many ways. It was such a conflicting feeling—training to protect yourself because someone is actively trying to hurt you, while simultaneously knowing the power has been in your hands the whole time. It was just a matter of learning about it.

I've been stuck in meetings all damn day, trying to tie loose ends for one of our campaigns for the governor in the spring. It's months away, but we need the extra time to plan.

Everything will be dripping in roses and diamonds. Important figures will be there. A good impression is imperative or else votes will go to shit. I'd rather not have to take out the other running governor, so you bet your ass Goodman's campaign is going to be unlike any other. Besides, I need to get on his good side since he's Shelby's father.

I have my plan now, I just needed the answer to all the questions I'd been chasing. That is blonde curls, round eyes, and a constellation of freckles.

Sitting at my desk, I rummage through the piles of papers for each company we partnered with today. I secured four major contracts and that isn't including the campaign in the spring.

I roll the sleeves of my shirt up and rub a hand over my face, looking at the mess on my desk. It was a good business day, but I'm fucking exhausted. The better half of my morning was spent completing hits to secure some of the contracts today.

"Don't look too stressed, this isn't even half of it." I hear Mitchell say in the doorway.

Flicking my eyes to him, I see he's wearing a suit like normal. A smug smile pulls his lips and amusement dances in his cold eyes. Not even a glimmer of pride for what I've accomplished today.

"I'm not stressed, just tired. It's been a long day," I say, keeping my eyes on the papers I'm sorting through. I don't want to give him the time of day. I have to give what little is left to Sunny.

"Get used to it. When you become owner, you're going to have a lot of these days." He sits in the chair in front of my desk. "And not only the company politics, but the social ones. The household politics. A wife. children. It's endless."

I roll my eyes. "Funny, I don't recall you being a hitman while running the company. As much as I'd love to sit here and talk about my future, I have obligations to tend to." I dismiss him.

He doesn't budge from the seat as a sadistic smile spreads on his face. "Unless it's a wife and children, or the company, those obligations don't matter."

"Interesting, because the wife and children obligation didn't seem to matter to you, either."

"I did what I needed to do to provide for my family."

"Okay, Mitchell. You keep telling yourself that. Now I need to go do what I need to do to support *my* family." I stack the papers and pack my things.

"You have an obligation to this company, Tyler. If late nights are necessary, then you just have to deal. You've learned your lesson about avoiding tasks in initiation."

I sling my bag over my shoulder. "Have a good night, Mitchell." I walk out the door and grab my phone to see a text from Cole.

She is doing really well. Small, but fiery.

I smile at my brother's words.
I already knew that.

SUNNY

With shaky hands, I bring the trembling water bottle to my mouth. I'm being put to *work*. The evidence of it sliding down my skin in sweaty tendrils. Cole and Anthony playfully swat and taunt one another, all skills they just passed onto me obliterated as they fight like two drunk girls.

"Don't be a little bitch come on, come on," Cole taunts.

Anthony somehow smacks Cole on the head, making sweat splatter from his long, dark hair.

"Ow! What the hell was that?" Cole asks, rubbing his head.

"It clearly worked." Anthony shrugs.

The two start grappling around like children. Tumbling on the ground as the air fills with their laughter, echoing around the light music filling the gym.

"You must've given me all you know if *that's* how you two fight," I tease. I won't complain, it's a nice view of muscles and sweat.

"Alright, alright. Sunny you're up." Cole waves me over.

Anthony fills the wordless air with chants and praises of encouragement to me, making me distracted and laughing.

"Okay, tell me more about yourselves." I swipe at a loose hair in my face.

"We are pretty boring people," Cole says as he swings an arm, and I duck from it. "Good job."

"Hey, speak for yourself. I'm a very interesting person." Anthony places a hand on his chest and bats his eyelashes.

"Okay then, pretty boy, tell her all about how spectacular you are." Cole takes a drink of water, giving me a second to breathe.

"Well then we would be here all night." Anthony smiles.

"Okay, back at it." Cole raises the pads for me to hit.

Mid punch I hear the door open as Tyler walks in. One glance tells me all I need to know about the day he had. If the flexed jaw and dark eyes don't say it enough, then the half buttoned dress shirt that clings to his tense muscles does.

While one hand holds his gym bag, the free one runs a hand through his once neatly groomed hair. He tugs at the already loose tie around his neck, flexing the exposed muscles of his forearms that showcase his scars.

"Sorry I'm late. It was just a crazy day." He throws his stuff down and starts unbuttoning his shirt. "I hear you're kicking some ass," he says, peeling the shirt off his body, revealing a white shirt underneath.

Somehow, that's a good look on him, too. *It all is a good look on him.* For a moment, I hope he'll peel that white t-shirt off too so I can see it all.

"I feel like my ass is being handed to me, if I'm being honest. These two over here can't stop bickering like an old married couple."

"Hey, what happens at fight club stays at fight club!" Anthony quips.

Tyler laughs as he places the now balled up shirt in his bag. He approaches, taking my hand in his and spins me around gently to see me in my athletic get up. "Look at you, huh? I'll be out in a few minutes. Just going to change really quick. Keep thinking about those ways I can make it up to you, little fire." He grabs the bag and heads to the bathroom.

A smile plays at my lips, but I'm a little sad I won't see shirtless Tyler. Bringing my gaze back to the other two men, I realize they are staring at me with smug smiles on their faces.

"What?" I try to play innocent.

"We know, he's pretty," Anthony teases.

You're right, he is pretty.

I make a mental list of all the ways he can make it up to me.

CHAPTER THIRTEEN
TYLER

FRESHLY SHOWERED, I TOSS A LOG INTO THE CRACKLING FIRE while my coffee steeps in the french press. After a morning spent in the gym with Cole and time in our downstairs interrogation room, a shower was necessary to wash the blood and sweat off my body.

We've made it to man two out of four. I want it as a slow burn so they each know what's coming their way—anxiously anticipating who is next and how it'll be done. They can run, but little do they know we find fulfillment in finding them. The guy who threw the drugs in Sam's drink will be my final kill. I have the perfect way to put an end to his existence—everything will come full circle.

Once my coffee is poured, I make my way into my downstairs office. The panoramic windows behind my desk give view to the gloomy day. The still heaviness of the dark clouds threaten a storm, only encouraging me to stay in my home rather than go to the event Mitchell dumped on me tonight.

I leisurely type and scroll away on my computer, waiting for my coffee to give me the energy necessary to pull my tired body upstairs and slip into a suit that'll be close to suffocating me all night.

With a sigh, I rub my tired eyes. There's only so much you can do with a name. Multiple monitors face me with an abundance of information, and yet it all does nothing for me.

All the tools in this room help me in my hunts. From the books lined on one wall to the weapons displayed on the other. Guns, knives, bows—each perfectly placed with a specific purpose behind them. Even in my place of peace that is my home, I need to be prepared.

After working on my computer for a few hours, I make my way to my bedroom to trade my sweatpants for a suit. I place my coffee on my dresser and go into my walk-in closet to sort through my selection.

Hearing my phone buzz on my nightstand, I pick it up to see two texts from my sister.

> Brace yourself, Shelby is making an
> appearance tonight.

I clench my jaw, regardless of the fact I knew this would happen. Shelby is chasing her forgiveness by showing up to events and putting a show on for what a good little wife she'd make. We didn't have a relationship, we had an obligation. One that still lingers over my head.

If she was a smarter woman and waited, we probably would've married for the sake of name and game. But she did what she did, and I met my little fire.

I read the second text.

> Also, I'm bringing Sunny as my date. I
> somehow convinced her LOL

I smile. *Sorry Sam, she's going to be my date soon.*

SUNNY

This time around, I was able to choose my own outfit. No longer falling victim to those dazzling amber eyes Sam utilizes as a lethal weapon.

My triumph faded quickly when my cream sweater dress not only failed to fight off the cold October air, but also made me look severely underdressed to the suits and cocktail dresses before me.

I instinctively wrap my arms around myself as we walk in. Meanwhile, Sam is wearing a fiery red cocktail dress that clings to her body with a black peacoat to fight off the creeping winter that is upon us. Her normally crimped hair is now straight in a high, tasteful ponytail. A glimpse at her gives me a mental note to allow her to dress me for the next event.

As a restaurant opening, I assumed the attire was casual, but the diamond studded necklaces and watches that are six months of paychecks scream otherwise.

Much like a lot of the city's architecture, the building has walls of red brick with wine bottle fixtures hanging from vaulted ceilings. Despite the cold night, the outdoor patio has numerous people talking and sipping their cocktails under twinkle lights and heaters. It's beautiful. Grander than any fancy restaurant from my hometown.

We check our coats, which I only ever thought was something that happened in movies, and make our way into the chattering crowds.

After living in such a small town, where our world seemed so small, I sometimes feel this version of my life is a dream. And I've just barely dipped my toe into it.

I stare into the crowd as memories wrap around my throat, taking hold of me and all my attention. Most nights I wake in a panic, thinking all this time I've been asleep, and I'll wake with

Ryan still next to me. Then I spend the rest of the night having to touch everything in my apartment to assure myself it's real.

Bringing me back to reality, I feel Sam's arm link through mine as she guides us through the masses of people. "I think Tyler and the rest are here already."

I already know because I feel it. *I feel him.* It's an indescribable, yet palpable sensation. My gaze is pulled to the patio where he stands, talking to a group of business partners. As we approach the patio to greet him, Sam is pulled by a man dazzling over her outfit.

I feel a drink get placed in my hand by Sam as she continues to entertain him. She introduces us, but it all feels like background noise to the beautiful outfit he wears of sequins and glitter.

I soon forget his name as my eyes trail back to where Tyler still stands, engaging in conversation. The businessman in him at the forefront while the Tyler I know isn't even an echo in existence.

A woman approaches from the crowds with a red lipped smile that matches her nails, and bleach blonde hair that looks too good for the color of blonde she is. She is practically a life size barbie. Stunning, with no flaws that the human eye can point out even if they try.

As she nears Tyler's side, she reaches her arms to him, slithering up his bicep and clutching him as she rests her head on his shoulder. I stare blankly, trying to decipher between the feelings that are fighting one another inside me, and why I'm allowing myself to feel them in the first place.

He looks unbothered, save for the slight flex in his jaw. She laughs, throwing her head back, baring perfect teeth, which was expected, and then continues her roaming hands on his body casually.

A primal rage sparks in my chest, ready to ignite. That festering flame warming as it flickers, getting bigger with each beat of my heart. A yank happens in my chest, something that feels so visceral. Tyler looks at me as soon as I feel it, almost like he feels it, too.

That invisible string.

When we lock eyes, it's almost like I can see it. That palpable thing I can't quite discern, manifesting into something just for us. Something only we can understand as we stare at one another from across the venue.

A smirk pulls his lips slowly. He keeps his eyes locked on me while he takes a sip of his drink, despite the fact the barbie and the men surrounding him are vying for his attention.

I arch a brow with a tilt of my head. His grin grows wider. The heat of his stare has my toes curling, but I don't break it. I hold those emeralds, determined to break down the man who screams predator to show I'm not afraid.

I won't let you win.

His smile only grows more, curving that scar that goes through his lips. *And I like it.* I like that his attention is stuck on me despite the fact everyone else is desperate for it.

He cheers his drink to me, but I don't exchange the offer as I hold his stare. A laugh sounds from him, only egging on the desperation of the barbie for his attention. Her red nails run up the lapels of his suit and then around his neck. And yet, he is still watching *me.*

When that doesn't snag his attention, her red nails sink into the skin of his cheek, forcing his head in her direction.

I grip my glass tighter as the fire that settles inside my chest rages to an inferno. It's when he looks down at her with *disinterest,* I almost feel relief. I don't know why. Maybe I don't like the idea of him liking someone like that. Maybe I don't like the idea of him liking anyone at all. No matter, I finally pull my eyes away.

"Fuck. Shelby is here," Sam says next to me.

"Shelby?" I ask, the name sounding distantly familiar.

"Her father is the governor. So naturally, our parents had to pawn Tyler off to wed her so they could place their foot deeper in the political realm. He hasn't actually done it yet. I think he is prolonging the inevitable, or he is formulating some sort of plan to get out of it. The parents gave him until thirty years old."

"What happens then?" I ask.

"I have no clue, but I also really don't want to find out," she says, eyes wide and off somewhere that isn't here.

"They can't do that. I mean, it's the twenty-first century."

"History repeats itself. It's been accomplished before, it can be accomplished again. Our world is very different from yours, Sunny."

I glance back at the couple. They do look good together. Their children would be stunning.

"Tyler tried for a while with her so that when they married it wouldn't be just for convenience. Also because a part of him thought maybe he could find something deeper to her than the bleach in her hair. But Shelby did something that Tyler refuses to speak about. So he broke it off and has been essentially biding his time since. Makes me feel like he has something up his sleeve."

"Do you think Tyler will change his mind and forgive her?"

Sam laughs. "No. If there's anything I know about my brother, you don't cross him. He's a powerful motherfucker. And a scary one. He's planning something, I'm sure of it. Regardless of the fact that Shelby's parents still have a deposit on the wedding venue."

They have a wedding venue.

"Understandable," I say. "She is gorgeous though."

"Gotta love plastic surgery," she laughs. "Come on, let's go snag a bar table. I'm hungry."

I take my time down the long, dark brick hallway from the bathroom to the main dining area. The sounds of the venue are muffled in here, a moment of relief before it's time to paste a smile on my face and be introduced to names I'll soon forget.

In the shadows, a tall figure emerges. "You didn't come say hi," Tyler's voice echoes through the muffled voices reaching through the hall.

"Mmmm," I hum as I wrap my arms around myself, trying to hide the clear difference in attire between us. "You seemed preoccupied."

He arches a brow as he walks towards me with his hands in his pockets. "Preoccupied, or annoyed?" He leans against the wall. A lazy smile sits on his lips, his greens softer in the dim lighting of the hallway.

"I guess you're the judge of that one."

He flicks his eyes to my dress, half covered by my arms. "I like that dress."

Despite myself, I feel a blush cover my cheeks. "I feel a little underdressed. Especially compared to Shelby."

Why did I say that?

Tyler laughs. Actually laughs. "So, Sam told you who that was."

"Why do you let her treat you like that? So maybe you could get laid tonight?"

Tyler's smile fades as fast as it came. "Why does it bother you, Sunny?"

He *knows* what he is asking. The right questions to reveal an admission of something I refuse and will keep sealed on my tongue, despite the words desperately pressing to get out.

"Because you spend all your time saving everyone else but yourself." I want to suck the words back in as soon as they are spoken, but what's done is done.

Tyler *winces* as if my words actually *mean* something to him.

"I don't need saving, Sunny. Why does it bother you, how *she* treats *me*?"

My brows crease, and anger kindles inside my chest. "Who touches another human like that? You expect me to not tolerate Ryan, but you tolerate her?"

It's how it started with Ryan. Small aggressions here and there. Grabbing my arm too firmly. Grabbing my face too firmly. Slamming a door too aggressively. Throwing an object near me but never at me. It's the same thing I told myself over and over— it wasn't anything serious until, *until it was.*

"There is nothing I can't handle." He smiles. A symphony of laughs rings from the dining area, taking our attention for a brief moment. We both look at one another again.

"Duty calls," I say.

He lulls his head against the wall and pushes off, slowly making his trek to the dining area in slow, measured steps.

"Tyler," I call out.

He turns around, his hands in his pockets. He keeps silent, allowing me to finish my sentence.

"You're...you're getting married," I say, the question desperately hanging on the end of the statement, hopeful a choice is an option.

"Yeah." He nods, walking backwards with a grin. "But not to who they think."

CHAPTER FOURTEEN

TYLER

Sunny's words echo in my mind as I sit in front of a man dangling from chains. My final prey of the four I've been hunting over the last few weeks.

You spend all your time saving everyone but yourself. Little does she know, saving people is how I save myself, too. It gives me purpose.

A simple hack of the club's cameras the night Sam was drugged identified each of the guys responsible for what happened to her and what almost happened to her. They wanted to play Russian roulette with their dicks and see which one of them could get her pregnant to merge their blood with the Caddell line.

Sam wasn't their first target, and she certainly wouldn't have been their last had they not ended up in the basement of my gym. In my interrogation room where they spill their secrets because they succumbed to pain.

So here I am, sitting before guy four of four as he pleads for me to give him grace. He tells me to let him go free and that if I do he will change himself for the better. I know he won't. They never do.

Max Chambers is just like his father and brothers. He takes what he wants, when he wants, and doesn't think of the repercussions. If you want to take, you have to be fucking smart about it, and he just simply isn't. His stupidity got him here, not me. He knew it was coming, it was just a matter of *when*.

The moment he slipped the pills in my sister's drink was the moment he gave himself a death sentence.

"I'll give you intel on some sick fucks. I know a lot of people you can take down!" The guy begs.

Just as everything has tiers, so does our world. He is the middle end of the rich. A trust fund baby that won't be missed.

"Go on," I urge him calmly, crossing my arms over my chest as false hope rounds his blue eyes.

Letting out a waivered breath, he tries to adjust himself. "There's a gentlemen's club."

"There's a lot of those, Max." I lean back in my chair. I notice my tactical pants are splattered in blood.

"It's called Barton's Babes. Lots of guys go there to get their drugs from him. Lots of guys your company has contracted with." He licks his chapped lips. "You could cut ties with them. If you take him down, you can have access to all those buyers and help the women there against their will. I can get you inside," he says hopefully.

The thing is, I already know this. Barton's Babes is an extremely high-end club where you need an invitation to even know it exists or gain access. The criterion for an invite is meeting a certain income a year, which I surpassed a long time ago. Two drinks max to avoid unnecessary drama and a mandatory five-hundred-dollar minimum cover which doesn't include services or drinks.

It's a place all these rich fucks go to so they can get what their wives won't give them. Anything additional comes at a cost, and you can be denied a service by a woman if she isn't comfortable with it.

"Is that where you got your drugs, Max?" I ask.

His eyes fill with fear and his body trembles. "It was a mistake!" he yells as I stand up from my chair.

"It's only a mistake to you because you got caught." I stand to my full height, getting inches from his face.

His panicked eyes move back and forth, searching for a semblance of hope in my own. But all he will be met with is calm darkness.

These things don't piss me off. I'm not angered. I'm *repulsed*.

"No! I know what I did was wrong! I'll do better. I'll work under you so you can see! I'll do anything you ask. I'm so sorry! Please, our fathers are friends, they will know what you did!" He thrashes in his chains, rattling them.

"Our fathers aren't friends, they are business partners, there's a difference."

"Please, let's just talk this through. We can work out a deal! Please."

I smile because *oh the irony*.

"See, you didn't listen to my sister when she begged you. So why should I listen to you when you beg me?"

The air fills with his stench and pleads, but I don't care. I look down to see the guy pissed himself.

"I didn't even actually hurt her!" he cries.

"That's because somehow, in the haze of the drugs you slipped in her drink, she texted me." I cross my arms. "But a simple hack in your phones gave me all the details you had laid out for her."

Walking up next to me, Cole hands me a bag filled with pills. I pour them in my hand and meet his eyes.

These will burn him from the inside out, because they are made with Carolina reapers. It won't be a peaceful slip into slumber. It will be with him screaming, melting from the inside out, starting with his mouth that lied to lure my sister. They will corrode his stomach and then move through his whole body, circulating into his bloodstream.

"Open," I command.

Shaking his head, he continues thrashing, as if he can actually stop me. This only makes a laugh slip from me. Cole walks over to him and forces his mouth open. The chains rattle, and screams that will soon be silenced fill the room and bounce off the walls.

I shove the pills in his mouth and clamp it shut with my own hand covering his lips. His screams are muffled, his bloodshot blues now wide as his body convulses.

I'll be the last thing he sees before he dies.

"Sweet dreams, Max."

SUNNY

The dreary day is only a small testament to how I feel. The loom of waking up with a sore throat only grew to panic when it wasn't washed away with a sip of water.

Hours later, here I am on the couch with a throat so sore it hurts to drink, congestion that makes my head want to explode, and a body that feels worse than the night I left Ryan.

Family dinner is tonight, despite the fact we all saw one another at the restaurant opening a few days ago. Sam includes me via video chat because I can't get the energy to pull myself from this couch and refuse their offers to bring it here so I don't pass this plague to anyone else.

They place the phone in my usual seat at Anthony's place. I can't help the smile that forms my chapped lips at the gesture. Lounging on my couch, wrapped in a blanket, I watch my friends through the screen. Everyone's faces chipper, smiling, laughing as they share food and conversation. It's the connection I realized I lacked and needed. The hole in my chest doesn't feel so big anymore.

"Okay family," Tyler stands up. "I'm going to bring our Sunny darling some food."

"Tyler the man!" Anthony chimes.

"I'll package up some food." Sam gets up.

"Guys, that's really unnecessary," I protest.

"I'll be over in fifteen minutes." He flashes a smile complimented with a wink. Soon enough, he's grabbing his keys and is out the door.

Shortly after, I say my goodbyes to the rest of the family and end the call. My eyes are heavy, and the sound of *Friends* on the TV settles me into a purgatory sleep. An in-between of reality and my own mind.

My eyes fly open as a knock sounds on my door. "Food service," Tyler calls outside my door.

I sit my aching body up, feeling the peak of the virus so profoundly that even my joints hurt. With the blanket still wrapped around my feverish body, I walk to the door and see Tyler standing outside through the peephole.

"You can just leave it on the floor. I don't want to get you sick," I say without opening it.

"Sunny, come on. I don't care. Open the door."

"I look awful. Like a zombie, really. You sure you want to see that?"

"I want to see every version of you."

You're good at this, Tyler.

I open the door.

TYLER

While it may not be her best day, I still like this version of her. Even with the wild bun and red nose. "Looking good, Sunny."

"Comical," she deadpans, leaving the door open and walking

inside, granting me access to her apartment. That fire may be dim but damn does it still burn.

"Tyler, you're going to get sick."

"I have the immune system of a god," I say proudly, placing the food on her counter.

I make sure to take good care of myself and with that, I'm rarely sick. But nothing would stop me from coming here tonight, even if it meant I'd get put on my deathbed.

"You need to eat." I pull the food out of the packaging.

"I don't feel very hungry." She sits on the couch.

I smile. My stubborn little thing.

"Why did you come? I already told Sam I didn't need anything. Really, I'm fine."

But she doesn't look fine. *Let me take care of you.*

"You should know by now, that I don't take no for an answer. And I always get what I want." I place the food in her microwave, eyeing her as I push the buttons to warm it up, further proving my point.

She scowls. "Yeah, yeah."

She gives up that argument quickly. Which means my statement is true; she isn't fine. She is tired and sick, and I'm ready to fix those problems.

I sit next to her on the couch. "What are we watching?"

A small smile quirks on the side of her mouth. I've been trying to get a full smile out of her. So far, I've failed.

"How do you not know this show?" She finally turns to me, her nose somehow redder.

"It's called *Friends*, right?" I ask. "TV was never a pastime in our house."

"Okay that's it, we are starting from the beginning." She grabs the remote, determined with wide eyes.

"Does this mean we get to have a sleepover?" I arch a brow.

Sleeping next to you would be even better.

She just looks at me, despite being tired, her eyes sparkle. I can only hope it's because of my sleepover suggestion.

I like your eyes, Sunny.

A smile pulls at the side of her mouth again. *So close.* "Don't you have work?"

"I guess that's the good thing about being heir to the company, I can pretty much make my own hours."

"This is the one where it all began," She says, putting the show on.

Yeah, it really is.

After a few episodes, I try coaxing her into eating, but she only takes a few bites. *Stubborn.* I fucking love it.

"Tyler, we need to talk about the conversation at the party." She tries deflecting my begging her to eat.

"What's there to talk about?" I ask nonchalantly.

I don't want her worrying about something that is in the past. I'm here to take care of *her.* Not the other way around.

"What do you need from me, Tyler?"

I need you to let me take care of you.

"I need you to eat." I hold the spoon back up.

"Seriously." She lays her head on the couch cushion.

"Don't make me play airplane with you," I say, holding a spoon in the air. With that, I get a smile. *Almost.*

"*Tyler,*" she laughs again "*Please.*"

"Please, airplane?" And I start making *fucking airplane noises.*

"Absolutely not!" She hops from the couch. "This is childish!"

Yet, she's laughing and smiling. It's the most incredible thing. I'd do anything for that smile—even playing god damn airplane. So, I continue to chase her around, making fucking airplane noises if it means those laughs will continue to grace me with their presence.

"Tyler, no!" She laughs, running around the apartment, still wrapped in her blanket. Her feet pad the floor as she runs around the kitchen.

Here we are—*just Tyler and Sunny.*

She stands on one end of the small island while I stand on the other, spoon still raised.

"No," she says with a grin full of laughter.

There it is. A full fucking smile. And I just stare, completely forgetting what I'm even doing as I watch her. Cheeks round with happiness, eyes wide with mirth, and those lips, pink and smiling and all because of me.

I did that.

What she does to me is something I can't name. I can only feel it. An undeniable pull between us, as if there is something deeply woven in my heart. The way it stutters and finds a new beat to be in rhythm with hers. The way I know the number of freckles that cover her nose. The way there is something so real between us, despite not being able to see it. What started as an obsession has completely morphed into something so much deeper. And yeah, we are far beyond friends now. Even if she doesn't know it yet.

She seizes my moment of failure, my moment of weakness, and dashes towards her room.

I never got to act this way. *At all.* She lets me open up that part I didn't even know existed. The *human* part. The childish part. The part I thought died the day I was nine years old, laying in that hospital bed.

She jumps into her bed, heavily breathing despite the grin on her face. *It's there. I did that.*

"A little out of shape there?" I tease.

She rolls her eyes. "I'm compromised."

"Well, since you aren't going to eat this, I'm going to go package it and put it in your fridge." I point behind me towards her little kitchen.

After I pack everything up, I come back to the makeshift doorway of what she deems her room and lean against it, my arms crossed.

I notice a book on her nightstand and nod towards it. "Whatcha reading?"

She turns the bathroom light off and walks over to the nightstand. Her face is bare of any makeup, glowy from her skincare routine I know she just did and *fuck*, despite the fact her nose is still red and she's sick, she's so fucking perfect.

She grabs the book. "It's called *Looking for Alaska* by John Green. It's basically my Bible." She hugs it to her chest.

"Read it to me," I say.

She blinks. "You might not like it."

"I like you," I smile. "Does that count?"

She breaks my stare, trying to hide the blushing smile forming her lips. "Okay." She sits on her bed, and I follow after, cozying myself right next to her. And *fuck*, my heart beats a little faster.

"What happened to the book?" I ask, noting it's ripped up with some burn marks on it.

Her eyes move from the first page, staring at the wall ahead of us. Something in her shuts off at my question. She's lost somewhere deep in that head of hers.

"*Sunny…*" Her eyes flick back to me. "What happened to the book?"

She toys with the tattered corner. "I was reading one night and he…wanted *attention*."

I close my eyes, trying to steady my hands that are trembling with an anger so visceral it's rattling my bones.

"I just told him to let me finish the page, and he got upset." She murmurs. "He said I loved my books more than him. That it was dumb, reading the same book over and over. That my literacy must be compromised since I can't read anything else," Her voice waivers. "So, he snatched it from my hand and tried to rip it but failed, which only made him angrier." A pause. "I tried to stop him but he…he pushed me down back in our bed and ran out of the room and grabbed the candle that was lit on our coffee table and tried to set my book on fire. Pieces of it fell on our carpet and almost caught flame. He almost burned our apartment down," she says with a moment of clarity. She shakes her head. "I should have left that day."

There's that look again—shame, guilt. The look of *had I left sooner, where would I be?*

"Anyways," She takes a deep breath looking at me with a small, weary smile.

My heart cracks open at the sight, bearing itself to her in offering to exchange for hers. It's broken too, but hopefully it can give her relief from her own. That thread I feel between us rattles in the wake of the heartbreak I feel emitting from her. That string has made one thing abundantly clear—her pain is mine, too.

"It can be easy to start melting together abuse and love. The lines between the two can become blurry." I place one of my hands on hers. "A starving person will eat anything. That's what he did to you—he starved you of the things you deserved. So, when he gave you a fraction of what you needed, you devoured it. Clung to it in hopes of the next serving to be just as special and substantial." I hook a piece of hair behind her ear as those beautiful, round blue-green eyes watch me. I'm almost certain she leans into my touch, just a little bit.

"I understand, Sunny, I do. And even if I didn't, you don't owe anyone an explanation to how you felt and why you stayed. What matters now is that you left." My thumb lazily moves back and forth on the soft skin of her face. "Now, are you going to read to me?"

I listen to that soft voice for an hour.

With my hands behind my head, I watch her. She's curled into me, gracing me with her soft vanilla and coconut scent. I want it covering my clothes, my hair, on my skin and all over my home.

Even in her sweatpants and oversized shirt, sickly and falling asleep, something inside me aches so desperately to have her closer. It pulls at my fucking heart, persistent and needy and inching me closer and closer to doing just that. I can't help that every fiber in my being just wants some connection with her. Whether it is by tracing those lines that define her stomach, or holding her hand or playing with the curls on her head.

Seeing her eyes get heavy, I motion for the book. "Let me."

She hands it to me and inches closer, getting comfortable for sleep. Her skin simply brushes mine, and desire blooms in me again to pull her closer against my chest and read to her until her eyes close and her breathing becomes rhythmic with mine.

I've never wanted moments like these until I met her.

It physically fucking hurts at this point that I really can't. I just need *some* contact. It scares me, because I feel things I have never experienced before. Quickly, too. So, *so* quickly.

When I look down and see she's fast asleep with her head against my chest, and still curled into me, every instinct in me says to not leave. I move closer, draping my arm along her back, cradling her to me. I pull her just a little closer so I can be her source of warmth. I read every single page of the book she loves so we can talk about it.

Every single word.

I want to stay like this all night, and I almost do, but tonight, I only get a few hours of this moment. *Of us.*

Once I finish the book, I set it down and face her as much as I can without waking her. I move the curls that escape her bun out of her face and start tracing all the features I've already memorized. From the dark eyebrows, the pert nose, and pink lips. I love it all. I don't fucking care if she knows or if she feels it. Maybe I *want* her to know.

It's pathetic, because I already ache and miss her even though she's right here. She's right fucking here but she's already running, already planning her next out. Leaving it all behind before it even gets a chance. Before *we* even get a chance.

As I memorize her features, the words come out before I can even stop myself, before I even realize I feel what I say.

Then, I feel it all at once.

In one single moment, my life completely changes its trajectory with four simple words.

"I love you, Sunny."

CHAPTER SIXTEEN

SUNNY

I slowly open my eyes, realizing I'm in a place that feels so familiar, yet I've never been here. All remnants of my sickness are gone, and when I look around, I'm surrounded by a collision of inky, starry sky and a dusky sunset bleeding into one another like vulnerable hearts.

It's all I see. It's all I feel. Somehow, it all feels safe. If peace were a place, this would be it. This is the place my heart has searched for my whole life. There is no beginning. There is no end. There is only *this*. And somehow, it's all I've ever needed.

I feel his presence, like a pleasant warmth in the back of my mind. When I turn around, there he is, standing underneath the starry night. As I glance up at the sky, I realize I'm in the dusky sky.

My head whips to him. "Is this a dream?"

Obviously it's a dream, Sunny.

"It's whatever we want it to be," he says, closing the space between us.

"What is it?"

He smiles. "It's ours."

I glance around again, taking in the beauty of it all. I've

never seen anything like it. Colors so vibrant, somehow speaking to the soul and making a person never want to leave. It feels too real, but almost too unreal to exist at all.

"Do you like it?" He asks.

"It feels safe. It feels right. I love it."

"I agree." He cups my cheek after hooking a curl behind my ear.

We shouldn't be doing this, but whatever this place is, it's telling me otherwise.

Looking up, I see where the night sky and fiery dusky sky become one. And somehow, that feels familiar too. Like it's something that exists deep in my soul and has finally been awakened here.

My gaze meets his, seeing a soft smile on his full lips, curving that scar in the right corner. He steps into my space, getting closer. We shouldn't...but I really want to. It's just a dream, anyways. There are no consequences here.

Just as my eyes close and I feel his lips whisper on mine, not a kiss but almost, *I wake up.*

The light of day peeks through the white sheer curtains of my floor to ceiling windows. Sitting up, I realize I fell asleep with Tyler in my bed. I won't vocally admit the disappointment of not finding him right next to me, considering his comments about a sleepover.

I wouldn't mind.

Huffing a breath, I'm crushed with reality as my shoulders slump. My heart aches for a place I didn't even know existed— a place only in my dreams. Where all the unexplainable feelings somehow have answers and can breathe without the repercussions that come with it.

I rub my face and swallow down the dryness, testing out my throat soreness. I actually feel a little better after a full night's sleep. I realize for the first time in months, I slept through the night. No nightmares. *Just sleep.*

Something feels different after last night. I can't put a finger on what exactly, but I know it's deeper. *Something has changed.*

Tyler, he's safe for me. Even if he is dangerous for others. Reaching over, I grab my phone and notice one single text from him in our private thread.

Sweet Dreams, little fire.

Things are *definitely* different now. Something about last night shifted our relationship. It makes me worry for myself, and him. I'm here on a travel assignment and will be leaving soon. Nothing will derail that plan.

My phone vibrates against my chest with an unfamiliar number. I send it to voicemail, because if it's important, they'll leave one.

Rolling back over, I see my book sitting on the nightstand with the bookmark sitting on top.

He finished it.

There it goes again, my heart being foolish and feeling those things I refuse to accept. Swallowing the knot in my throat, I get up and walk to my kitchen to see a coffee and a brown bag with a bagel and cream cheese.

I massage my weary face to try to distract myself from the somersault my heart is doing in my chest. A stupid smile forming on my face.

I can't like you, Tyler.

CHAPTER SEVENTEEN

TYLER

I WALK DOWN THE STREET, COFFEE IN HAND, AND THE BEST DAMN thing that's ever happened to me by my side. While the weather has been cooler, the sun is shining today, igniting the fire inside the blue-green eyes and sunshine curls that bounce around her head.

After a stop at Betty's Beans, we decided to shop around for some things because Sunny's hosting family dinner tonight for the first time. Her apartment is still practically empty, save for the few things she purchased when she arrived.

So here I am, helping her scour stores, clinging to that tether of hope that it's indication she's considering staying. Prior to her, I was a man with a reputation who didn't give a damn. Now, I can't stop fucking caring about this little fire, despite the fact she's burning every wall I ever put up straight to embers.

She's talking a million words a minute about her last few shifts, and I'm standing here, unable to take my eyes off her completely mesmerized.

I fell.

I fell fucking hard.

Flat on my face.

I sit in a mess of love for this girl. I never thought I would know love, but then I found her. She's here, standing right next to me. My ever-growing weakness, yet greatest strength all at once, shining her light across my dark soul, making me want to be a better man for her.

Fuck.

Sam buzzes around us, weaving in and out of shops, basically leaving me and Sunny alone for the majority of the day.

"Oh my god, a crystal store. Let's go in!" Sam says, running inside before we can even answer.

"Crystals don't help family dinner, Sam!" Sunny calls, shaking her head as we continue walking. "I have a question."

"Ask me anything." And god dammit there goes my mouth pulling into a too wide grin again.

"Have you ever had a desire to take over the company?"

"Yes and no. Either way I had no choice. Once I'm able to take on the company outside of Mitchell's reach, I'll lead a new era with it." I sip my coffee as the business plans I've built conjure through my mind. "I'd be a leader, not a puppet master. I'd change the way things are run. Sure, I'd get hate for it, but I don't care. I want to be a man who makes even better men. Who helps where help was never given."

She gives me a soft smile. "That's admirable. I know you'll do it."

I almost got a *full* one there.

"Tyler," She breathes as she approaches a flower shop, examining the sea of flowers that engulf the entrance. The glass doors are open, welcoming in customers. "Look how adorable this little flower shop is!" She glides a hand over the flower petals. "Maybe I can get some for family dinner tonight."

Sunny tucks her hair behind an ear as she bends down to smell the flowers. Her pert, freckled nose touches the petals and her eyes close. My god, I am so stupid in love. My obsession has grown so much deeper, and I'm not sure what to do with it.

"How about we go inside?" I ask, placing my hand on the small of her back.

She looks up at me and fuck, it undoes something in me, making my knees buckle. I'm about to make an idiot of myself if she keeps doing this to me.

"I'd like that," she says. "But what about Sam?"

"She'll know where to find us."

Smiling, I watch my little fire waltz inside one of my best kept secrets.

SUNNY

I'm captivated by the aroma of florals. The store is painted in a rainbow of flowers. The perfect little Boston flower shop packed with people. Standing behind a desk is a woman beaming as she arranges flowers and helps customers pick what they want.

Glancing up, her eyes lock on Tyler, her already beaming smile radiates. "Tyler!" She exits from behind the counter and wraps her arms around his neck in a hug. He gives me a crooked smile as he embraces the woman back.

She looks to be in her forties. Her blonde hair is up in a clip and her body wrapped in an apron to catch the excess water from the florals. Something in her screams motherly, nurturing, and kind that reminds me of my own mother.

"Oh Tyler!" She cradles his face in her hands. "I'm so glad you are here. It isn't already time for family dinner, right?"

Standing confused, I watch the interaction between the two. Tyler's family is well known, but I wasn't expecting him to know people in a random flower shop.

"No, no. We're just stopping in. My Sunny darling here was captivated by your florals outside and wanted to come in." He gestures to me, still standing in confusion.

"Oh, Sunny! How wonderful to meet you!" She wraps her arms around me. "I'm Leslie."

"It's very nice to meet you," I laugh in her neck.

"I'm so glad business is doing well. Even better that it's everything you wanted," says Tyler.

"Oh no, honey. It's so *much* more because of you. More than I ever could've imagined." She looks at me. "Tyler here is a dream maker, I swear. He's been buying arrangements from me for years. I'd been working out of my home and selling my arrangements on the streets. He was a regular weekly, and offered up a business deal with me. And I'd barely call it that. His only requirement is that I continue to make his mother and sisters bouquets. An angel sent to me."

He kneads a hand behind his neck while clutching his coffee in the other, that crooked smile still present. It's a rare occasion to see a humbled Tyler. I don't think this is a version he likes people to see, but he's letting me.

"I did nothing, Leslie. You did all this. You are the creator behind the art. I was just a customer who knew you could do big things."

"You are a miracle worker! Okay, I have to get back behind the counter, but please say bye before you leave! And don't forget to get this pretty girl something! I really hope to see you here again soon, Sunny." She gives me a genuine smile, squeezes my arm, and finds her place back behind the counter.

"Wait, so you helped her open this place?" I ask, looking at him.

"Kind of. She was the brains, and I was just the financial avenue to get her there." Taking a sip of his coffee, he walks around the shop examining the florals.

"I never pictured Mitchell contracting a small business like this."

"He wouldn't. So that's why I do. I try to give people a shot.

Small businesses like this deserve the same chance as the big ones. We all start somewhere."

"So, you do this? You help people open their small businesses without Mitchell knowing?" I clarify.

He's picking and prodding through the array of flowers. "It's really not that big a deal."

"Tyler," I stand next to him, meeting his face. "You are making people who have dreams become their reality. You are helping people who would never have had the help in the first place."

How many more small businesses in the city has he helped?

"I'm just doing my job, Sunny. Investing, contracting." He plucks a sunflower from a bunch.

"With nothing in return," I add.

He's trying to push aside this part of him to minimize such an incredible thing. The predator trampling the human. The darkness over taking the light. The one time he chooses to be humble, when normally he is kind of a cocky bastard.

"That's not true. I have my stipulations. Like Leslie not forgetting about me when she becomes a famous wedding florist." He smiles, handing me the sunflower.

Looking at it, I blink up at him. He's watching me but it's different now, somehow. I can't quite put my finger on what exactly those eyes say. *Admiration.* I take the sunflower.

"Oh, and the smiles on people's faces. That's the best part," he says with a wink and turns around, walking through the aisles of flowers.

"And how many do you do? Like, do you have a goal?"

"I try to aim for one or two a week. Sometimes more. Sometimes less. It all depends on who I meet, and if my other contracts are too consuming or not. These are the ones I actually care about. The ones that actually mean something."

"Show me more."

It's funny, seeing a man like him prowl through the aisles of flowers. Darkness among light. The black thermal that clings to his body in all the best ways as proof he seems so out of place.

He turns around with a smile. "Like Italian food?"

"I love it."

"Perfect. I'll take you to Leo's. We're opening his second restaurant soon."

"You know, recent scientific studies show that supporting small businesses makes your penis bigger," I joke.

"Huh," He looks down. "Thank god, I could use the help."

I bite back a laugh while he grins at me. *I can't like you, Tyler.*

"I got the goods! We are gonna be doing some manifesting tonight baby!" Sam says, holding a bag filled with an assortment of crystals.

Tyler and I just look at one another.

Then the laughter follows.

CHAPTER EIGHTEEN

TYLER

After Sunny's first training session, she asked if she could come on a weekly basis to continue. Obviously I'd never turn her down. Since then, she's spent the last few weeks coming in with each of us, training and learning more on self-defense while getting stronger. This helps me give her an ounce of leverage to protect herself in the moments I'm not there to protect her—without crossing any lines.

Somehow, I'm fucking nervous tonight, because it'll be just us. Cole and Anthony won't be here as a buffer between us.

I wanted to prep before she came here, so I sent a trusted car service to pick her up. A slip of a hundred dollar bill and a threat that if he doesn't get my girl here safely were enough to send him down the road without another word.

Wrapping my hands, I hear the door open as she walks in. *Don't fuck this up Tyler.* Had she been any other woman, things would've been very different. *But it's Sunny.*

Her trust is already fragile, and she's willing enough to trust someone like me, despite the fact she's had a glimpse into the person I can be. I'm already hers. In order to make her mine, I have to be cautious, meticulous, and dare I say, gentle.

She's still wearing her scrubs, and I can't help but think how completely *devastating* she is in them. She's turning me on while simultaneously making me an uneasy wreck.

Do not fucking get a hard on, Tyler.

That damn little fire in her has ignited a series of new kinks in me which are slowly burning down the foundation of who I am that I worked so hard for. The man who hacked a widely secured database, breaching the confidentiality of so many employees just to find this girl, can't even control his dick. All she has done is waltz in wearing goddamn scrubs.

"Hey!" she chimes, closing the door behind her. "I'm just going to change really quickly." She heads for the bathrooms.

Nodding, I watch her as my heart thrums against my chest.

She observes the place around her, eyes wider than normal with giddiness as if she's seeing it for the first time. "I really love this place."

"It's one of my favorite places,"

"Thank you for sharing it with me." Then she heads to the bathroom.

A grueling few minutes later, she emerges, making me more undone than when she walked in wearing her scrubs. Despite the chill of the October air, she chose black shorts that keep almost nothing a secret. Only further adding my dick's protests with a little cropped black shirt.

"Does this work?" she asks.

I give a twirling motion with my finger for her to spin around. She laughs, giving me a slow turn, showing the flex of her leg muscles, the grip the shorts have on her ass, the narrowing of her waist that spills into curves on her hips.

Of course it fucking works.

"Absolutely." I gesture for her to come to the punching bag.

Just a mere week prior, I admitted the one thing I didn't even realize was happening while she slept in my arms. *It changed everything.*

I'm ready to make her mine, and that's going to start tonight.

SUNNY

I'm panting.

Hard.

A sheen of sweat coats my body as I watch Tyler on top of me, pinning my arms down. I feel my heart in my throat at the sight, wondering how the hell I got here. Though I honestly don't mind.

It just kind of happened.

Looking up at him, my chest rises and falls fast underneath his. A feline smile spreads across his face with a tilt of his head. He is like the night sky, so tragically beautiful and you don't even know why.

"See, you were in a vulnerable position, and it was easy for me to reverse the roles," he says, still pinning my hands with one of his own while the other rests on the floor beside my head.

He's straddling my waist, and I try to ignore the generous parts of him I feel very close to the hyper aware parts of mine. He may have won this round, but I've managed to win the rest. Prior to this loss, I had him pinned to the ground while I straddled his waist.

Apparently that isn't just a vulnerable vantage point for my dreams at night, but also in a fighting ring. While I sat pridefully on top of him, he managed to flip me on my back. Somehow my mind started wishing we were naked in the process.

I've unfortunately grown accustomed to these thoughts that frequent my mind, chalking it up to the fact that he's devastatingly beautiful, and I haven't gotten laid in months.

"Get. Off." I scowl.

He doesn't move, and his smile grows wider. "*You* would be the first woman to complain about me being on top of them."

"Do you do this position with all the girls you bring home?" I taunt. He rolls his eyes, but he doesn't say no, and he doesn't say yes. All he gives me is that damn crooked smile.

"Okay," Tyler hauls himself off me, avoiding my question entirely. He grabs my arm and pulls me off the ground, sending me into a dizzy spell.

Chuckling, he places a stabilizing hand on my waist and that shit ignites a fire in my veins. It's nearly impossible to cool down at this point. Being here, all over one another's bodies, *sweaty*—it's doing something inside me. A brief glimpse of what only my own mind can conjure up.

"Let's go to the punching bag and teach you how to hit some more." He places a guiding hand on my sweaty back.

"I think considering my shot with Ryan, I did a pretty good job at hitting."

"Okay, so you did some damage. Now, I want to teach you proper technique so that you are prepared." He places his hands on the punching bag. "You want to make sure your feet are planted and firm on the ground and you want to brace your core with each punch."

There is something fundamentally different about him tonight. I can't quite figure out what it is. All I know is that the predator is long gone, and dare I say it leaves something vulnerable in him.

"Sunny?"

"Yeah?"

"You know, it would make teaching you a lot easier if you weren't staring at my lips every time I spoke. I mean, I can make all those curious thoughts go away by one simple action." He smirks.

There you are.

Leaning in, he braces his hands on the punching bag. The only barrier between us.

"Who says I was staring at your lips?" I ask, crossing my arms.

There's no escaping this, but I'll at least play along, like we always do with one another. Flirtatious banter isn't unfamiliar territory for us, but for some reason, tonight feels *different*.

"Your eyes." He leans an inch closer.

"And you know me so well that you can read my eyes?" I take a step closer, slowly closing the space between us.

We can't…but god I want to.

"I've been trying to navigate you for awhile, Sunny."

"Why?" I whisper.

He licks his lips. "Because I can't get you out of my fucking head." He takes a step closer. My heart beats frantically in anticipation.

"W-We're friends…we…we can't." I say, but the lie is prevalent as soon as it leaves my lips. It's breathless, needy and desperate.

Yet he takes another step into me. Those green eyes igniting with feral desire so wild that my heart skips a beat. He's so close, that the scent of citrus and salt become the very oxygen I breathe. I can practically taste him on my lips, only fueling that need to reach out for him.

"Friendship over." He grabs the back of my neck and pulls me in.

It starts as a whisper, a gentle brush against my lips seeking permission. Each gentle press is a whisper of words that can only be spoken like this. And I'm still trying to decipher the meaning.

So, I part my lips, allowing him in. He unleashes the predator who's been caged from this moment for so long.

His mouth captures mine, greeting me with the sweet mint of his taste. His kiss becomes fierce, possessive, wanting. A small moan leaves his throat as our mouths meet.

Letting go of the punching bag, he cradles my face with both hands while my fists ball in his shirt, fighting the urge to rip it off. We stumble back a few steps as his body collides with mine, but it does nothing to stop the talent of his tongue twining with mine.

His hands roam down my body, digging his fingers in my hips as he tugs me closer. While urgent, his hands are meticulous and gentle as they explore my body, like he's memorized it for this very purpose. As if he can anticipate each of my needs without ever knowing them.

Tyler possessively devours me, making me submit to him. Grabbing my neck, he pushes his tongue with delicate precision, knowing exactly how to navigate my mouth in a way that has my toes curling. Instinctively, I cradle his face, unwilling to let him pull away as a small moan leaves my mouth, eliciting one from him.

He is *good* at this. He knows exactly what he's doing. I wonder how he could've been so nervous when he's doing all the right things.

Temptation to cross that thin line between us catches fire in my body. The next thing I know, his hands are under my thighs, sweeping me off my feet as I straddle his waist, pressing our chests together.

He carries me to the front desk, setting me down so we can be face to face without removing his mouth from mine once in the process.

A smile plays on my lips when I feel the generous part of him getting hard beneath his sweatpants. Pressing myself harder against him, I tighten my legs around him, making him let out a deep, rattled moan.

"Be careful, Sunny," he warns. "You like to play games." He presses kisses along my jaw. "But so do I."

As he works his way down my neck, I feel an invisible branding on my skin that I don't think I'll ever be able to scrub off. Just as his lips almost meet the tender flesh of my scar, he pauses. His eyes fall to the stark pink skin while two fingers gently touch it.

It's my daily reminder.

My body belonged more to Ryan than it had myself for far too long. Because of that, I've only ever been okay with physical touch if I instigated it. I haven't been okay with a man's touch like this since. Yet, with Tyler, he's the only man I feel okay with when he touches me.

He gently places his lips on the scar—the one I can barely bring myself to touch. *And I like it.* It doesn't hurt so much with him.

My breath hitches, but it doesn't stop him from placing a hand around my throat and pulling me back to his lips. I trace the ropes of muscles in his arms, feeling the grooves of scars along them. He catches my wrist, practically ripping it from his forearm.

"Do they hurt you?" I ask. "Do your scars hurt you, too?"

The predator in him is alive, pacing inside his mind as his eyes frantically search mine. All he does is swallow hard, not saying anything as he watches me.

Grabbing the bottom of his shirt, I pull it up over his head, slowly. He doesn't stop me. Not when more scars are bared across his abdomen and chest. Not when the shirt drops to the floor in a pool of fabric. Not when his beautiful, scarred body is finally bare to me, like it's his very heart.

His eyes don't leave mine, searching me for a reaction, like I'll cower away, scared by them. By him. But I don't.

My fingers dance along them, noting how different each is. From white, pink, and red—jagged, clean lines, and circles that appear to be cigarette or cigar burns. I trace my finger down a raised, pink scar along his chest. He winces as his head tilts back slightly, but he lets me.

He lets me.

"What do you do when you're making love to a woman, and she touches these?" I ask, meeting his eyes.

"I don't make love, Sunny. I fuck." There is no mirth behind his eyes, no malice wrapped in each word.

"Mmm. And let me guess, you keep them tied up?" That earns me a smile.

"More often than not," he teases. Removing my hand, I try to hide my own smile. He catches my wrist, stopping me. "It hurts when people touch my scars. Not physically, but my entire fucking being. With you, it doesn't hurt so much."

I can understand that.

He presses a gentle kiss to the inside of my palm while watching me. I cradle his face, my thumb strokes the scar that pierces through his lips, and then press my own against them.

It just feels right.

Our breathing becomes heavy and the air between us becomes thick with desire. Yet, somehow, I feel like I can finally breathe. Like I've been suffocating, and he finally gave me oxygen.

My legs tighten around him as my need grows deeper. Feeling him against me is only a prelude to all the desires running rampant through my mind. His mouth around my nipples. His hands through my hair. His thrusts wild and unhinged as he pushes into me.

"Baby..." he whispers.

Just as we tread that fine line—where we both may have gone over the edge, a car door shuts and headlights shine into the gym, stopping us.

Tyler unwillingly pulls himself from me. His hands brace the counter I sit on as a barricade for whatever is outside. A glance over his shoulder has his jaw flexing when he sees who interrupts us. Turning back to me, his eyes fall to my lips then back to my eyes.

"It's Sam and the rest of the family," he says.

His eyes dart back and forth on my face, searching for whatever I'm thinking at this moment. And I'm not. I'm *not* thinking.

Biting my swollen lip, I contemplate. *I actually contemplate it.*

He stares at me, the eagerness in his eyes growing as our family walks closer to the entrance of the training center. The hope that is growing into a flame only to be dwindled by my next words.

I can't like you, Tyler.

"To be continued," I finally say.

The words are opposite of what I should have said. What I *need* to say. *How* could this be continued? It cannot be continued.

Swallowing hard, he nods with a smirk. "To be continued."

CHAPTER NINETEEN

TYLER

I still have the taste of her on my tongue, the smell of her on my clothes, my skin. A shower will practically be an impossible task at this point. I refuse to destroy any remnants of evidence of what happened.

Her final words before we faced our family plays over and over in my mind. *To be continued.*

I'd forgotten what it was like to simply want to kiss, to make out and enjoy that act alone. I could have spent all night making out like two teenagers. *Fuck.* I forgot how kissing could be so good.

It's always been a prologue, a necessary step towards the ultimate thing I wanted. Any kissing I've done as an adult has simply been a means to an end, an introduction to sex rather than what it is.

But it's her.

I can kiss Sunny all night, until our lips are raw and we are suffocating for air. If that's how death greets me, I'd go with a smile on my face.

As we sit at Martha's, I can feel the weight of our moment, this now secret, weighing heavy over us.

I kissed Sunny.

The memories of our night invade my mind, I have to shift in my seat just to adjust the damn hard on I can't fucking get rid of.

I kissed Sunny.

She's leaving, and I'm only growing deeper feelings for her. Maybe I'm just a rebound, but I don't care. I'll be anything for her if it means I get to have her and somehow make her mine.

I watch as she plays pool with Sam and Cole, as if our lips and hands weren't exploring one another just a mere hour ago. The remnants are still there—messed hair, swollen lips and hazy eyes.

I did that.

As though she feels my eyes on her, through that soul-bridge between us, she flicks her gaze to me. A whisper of a smile plays on her lips.

I think you like me, Sunny.

Something glimmers along that connection between us. An unspoken thing that somehow seems to scream so loudly now. Something unseen, but feels too real to not exist.

Now that I have her, I can't get enough of her. She's been my obsession since the moment I laid eyes on her. But that obsession has rooted itself much deeper, and I won't ever be able to escape. I never had plans to, anyways.

Every facet of my life now revolves around her. It is Sunny everything, everywhere, all the time. A dangerous line is being treaded here, but I truly don't fucking care.

Because I kissed Sunny.

SUNNY

Laying in my bed, I stare at the twinkling lights I put up on move in day. Along with the glow in the dark stars that scatter my ceiling, compliments of Tyler from our day of shopping.

He said he always had them in his room growing up since stars were far and few in between in the city. He'd wished upon each one on his ceiling as a child—that he still does to this day. I wonder if he's looking up at his right now, too.

My mind jumps from one thought to another. I count each light, each star, trying to distract my mind from earlier this evening in hopes it'll be like counting sheep and send me to sleep.

I kissed Tyler. And I liked it.

Pressing my palms against my eyes, I groan as I shift in bed. Desire that shouldn't be here takes over when I replay the way his hands felt against my skin and his tongue in my mouth tasted.

I knew something shifted that night he came over and read the whole book that still sits on my nightstand. Just so that we could talk about it during our day of shopping. I just didn't realize how much things had changed. While I try to deny the fact it's more with him, the truth still whispers in my mind—*it's always more with him.*

Continuing with Tyler would be selfish, considering I'm leaving. Ryan is alive, and I know in my very bones he is looking for me. His words were enough, but the tone that wrapped around each letter got the point across even further when I stepped out that door that night.

If you walk out that door and leave, I will find you.

It was just as much a threat as it was a promise he made to me.

Ryan is selfish for me, and he wants me back in his life, regardless of the fact he has no clue how to love me and that he hurt me. The better part of me tells me I need to have this discussion with Tyler to end things immediately. The immature part tells me to completely ignore it.

It has to be nothing.

I know deep in my heart that it's so far from the truth.
Because I kissed Tyler, and I loved it.

I immediately sit up in a bed that isn't mine, feeling my heart race as I grip the familiar gray blankets in my fist. Looking around the room, I realize I'm in my old apartment I shared with Ryan. My breath catches as the panic rises like bile in my throat.

"No," I breathe.

Ryan walks out of the bathroom. "I missed you while you were sleeping,"

The look in his eyes tells me exactly what he wants as he crawls over to me in bed. He *always* wants it. I used to find it endearing that he couldn't keep his hands off me, until one day he wouldn't stop despite my protests. He hovers over me, his dark brown curls falling in his face and his brown eyes fill with a terrifying hunger.

"Ryan, please," I manage to croak through my panic.

"What? You don't want to have sex with me?" he snaps and fear knots in my throat.

"I'm just really tired tonight," I try to sound sweet as I caress his face. I *have* to comfort him and make it seem like I'm the problem. To him, I always am. Yet, somehow, always the solution too.

When he rolls off me, he makes it a point to express his anger in everything he does. A drawer being closed too hard. His footsteps stomping with more frustration. Doors slamming rather than closing. Tossing and turning in our bed with sighs of frustration.

"Why are you upset?" I ask, even though I already know the answer.

"You never want to have sex with me," he snaps. "A man can only feel rejected for so long."

"That's not it, honey. I love you so much."

His gaze softens. "Then show me how much you love me," he whispers. "You know it puts me in a better mood."

How am I back here? What the fuck happened? How am I with him again? This isn't my apartment in the city. Reality and fallacy are melting into one, making it difficult to differentiate which one I'm in.

"I'm not really in the mood," I admit.

"What if I get you in the mood?" he asks, pressing kisses down my neck while his hands roam my body without invitation.

The thing is, if I say no, the night will continue in this back and forth. However, if I fall victim to this manipulation, we'll have a better night than the one that's already happening.

I don't say yes, and I don't say no. To Ryan, this means a welcome invitation to my body. I don't fight him. Not when he pulls my pants down. Not when he pushes into me, unaware of the silent tear spilling down my temple. Not when he finishes and thinks I did too, making me feel like a tool for his pleasure.

"I love you sweetie," he says, because he's gotten what he wants. "How about I make us a snack or something?" He kisses my cheek. "I can bring it to bed for you!" He calls over his shoulder.

Why did I stay for so long?

He leaves me in bed, feeling used and violated while he goes into the other room and doesn't come back for hours after. I roll on my side, squeezing my eyes shut as I work through the emptiness that has invaded my chest.

Wake up. Wake up. Wake up

I finally wake up.

When I sit up, I realize I'm crying. Shuffling out of bed, I run through my dark apartment, touching everything I can to know it's real.

I'm home.

Once I ground myself and make sure I'm where I think I am, I run to the bathroom and heave up everything in my stomach, sobbing into the bowl to the point I can't breathe.

I sit on the bathroom floor, my body trembling with a thick sheen of sweat on my skin. I lean my head against the cold tub, trying to steady my breath and heart.

As soon as I start to think maybe, just maybe I can build a life elsewhere, even here, I'm reminded of why I can't. Six months is already too long. I'd already made the mistake of staying too long once, I refuse to do it again.

Just like all relationships, we had the honeymoon phase for years, and then it just became a snowball effect. Each little thing he did piled onto the next until it all became too big and exploded in my face.

I spent so much time in school, getting my degree, then getting my experience, that it was easier to stay than leave. It was easy to brush off the things he did in the name of not being able to spend time together or as often or the stress of tight finances. The stress we both had of work, school, and life balance.

Of course, I justified the bad times with the good. Of course I told myself I was overreacting. Of course I said maybe, just maybe if I fulfilled his needs he'd treat me better. Of course I made up every excuse under the sun as to why I should stay and why I shouldn't leave.

Finally, pulling myself off the cold bathroom floor, I rinse my face and mouth off. One glance in the mirror tells me I'm right back where I started when I first came to the city.

Last I heard, Ryan is all the way across the country.

Still, before I go back to bed, I check every window and lock twice. Then, I grab my gun I keep in my nightstand, and sleep with it under my pillow instead.

CHAPTER TWENTY

TYLER

BEFORE WE VENTURE TO MARTHA'S FOR BEERS AND THE GAME, me and the guys finish up a sparring and lifting session.

"All I'm saying is," Anthony interjects "why not just say yes to at least one of them? You know, thousands of girls who try to shoot their shots at you? Apparently, eighty percent of relationships work when the girl initiates it."

I run a hand over my sweaty face. *I kissed Sunny.* Feeling a smile play at my lips, I think about the memory again.

"I'm not in the business of a relationship," I reiterate. I'm not in the business of a relationship *except* with Sunny.

"We hear that over and over. Come on, you're young, hot, rich. Why not take advantage of that? You already know your fate, why not just enjoy the freedom you have now?" Anthony shrugs.

Cole stares at me while a silent communication lingers between us. The only reason why Cole knows is because we had our morning sparring session right after I left Sunny's place, and he recognized the shift in me. I only shake my head, because I can't involve more people until I know what she and I are.

"Anthony, you and I both know I have to be careful of who I

affiliate with and am seen with. As soon as people see me even remotely romantic, word will spread like wildfire. I'm arranged to be married. I need to be careful with what I do," I deflect.

"Do it behind closed doors." He gives me a pointed look.

I laugh.

It's irrational, crazy, and too soon, but I'm not sure why it's something I simply can't stop. I can't stop *giving* myself to her. I love her, and I know I always will. I *know* that in my heart. Whether it destroys me or makes me the happiest man in the world, it's a privilege to love Sunny.

"Okay, how about this. Once you finally admit to Sam you're in love with her, I will advance to a date with another woman," I offer.

"I see what you're doing and that is not the same." Anthony points a taped finger at me.

Cole chuckles as a grin forms my lips. I hit a nerve with him.

"What?" Anthony asks.

"All I'm saying is, you tell Tyler he needs to get out there but you're pining after Sam. At least Tyler has a valid reason. You don't." Cole points to Anthony.

Anthony blinks. "That's not true. I date women!" But he doesn't deny his love for Sam.

"Like who?" I counter.

"Just, women." Anthony shrugs. "Here and there, you know. Nothing serious, of course. It's all just for fun."

I roll my eyes. "Because you're in love with my sister."

Somehow, somewhere, us three boys turned into three men head over heels for women we can't have.

"What about you, Cole? I don't see you getting out there?" Anthony quips.

"I'm spoken for," Cole admits.

Anthony's jaw drops. "I'm sorry, what?" His eyes dart back and forth between the two of us. "Are you too?" he asks me.

Well, this is going to be an interesting night.

Brace yourself, Brother.

SUNNY

A spam call lights up my phone, so I send it to voicemail and bring my focus back on the two girls I now call sisters. A girls night was necessary since the guys decided to watch the game at Martha's. So here we are, in Sam's paint studio, drinking wine and free painting while we gossip and giggle.

These are my favorite nights.

I still haven't told them about my kiss with Tyler. If I do, something about it will make it final and real. I can already imagine the looks on their faces and their squeals of curiosity. If I tell them, any chances of stopping it before something comes of it will be gone.

"Okay, I just have to ask, have you at least gotten laid?" Sam points her paintbrush at me.

"Sam! She literally just got out of an abusive relationship. I'm sure that's the last thing on her mind," Macey interjects.

This comment only fuels my curiosity if she feels the same. No conversation has been had about her being my patient, so I chalk it up to she either doesn't want to, or she doesn't remember.

"I have not. I'm also not opposed to it." I shrug.

Maybe a hookup will be good and help me shake the kiss from Tyler. Get whatever that kindled inside me to *calm down*. In the same breath, the idea makes me want to vomit.

"The Halloween party will be the perfect place for you to meet a good fuck," Sam says excitedly. "Or I can just cure that angst for you." She winks.

I roll my eyes. "I work Halloween, remember?"

"Just come after," Macey suggests.

"You can be a sexy nurse in your scrubs." Sam shimmies.

"I don't think sexy is the correct term after a twelve hour shift," I laugh.

"Oh, please. You're hot regardless, just accept it." Sam waves a hand. "So, Halloween we will hunt you down a good fuck buddy."

I laugh to mask my nervousness because I know when Sam is on a mission, she won't stop until it's accomplished.

"We'll see," I say.

"Oh no, it'll happen. I have to pee," Sam hops off her stool and saunters to the bathroom.

My phone buzzes again and when I go to grab it, Macey's hand collides with mine.

"Oh, Sorry Mace, I thought that was mine." My eyes fall to the screen. "You have a text from Cole."

Macey's face is unfazed as she grabs her phone. "He's fixing my parents' car. Something about spark plugs." She waves a hand, shooting a text back to him.

Macey and I are close, but definitely not as close as Sam and I. She's blunt while Macey is reserved. What you see is what you get with Sam, but clearly with Macey there's things that still need to be uncovered, if our history is any indication of that.

She places her phone on the other side where I'm not able to accidentally grab it again. "I admire you, Sunny." The comment takes me aback.

"Thank you, Macey. But for what?"

"I don't know the details of what happened with you and Ryan, but I do know he was abusive in all forms. The fact you're able to come here and just do what you do, just continue." Macey looks at me.

A knot builds in my throat. "Funny, I thought the same about you." I trace a finger on a dried spot on my canvas.

Her gray eyes flick to me, and a soft smile pulls on her lips. "I remember." She nods. "I just, I didn't want it to be an awkward thing for you. I mean, you were about to meet all of us. That's already so much. Add one of us being a trainwreck of a patient," she sighs. "I wasn't sure if you remembered. You helped me so much that day. Obviously he didn't do nearly anything close to what Ryan did to you, but still."

"You had me fooled," I laugh. "There wasn't even a glimmer of recognition or shock on your face."

"I should play professional poker," she teases.

"Trauma is trauma, Mace. Pain is pain. Comparison is just a losing game." I shrug. "It doesn't matter how big or small."

"I never got to thank you. You're such a good nurse. Because of Tyler, I won't ever have to worry about that guy again. He must have scared him off or something," she says, shaking her head with a chuckle, not realizing the gravity and reality of her statement.

"I knew once Tyler knew, that'd be the first and last time a man would lay hands on me." She looks back to her paint canvas. "How do you do it, Sunny? How do you stay so strong knowing yours is still out there?"

"I can promise you, it's not easy and I still battle a lot internally, but I couldn't waste anymore of my life by letting him have control over me." A lie, since I'm currently on the run from him. "I can't give him more than I already have. More than he has already taken."

"I just wanted to let you know." Macey gives a soft smile to me.

"That really means so much to me." And that's a full truth.

We wrap our arms around one another.

"Hey! I want in!" Sam runs towards us. "Ugh, I needed this," she says, wrapping her arms around us.

My sisters.

CHAPTER TWENTY-ONE

SUNNY

It's nights like tonight where I'm grateful I don't work the night shift. Halloween already gets crazy, factoring in the full moon is a recipe for a chaotic time.

So, I stand outside of my work, bundled and hyper aware of my surroundings as I wait for Sam to pick me up.

While it's gotten only slightly better, I still find myself looking around at every movement, each person who comes from the darkness to go inside the hospital. It's a hard feeling to shake when you're convinced someone is always watching you.

Sam pulls up in her purple jeep wrangler, beating with music while Macey sits in the passenger side.

"Get in, you sexy nurse!" Sam chants through her rolled down window.

I hop inside while *Man! I Feel Like a Woman* by Shania Twain plays in the car. They both turn back to look at me, revealing a glimpse of their well thought out costumes. Mace is wearing cat ears, her face painted with whiskers and a cat nose. Sam has devil light up horns and dark smokey makeup with black lipstick.

"Well you guys look fantastic," I say, buckling my seatbelt.

"Tonight, we are all gonna get a piece of some ass." Sam puts the car in drive and takes off into the night.

Ten minutes later, we're pulling up to a warehouse type building named *Curfew*. People moving in and out of it are dressed in various costumes. Sam tosses her keys to the valet, and we're led inside.

Different colored lights scatter across the warehouse as masked and painted faces whisk around. The air is filled with sweat, alcohol and sex. Sam drags us through the crowds with our arms linked as we bump into sweaty bodies.

"Where are the guys?" I ask.

"On the rooftop," Sam answers.

Somehow, we manage to make it through the masses of costumes and onto the cool rooftop, which serves as relief from the sweaty heat inside the club. There isn't much up here except for a few chairs and fire pits that can be mistaken as trash cans. It's quieter, calmer, which is something I soon realize I need after just a few minutes in the chaos of *Curfew*.

Approaching the guys is a treat, seeing what they all bring to the table for costumes. It doesn't surprise me when Anthony turns, revealing the iconic hangover costume. Sunglasses, baby holder with an old doll in it and the clothes to match.

A genuine laugh leaves my lips, because only Anthony would pull this off perfectly. Cole stays in Cole fashion, with simple dog ears as his only effort for a costume.

"Where's Tyler?" I ask.

"Right behind you," he whispers, making my heart skip a beat and my body react, unsure of whether to be scared or relieved. He places his hands on my shoulders, heavy in the most comforting way as he stabilizes my shaking body. "Hi, little fire,"

I turn around to face him, seeing his costume on full display. A half painted face like a skull, one side the predator, the other the human. A black hoodie and dark jeans.

"Where the hell have you been?" Sam asks.

"Someone has to work around here." He grins.

In what world is an outfit like this used for work?

Sam arches a brow. "Sure. If work is code for *laid*."

Tyler's jaw flexes as his eyes briefly fall to me and then back to his sister. "Don't talk about things you don't know, Sam."

"An outfit like that doesn't call for business," she counters.

"Your end of business and mine are totally different things." He stares at her blankly. "Consider yourself lucky for that."

What once was a lighthearted night has quickly grown heavy. The shift in everyone is prevalent. His tone changes, and everyone else does, too. Nothing else is said as he leans against the edge of the rooftop, bracing his forearms on the ledge, looking at the city.

By whatever confidence I've just gained, I say, "So maybe we should go dance?" I don't want to dance. Hell, I'd be content staying up here all night, trying to find stars through the light pollution if I had my way.

"My love language!" Sam says, skipping towards me, linking our arms together.

She grabs Macey, leading us off the rooftop. Looking behind me, I see Tyler watching me run off with his sisters, his arms crossed over his chest and a smile hooking the corner of his mouth, curving that scar I want to kiss.

I can't like you, Tyler.

Eventually, the guys follow after, because where we go, they go. Strobe lights dance around us as *Roses* by the Chain Smokers fills the venue.

As we navigate the building, I end up behind Tyler. His broad back serves as a shield through the chaos of people. The hoodie still hangs around his head and clings to his muscles in all the best ways. I tack it on to the ever-growing list of favorite looks on him.

The urge to place a finger and trace all the lines that build him takes over. As if I've lost control over my own body, that ache and need persists. My heart hammers in my chest, making it all seem in slow motion as my body reaches for his while we stalk through the crowd.

Somehow, a voice filters through the music and people, catching his attention. Just as he turns his head to whoever calls for him, Sam grabs my arm, pulling me into the dancing crowd. Soon enough, he disappears, relieving me from a lapse in judgement and a mistake that could've been made.

"Hey!" Sam squeals to someone nearby.

Standing before us is a tall man with jet black hair and ice blue eyes.

Damn.

"Connor, I want you to meet my new bestie, Sunny." Sam motions with her arms out, presenting me like a prize.

She wasted no time.

"I'm Sunny." I reach my hand out.

Smiling, he takes it in his. "Connor. I get the gist that you're *actually* a nurse."

"What gave it away? The mess of the hair or the bags under my eyes?"

He chuckles. "All I see is a beautiful girl."

Before I'm able to respond, Sam links her arm in mine and drags me to another spot on the dance floor.

"Hey!"

"I think we found you a fuck buddy. Gotta make him work for it! Connor is hot and already seems intrigued by you," Sam says. "Plus he's rich."

Maybe I am not ready. It's only been barely two and a half months since Ryan. How can the time feel so long yet so short?

After some time on the dance floor, Connor is summoned to my side with a hand reached out. "Mind if I cut in?"

"Not one bit." Sam winks and flips her hair while she drags Macey away.

I look up at Connor with a smile. In the corner of my eye, Tyler stands up straighter, adjusting himself so that we are in his direct line of sight.

"I have to warn you, I am not a very good dancer," I admit.

"By the looks of it, I'd have to say otherwise." He grabs my hand, bringing me closer to him.

"So observant."

"It's hard not to be with you in the room."

When I look up, Tyler is in the background, settling himself against a wall with his arms crossed over his chest. Despite the girl talking to him, his eyes are on me. I swallow back the guilt knotting in my throat.

He already knows where I stand anyways. He *knows* that I'm leaving. I just want a fling if I even want anything at all.

Tyler can't be just a fling.

He tilts his head, so animalistic as he watches me. I rip my eyes from his, though I still feel them on me. I always do.

The strobe lights hit Connor's face as he smiles down at me. For a brief moment, it feels good to just have fun, act young and stupid for a few moments. I never went through the phase most do in their twenties with random late-night hookups and flings. I *deserve* this part of my life.

As I dance with Connor, it's impossible to fight the instinct of my eyes moving where Tyler still stands. His eyes are no longer on me, but the girl standing in front of him. My eyes fall where her hand rests too comfortably on his chest.

Why does it bother me?

I can't explain why I feel the way I feel. It was just a fucking kiss. No more, no less. I don't have a monopoly over him because of it. He's young, wealthy, successful, and very attractive. He deserves to have as much fun as I do.

Those emeralds flick up to me, a smirk pulling at his lips

Looking at Connor who still has his eyes on me, I plaster a smile as I slowly glide my hands up his arms, feeling the cords of muscles along the way. He tugs me closer where I can smell the cedarwood of his cologne with a touch of sweat. Warm, but so unfamiliar.

In the dim background, Tyler watches us intently. I can *feel* his eyes on me even if I'm not looking.

Am I making you jealous, Tyler?

The smile he had dissipates with a flex of his jaw. The girl in front of him runs a hand up his chest, trying to regain his attention. He snatches her wrist, his eyes flicking to her as he murmurs something and then moves his focus back to me, fuming with wild rage.

I bring my attention back to Connor, trying to re-emerge myself in the moment. To allow myself this after denying myself for so long. So I force a smile, place my hand on his chest and try to combat the memories that are fighting for my attention.

Connor grabs my hand, spinning me around so that my ass is pressed to his groin. It's evident his plans for me considering the bulge I feel pressing into me. We sway back and forth as he tilts my head to the side—*exposing my scar.*

My body stiffens, but Connor has no clue into my body cues as he continues to try and nuzzle his way to the sensitive skin of my neck. My heart thrums against my chest in panic, pumping it through my veins like ice, freezing me in place.

I know it isn't his fault. It's *mine. I am not ready for this.*

The strobe lights dance around relentlessly, making my vision blind and compromised. In the haze of my spiraling thoughts, I see Tyler pushing through the mess of people. My perfect predator, ready to come claim his prey. His voice filters through the music and crowd, thawing the fear that once wrapped around my bones, leaving me frozen, and once again I can move.

I don't even need to look behind me to know it's him. I feel a sense of ease come over my body at the familiarity of his own.

Connor's body is replaced with Tyler's after a few indistinct murmurs. It doesn't take long before those scarred hands are gripping my hips, moving up my arms and wrapping around my neck. My head leans back into his chest, flushing our bodies together like two puzzle pieces that actually fit. That are *supposed* to fit.

"Eyes on me, little fire."

Gently, he tilts my head, exposing my scar. He is not only trying to prove something to himself, but to me, too, as he places his warm lips on the tender flesh.

"Funny how your body just *wants* mine," he murmurs. He grabs my arm, dragging me through the crowds as we navigate our way to the rooftop into the cold October night.

CHAPTER TWENTY-TWO

SUNNY

Our hurried steps are halted when he links an arm around my waist and throws me against a wall. He grips my face and meets my stare with something wild flaring in his green eyes.

"Tell me, Sunny, is that what you want? A man like Connor all over you? Don't lie to me, because I'll know if you do. Your body will tell me the truth even if you don't. Your body isn't very good at *lying*."

I swallow hard, trying to formulate words that don't seem to come, or that I want to admit. *I want a man like you all over my body*. But my anger gets the best of me.

"Tyler." I shove my hands against his chest in an attempt to push him off.

He grabs my wrist, spinning me around so my chest and face are pressed against the cold cement of the wall. With both of my wrists behind my back in one of his hands, he places the other against the wall next to my head.

"Don't think for one second I'm okay watching you with another man's hands all over you," he murmurs in my ear. "If it happens again, he will no longer *have* any hands."

He gently places his lips on the sensitive spot between my collar and jaw, whispering against my skin, "It doesn't hurt with me, does it baby?"

My thighs squeeze together but words refuse to leave my mouth. One of his legs goes between mine, kicking them open. "Do you need a release, little fire?"

I shouldn't want it like this after everything with Ryan, but because I trust Tyler, it's all I want. Desperately, I want those deep, dark, depraved parts of him. I'm not scared of what he is offering me, even if it feels like I'm looking at my biggest fucking predator in the eyes.

"Let me hear that body beg, baby." He nips at my neck while a hand ventures down the waistband of my scrubs. "Is this what you need? You need my fingers inside that perfect pussy? You need me to fuck that cunt to take this writhing edge off?"

My body trembles while my breathing grows heavier and faster, anticipation rising for his fingers. The hard length of him presses against me, indicating his need for me, too.

I realize the feeling it gives me can easily become addicting. I can make a man like Tyler so furious, so needy, so fucking flustered just by dancing with another man. It makes me feel... *powerful*.

"Use your words, Sunny."

It's so wrong, so wrong to say yes, but I want to so fucking badly. Before I can say anything, the word comes out breathy, desperate, and needy. "*Yes*."

One simple tug and the draw strings of my scrubs snap. He doesn't even bother trying to untie them.

"Can you *not* ruin my clothes?" I seethe.

"What fun would that be?" He chuckles while his hand slips through my waistband. His finger traces along me, feeling the embarrassing wetness there, making my body shudder. He pulls his hand out to examine his fingers now glistening with my arousal and tsks.

"Just as I thought—your body won't lie to me." He sucks his fingers clean and slips them back in my pants, creating soft, pressured circles on my clit.

My legs shake as need and desire build in me. He pushes two fingers inside me, making my knees buckle. I let out a small cry, trying to move myself but he has me pinned so firmly to the wall I can't do anything but stand here and take what he gives me.

His body covers mine, making it to where no one can see even if they tried. The green of his eye is stark against the hollowed skull paint. Such heavy desire as he watches what simply his fingers do to me. My heart rate climbs and my breathing becomes erratic when he starts using his palm as intricate friction against me. A moan slips from my mouth unwillingly as he curls his fingers in me just right.

"Shh. You are for my ears and eyes only," he says.

"Tyler...I'm..." But the words get jumbled in a mess of soft moans.

"I know baby, I know," he murmurs. "Now be a good girl and cum all over my fingers before someone finds us here. We don't need any more casualties tonight than there already have been."

I don't even have time to let what he admits register because he kisses my neck, my collarbone, and my scar as his hand works intricately on me. My knees weaken again. The moans coming from me are silenced by his hand wrapping around my mouth, pulling me flush to his front. I completely disintegrate from the fire that ignites in me.

"That's my girl," he praises.

Once I come down from the high, my body slumps back into his. Slowly he removes his hand from me, bringing his clearly soaked fingers to his mouth again with a groan. He spins me around and tugs me close so our bodies are practically one.

"Now taste how fucking good you are." He grabs the back of

my neck and pulls me to his lips. There is nothing gentle about any of it.

He doesn't waste time asking for entrance to my mouth as his tongue pushes past my lips, exploring in ways that make me let out an unintentional moan.

His chest moves up and down in erratic breaths. Seeing him so undone like this only fuels that growing power in me. So much so, I finally gain control of my wobbly legs and press myself into him.

Our bodies mold and melt into one another like two pieces of metal being liquefied by the fiery intensity between us. I wonder if we'll ever be able to separate ourselves. If we go any further, I know he won't let us be anything other than us. I try to push off of him but his grip on me only tightens with a low rumble leaving his chest.

"Tyler," I growl, finally shoving him off because if I don't this will go beyond anything we can recover from.

He stands tall, the hoodie still hanging over his head and the skull paint not even slightly out of place from our lips. The black hollow eye and human eye stare a hole into me while his chest moves up and down, much like my own.

It's in this moment as death stares me in the face I truly see how much power he has over people.

"*Sunny*," he grits out, stalking towards me.

Through my ragged breaths, I raise a hand up. He halts in his tracks, listening to my command. A low snarl bares his teeth as he rolls his neck, working out the sexual frustration coursing through his body. I almost smile, but think better of it.

"Tyler, why did you bring me up here?" I ask, bringing my arms to myself, rubbing away the cold now that the flames inside my body have died down.

He pulls the hoodie over his head, his t-shirt underneath getting caught and exposing the defined V and abs underneath.

He closes the space between us as he shoves the hoodie over my head before I can protest.

Considerate Tyler.

"You shouldn't get involved with a guy like Connor." He takes a step back from me, creating the distance I asked for. Giving me the respect Ryan never did.

"Oh? Who should I be getting involved with, then?"

We can't do this. We can't be jealous.

He pinches the bridge of his nose and runs a hand through his hair, threading them behind his neck. "I don't want you getting involved in anyone that isn't me."

"Tyler, it was just a kiss."

"And what about what just happened?"

"I…" I swallow hard and shake my head.

"So just to be clear then, we are just…"

"*Friends,*" I finish his sentence. *That's all I can give you, Tyler.*

"Friends don't know the way one another tastes."

I open my mouth and close it again. Words are impossible, so I fight him with an unsatisfied look of my own.

He chuckles, and just as quickly as the predator came, it leaves, giving me the Tyler that I know.

"Okay, want to hang out here with me? Just as friends though. I don't want you getting the wrong idea." He arches a brow.

"Sure," I take a careful step forward.

"Perfect." He lays on his back, placing his hands behind his head and looks up at the sky. "Let's watch the stars."

I tilt my head up and to my surprise, there are actually a few stars in the sky, despite the light pollution of the city. I lay down next to him, being sure to keep at least a foot distance between us.

"It can't be anything more than a kiss, Tyler. That's all it can be." I turn my head from the night sky to him. He's watching me, I realize.

"I know," he says softly.

We both look back to the sky, and I still hear the music thrumming beneath us.

"Tell me about your home," he says.

The ache of missing home comes with just the idea of it. Regardless, I know I want to tell him all about it.

You'd love it, Tyler.

"Well, it's definitely much warmer than here. Always warm, honestly. This weather has been a huge change for me."

"This isn't even the beginning," he taunts.

"That's the scary part," I laugh. "I don't even have snow clothes."

"You're in for a rude awakening," he chuckles.

"So encouraging."

This is what we need, Tyler. This is what we can do.

While I spend the rest of the night looking at the sky and telling him all about my home, I realize his eyes never leave me.

A sky filled with stars, and he's looking at me.

CHAPTER TWENTY-THREE

SUNNY

November somehow sneakily rolls in, etching time off here, and moving me towards wherever I'll go next. The colder weather continues to drop, serving as a reminder that I can't go home.

I'd think the silence of Ryan's whereabouts would bring relief, but in all honesty, it's only heightened my anxiety. I don't know where he is or his next move. Although I still live in a constant state of looking over my shoulder and checking the locks on my door throughout the night, it's become more... tolerable.

Tonight is a big event for the Caddell family. They have put a foot into politics. The opening of the brewery and its success for the Mayor is an introduction—a statement into what they could do for future and bigger politicians.

The indoor space is filled with lowlights, booths and tables with free flights of beers and burgers bigger than my head. The outdoor portion is adequately heated with stand up heaters, allowing people to sit comfortably on the couches and tables. Corn hole, giant jenga and many other games cover the outdoor space, entertaining people as the poll votes move along the numerous TV's inside and outside. The place is packed and filled with signs saying *vote for Hernandez.* Or *Secure your vote, get a beer on Hernandez.*

"Let's go outside!" Macey grabs both Sam and I, leading us to some couches that sit by a heater under a pergola.

Looking around, Cole stands tall with security around the venue, wearing a suit that's lined with a bullet proof vest underneath. An earpiece sits subtly in his ear while his eyes scan the venue, his hands resting on the holster that not so subtly pokes out.

After a few short minutes, everyone quiets down when we're greeted with a couple entering the back portion of the venue. Though older, age has done nothing to diminish their good looks. Whether it be the old money that's granted them such luxuries, it only adds to the power and sophistication that radiates from them. It's evident they're well-known by the way people greet them with eager handshakes and intimidated nods.

"Is that the mayor and his wife?" I ask Macey and Sam.

As the couple approaches, I get a better look. The woman's long brown hair somehow doesn't so much as budge from the delicate bun it's been placed in as she scans the venue. For amber eyes, they are still somehow cold, lifeless almost. Her stunning, emerald dress matches the man's eyes she clings to.

That's when I realize exactly who I'm looking at—*Tyler and Sam's parents.*

The man's salt and pepper hair is slicked and groomed, his face clean shaven, showing off the sharp features Tyler inherited. His eyes dance around the venue with amusement, almost like he is above everyone else here, and his appearance is more of a joke than a necessity.

"Nope. That's my parents," Sam groans.

"Mom and Dad are coming." Tyler appears behind us.

Sam completely drains of her normal color and is replaced with a gray hue as her parents approach. Yet, Tyler stands tall with his hands in his pockets, looking unbothered save for the muscle feathering in his jaw.

All I can see is a smaller, more vulnerable Tyler doing the same thing—trying to be brave for his sister in the presence of his parents. Suddenly, I feel anger ignite into a small flame inside me.

"Tyler, this place is a hit!" His mother says as they approach, her once cold eyes turning warm for her son. It's terrifying how easily she can shift. I wonder if that's where Tyler gets it from.

"Hi, mom." He gives her a hug and a kiss on the cheek. So tender and welcoming compared to his father.

"Mom." Sam gives them each a hug. "Daddy."

"Mitchell," Tyler says, shaking his father's hand like they just closed a business deal.

"Good job, Tyler." Mitchell pats his son on the back. I wouldn't be surprised if that's the most affection he's ever received from him.

"Mr. and Mrs. Caddell!" Anthony quips, hugging their mother and shaking hands with their father.

"Anthony, you always do such a lovely job getting these events together. It always flows so smoothly and is just so trendy." The mother smiles.

"What can I say?" Anthony strains a grin.

"It's so good to see you again, Mr. and Mrs. Caddell." Macey nods.

My heart thrums in anticipation for my introduction. The beat of it coursing an odd anger that I can't shake as the flames grow hotter inside me.

"Mom, daddy, this is Sunny. She is my best friend and date tonight!" Sam chimes giddily, no doubt to anger her parents.

The introduction feels like background noise. I keep my gaze on their father, who keeps his gaze on Tyler, who keeps *his* gaze on me.

"These are my parents Mitchell and Diane," Sam says.

Finally I come to, reach my hand out, and plaster a polished smile on my face. "Hi, I'm Sunny. I've heard a lot about you. Especially you." I turn to Mitchell.

The smile fades fast from my face as I look at the man who abused two of the people I love most. Sam huffs a laugh and a smile curves on Tyler's face.

"Sunny? Interesting name." Mitchell takes my hand, squeezing tightly.

"My parents are pretty unconventional." I squeeze back.

"Sunny is a trauma nurse here at Massachusetts General on a travel assignment," Tyler says, taking a step forward with his hands still in his pockets. Dare I say there is a glimmer of pride that passes his eyes.

"Sounds, *exotic*," Diane says, clinging to Mitchell's arm. I notice that a lot about these women, they cling to their husbands like they are their life source.

"We very much appreciate the service you do to our community. I'm not sure if Sam or Tyler told you, but we are actually part contributors of Massachusetts General. Specifically the pediatric ward." *Oh, do I know.* "I'm shocked you have the time to be at such an event as a working woman." Mitchell takes a drink from a waiter, his words no doubt a jab at my place in society.

"I know it's a big night for my family." I motion to them. "So I wouldn't miss it. Besides, if all these working people can do it, then I can too." I meet Mitchell's stare.

"Family," He gives a humorous laugh. "So when does your contract end here?"

"End of February."

"And then where will you go?"

"Wherever I feel like it. That's the beauty of free will."

"Indeed it is. Although everyone is always shackled by something." Mitchell places his empty glass on a waiter's tray and takes another one. His eyes scream, *and I will find what shackles you.*

"Sometimes people are their own shackles." I bite back maybe a little *too* harshly. All of a sudden, everyone finds interest in something else—the floor, the night sky, the surrounding mingling people, the bar.

"Let me refresh your drink for you, Mr. Caddell." Anthony has the right idea about removing himself by taking off into the crowd. I'm feeling a little too petty for that.

"You're a fiery one." Mitchell smiles.

An arm wraps around my waist, moving me away from Mitchell. I look up to see Tyler standing between us. Mitchell's face says he's formulating a plan to discover more about me and Tyler's reaction says he's ready to be the roadblock to that plan.

"That's our Sunny." Tyler keeps his hand on my waist and the other in his pocket. "Mitchell, have you seen Mayor Hernandez yet? Last I saw him, he was inside. He's very happy with the turnout tonight. We are up fifteen percent in votes already."

I don't need saving, Tyler.

Dropping his gaze to Tyler's hand on my waist, a muscle flexes in Mitchell's jaw. His eyes flick back to Tyler with a cold rage that has me shivering despite my proudness to stand tall.

"Shelby, darling!" Diane chimes as the barbie approaches the mess unraveling here. They give one another a hug and kiss like the French do, giggling over one another's outfits and the event.

Tyler's body stiffens and his grip on me becomes almost possessive. He's unmoving from my side regardless of his bride to be approaching. I look down to hide my ever growing smile.

"How convenient," Sam groans.

Macey downs the entirety of her wine in one swig and covers her laugh with a cough.

"Shelby, how lovely to see you." Mitchell gives her a hug

and kiss on her forehead. *Wow, so he is human.* "Where are your parents?"

"They're inside saying hi to Mayor Hernandez." She smiles. Scanning the group, her eyes land on Tyler's hand around my waist. I smile because I *want* her to see it and know she's no longer an option for him.

Tyler takes Shelby's hand, pressing his lips to it as a way of greeting, but still keeps his free hand around my waist. *Is this you making a statement, Tyler?* If it is, I'll gladly be the poster for it.

"Mr. and Mrs. Caddell." Cole comes from the masses of people. He shakes both their hands and guides them towards the brewery. "Let me take you to Mayor Hernandez. He's been looking forward to seeing you two all evening."

Tensions are palpable. Eyes are staring. *Hands* are clutching.

"Tyler, have you seen Mayor Hernandez yet?" Mitchell shoots his son a look.

"It was the first introduction I made when I got here," he assures.

"Tyler is truly so good at what he does! Born for it." Shelby takes a sip of her drink and places a hand on Tyler's shoulder. Though his blank stare remains, his body completely tenses.

What did she do to you?

He eyes her absently for a brief moment, then back to the parents who are now being escorted to the mayor by Cole.

"It's so cold tonight. My body is *not* used to this." I rub my bare arms.

Just as I thought would happen, Tyler instinctively pulls his jacket off and drapes it around my shoulders, knocking Shelby's hand off his shoulder in the process.

She watches every move, indicating my little trick is a success. She swallows slowly, clutching her champagne flute tighter, eyeing me up and down. "Who are you?"

"I'm Sunny. Who are you?"

"I'm Shelby."

I tilt my head in mock confusion. "I don't recall the name. No one has mentioned you before."

She stares at me. "I'm going to go find my parents. They've been wanting to see you, Tyler! Don't be a stranger." She squeezes his arm and takes off into the crowds.

Success.

A simultaneous breath is released from all of us. Tyler's once tense body becomes relaxed with my touch.

And his arm doesn't leave my shoulders.

CHAPTER TWENTY-FOUR
TYLER

My father is a smart man, regardless of his alcohol consumption. Down to who he is, what he does and who he does it with. He craves power and control, which is why he's started funneling money into politicians. Soon, when his strings are secured, he will be at the top.

The disapproval was already prevalent as soon as Sunny was introduced. Anyone outside of Shelby doesn't stand a chance to them. Yet, Sunny stood tall and didn't cower from them the way they expected. I fucking *love* that girl.

Walking to the balcony that overlooks the outside of the brewery, I find Mitchell there. He's leaning against the railing with a drink in hand, looking at all the people down below.

I find my place next to him while he continues looking out. Avoiding him is a coward's move. I'll face my biggest opponent and I'll do it with a smile on my face.

"So, that's why things fell through with Shelby," he says.

"I'm not sure what you mean?"

Downing the rest of his drink, he slams the glass down and meets my gaze. "You're in love with her." His eyes narrow below as a sadistic smile pulls his lips.

Following Mitchell's line of sight, I see Sunny, Sam, and Macey all huddled together on the couches outside, laughing. My suit jacket still slung around Sunny's shoulders—an unspoken claim to her.

Swallowing hard, I remove my gaze from her and look at him. "I don't know what you're talking about. Things fell through with Shelby long before Sunny came into my life."

Don't take her from me.

"Oh please, Tyler. It's written all over your face. You aren't very good at hiding your emotions. Never have been."

He knows the blow he just landed on me, considering I've spent my life mastering the death of my emotions because of him.

That's always been his play, to threaten the people I love most if I don't move when he tugs on my strings. Now he sees his biggest advantage.

"You better be careful, boy. You have a duty. I don't care what happened, you fix it. A promise is a promise, and she was promised to you."

I roll my eyes. "Free will exists, Mitchell."

He lets out an amused laugh, "Now you even sound like her. Have I not taught you better than to be whipped by pussy? Do not fuck this up more than you already have. You are *someone* and she is *no one*."

My jaw clenches as I try to bite back the words I want to scream. *She is everything.* Clearly the look on my face is evident, because he just keeps fucking going.

"That bad, huh? *Pathetic.* That will only make you weaker, Tyler. That's why we don't marry for love. Makes people too messy and irrational."

He's tugging at my strings, desperately provoking a reaction from me to further prove his point. So I close my eyes and take in a deep breath to calm the instinct inside me to move.

I start walking away before I do something to cause a scene and further prove his point.

"We marry for respect, politics, power, contracts, breeding, loyalty, names, bloodlines. Get that around your head." He taps his head. "You are twenty-nine years old and not married. You need a respectable woman by your side, so it makes you look like a respectable man. She is a *nurse*, that's all. She has a career and a woman by your side can't have that. Your wife's career will be you and your children. It will be supporting you. Her life will be *you*," he seethes. "You will marry Shelby, and when that time comes, you can fuck around with whoever. Just make sure you get the right one pregnant."

I stop at his words and turn around to look at the man I share blood with, forcing me into a world I never wanted to begin with.

"You mess this up and I'll make sure you never see her again," Mitchell threatens.

"You're pathetic," I say and leave the balcony.

Little does he know I'll kill him before that ever happens.

SUNNY

After a little bit of searching, I found a small balcony overlooking the outdoor portion of the brewery. My social battery is low, especially after working the last three days. It makes me wonder how these people do it. How they go to events like these filled to the brim with all the most important and powerful people. How they keep their social batteries charged with so much interaction and importance.

But it's like Sam and Tyler told me, they were raised and born for this. *Bred* for it. Products of their environment. If anything, this is probably just a normal Saturday night for them.

Hearing footsteps behind me, I peer over my shoulder to see Tyler standing before me, looking devastating with his hands in the pockets of his charcoal gray suit.

"Can I help you?" I ask, looking back out to the crowd down below while I try to stifle the heat flooding my cheeks.

"There you are," he whispers. The familiarity of his citrusy, salt scent settles against my skin and fills my lungs. A comfort that I didn't realize became one.

Reaching both arms around my body, he grasps the railing I'm leaning against. His hard chest presses into my back, bringing his face next to mine from behind.

I feel his heart beating against me so calmly. So confident while mine goes rampant.

"Thank you for coming," he whispers.

"Don't get used to it."

His laugh is dark as night but light as day. I feel the vibrations of him along my body as his warm breath coats the crook of my neck. Leaning my head as if I'm observing something, I welcome him instead—a delicate line we tread too often. He grazes his lips and nose along my neck and the side of my cheek, accepting the invitation.

"This. This is what I can never get used to," he whispers against my skin.

That soul bridge is just *begging* us to cross it. The more I resist, the more it pulls me closer, as if there's an invisible string tethering us together. No amount of untying will release me from him. My bloody fingers are proof of that.

He lays a hand over mine, removing it from the railing. "Let me see you." He spins me slowly like he always does.

Our eyes meet, his full with such a feral desire that has my breath hitching. He leans in close, breathing me in as if I'm his oxygen source. A feline smile spreads across his face as I hold his stare while he thumbs my bottom lip. I know the things he's done, and I'm not scared of him. A man trained to kill yet here I am, *challenging* him.

His eyes flick to something behind me, and all of a sudden a too wide distance is made between us. I attempt to turn and see where his gaze was focused, but he interrupts me as he pokes an arm out for me to grab. "Shall we?"

"We shall." I lace my arm around his, heading downstairs to the crowds of people I don't know.

What did you see, Tyler?

TYLER

We're parted within minutes because, well, she's technically Sam's date, not mine. One day, she will be though. No matter the look Mitchell gave me when he caught us on the balcony.

He thinks my love for Sunny is a weakness, but little does he know it's now my greatest strength. It's the thing I needed to finally take the step I've been contemplating for far too long.

"Tyler." I hear Shelby call my name.

Instinctively my jaw clenches at her voice. I don't want to deal with her right now, but curiosity has me wondering if her presence will summon my girl again. Jealousy looks so damn good on her.

"This place is awesome. The votes are up by a lot. I can't wait to see what your contribution will do for my father's campaign in the spring. You're going to become a big-name campaign investor. I feel it." Her hand falls on my shoulder, all while her brown eyes sparkle with a hope that should've been dead long ago.

I have nothing to say. The only reason she is here is because she saw the interaction between Sunny and I. It'd either send her running in the opposite direction or make her see the challenge and want to up it.

To my unfortunate luck, she saw the challenge and took it. The only upside is that Sunny will, too.

"Tyler, come on." She tugs my arm, trying to regain the attention she's been lacking from me. I don't have the fucking patience for this.

"What do you want from me?"

"I want you to forgive me. We are supposed to get married, Tyler. You can't prolong the inevitable." Her eyes plead, but I have no remorse.

"I think you forget who I am, Shelby." I eye her with a threat looming between us.

"You and I both know that won't work."

"Don't challenge me."

I want her to be afraid of me and what I can do. I want her to fear me so she will leave me the fuck alone. She gets off on my power and money, but I'll make sure it scares her shitless instead.

She swallows hard, and while I wish I cared if she cried, I don't. I also don't want to deal with a crying Shelby right now. I dealt with enough of that my entire life.

"We are supposed to be together, Tyler. We were made for one another." She tries to grab my hand.

I jerk away from her. "No, we are not."

Because I am made for Sunny.

"What can I do to make this better? It's been almost a year. How much longer are you going to punish me?"

"Punish you? Shelby, you know what you fucking did. You know what you took from me."

"I told you I was sorry and that I would do anything to make up for what I did. It was selfish. I know that. But we can fix it." She tries to place a hand on my face, but I step back from her.

"I will make your life a living hell if you don't let it go and leave me the fuck alone."

"Our parents have had this promise to one another since before we were born. *We* have had this promise. You and I have been promised to one another since before we were alive." She uses it as a threat, like she does most things. I'm not a man of words—I'm a man of *action*.

"I have no problem breaking promises, Shelby." I place my drink on a waiter tray and walk away.

SUNNY

Shortly after Tyler and I's separation, Sam wastes no time bringing me to jet black hair and ice blue eyes. *Connor*. He stands tall, wearing a black suit that frames his toned body well, clearly waiting for my arrival. Sam's on a mission, and unfortunately that mission is me getting laid by Connor.

"Look who I found!" Sam presents me like a gift.

"Fancy seeing you here." He grabs my hand, pressing his lips to it.

"It really is, isn't it?" Sam places her hands on her hips. "Well, I'm needed somewhere that isn't here. I'll catch you two hotties later." She takes off into the crowd.

"Sam!" I try stopping her, but she takes off before I can even attempt. Sighing, I look at Connor. "I'm sorry about my obnoxious friend."

"It's okay. I've known Sam for a while. I know what she's doing. But even if she weren't, I'd be lying if I said I wouldn't try myself." He grins.

I smile, considering somehow, even after years in a relationship, I still have *some* game. I'm not sure what to say or how to react, because just moments ago, Tyler and I were inches from one another's faces. The kiss we both so desperately wanted looming over our heads.

What I told him on Halloween still stands true. We can *only* be friends because he could never be a fling. But Connor, maybe he can be.

"Want to play corn-hole?" I motion to the game.

"Sure." He smiles. "So," he says, grabbing a sack and tossing. "I'm a little confused because as you know, this world is huge yet tightly knit. I've never seen you around the Caddell's or anyone for that matter. What brought you here?" He scores.

"Well, I'm a nurse here on a travel assignment. I met Sam in her paint shop. The rest is history." I throw a sack, missing pathetically.

He looks down at it and smiles. "How long are you here for?"

"My contract ends in February." I watch as he scores again.

"So Boston is temporary, then?"

I miss again. I hate this game. "That is correct."

"I don't suppose you have someone waiting for you back home?" His eyes meet mine.

"I do not."

We both know where this is going. We just don't know how to verbalize it. Honestly? I'm not sure I want to.

"So." He takes another sack in his hand.

"So."

He swallows hard. "I don't have anyone waiting, either." He throws the sack, missing this time—I have leverage now.

"Convenient." I throw my sack and I actually score.

"It is. Except, I did just get out of a long-term relationship."

"Me too."

"Convenient." He smiles.

"Yes, it is." I smile back.

This feels foreign, and it almost feels wrong, even though I know it shouldn't. I should be allowed to do this, even if my heart is trying to drag me back to that balcony.

He throws his sack and scores. "So."

"So."

"You're probably like me, and not really looking for anything serious, right?" His eyes flick up to me from under his dark brows.

"Right," I assure him.

"Perfect."

"Perfect."

I throw my sack and score.

CHAPTER TWENTY-FIVE

TYLER

Naturally, I'm pulled away by a group of businessmen who want to talk contracts with me. I'd be lying if I said I'm paying attention, because my sister offers Sunny on a silver fucking platter to Connor.

I watch as he takes her hand and presses his lips to her soft skin. Little does he know my own lips were on hers just weeks ago, and she loved every minute of it. I wish I could've branded myself there, so he'd know to back the fuck off. You'd think after Halloween he'd get the idea, but Connor was never a bright one.

They share smiles while laughing and playing cornhole and something inside my chest cracks. She *smiled* for him. So easily she gave him that precious jewel, when I spent weeks, fucking *weeks* trying to get that.

Connor's little heart just got broken by the love of his life. The girl he once was convinced he'd marry decided to ride another dick. He isn't looking for anything serious—he's looking for a fuck and fling.

Sunny is *not* that girl. No, someone like Sunny is for fucking life.

Shelby already pissed me off, so I'm not willing to sit here and let this happen tonight. Maybe Mitchell is right, because right now, I'm beyond irrational. Before I can even stop myself, I'm walking towards them.

Friends my fucking ass. Sunny and I are not just friends. We can *never* be just friends. Connor still tries to make a pass when another man's damn coat is around her shoulders.

"Sunny, can I speak with you?" I ask.

She looks me up and down. "No." And continues playing cornhole, ignoring me entirely now.

I can't decide if I'm turned on or pissed off by her confidence. My little fire is learning just how much power she has over me. I'm about to show her just how much power I have, too.

Connor observes us with a smug smile. I never liked the guy, and when I look at him, I plan out all the ways I'll make him pay for this. The first being cutting his hands off, the last will be carving his eyes out so that he can see everything I do to him, first.

"Sunny, please," I say through gritted teeth, giving her one last chance before I snap.

"Tyler, no." She tosses a sack and scores. "Yes!" she cheers, acting as if I'm not standing here like a fucking puppy dog begging for her attention.

Leaning my head back, I look up at the sky. If I don't fucking do something, she'll be going home with Connor tonight, and I'm not about to let that happen. She's going to be pissed, because I'm about to be the biggest cock block of her life.

Despite my fuming rage, I keep my calm demeanor as I stalk over to her and sling her over my shoulder in one simple swoop.

"Tyler!" she yells. She beats my back with her fists, fighting my hold. It's laughable, honestly. All our training down the drain in this single moment.

Turning to Connor, I smile. "Have a good night, Connor."

And I take what's mine.

CHAPTER TWENTY-SIX

SUNNY

Angry is an understatement. I'm fucking *livid*. I hit his back as hard as I can, but he doesn't budge as he carries me through the venue, not caring about all the shocked faces watching us.

He walks up the stairs taking two at a time in swift motions, bringing me back to the balcony we stood at earlier. He stares at me blankly when he sets me down.

Straightening my jumpsuit, I realize his jacket is still around my shoulders. I take it off and shove it in his chest. "What the actual fuck, Tyler?"

He pushes it back to me. "I told you not to get involved with a guy like him."

"It's none of your business who I involve myself in." I cross my arms, refusing to take the jacket back.

He sighs and slings it around my shoulders again. "It's my business when it involves my family," he growls, crossing his arms over his chest.

"Tyler, he is a perfectly kind man."

He shakes his head. "No he isn't."

"How do you know?"

"I grew up with him, Sunny."

"We have an understanding."

His jaw flexes at my comment because Tyler's jealous. He's jealous for *me*.

He places his hands in his pockets, looking down at his shoes. "And that's what you want?"

No. "Yes," I say before I say anything else.

"Well, then." He takes a step closer to me. "If a fuck is what you want, Sunny, then a fuck is what I can give you."

The human disappears as fast as it came. He's all predator as he takes each step closer to me. I can physically see it, the switch that happens in his eyes.

"Either way, at least I know that when his tongue explores your mouth but never in ways mine did and doesn't taste like me, when his fingers meet that spot on your neck that hurts with anyone else but me, when he doesn't satisfy you in the ways you know I would, I know you'll be thinking about me the whole time, the same way you did on Halloween night," he whispers in my ear. "The same way you always will when it isn't me."

He brushes my hair from my neck, exposing that scar for his lips to brand. My body betrays me as his touch manifests in goosebumps and shivers. When he pulls away, he looks down at me with stupid admiration.

"When that happens, because I know it will, you know who to call." He starts walking away, but I refuse to let him have the last word.

"Why are you so upset? Huh? I told you what I could give you. Why are you expecting more?"

He pauses and turns around, looking straight at me. I realize he looks at me like there is something worth looking at. For some reason, it brings unshed tears to my eyes.

"You smiled for him," he says.

"What? What does that even have to do with anything?"

"If there's anything I learned, those smiles are rare to come by. It's hard to get one. I've spent so much time trying, and I've succeeded a handful of times. In one night you gave him the one thing I've been working months to get." He looks at the floor, as if the words physically pain him.

I shake my head. "Tyler, that's…that's not how it is. But it just comes to show that I don't have a lot to give. I barely have anything. He…he took it all."

He steps into me again. "Don't underestimate yourself, little fire. You have a lot to give. But I'm not asking for anything. I'm asking you to accept what I am giving you. Take it all, Sunny. Take it from me. Take all you need, because I will always keep giving myself to you if it means I can keep that smile on your face." He thumbs my bottom lip.

Pulling back, he turns around, hands in his pockets and walks away triumphantly.

I still have his damn jacket around my shoulders.

"Dude what the actual fucking fuck?" Sam pulls me back to the couches we claimed for the night.

"I have no clue." I shrug.

"What was that even about?" Macey asks.

"Are you fucking him?" Sam asks curiously.

I shake my head. "No, not at all. I guess he just doesn't like Connor."

"Doesn't like Connor my ass. He barely knows Connor. Something must be up." Sam's eyes turn to slits, scanning the venue.

"What did he say to you?" Macey asks.

Tyler likes me. And I may just like him, too.

"He just said Connor isn't a good guy and doesn't want anything serious," I say.

Macey hands me a glass of wine while she settles herself on the couch. I take a sip, hoping it'll calm my racing heart.

"Doesn't he know that's the whole fucking point?" Sam raises her hands.

Nodding, I swallow down my wine. "Yes, I told him that. But you know your brother better than anyone, he gets protective of his family."

"What if he likes you?" Macey suggests.

"He doesn't," I counter.

"I mean it would make sense." Sam bites her tie dye nail.

"Guys, he doesn't. I promise," I lie.

"Okay well, we can't let my brother cock block your night. You deserve to be dicked and dined." Sam stands up. "I'm going to find Connor."

"Sam, *no*. He probably doesn't want anything to do with me after that whole debacle."

"He was practically drooling on the cornhole pallets." Sam scans the venue.

"How about we just let him come to me then?" I suggest.

"God, my parents are going to be pissed. It's going to be awesome." Sam sits back down.

Laughing, I agree. At least there will be one positive outcome of this whole scenario. I haven't seen their parents since our initial introductions, and I honestly don't want to, either. I know if I did, I'd do or say something that would get all of us in trouble.

"What a damn night." Macey shakes her head, staring off into nothing while she takes a sip of her drink.

"You're telling me," I say.

My body already hums with the warmth of the wine.

"Can we order something?" I ask.

"You read my fucking mind. Waiter!" Sam yells. "We need fries. Lots of fries."

TYLER

"Tyler, everyone saw that," Cole says. "What if it affects the polls?"

"Yeah, I know, and frankly I don't fucking care." I pace.

"You will care once Mitchell finds out, if he already didn't see," Cole mutters.

"People have done worse things in public, Cole."

"I wonder if Shelby saw," Anthony quips.

"Of course she fucking saw. The whole venue saw," Cole growls. "Fuck, her dad probably saw. Tyler, I am not in the mood to have to break up fights tonight."

"If Connor doesn't fucking stop drooling over Sunny and trying to get in her pants, then there won't have to be a fight tonight." I grip the table near us. "I kissed her," I finally admit. *And did more.*

Hanging his head between his shoulders, Cole looks back up at me. "Go on."

"This night just keeps getting better." Anthony leans against the wall with his arms crossed over his chest.

"I kissed her the night we trained together in the gym. And she kissed me back. It's there, you guys. I know she feels something. There is something fucking there." I sound like a desperate man, and maybe I am, but it's only for her.

"You're making this really fucking hard for me, Tyler," Cole sighs. "This, this changes things."

"We can't betray her trust. But we can cock block for you." Anthony shrugs.

"We have to be smart, not irrational," Cole reminds me.

"I know. I know." I say.

"Okay, this is what we can do –" Cole starts.

"Fucking shit, Tyler." I hear Mitchell say behind me.

"I'm not in the mood, Mitchell."

"Well, I wasn't really in the mood for you to walk through the event with a woman who isn't your bride to be over your shoulder, Not only in front of everyone, but her god damn parents," he seethes. The closer he gets, the more I can smell the alcohol seeping from his bulging veins and sweating skin.

"Well, it's a good thing they all know where I stand then," I challenge.

"Tyler!" He throws his glass, shattering it.

Cole and Anthony immediately step between us, but they're too late. I fist his shirt, slamming him against a wall. "Look who is irrational and making a scene, now. Don't ever fucking threaten me again." I throw him, watching him stumble on his feet.

He's got his teeth in me, but I'm about to fucking bite back.

CHAPTER TWENTY-SEVEN

SUNNY

A glass breaking in the distance captures all our attention. I hold my breath as we watch the fallout between Tyler and Mitchell. Now I understand why Mitchell has Tyler do his dirty work—Mitchell is sloppy and Tyler is practiced.

"Oh god," Sam groans. "Daddy is not happy."

"Jesus Christ." I get up. "Fuck this,"

"Where are you going?" Macey asks.

"To go find Connor and put an end to all the starting rumors."

"Yeah, Sunny, get it girl!" Sam says, mimicking a cowboy riding a horse with a lasso.

Laughing, I turn around to see Tyler stalking through the crowd with Cole and Anthony attempting to help Mitchell on his stumbling feet. He shrugs the two guys off, refusing their help as he shuffles towards the bar. When he notices me, his eyes follow me through the crowd while I look for Connor. No doubt does he assume I'm looking for his son, since Tyler is clearly looking for me.

They're all angry over one common denominator. *Me*. So I'm going to make a fucking point to all of them. Mitchell's eyes narrow on me, watching my every move. *I will fucking give you a show.* Statements are necessary in crowds like this, and I'm going to make one.

When I find Connor standing with a group of people, I march myself over to him, grab him by his shirt collar and press my lips against his.

At first, he's taken aback. His hands fall to my hips, tugging me closer so our kiss can get deeper.

And Tyler is right—he's always fucking right.

The only thing getting me through this kiss with Connor is thinking about what it was like with Tyler. Still, I continue working my mouth on his, making my fucking statement. Pulling back, I slip a piece of paper that has my number on it.

"We have an agreement?" I ask.

He looks at me wide-eyed. "Of course."

"Okay." I push him off. When I turn I have two sets of emerald eyes on me—one Tyler's, one his father's.

I turn to Mitchell and flip him off.

TYLER

I can't explain what happens inside me when I see her lips on his, but all I know—it isn't good. I don't care who he is, but eventually, he will be dead.

All I know is she wants to get her point across not just to me, but Mitchell too. And when she turned around and flipped him off, it only made me love her more.

I fucking *love* that girl.

I watch with a smile because I know when her lips were on his she was tasting me the whole goddamn time. My girl knows what she wants, but she is still confused about what she needs.

Slowly, she will learn.

I will make her mine. She will find her way to me. She just gave me a challenge, and little does Sunny darling know, I love a fucking challenge.

I start packing my things in my office to head to family dinner when I hear my phone buzz on my desk. Picking it up, I see a message from Mitchell with coordinates and a *task*.

> Darren Danforth. I want it done tonight. No questions asked.

I blink at the message. Usually, Mitchell gives me the courtesy of time and questions— the time to research our target to make it as clean of a hunt as possible.

I understand he's upset about what happened at the brewery, but he's usually smarter than this. Mitchell doesn't kill just to kill. But no questions asked means no questions asked. So I won't ask any and prolong my time to get to family dinner more than it already has been. It may bite me in the ass, but that's a mess for later.

Pulling up the coordinates has a pit in my stomach. I don't like completing hits without knowing exactly who it is and what I'm walking into.

Tonight, Mitchell is persistent, and I'm not in the business of challenging the threats he made to me at the brewery. My girl has enough to be running from, I won't add to that list.

Peeling off my work clothes, I exchange them for my gear. Boots a size bigger, filled in to leave no distinct print. A black hoodie and pants along with a backlav to make sure no trace of me is recognizable. I've mastered it so easily, it ultimately becomes another part of my day that doesn't require much thinking.

I get in my truck and drive to the place Mitchell gave me, playing music to distract myself from what I'm about to do—but it doesn't help. This one isn't sitting right with me.

I pull up to Harvard University; my alma mater. Entering the campus, I'm brought back to memories of me, Anthony, and Cole here.

Lots of nights throwing up in random bushes, pulling pranks on the trust fund frat boys who bought their way into this school. It's where we started our annual Christmas sledding competition. It's where we started our family dinner.

All the traditions I hope to see Sunny through. Thinking about her in a time like this grounds me. My heart started beating differently when she came into my life. It has more purpose now that she's here. A reason to walk out of a hit rather than let it go south.

As I walk through the building, I see the name of the man I'm about to kill on the signs leading me to his office in the building of fine arts.

Darren Danforth, Head of Fine Arts, Harvard University.
Why does Mitchell want a professor killed?

The name rings a bell. He was the professor that helped Sam when she was here. He let her use the art studio here as her outlet because she couldn't get a degree in art herself.

That can't be why Mitchell wants him dead, right? That was almost ten years ago. Sam got her degree in finance, and her art studio doesn't interfere with her work at the company.

The alternative comes to mind. Did he do something to hurt Sam? If so, that makes this job a hell of a lot easier than it initially was.

Standing at the door of his office, I pause. A part of me wants to turn away and just leave. But Mitchell will make me pay for that, and I know the first thing he will take as payment.

When I open the door, the man jolts in his seat and his eyes turn wide when he sees me standing in the doorway. He recognizes me and for some reason, something about him is familiar, too.

His brown hair is flecked with salt and pepper, his brown eyes wide as he watches me. He licks his trembling full lips, trying to formulate words. He knows who I am, and why I'm here—like he was expecting me. *What did you do, Darren?*

If it was anything involving Sam, I would've known. *I would've known.*

He lifts his arms in surrender. "Mr. Caddell. Let's just talk about this."

I stalk over to him. Though his panic is prevalent, he willingly lets me take his hands and tie them behind his back. Forcing him to his knees, I pause again. *I fucking pause.* Why is this so hard tonight?

Darren's shoulders shudder up and down with hushed cries. I finally turn him to face me, deciding to make this quick and look like a suicide. Bullet to the head is usually a man's choice of a way to go, anyways.

A knife is usually my choice of weapon, and I usually prolong the pain since the ones I normally kill are sick fucks. Men who have done bad things to hurt our name. But something tells me this hit is personal to Mitchell, and that the man in front of me isn't like the others.

Fuck.

"Please, I'll pay him whatever," he begs. "I'll disappear. I'll do whatever he asks. Just let me talk to him. Man to man."

Closing my eyes, I sigh as I lean my head back. I fucking hate this. I fucking hate what Mitchell has made me. Maybe I am just as bad as him.

"Sorry, man. Orders are orders." Turning my head, I close my eyes as I place the barrel of the gun to the side of his head. I pull the trigger.

The cries are silenced and met with a thud as his body hits the ground. I stand over his lifeless body, wondering if he had a girl or children at home. If I didn't do it, someone else would've. They would've been a lot less merciful than me.

Usually, I know every dirty detail of the hits I complete. I follow them and learn all about them. That's usually how I see the dirty, awful things they do behind closed doors. Something tells me this wasn't a bad man. I decide to not look further into him, even after this, because it'll only make me feel worse.

Untying his hands, I place the gun in his dominant one. I noticed it when he had a pencil in his hand. It looks like he was sketching something on his desk.

I could spend the night digging around, but I choose not to. I'm scared I'll find something that will make me regret completing this. So, I walk out of the office and shut the door behind me. When I get back to my truck, I peel my gloves and clothes off, dressing back into my work clothes so my family doesn't suspect anything.

I sit in my truck, rubbing my face and grab my phone to send a text to Mitchell.

Done.

CHAPTER TWENTY-EIGHT

SUNNY

Nothing more happened since the night at the brewery, and all seems to finally be right in the world. Sam and I walk into Cole's apartment, with Macey and Anthony already there. Tonight is pizza and movie night—a family favorite.

"Where is my twin?" Sam asks, placing wine on the kitchen counter.

"Late night in the office," Cole says, hugging the both of us. Macey follows with glasses ready.

"He's been having a lot of those, huh?" I ask.

"After what happened at the brewery, Mitchell has a tight leash on him and is swamping him in work," Anthony says, examining two movie cases.

I never found out what happened between Tyler and Mitchell. I'm not sure I want to know, but I also can't stand the idea of Tyler being punished for it.

"You still have actual DVD's?" Sam looks at Cole.

"He even has a VHS in his bedroom," Macey laughs, playfully elbowing Cole.

"Old soul much, Cole?" I toy.

"He always has been," Tyler says in the doorway. "I swear, by the time we were six he was writing poetry."

He looks...*worn*.

"There is our businessman!" Anthony chimes.

Setting his bag on the floor, Tyler gives his brother a hug. He makes his rounds, giving each one of us his greetings. I'm last, with his hug lingering a little longer than normal. A deep inhale is pulled from him, slowly being released as his tense body starts to settle against mine. His hand lingers on my waist when he pulls away, and only leaves when he grabs a beer from Cole.

He takes a seat at one of the barstools, tugging at his already loose tie. His once neatly groomed hair looks like a girl's fingers ran through it.

"Okay, the choices are Die Hard and the Lion King." Anthony holds up the two movies.

"After all that time, that's what you come up with?" Sam asks.

"Those are terrible choices," Macey says.

A smile forms on my lips while I watch them all banter.

"They are fantastic choices!" Anthony quips.

"I vote for the Lion King. I could use a good cry," Tyler takes a swig of his beer with a smile. The facade for his family is up.

"Daddy working you too hard there?" Anthony plays.

Raising his brows, he takes another swig of his beer and lets out a sigh through his nose. He says everything without saying it at all.

Our eyes meet, and he gives me a small smile before immersing himself into the conversation about which movie to watch tonight. His hand finds my thigh, giving me a small squeeze and resting it there.

He doesn't move. I don't move. We just sit there like that, as if it's normal. As if no one will see. As if we are Sunny and Tyler. A pair rather than two separate beings.

I cling to my glass of wine, certain I can shatter it with how hard I'm squeezing it. He's still immersed in conversation while my world is halted with his hand still on my thigh.

"Sunny?" I hear my name called.

"What?"

Biting back a smile, Tyler removes his hand from my thigh. The warmth that was there now replaced with the lack of him.

"Which movie?" Anthony holds up the DVDs again.

"Umm, Lion King."

"I think that's a fantastic choice." Tyler stands from the barstool and tosses his empty beer in the recycling bin.

"Your hair looks like you just got fucked. Were you really at work?" Sam asks, narrowing her eyes.

Cole and Anthony freeze at Sam's comment, making my stomach churn. What do they know?

Tyler only smiles as he walks up to his sister with his hands in his pockets. "Wouldn't you like to know."

"Yes, actually I would."

I just sit here spinning my wine glass, trying to ignore the skipping beats my heart is slamming against my sternum.

"I don't kiss and tell," Tyler says, grabbing the Lion King and waltzing to the living room.

"Lion King it is!" Anthony says.

"Pizza is ready!" Macey yells.

Cole grabs plates. Sam pours more wine. I continue to clutch my glass.

TYLER

When I put my hand on her thigh it told me everything I needed to know. *You like me, Sunny.* She refused to look up at me when it was insinuated I fucked another girl, reaffirming everything.

Mitchell's anger is exhausting, but it's fine. I'll use it as leverage to show him up and get it done with a smile on my fucking face. I'm good at what I do, and he knows that. He wants to see me crack—to see where my threshold is. What he doesn't know is I don't have one. All thanks to him.

Everyone is snuggled up on the couches. Sunny's legs are in my lap, toes painted white and with a toe ring of a sea turtle on her right foot. Even her damn feet are pretty.

She smells like a day at the beach. The contact with her is making me come back to reality.

A buzz between us draws our attention where our phones casually sit. Connor's name lights her screen, which has my jaw flexing. Her overtime hours at work had me convinced their agreement was a failed attempt. Then again, when a person is desperate, a late-night call is never off the table. We all know that.

I look at her phone and then at her, where her blue-greens stare at me. She quickly grabs her phone from between us and reads the message. I grab my own, pressing a few buttons and then set it back down. I take her feet in my hands and start rubbing them so that she's thinking about my hands while she's texting him.

"What are you doing?" she whispers.

"You've been working a lot. Your feet probably hurt," I say, running my hands up her legs, stopping at her thighs.

What she also doesn't know is how much I need this fucking contact.

"You aren't wrong," she says, still clutching her phone in her hands.

I continue my work on her feet while she types away on her phone.

"Cole, I think your wifi went down?" Sunny says.

Cole grabs his phone, checking the connection. "Says the connection is fine."

"Weird, my messages won't go through."

I run a tongue along my teeth, trying to avoid the smile that'll give me away. She hasn't responded yet, and doesn't try to further investigate the reason her messages won't send to Connor.

Instead, she settles into the couch, letting me continue to rub her feet like the good fucking girl she is.

CHAPTER TWENTY-NINE

TYLER

I CONTINUE COOKING IN MY KITCHEN AS PEOPLE HAPPILY WALK through my door, adding to the buffet already filling up the island in honor of Thanksgiving.

Typically, we invite a few more people when it comes to Friendsgiving. Those who don't want to attend the overzealous parties that their parents throw. Close enough to us to receive an invite, but far enough to not be a part of our family. Safe enough to allow in my home for a few hours.

After throwing my oven mitts off, I lean against the counter with my arms crossed as I wait for Sunny to walk through the door.

Each knock has my eyes flicking to the door, hoping to see her walk through with her wild blonde hair and a plate full of her now famous cookies she claims are the only good thing she can make. She knows by now knocking isn't necessary for her to gain access to my home. Still, each one has me glancing that way.

It's been three months since she's completed our family. She just fits in somehow, like a missing piece we never knew we needed. That *I* didn't realize I needed.

My black marble fireplace roars while everyone lounges on the couches and stands around mingling while sipping drinks and snacking on appetizers.

My eyes flick to the door, knowing she is about to walk through. Soon enough, blonde curls and round eyes walks through the door.

A smile pulls my lips, but falters as soon as I realize she isn't alone. A man walks behind her, following her lead into *my* home.

What the fuck is Connor doing here?

I fucking blocked his number off her phone. Her numerous overtime shifts were approved by the hospital, I made sure of that. Connor's apartment complex he invested in flooded. In what fucking world do these two have time for this?

My girl approaches the kitchen to place her dish down with Connor following her like a puppy on a leash. I keep my composure as he puts a hand on the small of her back. Every muscle in my body tenses, my heart hammering despite my neutral demeanor.

"Hey, Tyler," she greets me but doesn't meet my stare.

"Sunny." I wrap my arms around her, giving her a kiss on the head, placing my chin on top of her sunshine hair.

My eyes narrow on Connor while he stands behind her, holding another plate of cookies, shifting on his feet uncomfortably.

"Connor." I reach a hand to shake his, keeping my arm around my girl. I squeeze maybe a bit too hard by the subtle wince that flutters across his face. I'm making him nervous. I want him running out of here with his tail between his damn legs.

"Glad you could make it. Sorry to hear about the apartments. What a shame." I finally release his hand and continue to stare blankly when he stretches it.

He gives a strained smile. "How'd you hear about that?"

"Talk of the town." I shrug, knowing damn well I'm the

reason behind the destruction of his only source of income. "Have they figured out what happened?"

"Old pipes, I guess," he sighs. "I'm not even sure it's worth saving at this point."

I bite back a smile and turn to the food on the stove, noting the stare and creased brows Sunny gives me. They make their way to *my* living room and nestle into *my* couch together.

Fucking prick.

SUNNY

Shit.

That is not a good look on his face. Most would see it and not think anything of it. Probably indifference, but I know Tyler better than that. Despite the blank look he gave us walking through the door, I could see the details already being formed behind those eyes. And I'm truly fearful for Connor at this moment.

My relationship with Connor is for Tyler's benefit on many different levels. He has a bride to be, and that was almost up in flames the night of the brewery—so I set things straight.

I'm leaving, and Tyler's reactions have made it abundantly clear that his feelings go beyond the physical. Which is something neither of us should mess around with.

After not being able to text him for so long due to an automated update on my phone, Connor's contact was deleted and blocked from my phone along with a few others. He finally got a new phone considering his was damaged in the flood and here we are. Tonight is the night that I plan to actually do something. He's just for a good time, and he's willing to give that to me. We both are content in that agreement.

Squealing, Sam jumps in my arms and hugs me. Clearly very proud of her match making skills.

I'm introduced to the few unfamiliar faces here and remain

hopeful the extra people will serve as a buffer for any unnecessary tensions. We settle ourselves in the couches, Connor so comfortably wrapping an arm around me.

With ice blue eyes and jet black hair, it's hard to deny he's a good looking man. Yet, I find my eyes wandering away until they land on Tyler who is watching me without even trying to hide it.

I bring my attention back to Connor, determined to not let Tyler ruin this for me. I made my intentions clear.

It was a stupid kiss.

Just a kiss.

TYLER

The way she looks at me is more than just friends. That thought is only validated when the few seconds I count between each glance she makes at me grows shorter and shorter.

None of this between us is *just friends. We can never be just friends.* I look at her and I just…love her. I fucking love her, and it terrifies me what I'd do for her.

When Connor places his arm around her, I break my stare for a brief moment to gain my composure. When I look back up, I see blue-green eyes wide and watching me.

Friends don't look at one another the way we do.

I'm jealous and I'm possessive—I know these things. I get the feeling Sunny does too, which only further proves my point. *Do you want to see how far I'll go for you?*

A smug smile from Connor tells me he thinks he's won the battle. Little does he know it's only beginning.

Pushing off the counter, I start towards the couches but feel Cole grabbing me by the arm.

"Can you help me with my bike really quickly?" he asks,

dragging me out of the house and into the cold November night. "What the hell Tyler?"

The moment we step outside is the moment I realize the depth of my rage. From my labored breaths to the heat that you can practically see billowing off my skin.

"How did you do it, Cole? How did you deal with her being with other people?" I desperately ask.

Cole's head hangs between his shoulders. "I didn't have to, fortunately."

I nod, because some people are luckier than others, I guess. However, I'm not about to rely on luck for us. I know Sunny isn't blind, she's *avoidant*. Anything that makes her feel something sends her running in the opposite direction. Love scorned her once, so I don't blame her.

"You need to let her figure it out on her own. That's the only thing I can tell you. She will, you just need to give it time. But tell me what I need to do, and we will make it happen."

"We don't have time."

He winces at my tone but it's the truth. She's already been in Boston for almost three months, and only has a mere three more. Time is not in our favor.

"All I am saying is if you let whatever this instinctual thing is inside of you out, and you do something, you could ruin any chance you may have. I can't say I can relate to what it's like to see your girl with someone else, because I can't. I can say I know that deep innate desire to protect what you cherish most. You have always done that Tyler, but you need to be methodical this time. Remember, when we let feelings overcome, we get sloppy. We can't be sloppy here, okay?"

"Okay," I mumble. I have other plans, and he should already know that by this point.

CHAPTER THIRTY

TYLER

ONCE I COME INSIDE, I MAKE MY WAY BACK TO MY KITCHEN where I pull some of my finest liquor from a cabinet and a few glasses. I give a heavy pour in each glass and walk to the living room.

With a casual smile, I hand a glass to Connor. "Happy Thanksgiving."

He looks at it for a brief moment and then reluctantly takes the glass. "Thanks?"

"No problem." I sit on my couch and make myself comfortable.

My little fire's eyes are staring holes right into me. Wide and round and curious as to what my plan is.

"Cheers." I hold up my drink.

"Wait." Sunny grabs his glass, making me arch a brow.

"Do you want some, Sunny?" I offer.

She deflates. "No…no, I thought… it was something else."

With creased brows, Connor salutes his drink and sniffs it before taking a measured sip. "Blantons?"

"There is no other bourbon in my opinion." I take another sip.

"These are so hard to come by."

"I have a whole stock in my cabinet. Feel free to have at it," I offer.

He takes another greedy sip, giving me inclination that my plan is going to play out perfectly.

Let the games begin.

Every move he attempts makes my fucking body tick. But that's okay, because he is becoming sloppier by the minute. Words are starting to slur, feet are starting to stumble, and what little filter he already had is long gone.

I guess that's what happens when you can't say no to liquor and are six glasses of Blanton's in.

By the third glass, I don't even need to start handing them to him, and he is already long gone to realize I've held the same glass in my hand this whole time. What appeared as a peace offering has become my plan for the night. Nothing like a good bourbon to numb his broken heart.

He attempts his passes at Sunny, and I try my best to keep my rage at bay and let my plan unfold. It's only a matter of time now.

They play games together but hopelessly fail at each attempt. Connor uses the cliché leverage of teaching Sunny how to play each.

Come on Connor, you couldn't have come up with something more original?

To my surprise, Sunny plays along—she even seems to enjoy it. *I know you better than that, Sunny. Don't stoop to his level.*

Nancy, the girl who wouldn't leave me alone on Halloween night, is here. My statement remains true—she won't leave me alone tonight. I have no interest in her, but somehow, she becomes my partner for these stupid games.

Then I feel my girl call to me on that soul bridge. Looking over, I find her eyes trailing back to me.

You'll find your way to me.

SUNNY

Once the food digests and the main games are over, everyone either settles into watching a movie in the living room, playing a quiet game of beer pong, or mingling in casual conversation with one another.

I sit on the couch with Connor's arm around me. After drink three, I decided Tyler hadn't drugged it, and that maybe it was a peace offering. But the way his eyes are on me from across the room tells me something entirely different. He is waiting for something, and I have no clue what it is.

Connor's boozed breath is unavoidable as he continues to whisper drunken words in my ear. I know what he's expecting tonight, and as the clock ticks and the night starts to wind down, I feel myself wanting to run from the situation and agreement entirely.

I hadn't been with anyone else before. Ryan was my first and only, and I intended for him to be my last. I'm not sure if I'd count what Tyler and I did, but all I know is that it didn't affect me the way I anticipated.

Grazing his hands along my thigh, Connor goes up higher than I'm comfortable with, refusing to move it. He gives my thigh a little squeeze and I feel my heart sink.

I don't know if I like this.

I'm certainly all for a good time, but he's really drunk and I just…can't fucking focus with Tyler's eyes on me.

Connor's hand goes up higher making me jump from my place on the couch. Tyler's eyes flick up where I'm standing, letting his arms down from being crossed over his chest. He pushes off the wall, his analyzing look telling me he's trying to anticipate my needs.

"You okay?" Sam looks at me.

"Yeah, I'm just going to get some more food. Want anything?" I offer.

"Yes! I'll take a piece of pumpkin pie with extra whip cream please!"

"You got it."

Shortly after, the smell of alcohol is enough for me to recognize it's Connor behind me. It takes everything in me to not roll my eyes and groan. Maybe I should've taken up Sam's offer to get with her when we first met. Then I wouldn't be in this situation tonight.

Connor braces the kitchen counter with both arms, caging me in. I can't get out, and if I turn towards him, our faces will be inches from one another.

Pressing his chest into my back, I feel his bulge against my ass, pinning my hips to the counter. I'm honestly curious how the hell he is able to achieve that, considering the amount of alcohol coursing through his system. His body weight on mine is a reminder of how Ryan felt the night I left.

Leaning into my ear he whispers, "What if we get out of here?"

Panic rises like bile in my throat. I should've fucking known better. I should've known I wasn't ready for this. I can't...not after what *he* did to me.

Turning around to face him, I push on his chest lightly to get him a step away. "That'll be a no, Connor"

"Why not?" he asks playfully while his hand traces up my thigh.

I have a flashback of Ryan forcing my thighs open with his

knees. "Because I don't feel like it," I say matter of fact, trying to keep my composure despite my trembling hands.

"It'll be fun," he whispers again, tracing his fingers along the scar on my neck, giving me a flashback of my own stethoscope wrapped around it.

The disgust, the fear, the hate for myself and what he did to me, all of it rushes me like the very blood coursing through my veins. It's living and breathing inside me, reminding me that maybe I'll never be okay.

"Connor, no!" I jump away from his touch, pushing against his chest with my full weight.

Stumbling back, his ego is clearly bruised because a woman knocked him off his feet. He starts for me with rage prevalent on his face, fists balled, as if he's going to make me regret shoving him off.

Little does he know I've got a lot of rage inside me, caused by men just like him, *begging* for a release.

CHAPTER THIRTY-ONE

TYLER

All it took was a blink of an eye for me to lose my place leaning against the wall and to have Connor's neck in my hand.

Listen, I can't kill him. *Yet.*

I knew Connor would make a misstep because I know the type of guy he is. If he didn't make a mistake now, sending Sunny running the other direction, there's no way I'd let her leave with him.

If I killed him tonight, especially after what happened at the brewery, that would trigger a series of events that will create a target of not only me, but Sunny, too.

I unfortunately have to be methodical so that it doesn't come bite me in the ass. But soon, death will greet him, and I'll be the one to make the introduction.

Once I saw his fingers trace that scar on her neck, all fucking bets were off.

I throw him in the opposite direction before I even try to snap his neck. It wouldn't have taken much, honestly. But we unfortunately have witnesses tonight.

Connor tries to come after me, hoping I'll move from

between him and Sunny, but I refuse. I'll be the biggest cock block he ever experiences and I'll do it happily.

He doesn't realize he just pushed her right back in my arms and I'm ready for the pathetic fight he's about to give me.

SUNNY

"Tyler what the fuck?" Sam says.

Connor finally regains his bearings and starts for Tyler, ready to size him up. Ready to start a fight he'll easily lose. Tyler stands as a tall wall between me and everyone else, regardless of the chaos unfolding. He doesn't even flinch.

Cole and Anthony grab Connor, pulling him back on his stumbling feet. Tyler simply cocks his head to the side, watching Connor with amusement dancing in his eyes.

Does he think this is a game?

"I can handle myself," I scowl.

"That's enough, Connor. Get out of my fucking home," Tyler says, unmoving despite my words.

Everyone's murmuring around the room, watching us and waiting for the drama to unfold. As if they felt the palpable tension all night, waiting for it to erupt and finally witnessing its glorious explosion.

"Tyler, what is wrong with you?" Sam starts towards us.

"Get out of my fucking home, Connor." Tyler growls again, unwilling to move from my pathway.

Cole and Anthony let go of their hold on him, giving Connor the opportunity to make the right decision with use of force. Unfortunately, he doesn't.

I stand there, arms crossed over my chest, witnessing the chaos before me. If they want to fight, *let* them fucking fight. There really isn't much I can do. When Tyler's on a mission, he won't stop until it's accomplished. Though I know if anyone could knock him back in his place, it's Sam.

"Tyler, he probably doesn't even know what planet he is on right now. He's so drunk," I argue, hoping he will let Connor wander into the street and let fate handle the rest.

His head snaps at me. "And you think that's an excuse for this behavior?"

"You know what I meant…"

"No amount of alcohol excuses actions, Sunny." He turns back to the people in front of us.

"Okay, everyone take a fucking breath," Sam says to no one in particular. "I will gladly kick both your asses out if you decide to try anything again."

"This is *my* house." Tyler argues.

"Does it look like I fucking care?" Sam snaps.

He lets out a small laugh under his breath, only fueling Sam's annoyance. Cole's hands still rest on Connor's shoulder while they decide what to do with him in case Connor makes a split-second mistake of a decision.

Then, unfortunately, he does.

"Such a fucking tease. It's not cute. All you're good for is blue balls. Don't be a pussy and follow through with your promises," Connor mumbles as he stumbles towards us.

"That seems like a you problem. Be careful what comes out of that mouth, Connor. You don't seem very aware of your surroundings," I warn.

Connor takes a look around, realizing how minuscule he seems to the three men that tower around him. He shakes his head, and opens his stupid fucking mouth again. "Just a little slut who wanted a dick to ride and can't even follow through—"

Tyler takes another step in front of me, completely blocking the pathway between Connor and I. "You better pick your next words carefully, Connor. If they aren't *I'm sorry*, then you won't have a tongue to say anything else."

In a too swift moment, Anthony secures Connor's hands behind his back, and Cole's fist is slamming into his face before Connor can even realize what's happening. His body falls to the ground with a thud as he goes unconscious. My jaw drops, knowing there'd be a consequence, but not realizing it'd be *that*.

Tyler chuckles, a too wide grin plastering his face as his eyes bounce between me and Connor's unconscious body.

Forcing him back up to his feet, Cole grabs Connor by the shirt. Blood trickles down his face as he stumbles on his feet, trying to regain consciousness.

"You never talk to a woman like that let alone *my* fucking family. Get the fuck out," Cole seethes as he and Anthony shove Connor out of the house.

I know I shouldn't, but I find it endearing that Cole and Anthony defended me that way. *Family*.

Getting the idea, everyone starts making their way out of the house or helping with cleanup. Cole and Anthony don't come back inside, and something tells me I don't want to know where they are taking Connor.

Turning to me, Tyler's jaw flexes as he eyes me up and down. "Are you okay?"

"Tyler." I grab his arm, leading the way out of the living room, up the stairs, to the hallway, removing him from the situation. "What the hell is going on?" I confront him. I already know the answer to that question. *You like me, Tyler.*

The hallway is dark, and it creates shadows on his already darkened face. But his eyes are fire as they look down at me. "You think we would just sit there and let him do that to you?"

"I can handle myself. I don't need you, or Cole or Anthony to protect me."

He laughs but there isn't anything humorous in it. "You think that they will just stand by? Sunny, they will protect you upon instinct. You mean something to them. To all of us. They are your family now. Even if you push them out, they won't go far.

They'd sit outside your apartment if it meant your safety. They've done it for Sam. They've done it for Macey. They'd do it for you."

My heart feels heavy and airy all at once. The knot that's been sitting in my throat grows thicker, forcing me to try and swallow down the tears threatening my eyes.

"A man doesn't treat a woman that way. Any sane person would know that," he adds.

"Why does it concern you?" I ask, taking a step closer to him.

"It just does, Sunny," he says, walking away, towards the stairs, leaving me in the dark hallway.

"I'm not your mother, Tyler. I am not *yours* to protect," I snap.

Stopping in his tracks, he looks at the railing his fingers dance along. For someone who is so big, he looks so small right now.

"You're right. You aren't my mother." He turns to face me. "Because you actually left."

I blink at his response, my mouth opening then closing shut.

"When Connor touched you, it's like I had a preview of the sheer panic *he* put you through, and I...I couldn't stand it. I had to do something, yet all I could do was be a barrier for you."

"Again, why does it bother you?"

"It's what I do, Sunny. I protect those I love. There isn't a line I wouldn't cross for you."

He walks out of the hallway, back downstairs. Of all the words he spoke, one replays through my mind.

Love.

CHAPTER THIRTY-TWO

SUNNY

THE NIGHT CARRIED ON WITH NO MORE FRICTION, THANKFULLY. Everyone found their rooms to sleep off the alcohol and turkey that was consumed.

Tyler hadn't said anything else after the hallway intervention. No one really said anything to one another after the fact. Even after all the guests who aren't family left.

As usual, I share a room with Mace and Sam. Regardless of the fact we are all cuddled in bed, I stare at the ceiling wide awake with the events of the night playing over and over.

Of tonight.

Of the night at the brewery.

Of our kiss.

Of Halloween.

All of it.

I feel so stupid.

Tossing and turning, I decide it's useless. Sleep is not going to come to me. So, I roll out of bed, realizing all I'm wearing is one of Tyler's t-shirts and my underwear. I don't care, because I need to get up and do *something*.

I walk downstairs to the kitchen and see Tyler sitting on the counter, his head hanging low between his shoulders as he toys a glass of water in his hand.

"We somehow always run into one another here, don't we?" I say, and all of a sudden I become very aware of my lack of clothing.

"Are you okay?" His words are barely a whisper.

"I just needed some water." I open the fridge.

"I've heard that excuse before." He eyes me with a small smile. "Why did you bring him here tonight?"

I blink. "Why not?"

Grabbing a water bottle out of the fridge, I watch him, waiting for a response. A flicker of pain comes and goes across his face, and he doesn't say anything else.

"Goodnight, Tyler." I walk toward the staircase.

I hear him slide off the counter, gently grabbing my arm to stop me in my tracks. "Is that what you want Sunny? A guy like Connor?"

We stand in the dark living room, save for the dying fire which creates a soft glow on his face. He takes a step into me, making my back push up against the wall under the staircase.

His emeralds darken as his brows crease together, studying me. Darkness lurks around us. *In him*. A man so filled with darkness, trying to find light.

I don't say anything. Instead, I challenge his stare. This only grows his smirk while he threads his fingers through mine and gently spins me.

"Let me see you in my shirt." He presses my back to the wall under the staircase, caging me there with an arm braced against it. "What do you want, Sunny?"

His fingers dance along my arm. His eyes flick to my lips then back to my gaze where we stare at one another. My fight to hide his effect on me fails when goosebumps cascade along my skin. A smile toys at the side of his mouth, realizing what he does to me.

"I want… fun. No strings attached. I want *release*."

Maybe we can do this. Maybe we can just be one another's release. Friends with benefits—a way to suffice in a time where all we can give is this.

"What kind of fun?" His calloused fingers trace along the bare skin of my thigh.

"You know what I mean." I look up at him, despite the fact my voice quivers. His fingers feel like they're burning lines on my thigh, regardless how intimate and gentle the touch is. A contrast to the needy, desperate, possessive touches on Halloween night. It makes me wonder what he'd be like should he actually take his time.

A feline smile slowly spreads across his face, curving that scar that I love so much. Leaning into me, he slowly grazes his lips along the side of my cheek, down my neck, giving light, airbrushed kisses.

"Like this?" he whispers in the crook of my neck.

Yes.

His hands venture to my hips, running up my waist, pulling his t-shirt up and exposing my black underwear underneath.

"I like when you wear my things." He lets the t-shirt fall back down, draping the tops of my thighs.

A squeeze of my thighs does nothing to stop the ache, and tells me exactly how soaked I unfortunately am. I bite my lip to stop my protest. I asked for fun, and he's going to give it to me. Not even a touch of fear that bleeds from my past stains this moment. No, this…this I want more of. *I want more of you.*

"Is this what you want?" His hand finds its place between my legs. "because you know I can give it to you, little fire."

You'd think the damp panties would be embarrassing, but it's not. I *want* him to know how turned on he makes me fucking feel.

"These are soaked," he breathes.

Feral desire clouds his eyes, like he's ready to pounce on my command. Ready to give me what I want and to take what he needs.

My head tilts back against the wall as his fingers glide across my panties teasingly.

"You say the word Sunny, and I'll stop—no questions asked. Or, I can continue to do this." He toys with the waistband of my panties. "You tell me."

I'm not proud of myself as I wrap an arm around the back of his neck, push my chest against him, and seal my lips on his as I allow myself to relish in my selfish desires.

A moan escapes him while our tongues explore one another. His fingers hook into my panties, pulling them down. Gentle kisses are cascaded down my body as he falls to his knees. He looks up at me while he places my foot on his chest to take them off.

It's a powerful feeling, seeing a man like him kneel before me.

He slowly rises to his full height, towering over me while he keeps his eyes locked on mine, his hands gliding along my body in the process. He pushes a finger inside me, letting out a low groan. I finally feel the thing I've been craving, and *he* feels so fucking good.

Slowly, he works a finger in me while gracing my neck with whispered kisses, leaving no inch of my skin unmarked. His free hand moves over the thin material of his shirt that covers my breasts, using a thumb to circle my peaked nipple.

"Is this what you wanted?"

I nod against him.

"*Sunny*," he whimpers, continuing his fingers in and out, as if the feel of my name on his lips brings him pleasure.

"Do me a favor, little fire. Grind those hips until you make a mess all over my fingers." He brings his lips to my ears. "That way I can suck them clean."

His words become the very oxygen I breathe as my breathing becomes more sporadic with need. A sharp moan escapes my lips, and he places a hand over my mouth to silence it.

"Shhh," he gently whispers. "You are for my ears only."

My eyes roll as uncontrollable moans escape my mouth. Expertly, he moves his fingers inside me while his palm creates friction against me, diligently pushing me closer to the edge.

I grip his shirt, tangling my fingers in it as my forehead presses against his shoulder and my hips move in congruence with his fingers. Somehow, our bodies work, just know.

I wrap both arms around his neck, holding onto him because I don't trust my own legs. A loud moan slips from my lips, bringing Tyler to them and devouring each one.

I explode.

Fire courses through me, starting in my abdomen and flares throughout my body as if it is the blood coursing through my veins. It lights behind my eyes in the darkness, creating a night sky through its flecks that move across the black void. This moment becomes my very being. It's all I see, it's all I feel, it's all I breathe. It's all I fucking need.

"There it is." he whispers against my lips.

My labored breaths are erratic as I cling to him, because I can't trust my unstable legs. My arms are still wrapped around his neck with my face buried in him as our chests heave against one another.

He presses his forehead against mine. "I told you I have a list, baby. This is only the beginning."

He gently releases me and removes his fingers from inside me. Looking me in the eyes, he brings his glistening fingers to his mouth and sucks off every inch of me that's left on him.

"So fucking good." He makes it a point to lick his lips. "That was fun. Good night, Sunny." He places a kiss on my nose, walking away as if nothing happened.

I barely catch my breath while I watch him walk up the staircase, leaving me in the wake of all that happened. Fun is what I wanted. Fun is what I got.

Then I realize he didn't give me my underwear back.

CHAPTER THIRTY-THREE

TYLER

SITTING IN FRONT OF MY ROARING FIREPLACE, I SIP A GLASS OF bourbon with a book in hand. I couldn't sleep, so here I am instead. Hopeful a book will distract me from my own mind, and a glass of bourbon will put to sleep the body that refuses to.

It's supposed to be an early morning in the office to get a start on the Governor's campaign investment, but each tick of the clock tells me otherwise.

With a sigh, I rub my eyes and take another sip of the bourbon. The cruelest part of trauma is stealing sleep from a person who so desperately needs it.

Buzzing next to me, my phone lights with Sam's name on the screen. No matter how many times this happens, it still doesn't stop the kernel of panic that sets in when a phone call is received so late at night.

"Sam, are you okay?" I sit up, rubbing my eyes.

Greeted by pure reckless, high squealed chaos in the background, my sister squeaks and wails into the phone in a drunken mess. The shrills ring through my ears, making me pull the phone away.

"Sam, are you okay?" I ask again, my tone more urgent. I

patiently wait until the chaos is cut flat by a piercing silence that almost makes me leap from the couch and track her location to make sure she's safe.

"I'm fine!" she finally chimes. The vise around my heart decompresses and my shoulders slump in relief. "I need a favor," she singsongs.

"Go on." She either needs a ride or needs me to fuck someone up.

"So, I went out with some girlfriends and brought Sunny. She wants to leave, and she is adamant about walking. I obviously will not let her since it's one in the morning. Can you come get her? She's a little tipsy. I could call a car for her —"

"Yes," I cut her off. "I'll be right there." I stand, running upstairs to throw some proper clothes on.

"Okay, I'm trying to get her to stay but she won't have it. Like I said, she's pretty drunk, so she's being extra spicy right now," Sam laughs. "There's a girl I have my eyes on, so I can't leave, just yet. If you know what I mean. Mace is my wing woman, so she is going to stay." I can practically hear my sister wiggle her eyebrows through the phone.

"Try and keep her there. Don't let her go, Sam. I checked your location, it shouldn't take me any longer than ten minutes tops."

"Okay, brother. You're the best!" Then the line goes dead.

Fucking Sunny. That gnawing feeling in my chest dissipates as I grab my keys and walk out of the door. Ready to cross that soul-bridge to get my girl.

I'm coming for you, Sunny.

SUNNY

I blink at Sam while she tries to hold me hostage here. Prior to this, I had an internal moment of panic—convinced I somehow saw Ryan in this giant apartment party, despite knowing it's delusion.

"Sam, let me go," I say through clenched teeth.

While I'm confident I'm stable on my feet, the world spinning as the alcohol buzzes through my veins tells me otherwise. All the more reason to leave before I make another mistake to add onto my list of too many.

Sam kept handing me drinks. One turned to two, turned to three. My guard has become too weak as I've grown more comfortable here. Tyler is proof of that. I still haven't told Sam or Macey about Tyler. How can I?

By the way, Sam? Your brother fingered me by the staircase in his home Thanksgiving night while you and Mace slept right upstairs. My moans were so loud he had to cover my mouth with his hand. And I had one of the best damn orgasms of my life.

Yeah, I can't tell her. Not yet, at least.

Standing in front of the apartment door, Sam picks her long purple nails, totally unamused by my attempt to escape. "I already told you, Tyler is coming to get you."

"I don't want Tyler to get me. I want to go home and be alone."

"What has gotten into you tonight, Sunny?" Macey approaches.

I roll my eyes. "Do I have to say it in another language?"

"Listen, I know Tyler can be a little overprotective sometimes, but I called him here." Sam watches me.

"I just want to go home on my own without an escort."

I know I'm being a little unreasonable, but I want to go home, in my bed with comfy clothes on. If Sam let me leave when I wanted to, I would've been home in bed already doing that. Possibly hopping on the next flight out to get away from this almost Ryan. I'm in an unfamiliar place, with unfamiliar people, late in the night. I want out.

"Too bad." Sam continues to pick her nails, avoiding eye contact with me altogether. Still standing as a barricade to the door that's my freedom. It only serves as a reminder to all the times Ryan wouldn't let me leave our home. He used every excuse, when in the end, it was ultimately a control thing.

A knock on the door jolts me out of my almost panic attack.

"Thank god." Sam turns around, opening the door to a tired eyed Tyler. We stare at one another for a long moment. He watches me intently as his chest moves up and down steadily. I feel my pulse quicken and my breath hitch, becoming way too erratic.

"Sunny, don't." he takes a step forward, knowing exactly what's going through my mind.

"What—" Sam starts.

Ignoring his words, I take off, sprinting past him and Sam and somehow managing to dodge the arm he tries to wrap around my waist. My heart's thrumming wildly in my chest, but I'm free from that apartment.

I'm free.

"Sunny!" I hear both Tyler and Sam call.

Hurried footsteps chasing after me makes my heart beat even harder. Tyler's *tall*, which means tall legs that can outrun me.

Running down the hall and the stairs into the lobby, my long-lost athleticism from high school decides to make an appearance tonight. The guard at the desk eyes me and stands as I jet past, but he soon notices Tyler chasing after me.

"It's fine!" Tyler yells, following behind me.

I burst through the doors, and the cold November air knocks me almost sober. I gulp up its crisp, seething bite in my throat and lungs.

"Sunny!"

My heart is rampant in my chest, heaving up and down as I

try to get my bearings to where I am and how I can get home. I blink rapidly as I sway on my feet, trying to remember which way we came.

Before I can dash to my escape, I feel his strong, scarred arm curl around my waist. I fight him—kicking and flinging my fists with no rhythm or purpose.

"Let me go!" I grit through my teeth.

I try to break from his hold, but my normally average body is small compared to his, thrashing and fighting against his broad, muscled chest and arms feels almost pointless. Especially when he uses his other arm to pin my flailing arms and uses his legs to trap my own between them.

He's a trained killer, how can I think I'm a match against him? Yet somehow, that doesn't scare me. *He* doesn't scare me and I'm too drunk to remember the stupid training he gave me. I should be scared of him. *I should be.*

But that's the thing with Tyler—the reason I should be scared of him is also the reason I trust him. He doesn't hide who he is. No, he is undoubtedly himself and owns up to the bad parts of himself. He's bared himself to me, without me even asking. I know he'd never make me do anything I'm uncomfortable with, and he'd never do anything to make *me* uncomfortable.

"Sunny, *please,*" Tyler drawls. "I'm just trying to help you." His eyes are pleading. "Why won't you just let me take you home?"

I want to walk. I need to walk. I need the clear air, the night sky, the city around me to bring me back to reality. I need the reminder that it's real. Being trapped in a car right now or someone babysitting me and watching my every move the way *he* did will only further my spiral.

Something shifted between Tyler and I the night he came over when I was sick, but I was able to navigate that. This is a whole new maze I'm struggling to find my way through.

A labyrinth.

"I want to walk." I finally stop thrashing in his arms. He lets up on his grip, just a little.

"Okay, well if we are going to walk, One, I'm going to get you some food at a taco stand right around the block. Two, you're coming to my place because yours is too far," he finally says.

"Fine."

I appreciate he is respecting my wishes, even if it comes with reasonable stipulations. Tacos don't sound bad, either.

Easing up a little more on me, he takes a step back and watches me. I flick my eyes down the street, contemplating my escape once more. If I'm fast enough… I can bolt down the street. Then he can go home and not have to deal with me. I won't have to face him, what we did, how he *feels*. I won't have to go back to his place where it's just waiting for us to dig ourselves deeper in this hole.

I can make my escape right now. *If I run fast enough..*

Feeling the world flip, I realize he's slung me over his shoulder as he braces an arm around my ass and hips, securing me.

"I don't trust you," he says.

"Tyler!" I yelp.

As I'm flipped over, I'm met with a view of his ass through his jeans and the ground below us. I groan, because it's such a nice view.

I'm too drunk for this shit.

CHAPTER THIRTY-FOUR

TYLER

IT'S TWO IN THE MORNING, AND SUNNY HAS A TACO IN HER HAND while she dances down the street in front of me. A total contrast to the person she was just an hour ago. She just needed a little space, some food, and tough love.

She's free right now. And fuck, free looks so good on her. The glimpse of who she was before he stole it from her only fuels that primitive need in me.

I bite back a laugh, because once again, she's forgotten all about her training. *For the second time.* Then again, she's a little drunk, and it's me, not a stranger. I'll let this one pass. *Maybe she didn't want to escape that badly.*

Walking with my hands in my pockets and a stupid grin across my face, I watch the light of my life dance along the empty street as she takes in the city before her. She's twirling and laughing while taking bites of her taco in between. I can't help but watch her.

Her curls bounce as she skips and twirls. Her laugh is the only sound in the hushed, sleeping city. If this can be the rest of my life, I'll be the luckiest man alive.

She stops and turns to me, a crooked little smile spreads

across her face while her eyes trail me up and down. Little by little I'm getting that smile I ache for. A shiver goes over my body, and it isn't from the cold. It's from her, always her.

She giggles, and I have a feeling she knows what I'm thinking about.

"I smell rain." She turns around again and winks. "Looks like I'm getting wet tonight after all."

I fight a groan at just the thought.

"Why did you come?" The grin she had dissipates with each word. She stares up at me, and for someone so much smaller than me, she's so intimidating.

"You called," I say simply.

"Technically, I didn't call you, Sam did. That bitch," she scowls playfully.

I take a step into her, but she doesn't move. She stands her ground as she keeps her eyes on me. The lightning from the storm rolling in only gives me brief moments of her face, cracked through light and darkness.

"Sunny, it doesn't matter who calls, if it involves you, I'm there." I hook a curl behind her ear.

The Sunny from an hour ago emerges—the one who wants to run away from me, the one who is scared to let people in, the one who is scared to let herself live a little after what happened to her. I'm not about to fucking let her go.

My fingers gently tip her chin up, making her look at me while I lean in closer to whisper my lips on hers. I want to kiss her again so badly it hurts.

I can feel her breath hitch as our lips caress against one another. Her eyes close as she awaits the contact while her lips part ever so slightly, ready to let me in.

She's letting me in.

Lightning cracks as thunder booms in the sky so profoundly, I practically feel it rattle my bones. We both jolt, eyes flying open and an unforgiving space I don't appreciate is created between us.

"We better go, unless you want to see me wet." She winks, turning around and parading away.

Shaking my head slowly, I place my hands back in my pockets and follow whatever that feeling inside my chest pulling me to her is. If being wet is what she wants, then I'll make that fucking happen.

The rain catches us before we make it to my place. Icy cold bullets come down, piercing our skin with a frosty bite, unforgiving and relentless as it shoots down from the sky. But Sunny doesn't care. She welcomes it as she runs down the street with her arms open wide above her head, tilting her head back, letting each drop hit her face and her body. A glimpse of the person she was before someone stole it all.

Her clothes are skin tight against her, leaving little to the imagination as her nipples peek through the thin material of her shirt. Her once wild hair is flattened by the rain, plastering across the sides of her face.

I run a hand through my own that sticks to my forehead, slicking it back so I can get a good look at the way the rain droplets glide along her body.

We finally make it to the entrance of my home, and when I glance back at her, I can see her eyes roaming every part of my body on display by my wet clothes.

I open the door and smile, because we both know what happens when we're left alone. The grin doesn't leave my lips as I watch her walk through the doorway.

SUNNY

"Here." Tyler hands me a set of matching sweats and a hoodie. "You can use the guest bathroom down the hall."

I'm here. In his townhome. I'm going to be *naked*, in his townhome. I'm well sober now. If it hadn't been the tacos that sobered me up, it was the cold rain.

"Thank you." I grab the clothes.

Regardless of the cold, his hands are warm. As I grab the clothes, he firmly grabs my wrist. Looking up, I see his breathing is heavy as he stares at my hand. His fingers weave through mine as he watches them lace together.

"Yes?" I ask after a too long moment of silence.

His eyes flick up to mine, bringing him back to this moment and out of his head. It's late, or early. Whatever you would call this middle of the night madness. We've been up for hours, and he isn't thinking clearly.

He drops my hand. "Make yourself at home. There should be a variety of shampoos, conditioners and soaps to your liking. The guest room is all yours. Stay as long as you need to sober up," he says, like I haven't spent the night here before. Like we didn't sit on his couches, laughing and talking for hours at a time about nothing at all.

"Thank you." I turn, walking towards the bathroom.

I'm so utterly sober now, and I'm wondering if I should've just gotten in that damn truck and let him take me home. Because I can't stop thinking about the idea of our rain soaked bodies pressed together.

The warm shower thaws my bones while my mind festers with the thoughts of him showering, too. I grab the bottle of soap, realizing it's a coconut and vanilla scent. My brows crease as I look at the others, seeing the curl products I use there, too. Brand new bottles lined on the shelf. I stare at them, realizing he knew exactly what I use without asking. He sees me, and I realize Tyler is all about details. The little things you wouldn't think people would care about. Down to the simplicity of what soap I use.

As I dress, I can't help but notice how large his clothes are on me. The sweatpants are loose around the waist, making me firmly tie the drawstrings. The hoodie practically goes to my knees because he's so damn *tall*. But it's comfy, dry, and warm, and they smell just like him.

Peeking my head out of the bathroom, I see him walking out of his room with sweatpants and no shirt, his hair still wet from the shower.

The lightning gives illuminating moments in his dark home while thunder cracks. An unrelenting storm, most likely keeping me here for the night.

I watch his muscles flex as he pulls a t-shirt over his scarred back. The door squeaks and he turns around, his emerald eyes piercing me. Looking me up and down, he lets out a laugh. It's rich, genuine, and delectable.

Walking towards him, I start laughing too, but don't say anything because my heart is absurdly calm and that scares me.

"Are you tired?" he asks.

"Honestly, no," I admit.

"Good, I have some booze downstairs waiting for us."

CHAPTER THIRTY-FIVE

TYLER

"I'VE NEVER DRANK BOURBON BEFORE, BUT AFTER A FEW SIPS it's not terrible," she laughs, handing me the bottle.

The fire is roaring, and it creates a glow on her face that makes me want to kiss each subtle freckle flecked across it. My living room is dark, save for that firelight, and my couch looks a hell of a lot better with her on it. Especially in my clothes, covering them in her scent.

"It's my drink of choice." I take a swig, handing it back to her.

"Why don't you ever really drink at events or holiday parties?" She takes another drink. I think I may need to slow her down or else she'll be hating me in the morning.

I take the bottle from her. "In case of moments like Thanksgiving."

"Oh, so you can stare at me with those pretty eyes all night?" She snatches the bottle away from me.

I smile. Honestly, I haven't been able to get this stupid too wide grin off my face. Alcohol is making us bold but I don't mind.

Let's be bold.

She's drunk, but I'd rather her be drunk here than out there. She has a soft, small smile that hasn't left her lips and her eyes don't seem so alert anymore. Now that her hair is drying, her curls are starting to form in wild tendrils around her head. I want so badly to run my fingers through them.

"You caught me staring, but I caught you staring, too." I snatch the bottle playfully.

Shaking her head, she doesn't say anything. Then she looks at me, and we sit there for a moment, watching one another with stupid fucking grins on our faces. At the same time, we both start laughing.

"It's because you're pretty," she finally admits.

Our laughter subsides, but our smiles don't. The fire is crackling through the silence between us, complimenting the thunder rumbling as the only background noise.

"Why am I here, Tyler?"

"Because," I hook a curl behind her ear. "of that damn connection you and I both know is there. That feeling I know you and I both can't shake. Do you still think it's just a kiss, Sunny? Do you still think we are just friends?"

I see how my words impact her, one by one. "It'll pass."

"No, it won't. Something, *something* fucking pulls me to you. Connects me to you." I sit straighter, but my tone doesn't change hers.

She laughs. "I'm barely friend material, Tyler. How can I possibly be more than friend material? I barely have anything left to give."

"You keep saying that, like somehow my feelings expect something in return. I don't, Sunny. I don't want you to give. I want you to accept. *Take* what I'm offering you." I lean into her.

Letting out a slow breath, she shakes her head. "This is a mistake. This is how people get hurt." But the look in her eyes tells me otherwise.

Cupping her face, I thumb her lips as I give her a drunken smile. "Then hurt me. "

She swallows hard, but she leans in.

She leans in.

"I think you want me to kiss you, Sunny." My thumb traces her bottom lip.

"I think I want you to do more than kiss me, Tyler."

Fuck.

In the next breath, our lips are crushing together. I pull her onto my lap and grip her thighs, anchoring her onto me.

"Tyler—" she breathes but her hands find my face, keeping my lips on hers.

"Don't think, just do, baby." I flip us and put her on her back. The world flips with us and we somehow topple to the ground with me landing on my back and her landing on top of me.

She's giggling on top of me. "I thought you were good at this?"

"Oh, I'll show you." I stand up, hoisting her onto me.

I carry her upstairs to my room where I throw her on the bed. She's immediately on her knees, peeling my shirt off. But too short to get it over my head at her height, and it somehow gets caught on my face.

"Sunny." I pause, arms on my sides.

"I'm so sorry," she giggles.

Ripping the shirt from my head, I grab her and lift her onto me again. "Come here."

"Tyler!" she laughs as I lay us on the bed.

She starts peeling her sweatpants off. If the world is spinning for me, I can only imagine how much it's spinning for her. She rolls, trying to inch those pants off and tumbles right off the bed.

"Fuck, baby are you okay?" I ask, peering over the edge. My girl is laughing so hard, nothing is even coming out of her mouth. At least she got those sweatpants off. "Sunny," I laugh, getting off the bed and pulling her off the floor.

"What a shit show," she chuckles.

Then her arms are around me again, crushing her lips to mine. She pushes so hard into me that we stumble backwards onto the bed.

Sitting up with her straddling my lap, I cradle her face with both my hands. We're a mix of bourbon breath and desire, and nothing has ever tasted so good.

"Are we really doing this?" she asks.

"We don't have to do anything you aren't comfortable with." I assure her, pushing the hair out of her face, searching her for any semblance of not wanting this.

"I just...I want..." she starts. Her beautiful blue-green eyes are struggling to focus on me. "Oh my god. Tyler, I think there are two of you."

I start laughing. "Oh baby, you're so drunk. You are not going to be happy with me in the morning." I press our foreheads together.

"Then make it up to me."

She doesn't have to fucking ask me twice. I have my list of ways, and I'm ready to show her each one. Wrapping an arm around her, I pull her flush to me, right where she belongs. I flip us over so she's on the bed and kiss her lips one more time before I inch my way down her body. I start at the column of her neck, making sure I kiss my fucking scar there, because I want that scar to remind her of my lips, nothing else.

Working down her body, over my hoodie she still wears, I grab it in my teeth and pull. "I want this off." She sits up and does as she's told while I continue my exploring kisses on her smooth legs. "That's my girl."

She taunts me with a drunken smile, scooting away from me. "Tell me, Tyler." Each word is complete sultry, wrapping around my neck in a chokehold. "How do you like to please a woman?" she asks as her hand starts to graze over her naked body, touching that smooth skin my tongue is craving. Her back is against the headboard, legs spread open where I get a full view of her.

I sit on my knees simply watching her and taking in this moment. Helpless to the fact she has a power over me no one else will ever come close to having.

"I don't have to tell you. I can just show you," I say tightly. I'm dying to get my mouth on her. This visceral need squeezes like a vise around my chest.

Then her fucking hand makes it to that wet pussy my tongue is begging to be in, drawing circles on herself, creating a pleasure only *I* should be making. *Only me.*

"*Sunny,*" I warn her.

"What is it? Do you crave the taste of me, Tyler?"

"Yes." My voice cracks in a desperate breath. My mouth starts watering like a fucking feral animal, waiting for her to give me something. Anything. Her fingers continue to draw circles on herself, spreading her arousal that my mouth is begging for.

She lets out a small moan, making a growl form in my chest. I grab her wrist to stop her. Her breath hitches and I take those fingers covered in her, bringing them to my mouth and suck them clean.

Grabbing her thighs, I pull her back down the bed so she's underneath me. I sit up on my knees to take a long look at her, cherishing this moment I never thought I'd get.

"Sunny," I say against her skin. "The only way you will seek pleasure is through me. I will be your only source of satisfaction. No one else will touch you, not even yourself, understood?" I slip a finger inside her, feeling her muscles clench around me desperately. Her moans are enough of an answer for me.

So we have an agreement, then.

My tongue runs along her, taking in what I've been craving since the last time I tasted her. And I groan because I can only imagine what she feels like. *Soon.* I remind myself. Not yet, not like this, but soon enough.

I start working on her, flicking her clit and tongue fucking that cunt that's already quivering for me. I can see it; the way her body communicates with mine, each touch in response to my own.

Gripping her thighs, I continue to devour her, feeling her hips roll with the motion of my tongue, chasing that climax she's been craving from me. I remove my mouth and insert two fingers in her. Her moans become feral.

If anything this moment has taught me, it's that god exists. And god is a fucking woman. She's right here, giving me access to heaven. I've never been a believer, but I'll spend the rest of my life making it up to her by worshiping her on my hands and knees. She has become my religion, and I'm ready to bow down before her and beg her forgiveness.

"*Tyler...*" she moans.

I smile. Fucking poetry.

"Keep going, my love. Show me how fucking badly you want it."

The way her hips are moving only ignites a desire to experience it from a new angle. I want to feel those hips moving. *Now.* I remove my fingers from her and suck them clean. No part of her will go wasted. She lets out a small whimper but it's cut short as I wrap an arm around her, pulling her up onto my body and falling back so she's on top of me and her knees are on either side of my head.

"Tyler...too fast."

"Ride me, baby." I grab her hips, pulling her up onto my mouth. As if she even has a choice. Her hands instinctively grip the headboard as a gasp leaves her lips. Her body trembles at my tongue plunging into her. God, I want to drink her up.

One flick of my tongue is like a match to a flame. Then she ignites. I'm *so* ready to be burned.

There's truth in the way her body communicates with mine, despite all her words telling me anything else. There's truth in the way I watch my little fire turn into an inferno as the pleasure *I* created engulfs her, fueling the flames that had been almost dead for so long. It's there. She just needed the right person to light the match.

Finally her body relents, and she's panting hard, gripping the headboard like it's the only thing keeping her grounded. Removing myself from between her thighs, I push her back down on the bed and sit on my knees, watching how I satisfied my girl.

"Taste how fucking good you are." I bring my lips to hers, kissing her softer than the needy kisses from earlier. Pushing my tongue into her mouth, she welcomes me with another moan. She brings a hand to my face, cupping my jaw and pushing me into her more.

She rolls so that I'm underneath her and starts working her kisses away from my lips, along my jaw, down my neck, on my bare chest, over my scars. It doesn't hurt. Not with *her*.

I realize where she's heading too. I'm just worried once she crosses that line, I won't be able to go back over it. *I can't go back.*

Sitting up, I fist my hand in her hair, making her look at me. "*Sunny*." A smile grows on her face. "You don't have to…"

"I want to." She continues her path of fiery kisses down my bare torso. Once she makes it to the waistband of my sweatpants, she snaps them and demands, "off."

The moment my pants are off, her eyes fall to my dick. My need for her is evident in the veins and pre-cum beading at the tip. Those wide eyes are analyzing, planning how she's going to do this and how it'll fit.

She slowly lowers her mouth onto me, gliding her tongue from my base all the way up my shaft. My body fucking shudders as I hiss at the feel of that silk tongue along me. That mouth is heaven, in every single way. And I don't know what I did in this life to deserve to walk through the gates.

"Fuck, baby," I let out in a breathy groan. She continues her taunting and teasing on me. "Sunny," I growl. It takes all my willpower to not cum right now, needing to savor this moment because I don't know when we'll have it again.

Don't cum Tyler, don't fucking cum.

Her eyes flick back up to me, wrapping a hand around my base, she devours me, sucking off the pre-cum that's spilling from me.

My head rolls back as animalistic sounds come out of me. Fisting her hair again, I guide the bob of her head along me. My body is already tensing under the gravity of the pleasure she brings me.

I'm going to fucking cum.

My hips start to buck on instinct. I fuck my girls mouth, laying claim to it, and she takes it like she's supposed to. We are made for one another.

"You're doing such a good job, little fire. You're doing so good taking me. Letting me fuck that pretty mouth."

Pleasure rattles at the base of my spine and starts coursing through my body. All at once, my world cleaves, my vision goes out, and euphoria captures my body prisoner as I tense under the magnitude of the orgasm taking me over. My body practically convulses while my dick pulses as I fill her mouth with me.

I groan as my body finally relinquishes and relaxes on the bed. My chest heaves up and down as a sheen of sweat forms along my bare skin. And I watch as she swallows me fucking whole, completely making me rock hard again.

"Quick off the mark, huh?" she teases.

I groan and run a hand over my face. "Come here." I smile, hooking my arms under hers and pull her naked body onto my own. Her sunshine hair drapes around us, and I push it back so I can look at my girl. I press a gentle kiss to her lips where we can now taste one another. And us together tastes so fucking good.

Her body sways and her eyes fall heavy. She's no longer riding the high from the alcohol.

"Sleep, Sunny Darling." I trace her face. Those dark eyebrows, her pert nose, her pink lips swollen from my own.

"Here?" she asks.

"Nowhere else but here." I grab my hoodie she was wearing to help her get it on. "And no more rolling off the bed."

With a lot of effort, she finally gets the sweatpants back on and snuggles herself under the blankets, and to my dismay, she snuggles herself right up next to me. I tighten my arm around her, scared this moment will leave. Within minutes, she's sound asleep. I keep my arm around her as I stare up at the glow in the dark stars on my ceiling with a giddy ass smile on my damn face.

I think you like me, Sunny.

Running a hand over my face and through my hair, I look at her snuggled up next to me. She already has drool coming from her mouth, pooling onto my bare chest. I let out a loud laugh, but I know she won't hear it.

The amount of alcohol she consumed tells me there's a good chance she won't remember this. No amount of alcohol will make me forget.

Wrapping her arm around my torso, she buries her head in my bare chest. I tighten my arm that's around her, pushing the hair out of her face with my other and kiss her forehead.

"Oh Sunny, I just love you so fucking much."

CHAPTER THIRTY-SIX

SUNNY

I wake to the sun shining from a slit between the blackout curtains in Tyler's room. Rubbing the sleep from my eyes, I sit up and notice I'm not in his bed anymore.

That's where I was, right?

If the throbbing behind my eyes is any indication of the hangover looming over me, I am absolutely in deep. Looking around, I realize I'm on the floor wrapped in blankets.

What even happened?

My hands fist the hoodie and sweatpants still on my body. I huff out a breath of relief. That was a *very* vivid dream. I stand, swaying on my feet as I get my bearings and make my way to the nightstand. My head throbs with each step I take, and my stomach growls in protests of hunger yet somehow, I'm so damn nauseous.

Looking at my phone, I note it's already almost nine am. So we'd gotten at least a few hours of sleep. Maybe he's already left for work, and I won't have to face him hung over. A text from Sam lights up my screen in the dim room.

If only you knew, Sam.

Finding my way out of the room, I follow the aroma of coffee downstairs. The light from the morning seems way too fucking bright, and I wonder why a man who enjoys his privacy so much has so many floor to ceiling windows.

I hear him down there. Maybe he called out since he was up so late. *Because of me.*

I try to manage the mess of hair on my head in a bun and rub my face to make me look more awake. My body aches, my head throbs and I don't think I've ever had a hangover like this.

I make it down the stairs to see he's already up and dressed for work, wearing a nice collared button up shirt that has a tie secured around his neck. His hair is groomed back neatly and he doesn't even look slightly as disheveled as I feel.

In times like last night, I almost forget who he is, how important he is. Yet last night he was just a drunk guy, and I was just a drunk girl.

Leaning forward against the island, he reads the newspaper while sipping a mug of coffee. Who the hell still reads the actual paper?

"Good morning. Pour over okay?" he asks.

I simply nod. He grabs a mug and pours me some coffee while I find a seat at one of the barstools. He hands me the mug and I cradle it in my hand, letting the heat melt into my skin.

"Thank you." I blow on the coffee. "Shouldn't you be at work?"

"Perk of being the next owner of the company. I can make my own schedule. Well, for the most part." He takes a piece of bacon off a platter and takes a bite.

An assortment of breakfast foods lay in front of me. Eggs,

bacon, fruit, pastries. Clearly way too much food for only two people.

"Where did you get all of this?" My stomach growls, despite the nausea it's persistent on.

"I cooked it earlier. I figured you might be hungover. So you need all you can eat to soak it up. The pastries I ordered from Mike's." He takes another bite of the bacon.

"Let me pay you back for all of this."

He laughs and gives me a look like what I just said was absurd. "Money is not an issue, Sunny. And I'd never let you pay, regardless." He grabs the paper again.

I rub my temple, taking a sip of the coffee. "Why was I on the floor?"

"I don't know, not sure how that happened." He shrugs, though he fights a smile.

"You didn't even move me?" I ask, embarrassed.

"Well, for the better half of the night, you wouldn't let go of me. You clung to me like a sloth on a tree. But then, you basically kicked yourself off the bed and onto the floor. When I tried to move you, you somehow remembered all the training I taught you and fought me off. So, I decided to let you stay. Besides, you looked so *comfy*," he teases.

"Ugh." I pull the strings of the hoodie, closing my face inside because I am absolutely mortified.

"It's okay baby, we've all had those nights." He smiles at me through my little peep hole.

"How are you so okay?" I ask, finally emerging from my cocoon of his hoodie.

"I don't get sick, and I sure as shit don't get hung over."

I roll my eyes, only widening his grin. "What time did you even wake up?"

"Around seven."

"So that means you got what, three hours of sleep?"

"Yeah." He shrugs. "But that's pretty standard for me. So tell me, what do you remember from last night?" He leans into the counter again with a wicked smile.

I remember my sex dream.

"You picked me up from that party. We got rained on. We showered and got dry. Then, drank way too much bourbon. My head is reminding me with its persistent ache. We laughed way too much my abs hurt. Then we fell asleep in your bed after giggling around like two idiots." I pick apart the bits and pieces. It's honestly all just fragments in my memory. A bourbon blurred mess.

A too wide grin pulls his lips as he stares at me.

"What?" I ask.

He clears his throat as he takes a sip of his coffee.

"Tyler, what…Oh my god." I place a hand over my mouth. "So that wasn't just a dream?"

The dream is now becoming reality as the coffee and bacon absorb the alcohol in my system.

"Oh, so you dream about me, do you?" he laughs as he pours himself more coffee and then fills my cup.

I pull the hoodie over my face as my cheeks heat and slump down into the chair.

"Come on, little fire, no need to be embarrassed. A woman has needs."

"So, do you make breakfast for every girl you have over?" I ask, still shielding the redness taking over my face.

"Just you." He hands me two ibuprofens and a glass of water. "Take these now that you have some substance in your system."

"Not even Shelby?"

"Not even Shelby."

I take a bite of bacon and pop the pills in my mouth, flushing it with some coffee. I know what I'm about to ask can lead in two different directions of how this morning will go. I figure it's time I know, especially with all the parts we've shared with one another already.

And frankly, I'm nosy.

Shelby is a sensitive topic, but it isn't for the common reasons you'd think. He wasn't in love with her, and I need to know those reasons. He knows every dirty detail about me. Well, as much as he needs to know. I want to know every dirty detail about him, no matter how dark. We are sharing parts of one another that he shared with her.

The thought makes me sick.

"Tyler?" I look at him.

"Sunny?" He answers, still reading the paper.

"When are you going to tell me about what happened with Shelby?"

He sets the paper down and looks at me, making my heart thrum against my chest. He stares at me blankly, and I'm unable to read what's sitting behind those eyes.

"What do you want to know?"

"Everything."

Nodding, he flattens the paper down and leans back against the counter behind him with crossed arms. The flex of his forearms give me flashbacks to last night. I squeeze my thighs and take a calming breath.

"Well, you know that we've been arranged by our parents since we were kids. Her father is the governor, and he's a good one. His own father was governor before him. He wanted to lock in the biggest investors he could and my father wanted more ties inside the political world. So they made an agreement when we were kids. Before we were born, honestly," he sighs. "I'd prolonged the inevitable, with my thirtieth birthday as a deadline looming over me like a standstill storm. So, naturally, I did my part and tried things with her. We were together for about two years give or take. On and off, if you will. I was just so busy with work. Or just using it as an excuse to spend less time with her."

I nod, listening despite the fact it's hard imagining another world where Tyler is so heavily involved. Knowing it was with another woman.

"Shelby is the definition of an old money brat. She's never had a job and never plans to. Her parents pay for everything. She likes the finer things, but that's all it was. She wants to be a trophy wife, which is exactly what our parents want—a woman like that for me so I can look more powerful and respectable. A wife who can come to every event, plan all the parties, be just another puppet in the game."

Regardless of the fact I can't bring myself to look at him, he still stares at me with those greens.

"She wants me, but I just don't want her. I tried. I tried my best to love her. Hell, to even like her, but something was missing." He swallows down a gulp of his coffee and crosses his arms again.

The look on his face almost has me regretting asking, but he's telling me, and I know he wouldn't unless he wanted to.

He takes a deep breath and says, "I haven't told anyone this part simply because, it's fucking embarrassing. But I'll tell you. I'll tell you because I trust you, Sunny."

What did she do to you, Tyler?

I nervously trace the lines of the black and gold marble countertop, trying to create space for his voice.

"As you have observed, Shelby can be handsy. I just..." his voice falls. "Shelby is frail. I could snap her in two...if I was able to."

Rage kindles inside my chest. I don't even know what Shelby did, but it's enough to make Tyler hurt and that's enough to make *me* hurt.

"Shelby is a kinky bitch. I'm never opposed to anything," he chuckles, trying to create light in darkness.

It makes me...jealous, knowing Shelby got those parts of him and I didn't.

"She wanted to dabble in some bondage. I've never been one

to say no to any sexual endeavors. I'm all for it. I've done bondage before. Many times. Just not with her." He shrugs, but the tension that lines his shoulders tells me this is something more than casual. Those emerald eyes look at me. "I have one rule with anyone I've ever slept with—I will always use protection. I will never sleep with someone without a condom. It's just too intimate. Too risky. Something that should be shared between two people who truly love one another. And that wasn't me and Shelby, or anyone for that matter."

"I understand," I whisper.

"So, we tried the bondage thing. She had me tied up. Hands, legs. I couldn't move anything." He breaks our gaze, looking down while he rubs the back of his neck.

It's an unexplainable thing, what happens inside my chest. Simultaneously, my heart breaks all over again, only to be put back together by the melted pieces caused by the fucking rage that sets flame inside me.

She raped him.

"Tyler..."

"It's okay, Sunny. *I'm okay.*"

It's not okay, Tyler. This will never be okay.

"I noticed she didn't have a condom. I told her to unstrap me and that we needed to stop unless she put one on, but she wasn't listening to me." He shakes his head. "Despite my efforts to… make it not happen, my body betrayed me. Despite my protests, she continued. And despite any will power I thought I had, my body reacted, regardless." His eyes close slowly. *He blames himself.* Shelby violated him in a way no one should ever be violated, and he blames *himself.*

"Tyler, you can't possibly blame yourself."

"It makes it hard to trust your own body when it does the one thing you wished it didn't do. I should've known better than to be vulnerable enough to let her tie me up. Put me in a position where I wasn't in control." A muscle feathers in his jaw.

I shake my head.

"It's okay, Sunny. I know now it was just a reaction. That's all. Just my body reacting. But that reaction bit me in the ass. It made me feel so fucking powerless. So fucking stupid. I'm trained to take down a threat. Yet, I somehow let that happen to me."

"That's not fair," I argue.

"I ended up snapping the restraints. Too late, of course. I grabbed her by the neck and slammed her against the wall. I could've killed her. I let go before she passed out on me. Giving her back the life she doesn't deserve. And I hated that she got so under my skin that I was able to snap that way. I was a glimpse of Mitchell." He stares at nothing in particular. "I broke up with her immediately after. A few weeks later she told me she was pregnant."

My brain works out the math, realizing by this point, Shelby wouldn't be pregnant anymore.

"Yes, I should have a baby by now. That is if what she told me were true."

"So she lied about the pregnancy," I confirm.

"As soon as she told me, I started contacting all the best doctors we know. We are friends with a lot of doctors. Hell, we own part of the hospital. So I had an appointment booked immediately that week with the best OB in Boston."

Despite it all, he still cared enough for that. It's an odd thing to bring tears to my eyes, and yet it does. I blink them away quickly.

"She avoided everything involving the pregnancy. She just kept saying she needed time to process. What she needed was time to come up with another lie." He rubs the back of his neck. "Her plan failed. I know she wanted to actually get pregnant because she knew that's how she could lock me in. I could get out of just about anything, and she *knew* that. She knew I was planning to break up with her and formulate a different plan for her father. Pregnancy was the one way to keep me because how could I not stay for my child? But she didn't get pregnant, and she webbed a lie, catching herself in it instead of me."

When I finally look up, he's staring at me, the echo of his pain still prevalent in his stare.

"She took two things from me that day," he says. "The first time I could have sex with someone without any boundaries, and the first time I'd find out I'm becoming a father. I never really wanted any of those things, so it shouldn't bother me anyways."

"And now? Do you want those things now?" I ask.

He smiles as he leans forward on the counter, leveling his face with mine. Just mere inches from my lips.

"Like you wouldn't believe."

"Find your way out, Tyler. Find your way out of it." I meet his gaze.

"Only if you do, too."

"Then it's a deal."

"A promise." He gives me his pinky.

Smiling, I link my pinky with his. "A promise."

CHAPTER THIRTY-SEVEN

SUNNY

STEPPING OUT INTO THE COLD WINTER AIR, I'M HIT WITH THE crunch of snow under my shoes and the Christmas lights wrapping the light posts. *There's snow.* Which means Christmas is coming. I blink at the lights as the realization dawns on me—it's already December.

I worked Thanksgiving and went to Tyler's after for family dinner, so it didn't feel like a different day. But Christmas…the lights, the music, it's all a constant reminder that I'm not home with my family. Another reminder that Ryan's nowhere to be found and no other leads were made known. *Nothing.*

I'm actually enjoying my time here now, to the point I let time pass without regarding updates at all. And without any update on Ryan since October, it ironically put me at peace. I'm *living.* I'm actually moving forward.

Putting a hand to my chest, I realize that empty feeling is still there, but now seems so, so small.

And maybe, maybe this is a step forward.

Just as I took two steps forward, I take five big steps back. Who the fuck was I thinking I could move forward?

I spent the whole day focused on my lack of an update on Ryan. One minute, I think I'm almost whole. In the next breath, I'm plagued by emptiness. The illusion that my life could somehow become better while on the run from a man determined to chase me has dwindled and reality has sucker punched me in the gut. Festering thoughts erode my mind throughout my shift, making it hard to concentrate on my work until I get some sort of update.

On my walk home, I decide to call the detective working my case. He would've called anyway if there was an update, right? But to ease my anxious mind, I tap on his contact number.

"Detective Rodriguez, hi Sunny," he greets me.

"Hi Detective Rodriguez, is now a good time to chat?" My voice shakes.

"Actually yes. I was planning on calling you tomorrow as I know it's a little later there. But we can speak now since you reached out. I have an update for you."

Closing my eyes, I feel my heart drop. The world feels like it's about to cleave in two and I'm going to fall right through the crack.

"Okay," I breathe. "I'm ready."

I'm not, but I need to know.

The detective takes a long, deep breath. He's known me since I was a little girl, just as almost everyone else did in my small town.

"He left Oregon, Sunny." I hear the disappointment almost as much as I can hear my heart break. "So, what this means is, we don't know where he is, and we think he could be on the move to find you. We have nothing to confirm that, though. He could be moving to just prevent being caught. Staying in one place too long can leave too much for us to track him. It's hard to find someone that doesn't want to be found and hasn't committed any other crimes."

Closing my eyes slowly, my arms hang down by my sides. I tilt my head back to the cold night sky before me. This means staying in one place too long can leave too much for him to track *me*.

"Sunny?" The detective calls. "Sunny, you are safe. We have already alerted the local authorities there to keep an eye for a man of his description. You have a restraining order. I think he's aware of the repercussions if he tries to find you and violate that order. Warrants are out for his arrest."

"Right," I manage to say.

"It may not seem like it right now, but we will find him. He's going to mess up, and when he does, we'll be prepared."

I nod to no one in particular. "Thank you, detective. I appreciate all the hard work you guys are doing for me."

"We just want you safe and to be able to come home. Call if you need anything."

The words tear me apart. *Home*. I can't go home because of him. He can be anywhere now. At least with him being in Oregon, they knew that he wasn't anywhere else. That he wasn't *here*.

What if he is here?

For the first time in awhile, I feel unsafe walking home. Looking over my shoulder at every sound, I hustle my way back to my apartment through the cold night.

I lock the door as soon as I walk in and place my forehead against the door that no longer feels like a decent enough barrier between me and Ryan.

And I cry.

CHAPTER THIRTY-EIGHT

SUNNY

After a Christmas morning call with my parents, I stand on the curb as Sam pulls up to pick me up for an ugly sweater themed Christmas at Tyler's.

"Oh, my, god," I say, seeing what she's wearing. It's the absolute farthest thing from ugly and the farthest thing from *sweater*.

"You like?" Sam shimmies her shoulders as bells from somewhere ring on her. *She is literally a slutty reindeer.*

"How are you not freezing?" I laugh.

"It's called will power, baby."

Sam's outfit is barely an outfit to say the least, with brown shorts, big fluffy brown boots that go to her knees, and a cropped brown top with white accents on it. Reindeer antlers sit on top of her head and her makeup mimics that of a reindeer. *And she has a red nose painted on.* I won't be shocked if she even has a little tail on her ass.

"You are something else." I shake my head.

"Let's be merry." She puts her purple jeep into drive.

Wow.

That's all I can think when I walk into Tyler's home. Christmas music is playing, lights are flickering, bells are jingling. I stifle a laugh, because it's like I walked into a hallmark movie set.

"I guess I should've warned you, Tyler takes Christmas very seriously. That's why he hosts it every year. Oh, and because he's a fucking good cook." Sam walks inside, making no notion if she's cold, not even one shiver.

Seeing the rest of the family, I feel severely underdressed. Macey is my saving grace, and ironically, we both wear the same Christmas sweater.

When Anthony approaches is when I lose it. If Buddy the elf had a brother, it'd be him. Yellow tights, a green tunic and hat with a bell on the end.

"I thought this was ugly sweater?" I ask.

"Wait until you see Tyler," Macey says matter of fact.

As if he's summoned by her words, Tyler comes walking down the stairs. Arms spread wide in the Christmas onesie too small for his large body, he greets us, "Merry Fucking Christmas Family."

"It gets worse every year." Cole comes next to me and Macey.

Cole. *Cole* has an old green sweater on and duck taped a mirror to it. He literally duck taped a mirror *with a handle to his sweater.*

My laughing becomes uncontrollable, and it's freeing, because I can't remember the last time I laughed like this.

"It would be the two newbs who get a kick out of our bull-shit." Sam raises a glass and cheers.

"Sam! Seriously?" Tyler stands in his *Christmas threw up on me onesie*. "You didn't even slightly follow the theme."

"Sorry, I must have missed the memo." She sips her sparkling cider.

"Disappointed." Tyler looks at his sister.

"I think she looks great." Anthony chimes, some bell ringing somewhere on his body.

"You would," Cole murmurs, leaving me and Macey to sit with Anthony in the doorway. Tyler comes to the entrance, kissing me and Macey on the foreheads and takes our coats.

"Nice sweater." He smiles down at me.

"Definitely not compared to you." I observe the onesie.

Smiling, he gives me a wink and makes his way back to the kitchen to check on the food.

"Disappointed," He reiterates as he greets his sister.

Sam waives a hand and saunters to the living room.

And I'm right. Sam does have a tail on her ass.

After an indulging dinner, the family sits around the tree like giddy children on Christmas morning. Grown adults sitting criss-crossed anxiously waiting for their present.

"Okay, so Sunny had Cole." Anthony reads off a paper that has all our names. Cole grabs the present, gently shaking it and putting an ear to it in hopes to know what's inside.

"You know if you just open it, you will know what it is," I playfully bite.

"Alright, alright. Let's not get our panties in a bunch," Cole says, tearing the wrapping paper.

I found the record player at an old antique shop by my apartment. I saw it and knew he'd love it. I bought a few records, too.

"I remember one night at Martha's you said that it sometimes got a little too silent living alone. So, I figured this would help cure it just a little bit," I say.

He stares at it for a moment, a slow roll of his throat tells me that he's trying to conjure up words. When his hazels flick up to me, they say all the words I know he can't say right now.

"Thank you, Sunny," he says, the words slightly hoarse.

I smile, because sometimes words don't need to be said. A comfortable silence settles until Anthony breaks it.

"Okay, okay, Sunny is the best gift giver. We get it," he teases. "So, Tyler, you're next and you had Sunny." Anthony reads the list.

Of course. Naturally, Tyler would be my secret Santa because life said why not? Right?

He sits crisscrossed in his onesie, smiling boyishly at me as he pulls a box out. It's interesting seeing all the different versions of Tyler. This version is rare.

"Merry Christmas, Sunny." He hands it over to me, a smirk pulling his lips.

Laughing when I see what's inside, I pull out the brand-new scrubs.

"Told you I'd buy you new scrubs."

"A man who holds true to his promises." I smile.

"Only sometimes." He winks.

I unravel them to hold them up and gasp when something tumbles out and into my lap. When I pick it up, I see a brand-new limited-edition copy of Looking for Alaska signed by John Green himself.

Find your way out of the Labyrinth, Sunny.

He remembered.

I swallow the thickness growing in my throat and blink back the unshed tears threatening to fall. My shaking hands fan through the perfect pages, until something falls from it.

"Is this gift inception or what?" I smile, peering up at him as my fingers touch something metal. Holding it up, I realize it's a key. My brows crease and I look back at him. The soft look in his eyes has my heart picking up pace. I've never been so... admired.

"You buy me a new car or something?" I try to tease, but something tells me I already know what this is for.

"When your place doesn't feel safe, I want mine to be your safe. Everyone else has a key, so it's only fair you do, too," he says.

I gnaw the inside of my lips as I look down at the key I twist in my fingers. I nod, with no words able to leave because if they do, I'll lose the battle of my tears and start crying.

For so long, I didn't have a safe space. Now, I have several, in all of them.

I'm on my feet and jumping in his lap as I wrap my arms around his neck. He chuckles as he tilts back by the impact, but his arms curl around me in a hug.

"Thank you," I croak in the crook of his neck.

"Live by those words Sunny," he murmurs. "Find your way out of the labyrinth."

He remembered.

CHAPTER THIRTY-NINE
TYLER

I STAND AT THE TOP OF THE MONSTROUS HILL, EXAMINING WHAT we have deemed the Beast. Cole and Anthony stand on either side of me, holding their sleds as we prepare to start our annual Christmas Competition.

Much like every year, we didn't want to go home for the holidays, so we ended up at an Island themed Christmas party. On our stumble home after too many drinks, we came across this hill. Bring together three competitive drunk guys, and you find us sledding down the damn thing with just our bodies, despite the risk of frostbite.

Because of the alcohol coursing our bodies, lots of throwing up occurred and we decided that as proper elimination of the competition.

Did I mention we stole a tiki statue from the party? That somehow became the trophy for the Beast Race. The tradition stuck, and we told ourselves to pass it onto our kids, too.

The ultimate goal is to go up and down as many times as possible without throwing up. Last man standing wins the title *Conqueror of the Beast* and gets to claim Tiki, whom we named Sheldon, until the next competition next year.

Chuckling at the memory, I look over at the truck to see the girls all snuggled together in a blanket, sipping thermos of hot cocoa. Sunny clutches her mug, her pert nose red from the cold, the beanie on her head taming the wild tendrils framing her face, but there's a smile.

My girl.

"Are we going to do this or what?" Anthony jumps up and down, warming his body up.

"I think since this is Sunny's first year, she needs to conquer the beast too." I meet her stare as she hears her name. "Initiation, if you will."

"It's imperative," Cole says. "I think all the girls should have to start doing a run on the beast."

"No." Sam settles herself in the truck bed. "I'm not moving my ass from this spot."

"Come on! Yes you are!" Anthony trudges towards the girls.

"No!" Macey giggles as they all scramble to run away from us. Fresh snow starts falling from the sky, preparing a soft cushion for any wipeouts.

"New family members equals new traditions!" Anthony grabs Macey's hand.

"Hey, don't put that on me!" Sunny giggles as I slide her off the truck bed. The snow starts to grace her eyelashes and wild blonde hair. Her blue-green eyes are so bright against the white background.

"Come on, Sunny darling, it's time for you to participate in some more family traditions." I lead her to my sled.

After too much fucking protests, each girl is settled with a guy on the sled. Macey with Anthony, Sam with Cole, which I'm sure she's thrilled about. And my Sunny with me. She's settled right between my legs, leaning back into me. My heart fucking pummels.

"This is the biggest hill I've ever seen. It's practically a mountain." Sunny grips the front of the sled.

I place my hands over hers. "And we're going to conquer it."

"Speak for yourself," she groans.

I live for these moments with my family. It's even better now that I have my other half here to participate. *Finally.*

"Okay! On your mark!" Anthony announces.

"Just hold on as tight as you can. If we fall off, you get up and run as fast as you can. I'll grab the sled."

She nods her understanding. Regardless of her protests, I can see her eyes narrowing down the hill. She's competitive just like me.

"Get set!" Cole yells.

"Let's kick their asses," I whisper, just for her. "Go!" I yell, pushing us to our descent. I hear her little screams as we race down the hill. The cold air bites at us but the smile on her face is perfect.

We're both audibly laughing as we continue to make our way down. Her head is on my shoulder, my arms wrapped around her as I clutch the front of the sled. I peer over to see Cole and Sam tied with us. Macey and Anthony are just a few feet behind.

"Tyler!" Sunny yells as we go over a small bump.

We both fly off the sled and roll into the snow. Sitting up on her knees, she's laughing so hard, no sound is even coming out of her mouth. Cole and Sam get up and start their ascent up the hill.

"Run, Sunny! Don't let them win!" I get up and grab the sled. She immediately starts running up the beast, gaining on the two ahead of us.

I'm honestly impressed. My girl can *run*.

"And you want to chase that?" Anthony winks and starts racing up the hill.

Sunny makes it to the top of the hill, jumping up and down as she calls for me to hurry up. Sam and Cole get situated in their sled to make their descent. Macey keeps stumbling in the snow, falling as her feet sink in the soft powder.

"Macey," Anthony groans, throwing his head back.

Throwing our sled on the ground, I sling Sunny back on by the waist and push us down the beast again. This time, we have a lot of speed and pass Cole and Sam. Sunny flips the two off as we pass them, and I can't help but laugh. Sam sticks her tongue out.

God I love my family.

The sled halts this time, but we don't go flying off it like the initial time. Sunny gets to her feet as she meets Cole's stare. They both go running up the hill, racing one another. Sam and I stare at the two and then one another.

"Looks like someone is more competitive than you!" Sam takes off up the beast.

"Run, run, run Tyler!" Sunny yells.

I smile as I make my ascent up the hill. For a brief moment, the thought crosses my mind — *what will this look like with all our kids?*

After their third round, the girls tapped out and settled back on the truck. Despite their labored breaths, their smiles don't leave their faces.

Not a shock, Anthony ends up throwing up first, but he powers through as he trudges up the hill. I unfortunately tap out, knowing if I don't soon, I'll be looking like Anthony heaving at the base of the hill.

Cole stands pridefully at the top of the beast, holding his sled up with a deep *fuck yeah,* filling the quiet air.

"All right, let's pack it up and take our frozen asses back home for movie night." Sam slides off the truck bed.

Cole and Anthony know their cue as they jump into Sam's jeep wrangler. Cole takes the wheel and makes sure Sunny stays behind with *me.*

Packing up the sleds in the bed of my truck, I watch as the rest of the family drives away. They take off into the dimming sky, leaving me and Sunny behind. I turn around to see her sitting in the passenger side, rubbing her mitted hands together to fight off the cold.

I finally have her alone.

Opening her passenger door, I unbuckle her seatbelt without saying a word, making her eyes widen. I wrap an arm around her waist and pull her out of the truck.

"Tyler, what are you doing?" she asks as I drag her out of the truck, stumbling on her feet.

Slamming her on the hood, I knock open her legs with my own so I'm right between those jean clad thighs. Just a few inches closer to my heaven.

Looking down at her, I watch as her chest moves up and down, the steam from her breath floods the space between us. I inhale her, taking her in. Her nose is red from the cold and her body is trembling against the icy cold of the hood of the truck.

I have to have her.

I grab her thighs, tugging her closer to me so her jean covered pussy is flush against my hard fucking cock. Only four layers remain between us and I'm ready to rip those layers right off.

I lean over her and give her body a once over, admiring the way shock looks on her. *Are you scared of me yet, Sunny?* But as she looks at me, I don't see fear, I see a challenge.

When I grab her throat and she doesn't flinch is when I know I have her trust. With heady need, I slam my lips to hers. Her once tense body melts under me, only further proof her fire grows by my touch.

She wraps her legs around my waist, tugging me closer so my hard dick is pressed against her. When I groan, she smiles and *fuck*, I love how much power she knows she has over me.

I hit the hood of the truck, trying to calm my raging fucking hard on. That only makes her smile bigger against my lips. I want her so fucking badly, but I also want to keep playing with her, dangling her on this edge of almost. I want to rack up the score between us so she can never call it even.

Flexing my jaw, I remind myself soon enough we'll cross that bridge, stepping over the fine line we've been treading. Not here, not like this.

I've had to slowly prepare her, especially after her history. It's fragile territory and I'm going to do this right with her. I need to keep tallying off my list I subconsciously made. My list of ways to make it up to her for that night in the gym. It's somehow become a bargain for us, the only thing that she uses to allow herself to have whatever this is between us. I'll keep making my way down that list, because lord knows there's more things I'll be begging her forgiveness for.

My hands move under her flannel, meeting the soft warm skin underneath to then find her waistband, unbuttoning the jeans open for better access.

"Tyler —" she breathes against my lips.

"Shhhh." I slip my hand inside her jeans. "Fuck, baby," I groan against her mouth.

Frustrated, I work my lips on hers, nipping and biting my way down her jaw, her neck. Arching her back, she lets out a moan as I plunge my fingers inside her.

Removing myself from her, I grab her flannel and rip it down the middle, making buttons fly around us. Her scowl quickly turns to a whimper when she's met with the cold air stinging her skin. I pull her tank top up, revealing her pink peaked nipples just begging for my mouth.

As I slide my hand back into her pants, my lips and tongue find a nipple, eliciting a soft little moan from her. My body fucking trembles when my fingers sink into those, wet, tight muscles that wrap around my fingers.

"Tyler—" Hearing my name on her lips does something inside me.

Her knees are drawn up and her fingers claw my back deliciously. She opens herself up to me willingly while I finger fuck her. The cold may hurt, but my need for her hurts even more.

My body was made to please hers, and that's exactly what I'll do. Little by little I'll make my girl ache for me the way I ache for her. I want her *hurting* for me. I want her to experience the pain I feel when we are apart. She will be consumed with me the way I am consumed with her.

Feeling that sweet cunt squeeze my fingers, I stop my rhythm. She huffs out a breath of frustration as her nose flares.

God, she's fucking adorable when she's upset.

Grabbing her face between my fingers, I force her to look at me. "What do you want, baby?"

"You. I want you." She tightens her legs around me. And I love how boldly, how promptly she said it without hesitation.

"You'll always have me. Without you, there is nothing left worth living for me. So tell me, Sunny, whose are you?"

Her breathing quickens, and I can tell she's so close to the edge. I won't let her jump off unless she takes me with her.

"Yours," she finally breathes.

Continuing my fingers inside her, she lets out a breathy moan as I give her what she asks. "That's right Sunny, *mine*. Now say it again."

"Yours," she whimpers.

I use my palm to create the right amount of friction on her clit as I keep a steady rhythm of my fingers inside her. She squirms underneath me, her body writhing with uncontrollable need. Fuck, I love playing with her.

A quick glance at the sky shows me a clashing of colors. Night and day fighting for the sky's attention.

"Better cum for me, little fire, we're burning daylight. This opportunity may not present itself again tonight," I say against her fiery hot skin. She rolls her head back, closing her eyes as she grips me like her lifeline.

I grab her face again. "*Sunny*. Look at me." She bites her lip, trying to suppress the screams from her mouth. "Scream all you want, baby. No one gets the pleasure of hearing that pretty mouth but me."

Pinning her down by her neck, her body starts trembling under my grasp, and I get to watch every quiver, every roll, every moan escape her.

She sets fire right in front of me as I dowse her in the fuel of me. She unleashes as uncontrollable moans leave her. Her chest moves quickly up and down while she instinctively rides my fingers. I bite, suck, lick, and whisper across her skin until she finally relents to the pleasure. Making sure every single reaction is all because of me.

She finally lets go, and it looks so fucking good.

When I remove my fingers from her, I instinctively suck them clean. I bring my lips to hers and push my tongue inside her mouth so she understands *why* I have to taste her.

"What are we—" She starts.

"No questions, baby. We are whatever we want to be. My sole purpose is to give you the pleasure you seek. You will only ever get it from me. Now let's get home before questions are asked." I slide her off the hood. I shrug my jacket off and tuck it around her, because her lips are starting to turn blue.

I open the truck door for her and watch her slide in. Instinct has me grabbing the back of her neck and pulling her to my lips one more time, because once we go back home, we have to pretend this doesn't exist.

And I make sure she feels it as I brand myself there, because it's entirely too soon for me to say it.

I love you.

CHAPTER FORTY

TYLER

ONCE WE MAKE IT BACK HOME, EVERYONE HEADS UPSTAIRS TO change into their matching Christmas pajamas. Oh yes, it's a yearly tradition of ours, too. No Christmas goes without matching pajamas for my family. We're fucking adorable.

Sunny pauses in the living room as she stares at the fire.

"You okay?" I ask. She still has a bit of a hazy look after what we did earlier, and it makes me smile. *I did that.*

"You can't tell the others." She looks at me.

My brows crease together. "Tell them what?"

"That I broke secret Santa and got you a gift, too. Well, I made the gift." She pulls a rectangle from behind the couch.

She got me a gift.

"You told me your favorite place is wherever your favorite people are. So I figured, I don't know. Maybe I could paint your favorite places to hang in one of your favorite places." She shrugs and hands me the painting, shifting on her feet nervously while she chews her lower lip.

Gently, I take it and examine it, realizing all my favorite places are collaged so perfectly together across the canvas. From

Betty's Beans, Martha's, my home and the harbor, it's all somehow there, fit perfectly together.

"Sunny," I breathe. "This is incredible." I swallow the knot forming in my throat, and it's this moment I realize the true weight she has on me. Never did I think a fucking painting would choke me up, yet here I am.

She places a finger to her lips with a secretive smile. "Don't tell the others." Then, she turns on a heel and ascends the stairs.

When I can no longer see her, my eyes fall back to the painting. My fingers trace over the paint, noticing the finer details she put effort into. From the names Sam and I carved into a brick the day I bought this home, to the chipped paint outside of Martha's.

I fucking love her.

Once everyone is showered, mugs of hot cocoa are passed around as everyone settles in the couches. In tradition, everyone proudly wears their matching pajamas.

I'm at the end of the couch with Sunny right next to me. When she leans into me, I become completely still, despite my heart fucking pummeling in my chest.

How is it we go from what we did at the beast, where it all came so easy, to this, right here. Where simply leaning into me is something that so easily halts my world?

She gives a once over at the family so comfortably sprawled across the couches. And as she does, her soft smile grows bigger. When she looks up at me, there's something in her eyes that I can't read, but know I love.

Because it isn't so scared, anymore.

CHAPTER FORTY-ONE

SUNNY

Normally, the winter months call for busier days in the emergency room, especially on holidays. But not today. With the empty rooms and all my snacks already eaten, it looks like such a contrast to last week where we had gurneys lined in the hallways.

Amidst the chaos of the hospital holiday season, I haven't had much of a chance to see the family since Christmas day. Overtime shifts have been offered with generous incentives, so I couldn't say no considering my savings took a hit coming here.

Considering the down time, I decide to catch up on the family thread where several messages are waiting to be read about our plans tonight.

New Year's Eve.

Naturally, the celebration will be held at Tyler's place, with a rooftop firework show over the harbor and a fire-pit to roast s'mores.

It's like he knows he's been summoned in my mind, because a text in our personal thread pops up.

> Want to help me with dinner prep? You can come here instead of going straight home.

Either he forgot I'm at work or doesn't care. I glance around again, making sure there aren't any ambos or people in the waiting room.

I respond.

> Funny you text me at such a convenient time, looks like I may be getting off early. Low census today.

His response is within seconds.

> I'll be there in ten minutes to pick you up.

My brows crease as I type and delete, type and delete. Before I can even send my text, our charge nurse, Tara, is calling my name.

"Sunny! We are sending you home!"

Ten minutes later, I'm walking out of the hospital into the frigid air, where I see Tyler leaning against his truck with two coffees from Betty's Beans in hand. With each step I take, his smile grows bigger.

"Coffee snob buys coffee that he doesn't like?" I fake a gasp.

"Only for you." He winks, planting a kiss on my forehead.

It's effortless for him, isn't it? To care for me. Something I didn't think was but actually is.

"Thank you." I take a sip. It doesn't go past me the way he gives me a slow once over, taking in the scrubs and messy hair. Something switches in his eyes when they flick back up to mine.

He opens the door to the truck and says, "You look ravishing."

I blink up at him, feeling the weight of this moment over me.

Before I could even notice, Tyler and I have started to bleed out of friend-zone territory. No boundaries were set up when we decided to do, well whatever it is we're doing.

Yet, I can't help the way my heart gives an extra thump in my chest when I see those green eyes looking at me like there's something worth looking at. Coffee in hand because he actually thought about me on his way here. With a body on display in all the best ways by that thermal gripping his hard earned muscles. An added perk that sends my heart into its own personal spiral.

And I realize I'm in deep trouble. *I like you, Tyler.*

I clear my throat and break our too long gaze. "I feel ravished." I hop into the truck.

"You won't know ravished until I'm done with you." He grins. "So, is everyone too busy to be sick today?" he asks, bracing his arms above the door. His comment catches me off guard with how casual his tone is. Yet, it still does something inside me. Like there's stupid butterflies in my stomach.

So fucking in trouble.

"I guess so." I shrug. "So, why did you ask me to help you?"

He arches a brow. "Everyone else was busy." Then he closes the door and walks to his side of the truck.

"Mmmm." I hum in response.

"You don't have to believe me. But it's the honest truth." He flutters his eyelashes, placing a hand on his chest.

I hide my smile behind the coffee cup while I slide down in the passenger side. Was he always like this? Or have I somehow brought out a version of him that no one else gets to see? His friendship is one of my most cherished possessions. What will this unchartered territory do to that?

He starts the car and hits the road. We sit in comfortable silence while music softly plays and we sip our coffees. Pink cheeked glances and too wide smiles are shared along the short ride. And somehow, his hand finds my thigh, and I don't remove it.

Rolling the window down, I pull my hair out of my bun and stick my head out the window to feel the crisp air on my face while I rest my arms on the window frame. It's small moments like this that become my favorite. Ones that I wasn't able to cherish before, because silence usually meant something was wrong. In between moments like these were filled with dread about what was to come.

Pulling into the parking lot, I unbuckle my seatbelt. "What are you making for all of us tonight, Chef Tyler?"

"Pasta," he says, unbuckling his own.

I start opening my door, but feel Tyler's arm reach across me, grabbing the handle to slam it back shut.

"That's my job, Sunny. You should know that by now." He gets out of the truck and rounds it to open my door.

"Was that necessary?" I ask.

"Absolutely."

Once inside, he grabs a cart and wheels himself down the aisle, riding it with one foot and pedaling himself with the other.

He's a damn hitman, and he's wheeling himself down the aisles like a little boy. A glance over his shoulder reveals a boyish grin to further prove my point. For someone so lethal, he seems so harmless right now.

"Why do you keep looking at me?" I ask with a nervous laugh.

"I like to appreciate beautiful things," he says, wheeling ahead, leaving me in the crop dust of his words.

I shamelessly watch the muscles of his back move as he clings to the cart. The notes of sweat tell me he must've come from the gym. Either that, or maybe I make him nervous enough to cause a sheen of sweat.

I'd like to think it's that option.

"Okay," He interrupts my thoughts. My eyes move from where they were on his ass to where he stands in front of me now.

A devilish grin pulls his lips. "Were you just staring at my ass?"

"I don't know what you're talking about." I feign nonchalance as I take another sip of my coffee.

He chuckles and holds up two boxes. "Which pasta?"

"Whichever is cheapest?"

"Money isn't an issue, Sunny."

It's at this moment I'm sucker punched by the reality of who Tyler is, and the power he holds. He's important. He's needed. He's powerful. He's a goddamn hitman. He'll own that company one day and he's killed people to do it. And here I am, shamelessly flirting with him over boxed pasta. A nobody girl on the run from a man who may not even be chasing her.

"I don't know, aren't you the cook?"

Dropping his arms, he tilts his head. "Sunny?"

"Tyler?" I cross my arms.

"You're cute when you're annoyed," he comments and then *he kisses my fucking nose.* "You're right, we need pasta made from scratch." He places the boxes back.

I stand still, clutching my coffee cup so tightly I dent it. Still feeling the effects of his lips on my skin ripple through my body.

I hate that I like you, Tyler.

"Red sauce or white sauce?" he asks.

"Well, which goes better with champagne?" I swallow hard when I take a glance around and notice people are watching us. Noticing he's with me, *a nobody.* Tyler seems oblivious or just down right doesn't care. I know it's the latter.

"Honestly, I think white sauce would complement champagne more." He tosses cheese and heavy cream into the cart.

"I'll trust your judgment." I look at the contents in the cart.

He comes up behind me, bracing the cart so his chest is pressed to my back. The familiar scent of him encases me, only somewhat calming my frantic heart.

They see us, Tyler.

"It's good to know you trust me," he whispers low in my ear.

"Tyler, people know you here. They know who you are, and they're watching." I peer around again. They aren't *supposed* to know.

He removes himself from me, freeing me from the cage of his arms. "So?" he says, inspecting what looks like a block of cheese and then tosses it in the cart. "I don't care. So why should you?" He crosses his arms over his chest, making his biceps even more prominent now. It's hard to not notice these details of him when they are screaming at me.

"Aren't you worried they will say something?"

"To who? My parents? Sunny, you and I both know I don't care about my parent's opinions. I'm twenty-nine years old. I don't need mommy and daddy's approval." He tosses another item into the cart. "I'm a regular in this store. That's the only reason why they know me. It's not like they know who I am and even if they did, I don't give a fuck. My reputation would be the one thing to deter them."

I feel his large, calloused hand lace into mine. Looking up, I watch as he brings my hand to his lips and presses a kiss to it. "See? I don't give a shit."

Which would've been fine, except he doesn't let go. He still clings to my hand, our fingers still laced together as we walk through the store.

I don't stop him, either. I keep my hand in his, unaware of how to let go because it feels too good.

It's kind of funny, everything we've done intimately was behind closed doors, in the middle of the night without anyone knowing — to this.

We never really explored this portion of our relationship. The small, flirty, butterflies in your belly gestures such as hand holding in public.

We aren't supposed to. We shouldn't.

We are supposed to be friends with benefits. Only fulfilling one another's sexual desires behind closed doors, despite the fact we haven't even had sex yet. Not kisses and hand holding and coffee.

Yet, I don't remove my hand from his.

CHAPTER FORTY-TWO

SUNNY

"Alright." Tyler puts the last of the groceries away. "I have to take a shower. Everyone should be here around eight." He glances at his watch. "That gives you plenty of time to join me in the shower." He winks.

"Tyler!" I throw a pillow at him. He chuckles, disappearing up the stairs. I catch a glimpse of his muscled back as he pulls his sweaty shirt off and I groan internally.

A few minutes go by and thoughts flood my mind of Tyler naked in his shower. Thinking about it isn't nearly as bad as actually doing something about it. I grab the remote and flip through channels in an attempt to distract myself.

When the tv doesn't suffice, I peer around the house that has basically become my second home. A smile pulls my lips when I see my painting proudly displayed in the living room for all to see. His office door is slightly open, and of all the times I've been here, I've never been in there. Frankly, I'm not sure I want to.

I toy with a curl, fighting the urge to even the score in whatever match this is we've started. Technically, we're three to one, and I refuse to let him have the upper hand. That's when I decide that's enough of an excuse to toss the remote to the side and make my way up the stairs, following that pull that's tugging me.

The steam from the hot shower spills through the open doorway like a smoke trail guiding me to my destination. The mirror is fogged and I can see the shadow of Tyler's naked body through the glass doors of his shower.

You're just evening the score.

With a deep breath, I open the shower door. I remain dressed to prove my point.

I have a full side profile of him. Every muscle completely on display as water droplets dance down the groves of his body. He runs his hands through his wet hair, slicking it back to give me a perfect view of all the angles that make up his face.

I shut the door with a click, making a smile curve the side of his mouth before he even opens his eyes.

"I'm here to level the playing field. Even our score," I say.

Finally, he opens his eyes, that smirk never leaving his lips. His scar standing proud whenever he smiles. Before he can say anything, I push him against the wall and lean in so that my lips are a whisper across his. He doesn't give me the chance to tease when he grips the back of my neck, sinking me deeper into him.

Once I'm able to rip my lips from his and come up for air, I slowly work my way down his neck. His fingers dig into my skin, his jaw flexing as a moan rumbles through his throat.

My lips shamelessly move across his body, relishing the way he feels underneath them. His muscles are carved perfectly from hard work and dedication. Pieces that somehow fit so perfectly with me.

Despite my efforts, he peels my scrub top off. His eyes roam my body as fervently as his hands do. The needy desire of them ignites across my sensitive skin.

My eyes fall to where I feel him pressing against me, so ready for what I'm about to do. When I look up, those emeralds are staring at me. No longer is he the Tyler from the grocery store, but the one from Halloween night.

A firm hand fists my wet hair, forcing me to my knees. When I look up, I see his labored breaths despite his calm, animalistic eyes.

"Open," he growls.

He shoves me forward, making my hands slap the shower wall behind him. I open my mouth willingly, ready to make this predator of a man fall to his knees for a woman like me.

I taunt him a bit, using my tongue to write all the words I'll never say. It doesn't take long until he is moving my head forward so I'm sucking him in.

Barely halfway, I already feel my gag reflex kicking in. Hissing, he leans his head back as I suction my lips around him.

"Fuck, Sunny," he growls as his hips thrust deeper into me. He takes his time pushing into me, working me slowly so I can take him fully without resistance.

Tears sting my eyes and streak my face, but the shower masks it. I want him deeper. I want him to fall to his knees because of me. The fire he claims me to be, burning everything that was ever before me, and my flames so harsh that it'll ruin anything after, too.

My hands claw his thick thighs, drawing blood as he pushes deeper into me. I can feel his body writhe as he inches himself into me, trying to contain the urge I know he has to take me desperately rather than adapt me instead.

"That's my girl. Taking me so well. *Devour me*, Sunny." He pushes more.

I wrap a hand around his base, covering the area I know my mouth simply can't. His head tilts back against the shower wall while his body trembles at my touch.

I *love* the power I have over him.

I gently glide my teeth over him, knowing he likes a little

pain with his pleasure. As he lets out a snarl, I feel his body start to tense as his release starts to take over his body.

"Fuck Sunny, fuck!" His thrusts become wild as he fucks my mouth, becoming the Tyler I know he is, taking my mouth with no regard as pleasure starts to possess him.

His fist tightens in my hair while his other hand slams against the tile wall behind me, curving his body forward.

Lose control.

Then he does. I'm met with unhinged thrusts. My body instinctively fights him off, despite the fact I don't want to stop. And I know he wouldn't let me, anyways.

"I want you covered in me," he says, his voice so low and hoarse.

He pulls out, using that hand fisted in my hair to make me look up at him as he spills all over my chest with a groan.

Seeing him become undone because of me is intoxicating.

Leaning forward over me, his dark, wet hair hangs as water droplets fall from it. Those emeralds stare at me, so animalistic like, I start to feel a kernel of fear bloom in my chest.

Is this the man all his victims see before death greets them?

He swipes his thumb through his cum that slides down my chest and brings it to my mouth, running it over my bottom lip.

"Taste what you did to me and clean up your fucking mess." He presses his thumb in my mouth.

I do as he says, sucking him clean. This only gives me another groan, and to my shock, makes him hard all over again.

Before I'm able to do anything about it, his hand is around my throat and bringing me to my feet. No words are said when he peels my scrub pants off and tosses them outside of the shower.

He grabs my face, making me look at him. "You really think I was going to let you come in here and have your way with me?" He leans into me, his lips whispering over mine. "Jokes on you."

With a spin, he turns me around and slams my back against the shower wall. His arms create a cage around me. "I always get my way. And I always fucking win."

He presses his lips against mine, invading my mouth in an attempt to distract me from his roaming hands down my body and between my legs. An unsolicited moan leaves my mouth, only adding to his ever growing smile against my lips.

He works his lips down my neck, taking extra time on my scar, giving it the love that was stripped from me. A swift movement and my bra is on the floor, his mouth circling one peaked nipple while his fingers tease the other. I bite my lip, unwilling to give him the moan he is pushing for.

A dark look in his eyes tells me he is going to get it no matter how hard I fight it.

As he makes his way down my body, he slides my panties off, leaving a trail of kisses over my skin, a silent writing of all the things he wishes he could say.

"Open my legs." He slaps a hand on my thigh, making me spread them wide for him. "Let's see how long you can fight this."

My argument is silenced when his mouth is between my legs. It's not fair, how fast the orgasm tries to rip through me, no matter my attempts to stop it.

Just as I'm about to fall off that edge he's dragging me over, he removes himself from me. Two fingers are pushed inside me, curling just right that a moan finally slips free.

"You're fighting it," he murmurs, getting to his feet again.

With his face inches from mine, he nips and toys with my lips while treacherously moving his fingers in me. Another pathetic whimper sets free when I feel the orgasm lighting up inside me.

"There it is." He smiles.

I see what he is doing, getting me so close to then take it

away, that way I'm begging for it. Asking him to be the reason I seek pleasure. Just like he wanted.

He grabs my face, making me look at him when he says, "*Cum.*" Through clenched teeth.

My ragged breaths are filled with the water pouring down on us. Fighting it is a losing game at this point. So I roll my head back, allowing the flames of the orgasm to engulf me.

The fire floods my veins, warming me so deeply I can't help but succumb to the melting it forces me into. I fall into him, unwilling to fight any longer as my knees give out.

"That's my girl," he whispers in my ear.

Our bare chests move in rhythm to one another while he cradles my face, pressing our foreheads together. We sit there for a few silent moments, catching our breath, eyes closed, the water still beating down on us.

He pulls away from me so he can look at my face and brushes away wet hair that plasters my forehead. "Looks like I win again." A smile curves at the side of his mouth.

He presses a kiss to my lips and starts picking up my scrubs that lay on the shower floor. "I'll wash them for you." He wraps a towel around his naked body. "See you at dinner."

CHAPTER FORTY-THREE

SUNNY

I find myself in another set of Tyler's sweats while I sit on a barstool, formulating a series of plans to side step questions.

Toying with the too loose material, my thoughts fester. How will I explain this? Especially to Sam. She already traveled down that path of questions with Tyler and I, even if for a brief moment.

"Tyler," I say, looking up to see him cooking happily. With a toothpick in his mouth and the white t-shirt and sweats combo, it makes it hard to have a conversation beyond this moment.

"Yes, baby?" he asks, rolling the pasta dough along his black marble countertops, flexing those cords of muscles in his forearms.

I get up from the barstool and come up next to him. "What are we going to tell Sam?"

He side eyes me. "We can tell her the truth."

"*Tyler,*" I groan. "We can't do that."

"And why can't we?"

"Are you serious? You know why Tyler. This isn't..."

"It can be whatever we want it to be, Sunny. Weren't you the one who told me the night we met, well, for the second time, that there is always a choice. Right?" He glances at me. "We always have a choice, and we can shape our own path, do whatever the fuck we want because it's *our* life. I already live by my own morals. Why don't you?"

We stare at one another for a beat, and he slides the dish cloth off his shoulder to wipe his hands. Tossing it to the side, he brings both hands to cup my face. "Does the idea of hiding behind closed doors turn you on, little fire? Is that why you don't want to tell anyone? Sneaking around just does something inside you?"

"*You* do something inside of me," I admit.

"Oh baby, this is only the beginning. I've only checked off a few items of my list of ways to make it up to you."

"Then show me."

"I plan to take my time with you." He grazes his lips along the column of my neck. A sigh leaves my mouth and that fucking fire starts to kindle inside me again, aching for him to fuel it and set it aflame.

"Tyler…" I swallow hard while his lips keep whispering along my neck. "Anyone could walk in right now." He picks me up and sets me on the counter. "Hmm. I don't think you mind that at all. I think you like knowing we could be caught at any minute." He tucks a curl behind my ear. "What would you do, baby, if we got caught?" He nips at my neck, then traces his tongue along my scar.

"I…" I open my mouth to speak but the sound of a knock on the door has both our heads snapping in that direction."Okay," I start, panickedly. "I got shit on at work, decided to just come straight here and shower since your place was closer and I just wanted to get the ick off."

"Shit on?" he asks. "You really know how to make a man go from rock hard to soft instantly," he jokes, pressing a kiss on my head and starts washing his hands.

"Tyler, I'm a nurse, that's not uncommon"

The knocking continues and the knob jiggles because no one ever knocks. They are family. *We* are family. We all come and go as we please. He looks at me, not fully committed to the lie we're going to continue.

"Tyler," I say through clenched teeth.

He rolls his eyes, jaw flexing. "Fine. Okay. I can't promise I'll keep up with this Sunny." He points his spatula and I bite back a smile.

His blank stare tells me he isn't amused. But when he walks away to answer the door, I see a hint of a smile on his lips.

And here we go again, lying to our friends' faces once more.

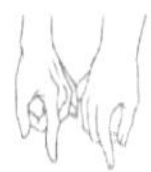

To my luck, today is the one day that Anthony forgot his key. I shudder at the thought of him walking into what we were doing.

My thoughts are interrupted by Sam bursting through the door, announcing her presence as if it's unnoticeable to begin with. "The party has arrived." She places a hand on her hip, the other hand holding a bottle of champagne.

"Why are you wearing Tyler's clothes?" She blinks between the two of us.

The lie rolls off my tongue so easily, but I shouldn't be surprised, considering the last few months.

"You wouldn't even believe the day I had at work. I got freaking *shit* on," I exaggerate.

Tyler eyes me, the silence growing between us with each passing second. His jaw flexes when he sees the plea in my eyes. He is what stands between Sam and the truth.

"She smelled awful," he finally says.

I release a breath. The vise around my heart finally loosening. "I had planned to come straight here anyways for New Years, so I texted Tyler asking if I could just use his shower and borrow some clothes so that I wouldn't have to back track going home." I explain in every dirty, lying detail.

"I don't know how you do that, Sunny." Anthony crinkles his nose as he takes the champagne from Sam.

"Well, sounds like a shitty day, pun intended." Sam waltzes to the room to greet everyone, but I still feel her eyeing the two of us.

Fuck. *She knows. She knows. She knows.*

I feel a hand brush my own and when I look up I see Tyler next to me. He nods towards the living room to greet our family while he finishes up.

Despite things being left at that, I can't help the pit in my stomach.

"Okay, this is the plan. I'm going to kiss Cole, Anthony is going to kiss Macey and Tyler is going to kiss you," Sam says with her arm linked through mine as we stand on the rooftop of Tyler's home.

"Why does it have to be like that?" I ask.

"It's just how it worked out." Sam shrugs.

Regardless of her nonchalance, a part of me is wondering if this is a test from Sam. Too quickly she picked up on me wearing Tyler's clothes. Suspicions started long ago, and I just keep feeding into them.

She's either totally oblivious to me and Tyler or now totally aware and using this New Year's kiss to confirm. So, I try to play it off. I hate that I have to, but I can't tell her. I need the right time. The right place. With wine. *Lots* of wine.

"Okay." I shrug. "Does Cole know he's kissing you?"

"No. But he will." She smiles and wiggles her eyebrows.

I roll my eyes and laugh. "Sam, you have to tell everyone who they are kissing."

"Alright, alright. I'll tell everyone the plan." She grabs her glass of whatever is in there and heads inside. "I'm kissing you if I don't get my plan A!" she calls over her shoulder.

I look out from Tyler's rooftop, imagining what the fireworks will look like from here. I angle the chairs so that they are all circled around the fire pit but towards where the show is supposed to be.

Once I feel I've made my contribution, I head back inside because without the fire and blankets, my hands are starting to turn blue. I keep my head down as I make my way back inside, almost bumping into Tyler in the process.

"Haven't you learned your lesson from Betty's Beans?" He arches a brow with a grin pulling the side of his lips. One arm holds firewood while the other is heavy on my shoulder.

"I guess not. Had I stayed out there any longer you'd come back to a frozen carcass." I wrap my arms around myself.

"I was just about to come up and start the fire," he says.

"Change of plans." Sam grabs me, shoving past her brother.

He gives a little shake of his head and rolls his eyes, starting for the rooftop. Does he know the plan?

"What is it?" I ask.

"Apparently Cole and Macey already made a pact to kiss one another tonight. Probably because Anthony wants to kiss me. I can't kiss my brother. So, Anthony it is. Thanks for taking one for the team." She raises her glass to me.

The phrase my pleasure comes to mind, but I know that isn't a smart choice in response.

"I don't get to kiss you?" I feign disappointment.

She scowls and rolls her eyes, so similar to her brother just moments ago.

"Okay, everyone! Ten minutes til! Grab your blankets and sweaters, drinks and all and let's go outside!" Anthony chants.

With a smile, Tyler approaches me with a fluffy blanket. God he is so observant, only feeding into my spiraling thoughts of what he does for a living. He sees the details.

"Let's ring in the new year?" He secures the blanket around me.

"Let's," I say, looping my arm in his.

CHAPTER FORTY-FOUR

SUNNY

FIREWORKS CASCADE THE SKY DESPITE THE FACT WE STILL HAVE a few minutes until the new year. I look at Tyler, and see he is staring at me. A softness takes over his normally lethal eyes and I wonder why it's me that has somehow delivered this part of him.

It's at this moment I realize, being loved isn't the same as being seen. And Tyler, he sees me. No matter how much I try to hide myself from him.

Something about being able to kiss him in front of all our friends feels absolutely freeing. It's my fault that we have to hide behind closed doors, I know that. But it isn't fair to make something more than what it is, what it should be when I have plans on leaving in a few short months.

I turn to him, bringing a hand to his face where my thumb traces the lazy smile that curves his lips. He leans into my touch, closing his eyes as a hand of his covers my own.

And I'm smiling.

Not like the half smiles I've had. It is a too wide grin that pulls my lips so desperately that it hurts my cheeks.

And it's because of him.

Them.

My family.

It's because of these small, wonderful moments I've spent my life chasing. Moments surrounded by people I love and who love me. And here it is. It exists. *I have it.*

Being with Ryan was isolating and lonely. I not only lost a part of myself but a lot of friends, too. In a world where it seemed like he lost everything, I tried to replicate that in myself. And he let me. He let me be his everything in such a deep, profound way that became harmful. In becoming his everything, I lost everything.

"Beautiful," Tyler whispers. "I have spent so long trying to get a smile like that on your face." His thumb traces my lips, memorizing their curve.

Fireworks continue to grow more and more by the second, leading up to the final moments of the year. The year that has caused so much pain, yet so much happiness, all in one.

"Do it again," he says. "I'll do anything, anything to keep that smile." He kisses my palm.

So I smile, because I am so goddamn tired of the frowns my sadness has caused.

"Five, four, three, two, one!" I hear our family countdown.

Each second he gets an inch closer, until his lips are a whisper against my own. His fingers wrap around the back of my neck, his thumb stroking my cheek. And I feel that tether, stronger than ever as I look into his emeralds.

"Happy New Year!" they all chant at once.

"Happy New Year, Sunny darling," he whispers against my lips.

We kiss and it feels like... *finally.*

His lips press into mine, using his tongue to write all the silent, lost words that I won't allow him to speak. They melt on my tongue and flood my system, coursing through my veins as they fill the cracks in my heart I thought were irreparable.

I feel it between us, stronger than ever, as my broken heart tries to run from a glimpse of being loved properly, regardless of that thread slowly suturing my broken pieces.

But maybe my tired heart will finally relinquish to the chase. For once, I'll allow myself this, because it's at this moment I know he will never stop. He will never stop chasing until my heart finally screams *I'm yours*.

And it's there. I know it is. The words echo in my mind and beat with each thump of my heart despite the denial of it all.

Yours. Yours. Yours.

The day that I met him was the day my heart started beating differently. I'd chalked it up to being broken, but Tyler somehow went through the rubble, found the wires and rewired it all to love him.

I don't care if they know.

I *want* to kiss him.

We deserve it.

We are well past the mark of a New Years kiss, but we don't stop. His hands trace all my broken parts, not caring if it makes them bleed.

I didn't realize this is something I'd been craving for far too long. The freedom of kissing him without barriers, without worrying. With just simply allowing myself something after so long of denying it.

It's when we finally pull away, the words of the outside world interfere with our silence.

"Um, is there something I need to be made aware of?" Sam asks.

CHAPTER FORTY-FIVE

SUNNY

WE BOTH GLANCE AT SAM AND THEN BACK TO ONE ANOTHER. I can't even be mad at him, because I'm just as guilty.

Realization dawns in those amber eyes, and I know no amount of lies will fix this one.

"Oh my god." She blinks between the two of us. "So you two are fucking?"

"What?" Tyler asks, trying to salvage what little privacy we have. Trying to undo what we did in front of everyone. And I know it's only for me. Hiding *us* because I asked him to.

"Oh my god." She brings a hand to her mouth. "So, when did that start? Because that's more than just a kiss. That's more than just a physical attraction."

My chest caves in at the tone. This is what I was afraid of.

I don't even know what it is, Sam.

"Sam, please." Tyler dismisses her. "We all know I'm just a fucking good kisser. Shove your assumptions up your ass."

My mouth drops the same moment I practically see smoke fuming from Sam. By the way Cole is staring at Tyler, it tells me he knows far too much. Did Tyler tell him?

Sam follows my line of sight to Cole, seeing exactly what I

see, too. The silence stretches between all of us with every passing second.

"So, you knew, too?" Sam seethes to Cole. "These aren't just assumptions." Her eyes narrow on her brother.

"Sam, there are a few things you should know," Cole says, rolling his lips.

The confusion and hurt in her eyes are prevalent as they dart between Tyler and Cole, then finally on me. But at this point, I'm almost as confused as she is. Anthony practically avoids any eye contact.

Did he just tell *all* of them?

This whole time I did everything I could to keep this secret and he just fucking told them everything. It explains everything that's happened that lead up to this point.

I look at Macey who stands wide eyed at Coles side. What are *they* not telling us?

Cole takes a deep breath. "I should've told you this sooner because I honestly just drug it on for too long, and it's not fair to you. I knew your feelings for me, but I just let you have them instead of telling you the truth."

How could we have been so blind to it this whole time?

"I didn't kiss you tonight because of Anthony. I'm in love with someone. I have been for a while and we have both made it clear we'll be with one another, we just didn't know when the right time would be. But now that it's all getting put out there." He grabs one of Macey's hands that's wrapped around her body. "Macey and I are together," he finally announces.

Despite the panic that rounds Macey's eyes, she leans into Cole trustingly. I admire her for it. Clearly I wasn't the only one trying to hide my secret love affair. But at least they had a valid reason.

Sam takes a faltering step back. "Am I crazy or just blind?" she asks. "Am I the only one who didn't know?"

"No. I didn't know," I say.

Her amber eyes snap to me. "How convenient." Grabbing her blanket off a chair, she storms back towards the inside of the house.

Anthony follows after her but then she stops in her tracks and turns around where Cole and Macey stand. She isn't finished with this moment. She's on a warpath now, trying to hurt the way she's hurt.

"Well it's a good thing I fucking miscarried *your* baby Cole, otherwise you'd be unhappily stuck with me for life." The look in Cole's eyes tells me he was told an entirely different story.

"What?" Tyler breathes, his whole body stiffening next to me.

"I thought you had an abortion?" Cole asks, confusion evident on his face.

I practically jerk back at the remark. In what world did he get this idea?

Cole's eyes move back to Macey who pales. Her gray eyes turn wide with guilt. My chest caves in.

Oh no.

"*What*?" Is all that comes out of Sam's mouth.

"Fuck," Tyler mumbles, pinching the bridge of his nose.

"You told me she had an abortion?" Cole snaps at Macey.

"I –" Macey starts to defend herself.

"A fucking abortion?! You took me to the emergency department when I was bleeding everywhere having a miscarriage!" Sam roars, throwing her hands in the air. "I wanted that baby more than *anything*."

Tyler winces at his sister's words. "Can someone just tell me what the fuck is going on?"

"Oh sure, hero Tyler is trying to save the day again. Get rid of your savior complex. It's not going to help anyone right now," Sam snaps.

"Maybe if you weren't so goddamn self-destructive I

wouldn't have to have such a fucking complex, Sam." Tyler sighs.

"Okay everyone take a breath," Anthony shouts to my surprise.

Everyone turns at that, and I realize Cole is no longer holding Macey's hand. Her arms are wrapped around her body, trying to make herself small among the wreckage she's created.

We all have secrets, and this is proof that one day it'll all come out.

"Why did you lie?" Cole snaps at Mace.

"Cole, tone it down," Tyler says.

"No! She made me think this whole time that Sam made a life altering decision without me. And I won't lie, I've had some resentment towards you because of it. Was this your plan, Mace?" Cole swings his head back to her.

Tyler closes his eyes, slowly letting out a breath. "This is something you two should talk about in *private*, Cole."

Regret fills Macey's wide eyes, and I can tell remorse is already weighing her heart. *We all have secrets.* It's just a matter of whether they become uncovered or not.

"I was selfish," she finally admits. "I...I had an abortion with my ex. I was already too far into us, and I couldn't imagine going through with the pregnancy. I thought I was seeking your best interest when I lied because I knew a miscarriage would hurt you more than Sam making a choice." Her voice is small. "We had such good momentum, I didn't want anything to ruin it. And you kept asking me what was wrong and...that came out instead of the truth. I thought putting my truth as a lie in Sam would give me a glimpse of what your reaction would've been to me."

Sam huffs a laugh. "Yes, let me not tell him the truth and instead just tell him a downright lie so that he'll be angry at Sam and love me more. Smooth, Macey."

"Hey!" Cole snaps.

"Oh please." Sam waives. "The fact you're still taking her side tells me everything." She rolls her eyes and turns where Tyler and I stand, her amber eyes ablaze with an anger so hot I'm worried we will physically be burned.

"It's one thing to have a crush, but it's another to have a full blown whatever the fuck you guys are and hide it from only me." Sam huffs. "Clearly, I am not let in on a lot of things in this group and it shows." With that, Sam leaves the rooftop and Anthony follows after her.

I shift on my feet, unsure of what to do. Give her space or go after her. This somehow ended up as an involuntary attack on her.

"Thanks for deflecting," Tyler grumbles to Cole.

"It needed to be done, anyways. It hasn't been fair to Macey having to watch Sam's continuous flirtation with me. And clearly there were some things that needed to be aired out." He puts an arm around Macey, who again melts in his embrace. Thankful this didn't end what they had going for so long. "We have a lot we need to go talk about," he says to Macey, guiding her away from the mess.

I feel a hollowness in me, a longing to finally be able to give into something like that with Tyler. I wish that it could be as simple as that for us, but it isn't.

Not with all the dark and broken parts of me.

"Oh god." I place my face in my hands.

How much longer can I do this? Being a girl on the run means no roots, and this is proof of the pain that it'll cause when they are pulled.

My best friend is hurt. Tyler is going to be hurt. Cole and Macey are fighting for a relationship that just barely became public.

I didn't fucking *think*.

Tyler sighs, wrapping an arm around me. "Talk about ringing in the new year with a fucking bang."

After much deliberation, we decided to give Sam the time she needed. In our wait, Tyler and I sit by the fire while Cole and Macey hash things out. From a distance, their words are muffled but their reactions are not.

I'm not aware of what was said, but a lot of hand slashing, tears, raised voices and laughs are shared all to be sealed with a kiss that made things look up for the new couple.

We sit quietly by the fire as they approach holding hands, and make themselves comfortable. With Tyler's chest to my back and my head in the crook of his neck, the anger my heart once felt has calmed to a quiet. He is warmth, salt and citrus and everything I want to belong to me that I'll never allow myself to fully have.

His laughter rumbles through me, the vibrations of it running along my skin and rattling my bones as I sit here casually with him.

I hate that I like this with you, Tyler.

A conversation is held between Tyler and Cole, as if nothing happened just thirty minutes prior. As if nothing in this moment matters right now except this small, safe space where the four of us no longer have to hide.

Without second thought, his callused hands gently caress my bare skin. A gentle kiss is pressed to the top of my head with a subtle inhale, no doubt his memorization of what I smell like so intimately close.

And for now, I don't want to leave this spot, this moment, and that scares me shitless because I *have* to. I have to leave, and he has to stay. That's our reality.

I can't keep doing this.

Standing to my feet, I immediately feel the void of where he was. The *lack* of him.

"What's wrong?" He asks, his arms still open as if I were there. Is that what it'll be like when I leave? A void nothing can replace left inside him?

"I need to go talk to Sam," I say, still standing with the blanket wrapped around myself.

"Do you want me to come?" Tyler offers, standing up.

"No," I immediately say with a hand up. "I need to do this alone."

"Okay." He nods. I wasn't Switzerland per say, but I'm closer to it than Tyler is.

"I'll come back up once I'm done," I say. "And Mace, you need to, also. Okay? You're sisters. You need to figure this out."

"Good luck," Cole wishes.

"Oh, it's not me I'm worried about."

CHAPTER FORTY-SIX

SUNNY

The warmth of Tyler's home dowses my body as I enter, but a shiver runs down my spine nonetheless. When I make it to the living room, I see Sam and Anthony on the couch together.

"I'm going to go on the roof," Anthony says, getting up and dismissing himself. He squeezes my hand as he walks by. I can't determine if it's a warning or a go ahead.

Picking her nails like she always does, Sam watches the fireplace. "It's about damn time."

"You really need to stop doing that." I sit next to her.

"You really need to stop doing my brother."

I choke on the laugh trying to escape from me to keep the moment serious. *If only you knew, Sam.*

"I'm sorry. That was a low blow." She finally looks at me.

"If it makes you feel any better, we haven't done...*that.*"

"That right there tells me all I need to know about how he feels for you."

I sit up straighter. "What do you mean?"

"Tyler won't wait around or chase a fuck. He can get a fuck whenever, wherever he wants. He could close his eyes, tap a number in his phone and the bitch would be there before the hour ends. Yet, he still chooses to refrain from that and do…whatever he does with you. That means he cares, Sunny. He cares about you if he hasn't fucked you yet."

I stare wide eyed at Sam, not really sure what to say. I have no other explanation as to why that line hasn't been crossed except for the fact it could mean more than it's supposed to.

"People talk, Sunny. I've had the unfortunate encounter of hearing women talk about my brother's bedroom skills."

The idea of Tyler with anyone else does something inside me I don't appreciate. I toy with a loose thread on his hoodie. A small imperfection among his perfect clothing. A fatal flaw. Kind of like me. One pull, one wrong move and the whole thing can come apart.

"I'm not mad that you're with, or doing, or whatever it is you have with my brother. Which, I don't even think you two know what it is." She gives me a pointed look.

"That's fair," I agree.

"I'm mad at the fact you hid it from me. And I'd be lying if I said my ego wasn't bruised by Cole basically announcing to the world my feelings for him while simultaneously picking another girl over me. Not to mention, said girl is supposed to be one of my best friends, my sister, and lied to make me look bad and save her ass." She rolls her eyes.

"What do we do?" I ask, genuinely unsure of how to approach this.

"It's something I need to talk to Mace about. I just can't believe we were so blind to it? Like how did we not see it?" She picks her nails again.

"I have no clue. But once it was aired, it honestly made so much sense." I watch the fire.

She shakes her head. "Anyways, tell me more about you and Tyler."

I gnaw on my lip. "I really don't know what we are. A lot of factors play into it. I just figured we were just friends, with benefits…maybe?" I let a nervous laugh out. "I don't think it's like that for him anymore."

"Tyler is… so intense," Sam laughs. "He loves so deeply. He loves his friends more than anything in the world and though he doesn't want to admit it, he will destroy himself if it means healing the people he loves." With a sigh, she looks at the fire. "I had my suspicions about you two, I just didn't know it was the extent that it is. I just thought maybe it was innocent flirtations, a chemistry between you two, maybe a good fuck every now and then, but I saw the way he looks at you." She meets my eyes. "Only a man in love looks at a woman like that."

I break her eye contact, trying to hide the damn tears that threaten my eyes. God, when did I become so emotional?

"I was too caught up in myself to see what's happening to my brother. I always wondered who the girl would be, the one to finally make him fall flat and wipe that stupid womanizing grin off his face. But it makes sense it's you, Sunny." She smiles. "Something shifted in him when you came around. He became more alive. I got worried there, for a while. Not to say he wasn't present, but he was just on autopilot. Especially after Shelby. I don't know what she did to him. He needed something to pull him out of that and you did it. I was shocked he so willingly invited you to family dinner after only meeting you twice."

"He…He invited me?" I ask, clearly shocked. I'd thought it was Sam all along.

"Yeah," she says. "I see a lot, Sunny. I just choose to not acknowledge it. Which is why I'm still shocked I did not see Cole and Macey. Too blinded by my own feelings," she sighs. "I know that you've been hurt badly and it might feel so foreign to be feeling what you feel so soon after Ryan. I may be biased but Tyler, he's incredible, Sunny." Her eyes start to water. "He'll never hurt you the way Ryan did. I know you're leaving, so this must all be so confusing, but definitely try to talk to him. Because like I said, Tyler is intense and once he's committed, it's hard to sever that commitment. And we can help you. We know lawyers, judges." She places a hand over mine trying to comfort me.

"I..I.." The words are caught on my tongue.

"We don't have to figure it out now. I just wanted to tell you that." She smiles.

I do what I do best—I shift topics. "So, are you okay after hearing the Cole and Macey news?"

Sam blows a breath and then laughs. "I have to be. I guess I should've taken a hint, but I was so blind to it. After we hooked up, I just wanted more of him. I guess it was just a moment of weakness on both our parts. Even with the miscarriage, it honestly was probably for the best." She takes a sip of her champagne. "They make sense though."

I won't say it out loud, but I couldn't agree more. Macey and Cole *do* make sense.

"And what about Anthony?" I ask.

In a perfect world, I'd be with Tyler, Macey with Cole, and Sam with Anthony. But this isn't a perfect world. This is reality and we don't always get what we so wish for.

If only we could.

"Don't get me wrong, I love Anthony. When we hooked up, I'd be lying if I said I couldn't imagine doing that for the rest of my life. I'm just not there. Maybe one day. Or maybe I'll find a hot MILF."

We both start laughing together until tears come from our eyes. Once we finally settle, I make my apology.

"I'm sorry. I'm sorry I hid behind your back with your brother, and you had to find out the way you did. I feel like we kind of cornered you and bombed you."

Sam waives a hand. "It's fine. You know me, always gotta be the center of attention. I just want you to know, I'm only slightly bitter he got you and I didn't when I clearly made the bolder first move."

We hug one another then I grab the bottle of champagne on the table. "Alright, now let's fucking party like it's the New Year."

TYLER

She's left an imprint on me, one so deep that it'll simply never go away. If she leaves, I'll spend the rest of my life missing everything we could've been.

Which is why I simply cannot let her.

Our family knows now. There is no more hiding. And I know they will do everything they can to make her stay, too.

Don't run from me, Sunny. We were doing so good.

I was given a taste of what normalcy would look like with her. Now that it's gone, I feel starved. I want everything with her—the sweet moments of hands holding, forehead kisses and pink cheeked glances. And I want all the depraved parts—the hands tied, bite marks and tasting one another.

And I'm determined to get that.

"Okay." Anthony sits down. He points to Cole and Macey. "All I want to know is when, how, why." Then he points at me. "When, how, why and what the fuck you gonna do."

A laugh escapes me because I don't even know the fucking answer to the question. I battle it every day. My girl needs time we don't have, but I'm doing everything in my power to give it to her.

"One night at Martha's." Cole starts the story he shared with me just a few months prior when we sparred all night long.

Anthony knew Cole was seeing someone. He just didn't know it was Macey. And Anthony knew I'm in love with Sunny, he just didn't know that she's starting to reciprocate with me.

"I was giving her a ride home and for some reason, she just

didn't want to leave the truck." He smiles down at Macey. I feel the void in my own lap with Sunny gone. A prelude to what my life will be in the next few months if I don't do something about it.

"We just started talking and by the time we realized it, hours had gone by," Macey says.

"That was the night it changed for me. Something just snapped in place. It was like, there was something tying us together and I didn't want to let it go," Cole admits.

And I understand, I really do.

"It just kind of spiraled from there. We found ourselves coming and going to family dinners together just so we could have more truck moments. I'd pick her up and drop her off. Until finally one night, I told her that I didn't want her to go home. I told her I wanted her to come home with me," Cole says, tightening his grip around Macey.

"So, I did." Macey giggles.

"That's when we decided there was no one else for us." Cole kisses her head.

"So, to answer your question, about a year," Cole says to Anthony.

"Y'all make me sick," Anthony jokes, shaking his head. "Alright, you're up Tyler."

Before I'm put on trial, we're greeted by a giggling Sunny and Sam. Their arms linked together as they pass a bottle of champagne between one another, taking sips. A sigh of relief leaves my chest seeing they made amends. I knew they would. They're sisters.

Now let me make that legal, Sunny. Let me make you and Sam sisters when you marry me.

"We brought champagne to celebrate!" Sam says, holding up a bottle while my girl holds the other. "To new relationships, well, new to me at least." A choked laugh escapes the group while a groan leaves me. "And to a new fucking year and this fabulous family of mine." She passes glasses around, filling them with champagne.

Sam pulls Macey aside, both of them wiping tears from one another's faces and hugging it out. I know things won't be okay immediately because the wounds need to heal, but at least this is a step forward, and we have at least stopped the bleeding.

Seeing my girl look around, I can tell she is contemplating where to sit.

As if she even has a choice.

The only place she's allowed is in my lap. Grabbing her hips, I pull her back into me.

I feel the void go away almost immediately.

CHAPTER FORTY-SEVEN

TYLER

I sit in my office, phone in my hands like a giddy fucking teenager texting his girlfriend. A smile pulls my lips thinking about that label with Sunny, despite the fact it feeling and sounding way too juvenile for people our age. *My girlfriend.* It's simply too casual a term for what I feel for her.

I send her a text.

> Train tonight?

It's only been a week since New Years Eve, but with the time off for the Holidays, we've both been buried deep into work.

I place my phone down on my desk and look out the window to the gloomy January day. Footsteps catch my attention. Looking up, I see my father walk in.

"Tyler," he says, giving me a nod.

I put my hands in my pockets and lean back against my desk. "What can I do for you?" Mitchell always likes to drop in unannounced to check on me.

"I wanted to see where you're at with Shelby. The campaign is in a few weeks, and we really need to start making it our main focus." He makes himself comfortable in the chairs in front of my desk. "You know your duty. You know why the two of you have been arranged. I need to make sure you hold up your end of the bargain. Since you haven't yet. The campaign would be a great way to announce your engagement or even propose."

"I never said I wouldn't invest in his campaigns even if I didn't marry his daughter." I cross my arms over my chest, keeping a blank look on my face despite my suit feeling tighter than it already is.

I'm already drawing up the contract as we speak. A contract like this takes deliberate precision. There cannot be any loopholes in which Matthew can get through. Both our lawyers will review it as many times as it takes until every word is memorized and recited perfectly.

This not only gives Matthew a set number of campaign money funneling into him, but it gives the Caddell Company political gain without having to reap the repercussions. He will question it because in our world something isn't so easily given without something being taken. An exchange. But the only thing I want is Sunny, and this is how I'm going to get her.

If this doesn't pan out, I have my other ways. I figured I'd do the professional route first. Give Matthew the chance to make the right decision without my use of force.

"Tyler, what the hell happened? This has been in the plan for twenty-nine years. Now you're unwilling to follow through on your part. You two should've been married by now and with a child here or on the way. The easiest and best option is to marry her because that's the only contract we need. If we need to change things, do what we want, we don't have to live by the rules of a *real* legally binding contract. Do you realize that? You can fuck whoever you want after you marry Shelby."

"Is that what you do? Fuck whoever you want outside of mom?"

"What I do is none of your business. I have myself established. And while you have your spot in this world, you need to make yourself a man of your word or else you will lose all that." He pinches the bridge of his nose. "People will think you're flakey, unreliable, not loyal. Every day that you don't have a wife and don't produce an heir, our family weakens. It leaves all we have built left to no one."

"I know what I'm doing, Mitchell. As far as I'm concerned, I'm not marrying Shelby. I already have a contract drawn up. I'm just waiting on Matthew's lawyers to get back to us."

"*Tyler*," Mitchell snaps. "You are twenty-nine years old and have no heirs. No wife."

"It's done, Mitchell. Leave it alone. I have it covered. If you'll excuse me, I have work to get to."

I'm working on Leo's second restaurant. Business is doing well for him. I made it a note to take Sunny to his second restaurant opening. She loved the first and Leo loved her. He's the one who taught me how to make pasta from scratch and offered for us to come in to teach Sunny.

"You better hope this fucking works. If not, you're marrying Shelby. Even if I have to drag you down the aisle and tie you to a chair to do it." he seethes and leaves.

I lean back in my chair and laugh. How quickly Mitchell forgets who he made me to be.

My phone buzzes on my desk, making me smile when I see Sunny's name light up my screen.

Sounds good to me.

The things I do to be with you, Sunny.

Pulling up outside of Sunny's apartment complex, I see her waiting on the steps for me. I shake my head as I put the truck in park, because she knows that I hate it when she waits outside.

She stands up, wiping off her pants and walks over to the truck. I get out immediately and open the door for her. She gives me a weak smile, but something seems off.

When she gets into my passenger seat, the silence looms over us like the standstill of a storm on the horizon. I brace my arms on the truck, ready to break the heavy rain cloud above us.

"Are you okay? We don't have to train tonight if you're tired," I offer. "A storm looks like it's coming in anyways. We can have a lazy rainy day. Books, Friends, blankets, hot cocoa, and a fire." I smile, hooking a curl behind her ear.

She shakes her head. "I'm fine. Let's do it. I need to train."

"Okay." I smile, closing the door. I'll find out what's bothering her.

I put the truck in drive and pull away from her apartment. The silence maintains, because if anything I've learned about her is when she's quiet, her mind is very loud. She seeks asylum in the silence when things are too loud in her own mind.

My own thoughts start to fester, asking all the what if's she won't give me right now. From what I gather, it's been awhile since she's had any update on Ryan.

"Have you heard from the detectives at all?" I ask.

"No."

"That's a good thing, right?" I glance at her. She's staring outside the truck window with a sadness I haven't seen on her in awhile. It hurts. It fucking hurts.

"I honestly don't know," she whispers.

I know how it goes with these things. After a few months of inactivity, there is only so much law enforcement can do. He becomes just another name on their list. The police will still always be "looking" and there will always be a warrant out, but it'll never be the man hunt I could make it.

It's my obsession, but their profession. They won't waste their time and resources on a man who doesn't seem to pose a threat anymore and doesn't want to be found. He isn't a priority criminal for them, but he is for me.

Let me find him, Sunny.

"Tyler…" She looks at me.

"Yes, baby?" I ask, glancing at her again. "What is it?" I brush the loose strands of sunshine hair from her face.

"Us."

I see her running already. She's sitting here but she's already fucking mentally running.

We were so close.

So close.

CHAPTER FORTY-EIGHT

SUNNY

With a sigh, he grips the steering wheel, head hanging between his shoulders. Like he can no longer withstand the weight of my words. When he looks at me, I see the devastation that hits him. It flexes in the muscles of his jaw and strains the tendons in his neck.

"Sunny, no. Don't do this. Don't fucking do this." Each word builds with anger.

I wince, despite the fact I'm the reason behind this. Immediately his tone calms, and he runs a shaky hand through his hair.

"Please, Sunny, let me help you. I have the best lawyers. I have the best security. *I am the goddamn best*. We can make this better and even if you don't stay here, at least you can just stop running and living in fear." He presses his palms together, as if he's sending a prayer up to whatever that will take his offer.

I'd considered it. For a brief moment in one of my panics, the idea of having someone like Tyler to bring me justice and find the man I've been running from sounded poetic. But then I remembered what he'd told me about Mitchell and the ever growing list of hits he's forced onto his son. Although Tyler will never admit it, I know it haunts him at night. Who could he have been had it not been for Mitchell?

I'd spent so long somehow dependent on a man, and I'm not going to do it again. I shake my head slowly indicating my no.

"Believe it or not, my parents do not control every aspect of my life, Sunny. Me utilizing our resources doesn't give me a life sentence. And don't act like because I'd do this for you that I haven't done it before or wouldn't again. I've killed people, Sunny. Ryan won't be my fucking first."

It's a sucker punch to the gut, hearing the words so violently from his mouth. It's always been an unspoken thing, a silent understanding, much like a lot of what we have. Breathing those words to life only anchors my decision.

"He may not be your first, but I won't be responsible for making you add to your list. I see what it does to you, Tyler. I will not be the person responsible for that."

"The damage is done, Sunny! The damage is fucking done." He hits a fist on the steering wheel. "It's no one's job but mine to live with the choices I've made. You think it bothers me? It fucking doesn't. It's what I was made to do. It's who he built me to be. I am not some good person who does bad things. I am a bad fucking person who does bad things. Stop trying to justify my actions with remorse that doesn't exist."

"It's no one's job but mine to live with the choices I've made! Tyler, it was no secret that I'm leaving and whatever the hell this is would come to an end. You and I both know that." I'm not going to allow him to make me feel guilty for this. I already feel guilty enough.

"What I can't wrap around my head is why you won't let me fucking help you," he growls.

"Because it is no one's job but my own to help me!" I yell, my arms spread out. I can't get why he can't wrap it around his fucking head. "Sam was right, you do have a savior complex."

His jaw flexes as his grip tightens on the steering wheel. *Good.* I need to make this unforgivable.

That way he will finally let me go.

TYLER

She looks so small, so fucking small in that passenger seat. I blow out a breath, trying to calm my trembling hands and harsh voice.

She's trying to run, but I'll be damned before I ever stop chasing her.

"Sunny, stop. I know what you're doing. It doesn't matter what you say, I will not stop trying for you. And you can drop the miss independent act, okay? You don't have to keep fighting alone."

She sits there with a blank look on her face, trying to put a façade up. Covering the emotions I know are trying to burst out of her. My little fire tries her best to put her own flame out. It's what Ryan groomed her to do, but it doesn't fucking work with me.

"Baby, you have to stop holding onto it. Just let it go. Let go and live your life," I say, gentler as I trace a finger along her jawline.

She swallows hard at my touch. "And where do I put it down, Tyler? What do I do with it?" her voice cracks.

Her pain is my pain.

"Give it to me, baby. Give it to me if it means it will set you free." I cup her face. "Give your body and mind rest and let me handle it. Let me take care of you."

She contemplates, but then something switches, and the flames erupt. "I'm not just some broken thing for you to fix

Tyler, okay! So you can just stop already," she snaps, jerking her face from my grip.

I can't even stop the words before they leave my mouth, much like the night they first came out.

I couldn't stop it then. I can't fucking stop it now.

"I'm not trying to fix you Sunny, I'm trying to love you!" I yell.

I run my hands over my face again, because I know what I did. What I said is going to send her running faster than she'd been from Ryan. These words are going to scare her shitless because they scare me shitless, too.

Realization dawns on her as my words linger in the air between us, the torrential downpour of it all a threat right above us.

If she's going to run, then I'm going to fucking chase her.

And I will catch her.

CHAPTER FORTY-NINE

SUNNY

I LOVE YOU.

The words echo in my mind, no longer a silent understanding but an outspoken declaration. They embroider across my heart with that invisible string between us, branding it as his, regardless of the fact it never belonged to me in the first place.

We'll always be like parallel lines, so close, *always so close*, but never together because honest feelings and bad timing make the most painful combination to exist.

"What?" I breathe, meeting his eyes, regardless of the fact he is loud and clear.

"Sunny." He tries to reel back.

"No." I put a hand up to stop him. "You're in love with me." I wish the more I say it, the less it'll be true.

Rubbing a hand over his face, he looks back up at me and lets out a small, humorless chuckle. "That's an understatement."

The truck feels like it's closing in on me. It feels so fucking hot. My clothes feel suffocating, no matter the heavy breaths I keep taking. And I feel the urge to do what I always do best.

Run.

"Sunny, please," he begs as he puts the truck in park.

"I need air." I open the door, rushing out and slamming it shut behind me.

And I run.

I run all the way to the end of the massive parking lot that seems too big to belong in Boston. I hear him chasing after me, footsteps hitting the ground in a desperate attempt to keep me. I don't care, because I need to get far away. As if going farther away will make him love me less.

"Sunny, stop please!"

Halting with a hand on my chest, I try to suck in air but I can't fucking breathe. These feelings are so big that they are crushing me.

"When?" I turn back to him. "How long, Tyler?"

He swallows hard. "Does it matter?"

"Very much so."

He shifts on his feet and looks at me finally. "I knew I was in love with you when I realized I could never love anyone else. Even just the thought is simply impossible."

Biting my cheek, I try to force the tears back down that want to sting my eyes. "It was before everything, wasn't it?"

"Yeah." He nods. "I knew the night I came over when you were sick. So yes." He looks up to the gray sky.

There can no longer be any more rainy days for us because there can no longer be an us. If I had known. *If I had known.*

"It wasn't supposed to be like this." I shake my head.

"I am not capable of being casual with you, Sunny. *I am not capable of being casual with you,*" he emphasizes. He takes a cautious step towards me. "Sunny, you have given me a reason to keep breathing. I am a man willing to admit that I cannot exist in a life without you," he exhales a shaky breath. "Because without you, I am nothing but skin, bones and a heart that has no purpose to beat at all. All of you belongs to me, just as all of me belongs to you."

I break his gaze, unable to hold myself under the severity of it.

"Look at me," he commands. "Look at me when I tell you this—make no mistake, little fire, you can run from me through lifetimes, trying to deny that string connecting us, but I will keep fucking running, yanking it to drag you back to me. No matter how hard you try to prevent it, I will love you through lifetimes." He shakes his head and shrugs. "I can't lie anymore."

CHAPTER FIFTY

TYLER

Simultaneously relief and fear thread through my bones. The words have been a desperate, silent cry on my tongue for far too long, begging to be released. But now that it's said, I can see the look in her eye. One by one, I see the weight of my words and their effect as they land on her.

Her arms hang loosely at her sides in defeat as she blinks at the parking lot ground. The silence between us louder than any of the words we've spoken.

I wait patiently. I always will.

"We agreed to be casual, Tyler. Why would you agree to that when you already knew your feelings for me?" The emotions flick through her like a film switching to different frames. Anger, sadness, shock. Repeat.

The thing is, we never fucking agreed on anything. We never made a pact. We never signed a contract. We never promised. We're people of action, not fucking words. Too little words were spoken between us. Instead we were in a tangle of limbs, mouths, and moans.

I huff out a breath because honesty is all that is between us now. "We never agreed to anything, Sunny." I step into her. "But even if we did…If that was all that I'd get from you, even if you didn't love me back, it'd be worth it. If this is all the time you and I are allowed to have, if this is it, then it's worth it, too. And I'd do my life over again so I could keep having this small portion with you," I growl. "Maybe I thought you'd fall in love with me too, maybe a small portion was hopeful. That part of me is selfish. I'm being selfish, Sunny. Asking you to stay and to let me help you is me being selfish again. And to be frank, I don't fucking care."

Her brows crease, the anger pertinent on her face as I step closer to her.

"I don't care if it's selfish because if it means that you are safe and you are cared for and you are loved the way you deserve then yes, I'll be fucking selfish. I'll also respect you. Even if I don't believe the words coming from your mouth. I don't believe you want to leave, and I don't believe that you want this between us to end because if it truly is what you say it is, then you wouldn't have let it get as far as it did. And you wouldn't be running right now because you realize you have feelings, too. I get you had this plan but life changes, and we need to learn to change with it."

Running a hand over my face, I start to pace the parking lot. I watch the slow roll of her throat as she tries to swallow back the tears.

"Is this what you want?" I stop my pacing.

Her eyes flick from the ground to me, but no words come from her. She's a blank sheet. No more film roll of emotions. She's shutting down.

"Is this what you want, Sunny? For me to just move on from you? You want me to let you go so you can go running to the next place?" I press, taking another step towards her.

I realize that I gave a part of myself to her, and I'll never get it back. I don't want it back anyways, because I'll never be the same now. Not after her. I'd rather never be the same again than never know what a life with her was like.

"Yes," she whispers, her eyes on me now. And I see nothing in them save for a glimmer of pain. "I want you to move on."

Impossible. No one else makes sense.

I shake my head slowly at her words. "This is ridiculous. You're a *liar*."

"It's what needs to happen, Tyler. We both know it. You need to move on from me because there will no longer be me in a few months."

"Don't be a fucking coward then and say it louder." I seethe through my teeth.

"It's what I want! I want you to move on," she emphasizes, but her voice still shakes.

"Do you know exactly what you're asking me?" I take a step closer to her. "You want me to kiss another girl?" I take another step. "You want me to buy her flowers?" Another step. "You want me to explore her body in all the ways I explored yours? And then more?" Another step.

She doesn't move. She stands where she's at, taking it all. She isn't scared, and she never was. I just wish she would see that, too. Because maybe then she would stop running.

She needs to understand the depth of what she's asking. This wall she's placed is preventing her from thinking clearly. I just need to create a crack, to know that it's actually her and not this wall. Some sort of reaction to see this hurts her as much as it hurts me.

"You want me to fuck her until she is screaming my name? Maybe even put a baby in her? Fill her with me. Owning her and making her *mine*." I seethe.

Her eyes flutter at my words, my tone. *A crack in the wall.* But a reaction, nonetheless. Slowly I'll break through this fucking fortress she put up.

"You want me to tell her I love her, the way I love you, if not more?" I take another step.

That part is impossible. I now know why I've never loved before, because all my love belongs to her. It always has, and it always will.

Just mere inches from her now, we practically share breath. But her eyes never leave mine.

"And you want me to just forget about you, and all the things we've done, all the pieces of ourselves we shared, as if you just never existed?" The words are practically a whisper against her lips.

I search her face, hopeful for another small reaction. Something for me to cling onto in hopes that I know I'm not fucking crazy about the feelings we have for one another. Then, her lip quivers.

Another crack.

I cling to that hope like a fucking life line, but as quickly as I held on tight, it shatters in my hands with one simple word from her lips.

"Yes." She nods. No quiver in her voice. No breaking our eye contact. No, this time, she means it.

I scoff and I pull back from her. Placing a hand over my mouth, I shake my head, knowing she's lying to both of us, but she's too fucking stubborn. That fire inside her destroys everything good for her. So, I'll fucking give it to her. Because how much more, how much longer can I do this with her?

"No one else makes sense but you, Sunny. No one else." I point at her. "But if this is how you feel, then okay."

Turning around, I walk back towards the gym, feeling my god damn heart she brought back to life shattering as I take each step.

CHAPTER FIFTY-ONE

SUNNY

I stand at the island in Cole's apartment, chopping mushrooms. My frantic heart makes it impossible to focus. I'll be seeing Tyler for the first time since…*everything.*

With frequent work trips, he's barely been present at family gatherings over the last two weeks. No doubt in avoidance to the ever continuing heartbreak that I cause. It seems to be a consistent trend of mine. Broken people break people—I'd warned him.

Tonight however, he's supposed to finally make an appearance. Naturally, he'd be the last to show up, which does nothing to my ever growing nervousness. Staring at the mushrooms, I realize my hands aren't even doing anything.

"Hey," Cole says, putting an arm around my shoulders. "Do you want me to take over?"

I shake my head. "I just feel like this is my fault." I look at him.

"Don't blame yourself for his inability to control his emotional lows." He shrugs. "His hero complex makes him think anyone who battles hardships needs saving."

Something in his eyes tells me he knows more than he's

letting on. His loyalty to Tyler runs deep, and I know his words are to validate me regardless of the fact he doesn't believe them.

"That is the truest thing I have ever heard." Anthony takes a grape from a bowl and pops it in his mouth. "We all have our thing. That's just his. It can be very good, and it can also be very bad."

"Where the hell is he, anyways?" Sam sets her wine glass down on the counter.

Something tells me he is right outside that door, and the turn of the knob indicates I'm right. It's a feeling that happens in my chest I can't quite name. Something that I can only feel with him, or whenever he is around. It bangs against my sternum with each beat of my heart, refusing to allow me to ever forget it exists.

He walks through the door, wearing a charcoal gray suit perfectly tailored to his body. Tense shoulders and a hard set jaw tell me his day at work was long.

His gaze flicks to me briefly, then back to the family. The slow roll of his throat catches my attention while he looks over the room, analyzing and preparing.

For what?

"There he is!" Anthony quips.

"Sorry I'm late." He steps through the threshold cautiously.

He pauses there with the door still ajar while everyone stares at him. I can't read what's on their faces, just as much as I am unable to see whatever it is they see.

When I glance back to where he stands in the doorway, I watch as he ever so slowly turns around, grabbing red painted nails in his hand. Walking through the threshold right after him is blonde hair, brown eyes and a smile too pretty to exist.

Shelby.

I watch as he moves his hand to the small of her back, guiding her inside with every bit of caution, like he knows the explosion waiting to happen. And she is the fucking bomb ready to be detonated.

Or maybe I am the bomb that's going to ignite, because…

Because…

My heart crumples in my chest when I see the glistening of the biggest fucking diamond I've ever seen in my life placed on Shelby's delicate ring finger.

CHAPTER FIFTY-TWO

TYLER

You wanted this, Sunny.

She made it clear what she wants, and that's to let her go. That's not a viable option, so this is the alternative. If it pisses her off, so be it. In fact, I hope it does. She doesn't want me doing this, and I don't want her doing what she's doing. *Call it even, baby.*

Yet, one glimpse at her is almost enough to make me backtrack every single thing I've done since the moment she shattered my already broken heart.

The looks on everyone's faces tells me this was not the way to go about this. I know they'd try to talk me out of it. I'm not going to sit through a fucking lecture about what I should and shouldn't do. It's *my* life.

The love of my life is walking out of my life, taking a part of me with her. I know what a great love is now, and I know I'll never get that again because if it isn't her, then it isn't anyone else.

I had the contract ready for Shelby's father, but then Sunny ended things, and it wasn't worth the fight anymore because Sunny is the only thing worth fighting for.

So fuck it, right?

Unwillingly, I feel that thread woven deeply in my bones pull my eyes where she stands. The look on her face is enough punishment as it is. Dark brows crease, pink lips part, and I watch the very betrayal she feels ripple across her face and body as the defeat of it all decompresses her, weighing on her slumped shoulders and caving her chest in.

I avert my eyes everywhere but her, trying to swallow back the thickness forming in my throat. Maybe it's for the best, because no person should have a power like this over me.

While she may be my greatest strength, she has proved to be my greatest weakness, too. That's something I can't afford.

Still, my eyes move back to where she stands, looking so alone in the kitchen. Gone are the flames of her emotions, and back is the ash of who she is.

The sad girl who refuses to give me anything.

This is what you wanted, Sunny.

SUNNY

He already proposed to her, and he told *no one*. The looks on everyone's faces is proof of that.

When his eyes meet mine, it's like the world goes into slow motion. I can't read a single thing behind those emeralds. Maybe I don't want to because I'm scared of what I'll see. The pain *I've* caused.

"Hi everyone!" Shelby smiles big, baring her white, straight teeth. She's so beautiful on the outside…but the inside.

"Shelby. *Wow*. What a surprise," Anthony says.

"I hope we have enough food," Sam groans in her wine glass.

"There *will be* enough food," Tyler snaps.

I hate his defense for her. This is not what was supposed to happen.

"It's so good to see you all!" Shelby clutches Tyler's bicep harder. A muscle feathers in his jaw.

"So what brings you here tonight, Shelby?" Cole braces his forearms on the counter next to me. He knows the answer to that question. We all do. That massive ring is indication enough.

"Well…" She looks at Tyler who stares vacantly to nothing in particular.

She nudges him, and I watch the slow roll of his throat as he prepares to say the words he knows all of us are waiting for.

How do we undo this? I was willing to let him go to *anyone* other than her.

I already know by the ring on Shelby's finger that it's happening. But to hear it from Tyler's lips, that will just make it all the more real. It'll make it *all too real.*

"We are getting married," he says blankly.

"Oh my god. Wow." Anthony breaks the too loud silence, his sarcasm staining each word.

Shelby jumps up and down and *squeals.* Hanging her hand out, she shows off the massive rock that's impossible to go unnoticed. There's no way Tyler picked that out himself.

I clutch the counter, white knuckling it as I hold back the bile stinging my throat.

"Oh god," Sam groans.

"Well, this is a shock," Macey finally speaks.

"It was a shock to me too!" Shelby says excitedly. Clearly not reading the energy of the room, or maybe just not caring.

"How was it a shock when you're arranged?" Sam asks, but Cole nudges an elbow to her.

"Well, congratulations buddy." Cole slaps Tyler on the back. "Let's get you two a drink."

I still stand at the counter, looking down at the stupid mushrooms. I still haven't said a word, and I don't want to. What do I even say?

My breathing becomes heavier as I watch them move towards the room full of shocked people.

Clutching the bottle of wine in one hand, Tyler uses the other to guide Shelby while she holds his bicep with her perfect red manicured nails. The perfect wife on his arm that they wanted for him.

I look down at my own short, un-manicured nails, swallowing hard about the fact I am so unkept while she looks absolutely perfect.

Maybe they do make sense.

I'd thought the moment my body became a canvas for his abuse was the moment I knew heartbreak in its rawest form. This has somehow surpassed that.

He made a promise, and he broke it. The moment we linked our fingers the agreement was set. But much like everything else in my life, it has been broken.

I feel his eyes on me, the weight of those emeralds something I'll never be able to unknow. When I meet them, I scream internally.

You promised.

A crease of his brows and flex of his jaw makes me almost believe he was able to hear it.

"What do you need from me?" Cole asks, leaning his head into me for a semblance of privacy.

When I came to Boston, I never imagined finding people like this—friends who became my own family. But Cole is Tyler's brother and partner first, So, the fact he didn't even know about this terrifies me.

"I just need to finish these mushrooms." I give Cole a weary smile.

He nods and kisses my forehead. He understands.

They all do.

TYLER

You promised. You promised. You promised.

I hear it clear as day, the pain that laces her voice in a way I'm unsure I'll ever be able to undo. But promises get fucking broken.

She made her intentions clear. So I will make mine clear, too. I was convinced I was prepared for the outcome of tonight. But Sunny is living proof of the fact she has completely altered any semblance of the person I was. Because I am not fucking prepared for the way she is acting.

I understand that a shock is to be expected since I proposed to Shelby without telling a soul. Well, it wasn't so much of a proposal but me and Shelby going to the closest Tiffany's to let her pick out whichever ring she wanted. She had no complaints about that as she picked the biggest damn ring and I handed my card to the cashier without a second guess.

It's *so* different from what I had gotten Sunny.

If I was going to marry anyone, it was going to be her. *Of course it would be her.* The day after I knew I was in love with her, I researched every nontraditional ring I could. I scoured stores all day, going to every jeweler I knew once I picked the type of stone that would be perfect.

And I bought the ring.

A beautiful stone of moss agate, elongated into a hexagon and haloed by diamonds on a thin golden band. Custom made by me. Simple, but beautiful *just* like her.

I'd never been one to believe in the power of stones, but I know she is. So I researched all the ones I felt were fitting for us until I finally landed on this one—healing and growth that occurs when you're with a loving partner. That's exactly what she's given me, and I can only hope that's what I've given her too, even if it's short lived.

It still sits in my closet to this day. I won't return it, because it's a reminder of my greatest accomplishment and biggest failure.

Shelby walks through the apartment with her head held high and a big smile across her delicate face. She's proud, and feels like she won. Maybe she did.

My perfectly detailed plan has failed. *I have failed.* That's a tough fucking feat to swallow.

By the way her hands are exploring me, I know what Shelby will want by the end of the night, and I just won't be able to bring myself to do it. If I can't now, will I ever be able to?

I experienced more damn pleasure in the handful of times me and Sunny fooled around than in the two years me and Shelby fucked. It was just… sex. It was just my body fucking reacting, not connecting. After what she did, I know it'd always remain that way.

But with Sunny, we hadn't even had sex, but anytime we found ourselves together, I felt more connected to her, to myself, than I ever did before.

Things needed to be set straight, my affairs all in order before I ever crossed that line with Sunny. Because once I did, there would absolutely be no way I could go back. Now we will never get the option.

Swallowing hard, I blink away the thoughts as Shelby places her hand on my thigh, pulling me back into reality, laughing at something Anthony says.

"Well, Tyler and I have stayed in contact this whole time, I mean how could we not? And finally, we just decided to hang out one day and it took off from there. Here I am once again!" Shelby smiles at me.

That's a fucking lie.

There wasn't a week that went by without a text from her. No doubt her parents trying to push her where they need her. Every single one went unanswered until two weeks ago when I finally told Mitchell I'd follow through with his plan.

To say our parents were excited is a fucking understatement. No actual legal contracts were necessary anymore except for the marriage license. Something so much more malleable if need be. Because how could his son in law promote any other governor but his father-in-law?

I watched as Mitchell and Matthew threw the contract I drew up in the fire. Putting an end to the out I formulated for months. They brought out their finest bourbon and clinked glasses with me as I watched every shred of hope I had left burn to embers.

Matthew was never going to accept the contract. He just said he'd consider it to play with me and buy time until I finally caved.

It'd all be so, so perfect because how could it not, right?

Because I love you, Sunny. It will never be anyone else.

CHAPTER FIFTY-THREE

SUNNY

"Here." Sam places a glass of wine in front of the cutting board I'm still standing in front of. "We're all going to fucking need a drink tonight."

"You had no clue?" I ask, but I already know the answer.

She shakes her head. "I had no idea. And to be frank, I'm fucking pissed." She sips her wine.

"I just don't get why he wouldn't tell anyone? How could he not say anything about this to any of us? I mean I know I'd be the last person he would – ow fuck!" I yell as I feel the knife slice through my hand.

"Sunny!" Sam yells as the blood starts pooling all over the cutting board and mushrooms.

Stupid fucking mushrooms.

Sam runs to the sink, turning it on so I can clean my wound. The blood is spilling fast, coating my wrist and forearm.

Within seconds I feel Tyler by my side. "What did you do?"

"What did I do? What did you fucking do, Tyler?!"

"Sunny…" He tries to cradle my hand.

"Leave me alone." I pull from him as Sam guides me to the sink.

"I have a first aid kit. I'll go grab it," Cole says, leaving the room.

Macey starts cleaning up the stupid fucking mushrooms and the cutting board. From the couch, Shelby watches as the family moves fluidly to aid me. The family she clearly isn't a part of.

"Okay, let's see it." Anthony shuts the water off, grabbing a dish towel to wrap my hand.

"Do you need stitches?" Tyler asks.

"No," I snap. He wants to see a fucking fire? Well mine is ready to rage.

"Are you sure?" he presses again.

"I'm a fucking nurse, Tyler. I know what I'm looking at."

"Maybe just go sit down with your fiancé?" Sam suggests.

"No," he growls through clenched teeth.

"She's not your concern anymore, Tyler," Sam snaps.

Shelby's eyes flick back and forth between all of us, watching the tension unravel. And dare I say there's a glimmer of amusement.

"Got it." Cole holds the first aid kit up in the air. "Okay, let me take a look." He unwraps the towel from my palm. "Damn, you got yourself good. How did you do that? It's not even a finger, it's your palm."

"I was distracted." I meet Tyler's eyes. His back is to his fiancé who now stands behind him as her eyes bounce between us. She curls her hand on his shoulder and around his forearm.

"I can do this myself." I try grabbing the kit from Cole.

"Not with one hand you can't." He takes the kit back.

Everyone is around me now just watching. *Stupid fucking mushrooms.* They're my least favorite food now.

"Mace, can you take over the food for me? Anthony, maybe you can pick a movie for us to watch tonight? Sam, maybe get a glass of wine for Sunny. And you two love birds, go sit down and relax. I'm sure all the *excitement* has been tiring." Cole takes lead.

Everyone springs into action, except for Tyler. He stands still, his emeralds on my hands, but his thoughts somewhere else.

"Come on." Shelby tugs his arm, trying to bring him back to the living room.

"I'll be over in a second," he says, not taking his eyes off me.

Shelby glances between us again. *She knows.* Tyler isn't necessarily being subtle, and neither am I. How can we be? How can we keep going like there's nothing there, when it's so prevalent to everyone in the room? When *everything* is there.

And how, *how* could I have asked him to pretend, to shut down his feelings and move on. And *how* could he have broken such a vital promise between us, running straight into the labyrinth instead of getting out of it? Because of course, *of course*, that is not what I want at all. Not in the slightest. Seeing him do it makes me wish I took back all those promises.

Or just never made them at all.

CHAPTER FIFTY-FOUR

SUNNY

The cooking is a little delayed due to my mishap with the stupid fucking mushrooms. So everyone mingles as they wait for dinner, munching on appetizers and sipping the wine Tyler brought in hopes it'll ease the clear animosity that lingers. Suffocating us all and sticking to our skin in the most grotesque ways.

I refuse to leave the kitchen. Instead, I keep myself perched on a barstool, observing the life size barbie invading our family ritual. The way she walks with such pride and confidence on Tyler's arm like the sweet little accessory she is. Her bleach blonde hair perfectly curled, wearing cute slacks and a knit sweater. The brightness to the brooding, scarred Ken sitting next to her. And she's responsible for some of those scars. I suppose I am, too. No one is innocent here.

It all makes sense now, why the parents want them together.

I mean look at them.

Meanwhile, I stand here, in the same scrubs I started the day with, the scent of hospital still clinging to me. Bags under my eyes as evidence of a long day. A bun barely managing to keep my seven day old curls at bay.

It isn't until I see a blurry figure getting closer that I realized I've completely dissociated. When my vision finally clears, Shelby is in front of me, smiling wide as she looks down at me.

Shit.

She places an elbow on the counter, tucking her chin in her hand to obviously show off her gaudy ring right in front of my face.

"So, you're the famous Sunny?" she says whimsically.

"Ah," I let out a nervous laugh. "I wouldn't say famous. But yes, I'm Sunny. You must be the famous Shelby."

"The one and only." She smiles and laughs. "I think we met at the brewery event though, right? Back in October?"

"Yes, that's correct." I take a sip of my wine.

She pauses for a brief moment, eyeing me up and down, like she's trying to find a weakness. "So," she continues as she eats from a bowl of grapes. "Tell me how you measled your way into family dinners after being so new to the group."

"Um, you know Sam and I just hit it off. She truly is my best friend here."

Swirling his drink in his hand, Tyler's head peers up, watching the two of us with his elbows on his knees.

"Tyler has been a great friend too," I add as I eye him behind Shelby. "He's the one who actually invited me to family dinners."

She purses her lips together as she takes in the words. I want her to choke on them.

"Tyler really is the best, isn't he? I'm so glad we were able to rekindle our relationship. To think, we're getting married in just a few short months. I'll be able to have the *best* sex of my life for the *rest* of my life." She leans on the counter, smiling at me. "Don't you leave in a few months?"

I just blink at her, unwilling to give any reaction since that's clearly what she's seeking. "Yeah, my contract at the hospital ends in February."

"What a shame. Spring weddings in Boston are absolutely gorgeous. It's too bad you'll miss it."

Letting a smile curve across my face, I raise my glass up. "Cheers to you and Tyler. And the best sex you've ever had, for life." I clink my glass with hers.

"Cheers!" she squeals.

TYLER

Shelby will always be the second choice, if you'd even call her a choice, and she knows that. It's prevalent in the way she tries to stake claim to me. Whether it be keeping a hand on my thigh or rubbing my arm and playing with my hair.

It's when I don't reciprocate that her frustration grows. Regardless of the fact my body clearly is repulsed by her, she doesn't stop.

When I look up, and see wide blue-greens narrowing where Shelby's hand is too comfortably on my thigh, it takes everything in me not to smile.

She notices.

Clearly she's pissed off that I broke our promise, but she isn't necessarily keeping hers either, because running away is not finding a fucking out. She's learning quickly that I do what I need to do, even if it means promises are broken and feelings get hurt.

I never said I was a good person.

The moment Shelby saw my line of sight and got up from the couch was the moment I knew I fucked up. Even with a desperate grip of her wrist, she somehow managed to slip away towards the one thing my focus is on.

I never got to really meet Sunny, she'd said.

Sunny's eyes flick to mine when she holds her glass up to

Shelby. When they clink in their cheers, it's then I realize the problem I just created for myself.

I have to do a double take when I see Sunny finally remove herself from the barstool she'd been glued to all night. She brings her plate to the sink where she starts loading dishes. No matter whose home we're in, she always tries to bring the task upon herself.

"Excuse me? What do you think you're doing?" Anthony bumps his hips against hers, playfully knocking her out of the way. She laughs at my brother, bumping him back.

That's the moment I realize that Sunny is permanently in this family, no matter where she goes, no matter how far she runs, she is not only tethered to me now, but to all of them, too.

"You have that massive cut on your hand. You can't get an infection. Ms. *Nurse*."

She raises her hands up in surrender. "Fair enough. I actually think I'm going to head out. It was a long day at work."

I frown at the same time Anthony does. Immediately I'm on my feet and Shelby looks up at me in confusion. This is my only chance at contact with her tonight. *Direct* contact. And I'm ready to fucking indulge in it.

Consume me, little fire.

"You aren't going to stay for the movie?" Anthony frowns.

She just shakes her head and gives him a look. He nods, giving her a hug, then goes back to the dishes.

She makes her way around the room, giving hugs and saying goodbye to everyone. I'm still standing, watching her when I feel Shelby's hands snake herself around my damn arm, laying her head on my shoulder. I roll my eyes. She's fucking cock blocking me. I don't want anyone jealous for me except for the one girl in this room who is showing me absolutely nothing.

How did she even get here anyways? I fucking hate when she walks the city alone. Especially at night, in the cold.

My heart thuds against my chest with each hesitant step she takes towards us. A weak smile pulls her lips as she stops a foot away. A side hug is exchanged between Shelby and Sunny, no doubt because Shelby is off put by the scrubs. But they are my favorite look on her.

Soon enough, Shelby's hands are immediately wrapped around my arm again, shackling me from the one thing I want most. I shift on my feet, removing myself from her and wrapping my arms around Sunny. I press my nose into her curls, indulging in the subtle scent of vanilla and coconut that has easily become my favorite thing. The scent only few are lucky to know if given the chance to be close enough.

I hold on for a little too long, but I don't care.

Stay with me, Sunny. Just stay here.

"How are you getting home?" I ask, my lips press in her hair.

Her body tenses under mine, but she doesn't answer me. I pull away from our embrace and cradle her face. Her eyes are tired, too. My little fire is burning out.

"How are you getting home, Sunny?" I say the words slower, my eyes searching her face.

"Goodnight, Tyler." She turns around.

"*Sunny*," I call out to her.

Then Shelby's hands wrap around my fucking arm again. "She'll be fine, Tyler. Seems like she walked here anyways."

But it feels distant as I watch Sunny leave the apartment. Why didn't anyone pick her up? Why didn't anyone take her home?

I still feel Shelby eyeing me as I watch half of my heart walk out.

Come back to me, Sunny.

SUNNY

I try to walk home, but it's mere minutes before Sam is bursting through the apartment doors telling me to get in the jeep.

So I do.

"I can't even fucking believe it." She slams the door.

My anger licks flames across my skin, burning up my throat, forcing me to swallow hard, taking all my words with it. I know I shouldn't have a right to feel jealous but I do. *I just do*.

"He had the audacity to be concerned about you walking home. He literally was practically begging everyone in front of Shelby to take you home. Which I obviously would do on my own but like what the actual fuck?" She starts the jeep.

I blink at the road ahead of us. "All our plans got ruined tonight. We were too late."

"It's never too fucking late, Sunny. No one has said 'I do,'" she says, eyes on the road.

"You're right," I say flatly.

We look at one another.

"What are you going to do?" she asks.

We stare at one another for a beat, and soon enough, a smile pulls her lips into a too wide grin.

"I need to even our score."

CHAPTER FIFTY-FIVE
TYLER

I could've been on my hands and knees begging, and you wouldn't have been able to tell the fucking difference.

The car ride is silent for the most part. Save for the few times Shelby tries to stir up conversation. She sits in the seat that once belonged to *my Sunny*.

"Will you ever get a new car? You've had this old thing forever," Shelby says.

"No," I manage to get out.

"Why not? Isn't it super old." She peers around the truck I love.

"Because Cole and I built it."

She purses her lips as she contemplates. "Well can't you imagine yourself in a Mercedes or even something a little lower class like an Escalade?"

Lower class.

"No." I rub my jaw. My suit feels extra tight around my aching chest. I'm not in the fucking mood for conversation. Especially with her.

Maybe this agreement isn't fair to her either, because I don't care about her. But in the end, she'll get everything she always wanted. Everything she was bred for. The only thing Shelby wants more in this world than money is me. And she's going to be able to get both.

"What about when we have babies?" She eyes me, waiting for a reaction.

I give her none, regardless of the fact my heart beats a little faster in my chest. The only person I want to put a baby in is in another person's car right now.

The image of Sunny pregnant with my child does something inside me. A primitive need I never thought existed awakens in my chest.

"Then we will cross that bridge when we get there," I reply, hoping we never do. I'd get a vasectomy so I could avoid that happening with her.

"What if… what if we tried to start crossing that bridge now?"

My eyes slowly pan over to where she sits. We haven't even so much as kissed when I decided to follow through with my end of the bargain. Yet here she is, already trying to get me to put a fucking baby in her.

"Not before the wedding." I grip the steering wheel a little harder.

"Oh, come on. The wedding is going to be in like two to three months max. No one will know. They'll just think it's a honeymoon baby." She leans in closer to me.

Propping my elbow on the door, I keep a hand over my mouth, trying to create as much distance as possible between us. "People will do that math, Shelby."

She knows it's the way to lock me in for good. She's tried once before and fuck, she's trying again. She won't bite the hand that feeds her again, I try to tell myself. She has no other ambition outside of this life.

No fight.

No *fire*.

She leans back into the seat with a huff, finally realizing I won't budge on this topic. The remainder of the drive is silent and I'm grateful for the quiet. But her damn hands still keep trying to toy with me. Running through my hair. Tracing circles on my hand. Rubbing my thigh and going up a little too high.

I keep my eyes on the road, trying to not acknowledge it. But my fucking dick decides otherwise as it twitches in my pants. I hate myself for it.

Just your body reacting.

She lives in a luxury condo her parents still pay for. When we pull up, I send a silent prayer to whatever exists that she won't try to convince me to move in here. Yet, I can't imagine allowing her in my home. There's too many precious memories there I refuse for her to taint.

I put the car in park and hop out to open her door. The damp cold is prevalent with the cloud that forms around me with each of my labored breaths. I offer a hand to get her out of the truck, and she smiles at me like it's the kindest gesture.

"Come inside." She holds my hand, looking up at me.

All I can imagine is Sunny looking up at me with her big blue-green eyes round as she observes my face.

Each beat of my heart brings a reminder of the ache. I won't move on from her. My heart resurrected from a grave I shoved it into the moment I laid eyes on Sunny, giving it a reason to start beating again. But now it aches as it slowly loses its lifeline, desperate for her again.

I shake my head. "No. Not tonight."

"Come on," she gently coaxes me, tugging on my hand. "We need to celebrate. And I need to thank you for this gorgeous ring."

I run a hand over my face. "I'm tired, Shelby. It's been a long day."

"I can make you feel better." She leans into me.

No you can't.

She licks her lips, readying them for mine. I know what she wants. I'm just not sure if I can give it to her.

"Come on, Tyler. Just come inside. Nothing has to happen. *Or* I can do all the work. Let me show you how grateful I am for this ring," she pleads seductively with her hands on my chest, rubbing up and down. But something in her eyes tells me otherwise. A small smile curves on her red lips when words don't leave my mouth.

I know when I'd do this with Shelby it'll be with my hand pressing her face down on the mattress. There's no fucking way I can watch what I'm doing and be okay with it. There's no way I can fuck her and not think of Sunny the whole god damn time. I'll fuck her feeling like I'm betraying the love of my life.

But she made it clear what she wants, what her intentions are. She is going to stay running around in her labyrinth, never finding a way out, so I may as well, too.

I look up to the sky that's now polluted with light from the condos as I contemplate. There are no stars for me to wish on tonight. Nothing to hear my final cry.

Let me let you go.

I fist Shelby's hair with one hand, maybe a bit too firmly, yanking her to look up at me. Her lips part, waiting for mine. Feeling my jaw clench at the sight, I swallow the knot in my throat.

A smile creeps on her face, and I fucking hate it. Her hand clutches my shirt as my hand tightens in her hair, keeping the other deep in my pocket to prevent myself from strangling her. Take her air the way she has taken so much from me.

"Okay," I breathe.

I toss my keys to the valet driver as Shelby leads me inside her building, tugging me one way while my heart is being pulled another.

CHAPTER FIFTY-SIX

TYLER

She opens her apartment door and leads me in by my hand. I step into the familiar place with a weight sitting on my chest. It feels wrong, so fucking wrong. This never was an issue before.

Before her.

If I don't do this now, I'm not sure I ever will be able to. If I don't do this now, Shelby will start suspecting too much. I don't need her running to her daddy, telling him her fiancé is in love with another woman, posing more of a threat to my little fire when she's already running from so much.

Eventually, I'll be expected to produce an heir shortly after our wedding, so I need to be okay with fucking her now or else I never will be.

Something breaks inside me that I never thought could be broken, knowing it'll all be with Shelby and never with Sunny.

Hearing the door close with a click behind me, I turn around, my body tense as I prepare for what's to come.

Shelby's hands linger on the doorknob behind her, a lust sits in her brown eyes as she grazes them over me. Ready to show me just how thankful she is I gave her a second chance, and put that ring on her finger.

She's delusional to think it'll ever mean anything.

Slowly, she steps towards me, taking cautious steps considering I'm still a flight risk. *Run. Run. Run.* Her red painted nails reach for me as she gets inches from me, grazing up my suit covered arms and sliding it off.

"It's so nice having you back here, Tyler," she whispers in my ear.

I don't say anything back. I'm not in the mood to talk. I just want to fuck her and be done with it. And I'm not even in the mood for that either.

Fuck. What has Sunny done to me?

"Let me show you, Tyler. Let me show you how grateful I am." Her brown eyes peer up at me. She starts lowering herself down on me. I close my eyes as my chest caves in. The last set of lips around me were Sunny's. Shelby won't replace and erase that.

She fiddles with my belt and pants, but before she can release my soft cock, I fist her hair, forcing her to stand back up.

Her brown eyes widen to saucers as she meets my cold stare. "Let me do this, Tyler," she pleads.

I throw her towards her bedroom. "In the room."

Stumbling on her heeled feet, she listens to me as she enters her massive bedroom.

I could try and say I'm not normally like this when I fuck a woman, but that'd be a lie. I've always been in the business of a fuck and fling. I'm not going to hover. I'm not going to do after-care. I never believed in making love. I get what I need and leave.

Shelby sits on her bed like the good little submissive slut she is. "Tell me what you want."

I don't *want* her. I want my Sunny.

I swallow hard as I unbutton my dress shirt, because I actually like this one, and I'm not going to let her ruin it. "Get undressed."

She listens as she peels her clothing off, revealing the matching lacey red set she wears underneath. She was prepared for tonight. She was *expecting* it. And I'm so fucking mad at myself for falling into her predictions.

I peel off the dress shirt, but that's all I take off. She doesn't deserve to see the rest of me. Staying clothed will make this faster. I'm not going to give myself to her the way I was supposed to give myself to Sunny.

I approach her on the bed, stepping into her. She looks up at me from where she sits, her brown eyes hopeful.

"Tyler.." she breathes. "Get undressed, baby. Get undressed for me."

Grabbing her by the neck, I bring her face inches to mine. "I do what I fucking want."

I feel her swallow hard under my grasp, her chest starts moving faster as her lungs search for the air I'm slowly constricting from her. But she nods. *Good.* She knows her place.

"Have you slept with anyone else?" I ask.

Her eyes widen, and I feel her body tremble because she knows she can't lie. If she does, she knows I'll find out.

"*Yes*," she chokes as I take more of her air.

"Such a little slut. Good, because you'll be begging for the pleasure they brought you while stuck in a lifetime of pain with me. You are a pussy to be fucked and a contract to be signed."

"What can I do—" I cut her off as I flip her onto her stomach.

I can't fucking watch what I'm about to do.

"There's nothing you can do." I yank down her underwear. I unzip my pants and fist my fucking limp dick in my hand. I stroke myself over and over to try and get something.

What are you doing to me, Sunny?

Shelby tries to turn her head back to me, but I push her face down in the mattress. Once I finally get my dicks attention, I grab the condom from my pocket and tear it open with my teeth, rolling it on my half hard cock.

I grab her hips, ready to sink myself into her. But I pause, I fucking pause as my stomach pits, my chest caves in, and I'm pretty fucking sure I feel bile rise in my throat.

What the fuck is happening to me?

Just fucking do it, Tyler. Do what you're expected to do. If I can't even do it with a condom, how the fuck will I ever be able to make an heir? If I don't do what I'm supposed to, Mitchell will attack where he knows it'll hurt.

"Tyler, Tyler please. Let me help you," she murmurs.

She needs to fucking shut up so I can focus. That's how she'll help me.

I smack her ass hard, making her whimper. "Shut up and let me fuck you," I growl pushing her back down into the mattress.

"Yes sir," she says too amused, too fucking turned on by my aggression. I roll my eyes and clench my jaw as I close my eyes, trying to will myself into what I need to do.

And I finally push into her.

Every muscle in my body goes absolutely rigid as I work my hips. It feels *wrong*. It feels so fucking wrong. I try to imagine Sunny. Try to imagine being inside her instead as I push into Shelby, but she fucking moans, interrupting me.

I rip off a piece of my dress shirt with my teeth, ball it and shove it in her mouth, muffling her and making her gag. I rip another longer piece, tying it around her head to secure the gag I placed in her mouth.

I can't be reminded of what I'm doing.

I start pounding into her, trying to imagine my little fire's face when I worked my fingers in her and she rode my face. The sound of her completely making me unhinged and needy and desperate. It's working, I think. I feel my dick finally awaken and decide to do its goddamn job.

Then Shelby lets out a loud moan over the gag, and I'm brought back to my reality. My jaw flexes as I grit my teeth and fist her hair, pushing her head further into the mattress to stifle her.

She enjoys anything I give her. I can already feel her pussy clamping down around me.

Just fucking finish, Tyler. Just fucking do it.

I can't get there, no matter how quickly my hips move. No matter how much focus I put into this just to get the damn job done. *Fuck.* Why can't I finish?

Shelby becomes unraveled. Her body seizing as her pussy ripples around my cock. *God dammit.*

"Get up." I grab her by the back of the neck, getting her up on wobbly feet. Her legs shaking from the orgasm I just gave her. And I hate myself for it. She doesn't *deserve* it.

I slam her against the wall, frustrated I can't get my fucking dick to work right. Shelby cries out at the impact, but doesn't complain because like I said earlier, she won't bite the hand that feeds her.

I push into her again more aggressively this time, working my frustration on her.

I swear to god if Sunny fucking ruined this for me…

She tries to bring her hands around my neck but I grab each and slam them against the wall above her head, pinning them there so she can't touch me. Her hands don't belong on me.

Each muscle in my body grows tenser with each thrust into her. My dick does its job of staying hard, but it won't complete it's fucking task.

I slam my hand on the wall next to Shelby's head. "Fuck!" I yell as I continue working in her. When I remove my fist, there's a hole in the wall.

She starts to moan again under my aggression. Her happy fucking pussy chasing another orgasm. She's going to think this is the best night of her life. Engaged to a man who gives her multiple orgasms, when in reality I'm selfishly trying to find my own release. Trying to prove a goddamn point to myself.

Grabbing her by the hair again, I throw her on the bed. Facing me now, I grab her by her thighs, pulling her to the edge of the bed. When I push into her again, I try to look everywhere but at her. Yet she's still all I can see.

"No," I say out loud and flip her back over on her stomach, forcing her head back into the mattress to hide my reality.

Whipping my belt off, I grab her arms, bending them harshly and tie them together behind her back, stretching them painfully to the point she cries out again. But she doesn't ask me to stop.

I start hitting her from behind again, trying to envision my little fire instead. *Come on...*

I shove her face deeper into the mattress, knowing I'm slowly cutting off her air supply. If I just hold her there long enough...I could put an end to all of this. Soon enough, she'll stop breathing if I could have it my way. I could put an end to her the way I've always wanted to.

I shake my head and redirect my thoughts to my Sunny.

I imagine the night we got drunk together. The way her hands explored my body. The way it didn't hurt when she touched me. How much I craved her. I imagine those blue-green eyes meeting my stare while she devoured me. Those perfect pink lips around my cock, taking me the way she was made to. My eyes remain shut, envisioning that night. Working myself so hard into Shelby our skin is slapping and stinging.

She groans under the gag, but I tune her out as I imagine me and Sunny in the shower on New Year's Eve. Her body under the shower water. The way she cried for my dick as I fucked her mouth.

"Yes baby," I whisper, imagining it all.

My fist in her hair, making her look up at me with those blue-green eyes, the desire sitting heavy in them. The way her mouth parts as my fingers push inside her. Feeling every bit of her. The fucking wetness that my mouth craves to taste. Her hips rolling with my fingers, chasing that climax.

"Just like that," I breathe as I keep working.

The orgasm starts to approach. It's kindling at the base of my spine, trying to work its way to me. I keep imagining my girl, trying to keep this moment. Trying to keep *her*.

My forehead pressed to hers as I breathe her in. Her breath becoming rhythmic with mine. The way she sat in my lap on New Year's Eve. So comfortable and content. The way her soft fingers traced the jagged scars on my body, seeing them as beauty rather than tragedy.

I realize I don't even need to think about our sexual encounters just to get me off. No. All I need to think about is her. Because it's her. It will always be her. So, I imagine her lips on mine. The way they tell me everything she refuses to admit herself.

I love you.

And finally, I find my fucking release.

The orgasm invades my body, taking hold of me as I imagine my Sunny. "Fuck!" I groan as I finish.

I open my eyes as I realize the reality I'm in. My hand is shoving Shelby's face so deep into the mattress, I wouldn't be surprised her air supply is cut off and I succeeded in what my thoughts were screaming to do.

The weight of everything crashes on me.

I fucked another woman.

This isn't Sunny.

No, this is my worst fucking nightmare.

I ripped the condom off and zipped up my pants, leaving Shelby on the bed to figure out getting the restraints off. My chest felt cracked open and exposed as I stumbled out of her apartment.

Dirty. I feel fucking dirty.

The clothes I wore end up buried in flames inside my fireplace and I spend the rest of the night in my shower, washing myself over and over and over but never feeling clean.

I scrub my skin until it's raw and bleeding, and it still doesn't feel like enough. Ragged breaths do nothing to give me the oxygen my body is screaming for. All my mistakes wrap around my lungs and ribs, making each breath practically impossible.

How will I spend the rest of my life doing this? How will I give an heir when I feel this dirty after using a condom and keeping all my clothes on?

I continue scrubbing my skin, watching the water turn pink from the blood trickling from the angry red patches across my body.

I'm so sorry, Sunny.

CHAPTER FIFTY-SEVEN

SUNNY

Sitting on my couch, I look at the envelope placed on my coffee table. The embroidered silver words on the cream colored cover blatantly stare at me.

To: Ms. Sunny Mason

I bite the inside of my cheek while I contemplate facing it or throwing it in the trash entirely. My phone is a useless distraction as another spam call floods my screen. Denying the call, I toss the phone on the other side of the couch in frustration. I prop my elbows on my knees and run my hands over my face, through my hair with an audible groan.

"Fine," I say to my empty apartment and grab the envelope, tearing the pretty packaging to find an even prettier announcement inside.

We are pleased to announce the engagement of Shelby Marie Goodman and Tyler Michael Caddell. Please join us in the celebration of this union.

Even though I know what I'd see when I opened it, the blow still hits all the same. I read it over and over, each time hitting harder and harder.

It's only been three days. *Three days*. And their families are already throwing an engagement party.

I fight off every urge to make this right. To reverse what's been done before it's too late. However, in the same breath, I tell myself I need to at least stick to one plan. Clearly I've strayed so, so far from the one I had planned for Boston.

The detectives told me that at this rate, it's important that I try to move on with my life. We still have absolutely no clue where Ryan is, but they don't think it's here. For now at least.

I know doing what I want to do will only stray me from my original Boston plan. But now that Tyler is about to sell his soul to the devil, I'm ready to formulate a slight detour. God knows I've already taken so many.

I'm the reason he's stuck in this problem. So I'll be the reason he gets out of it.

It's time I even the debt between us.

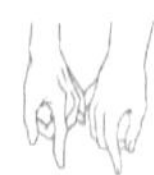

Next thing I know, I'm at the front door of his townhome.

The red brick gleams in the string lights that hang outside his home. The ones I made him put up because I'd said you can't have red brick without string lights, just like he said you can't have a bedroom without glow in the dark stars.

The next day he had a box of lights sitting on his counter, and we'd spent the afternoon hanging them up while immersed in conversation or moments of silence.

That'd always been one of my favorite things about my time with Tyler, conversation wasn't always necessary to fill up the silence, and we could sit comfortably in that quietness, knowing we both need it to calm our festering thoughts.

The small front yard is frosted over with ice crunching underneath my boots as I make my way to his door. Walking up the few steps to his porch, my heart beats wildly in my chest. In Tyler fashion, he'll be upset that I walked here alone, in the middle of the night, but that just may work to my advantage.

Standing in front of his door, the bite of the cold night gnaws at me while I contemplate following through with this plan. If I pay this debt, the hope is that he'll drop everything with Shelby and I'll call it even.

He is five-to-two in this game, and I'm a competitive bitch.

I need to make him put an end to it.

With a trembling hand, I knock on his door. Patiently I wait, despite the cold air biting at my hot skin.

A grueling few minutes later, he opens the door, baring a shirtless chest and gray sweatpants that hang low on his hips. His scars are stark against the moonlight that cascades the city. Those emerald eyes are a beacon in his dark home as they stare at me.

The warmth of his home blankets over my shivering body, giving me a brief smell of the citrus and salt that coats his skin, the familiarity of it beckoning me to step through the threshold of his door.

"Sunny, what are you doing here?!" His sleepy eyes become wide. "It's freezing, and so late. Are you okay? What's wrong?" he asks, pulling me inside his home by my arm in one swift movement. Rubbing my arms, he tries to warm me up, despite the fact he's wearing less clothing than me.

"Why do you keep walking out here alone?" he groans. "Fuck, you're so cold." He pulls me flush to his body, trying to warm me.

"I came to repay the debt between us." I look up at him.

Grabbing my chin, he makes me meet those darkening eyes. "What do you mean?" His voice is breathy because he knows exactly what I mean.

If there's one thing I know about Tyler is that he's possessive of me. He wants me to be his and only his. *I know.* I always have since the moment we kissed in the gym. His mouth on mine told me everything he couldn't say.

He brushes a thumb over my lip, patiently waiting for my response. "Sunny…"

"You're an engaged man now. I'll have to take care of things myself or get someone else to." I trail a hand to my own waist band.

He snatches my wrist. "Sunny, no…" His voice is low, raspy from the sleep I woke him from. *But pleading.*

He doesn't like the idea of anyone touching me. Or even myself for that matter, because he wants to be the one to do it himself. The *only* one. I'm stooping to a level I shouldn't. I *have* to.

Maybe I am jealous for you too, Tyler.

"Maybe Connor can help me," I say, looking up at him.

My words unravel him. The predator that is normally calculated is losing it before me. The rage that flames in his eyes gives me all the validation I need. I see something in him I've never have before.

"*Sunny,*" he warns me. "No.".

"*Why?*" I challenge him. Still holding my wrist in his hand, his grip tightens.

"Because you're *mine*," he growls.

There it is. The words that will bring a crashing end to the short-lived engagement of him and Shelby.

I rip my wrist from his grip and taunt my fingers around his waistband.

"Sunny…" he whispers with a hard swallow. But he doesn't stop me. He keeps his eyes on me, intently watching each move. He won't stop whatever will go on tonight between us. Because it's me. Because it's him. Because it's *us*.

I push him against the wall and my knees meet the ground. I'm met with the large press of his dick in his sweatpants. Fisting them in my hands, I pull them down, being greeted by his length springing free.

I don't start there. Instead, I trace my tongue through every groove of muscle, every line, every curve that builds his chest. I kiss the inside of his neck, inhaling all that is Tyler. Citrus, salt and *need*. His head leans back, hissing in pleasure.

Yes.

This is what I want. I want him unraveled by me. I want him begging for more of me. Slowly, I work my way back down, nipping, biting, licking to tease him in any way I can. I trace my tongue from his base up to his shaft, feeling him tremble by my touch alone.

"Baby..." he murmurs as I glide my tongue along the long length of him. Then I stop, making him look down at me in confusion. I give him nothing when I meet his stare. His chest moves up and down with labored breaths, and I can see the way I make his pulse grow faster in the base of his neck.

"*Beg*," I demand.

"Please, baby," he whimpers. "Please." His hips thrust the air, his need taking over.

I smile, because I want him to become undone for me. I want him to scream my name. I want him to end it all because of me.

His hands weave into my curls, grabbing me so firmly to keep my eyes on his.

"Again," I demand, taunting him with a flick of my tongue. The way his body trembles has me intoxicated with power.

He swallows hard. "Please, little fire," he rasps. "Please, just put my fucking cock in your mouth."

Satisfied, I trace my tongue along him before taking him entirely into my mouth until he hits the back of my throat. This undoes him so deliciously. From the way a feral groan leaves his throat, to the way his fingers tighten in my hair, to the way every muscle in his body flexes under me.

It's addicting.

"Fuck," he mumbles. His head leans forward as his emeralds watch me. "You take me so well, baby. You're doing such a good fucking job."

His words only encourage me. I continue my mouth along him, using a gentle glide of my teeth that have him practically bucking and thrusting while his hands hold me in place.

I want him to fuck my mouth. I want him to tell me how good I'm doing. How I'm his good fucking girl making this predator of a man unravel and fall to his knees for me. I want him to see stars as he fills my mouth with him. I want him to own every part of me.

Groaning, he bites his lip and his head leans back again against the wall. So I let out a loud moan to encourage him and let him know he's fucking my mouth perfectly. His mouth falls open in desperate breaths, brows creased as he tries to keep his composure he's losing so quickly.

He continues beating his hips, slamming in the back of my throat. Tears sting my eyes, but I don't want him to stop. I feel them trickle down my face, and my body fights the urge to gag, despite the fact I love the way he fucks my mouth.

"You look so fucking gorgeous choking on my dick," he growls as he pulls my head back to get a good look at me. He swipes the tears that roll down my face with his thumbs, meeting his emeralds with my watery eyes.

Just as I wanted, he becomes undone and unhinged. My mouth fills with the warmth of him. Hot, thick, and heavy as it rolls down my throat and I swallow every bit, drinking him.

His knees buckle as he continues to thrust, groaning as he cums and releases everything he has to me. His trembling body is proof that I've done my job. The fucking predator taken down by his goddamn prey.

The score is even.

"Fuck, Sunny," he whimpers.

Removing my mouth from him, I keep my eyes on his as I

swallow what's left of him. I stand on my feet and use a hand to wipe my mouth clean.

He lunges for me, pressing his lips to mine possessively. His tongue laces around mine, describing all the ways he wants me to be his. Linked by that unavoidable, undeniable string between us, not only woven through our hearts but through every fiber of our being.

That might be the only explanation as to why we are always in this dance, this labyrinth of us, because fate simply won't have it any other way. Our souls forever threading together in this life, and all the rest.

It takes everything in me to step out of his embrace, no matter how much I want this. He lets out a snarl as I remove myself and tries coming for me again, but I raise up a hand.

He stops instantly.

"Consider my debt paid." I turn around and leave into the night before he can protest otherwise.

CHAPTER FIFTY-EIGHT

TYLER

I CAN'T STOP THINKING ABOUT ANOTHER WOMAN AT MY OWN engagement party.

People saunter around the venue in their suits and dresses while waiters walk around with trays of food I can't pronounce. Shelby clings to my arm, her white dress flowing behind her as a prelude of what's to come in the next few months.

Yet all I can think about is Sunny's lips around my dick. I'm so confused, so fucking confused.

"Here come mommy and daddy." Shelby clutches my arm, her smile beaming.

Her parents approach us with wide smiles on their faces. She shares the same brown eyes and blonde hair as her father, but the rest of her features are just like her mother. Dainty, sharp and feline.

"Tyler." Governor Goodman takes my hand in his. "We are so thrilled about this. Congratulations to you both."

Shelby smiles between us as I take her mother's hand in my own and place a kiss on it.

"Oh Shelby, you really do have a good one." Mrs. Goodman smiles at her daughter, her cheeks flushing by my touch.

"I know," Shelby says, laying her head on my shoulder.

"Fancy running into you here, Matthew." Mitchell approaches with a wide grin and shakes hands with Matthew. Ironic everyone is smiling tonight except me.

"Look at these two! They belong in a magazine," Diane chimes as she makes her rounds and greets us.

"Truly they do. There is no better match," Mrs. Goodman says to Diane, both of them clearly giddy over this match. "Can you imagine what their babies will look like?"

As they continue their conversation, I analyze the venue. The conversation ultimately becomes background noise when Sunny walks in.

Her gown is stark black like night, as if this is a funeral over a celebration. A death to something that could've been ours. A two piece dress that reveals just enough to make anyone curious about the rest underneath.

Her blonde curls are a wild mess around her head. She toys with a curl in one hand while the other holds a flute of champagne. Blue-green irises flick to me, as if she knows I'm watching her, like she can feel my presence just as much as I can always feel hers without even looking.

Our stare lingers. *Stay with me.* I wish she could hear me. *Stay in this moment. Stay with me.* But then her eyes go back to whatever it is our family is saying to her. And I realize my reality crashing down on me.

I'm over here. They're over there. A distance I don't like. A reality I refuse to accept.

I clear my throat. "If you'll excuse me."

"Where are you going?" Shelby doesn't let go of my arm.

"I have people I need to greet," I say, removing my arm from her.

Her eyes trail to where my family stands and back to me. "Well let me come."

"No, it's fine,"

"Tyler, bring your fiancé with you." Mitchell's eyes are on me.

"I'll be just a minute," I say, walking away

With each step I'm given a flashback of last night. Sunny's lips exploring my body, as if she were trying to memorize it. My hands in her hair and that look in her eyes as she swallowed me entirely.

Fuck.

"The man of the hour." Cole gives me a hug. "You okay?" he asks, placing his hands on my shoulders. *He knows*. He always does. That's why he's head of security.

I just nod.

"We'll talk later." He pats my shoulder and releases me.

"Congrats man." Anthony hugs me.

I give Macey and Sam hugs and kisses, though my sister is clearly reluctant and pissed off at me. I can't blame her. I kept secrets from her. I don't like it, but I knew how she'd react if I told her before the agreement was done. That I was fulfilling at least one promise made, even if I never made it myself.

I approach Sunny, my heart beating a bit louder in my chest. "Can I talk to you?"

She just blinks at me. "About what?"

I shake my head. I see that fortress trying to come back up. She's so damn stubborn, and it's turning me on instead of pissing me off.

Not saying anything else, I grab the flute of champagne from her hand and set it on a tray. With her arm in hand, I take her to a place where I know no one will find us.

"Tyler!" she snaps as I continue to drag her down stairs into a dark cellar filled with hundreds of different wine bottles.

We need a quiet place to talk without any disruptions.

A place where I know no one will hear her screaming my name.

SUNNY

Before I can say anything else, he pushes me against an old brick wall in the dimly lit room lined with hundreds of wine bottles. The thud of my back against the wall is the only other sound in here besides his heavy breathing.

The sharp angles of his face are hallowed in the dim lighting, and it makes me wonder if this is who his victims see before he introduces them to death.

I know he was thinking about me all night. And I know he was thinking about me all day, even here, at his own engagement party. Yet, here we are, still at the damn engagement party.

He didn't call it off.

"What do you want, Tyler?" I cross my arms.

"Me? What do you want, Sunny?" He starts pacing in front of me.

I don't say anything because I don't know what to say. I don't know what I want except for one thing.

I don't want him to marry her.

"We are at your *engagement* party, Tyler. You are engaged when you promised to find a way out. You didn't just break the promise but you locked yourself in instead!"

"How is what you're doing any different? How is it any better? It's not a solution. It's a fucking cop out," he growls.

"I'm running *from* him. Not *to* him," I bite back. "You broke the promise we made."

"I've broken a lot of promises, Sunny. This wouldn't be my first."

"What the hell is that supposed to mean?" I take a step towards him.

He stops in his tracks and gets so close to me that I can practically taste his anger on my lips. He braces his hands against the wall on either side of my head, caging me in without escape.

"Let me let you go, Sunny. *Let me let you go*," he whispers, the pain laces each letter, cracking my heart.

I can't. *I can't.*

I can't let him go because of this connection. I want to scream at this bond so deeply woven between us. My frantic fingers have been desperately trying to undo it. And even then, I still don't know if it'll ever separate. It's deeper than anything I've ever felt in my life.

I've felt more love between us than in my ten years with Ryan.

The realization of this hits me so hard, I practically feel the sting of it across my face.

It's in this moment, as I watch his emerald eyes searching mine, I realize I am in love with Tyler Michael Caddell.

I'm so completely in love with him.

It comes crashing on me, and I don't know how to stop it. Something changes in me. My heart starts beating differently. By the look of Tyler's eyes, I think he sees it too. His pupils dilate, his nostrils flare as his breathing picks up and catches.

"Sunny…" he rasps.

But this is all we get. All we'll ever get. I'm still leaving because Ryan is still out there. As long as he is, I have to keep running, regardless of my love for Tyler and his love for me. And even that feels too weak of a word to describe what we have.

What we feel.

How *I* feel.

"Let's just let it go then," I say, meeting his eyes, my heart screaming at me for pushing him away. *Stop. Stop. Stop.*

"If it was that easy then I would have done that a long time ago."

"You knew," I seethe. "You knew I was leaving and still made me feel the way I feel."

The pain and the anger take over, prevalent in my voice and

shaking hands. I'm so angry that he let me feel this way. That he made me love him. That he made me fall in love with him.

All of it.

"You knew I was leaving and that no matter what this would be the end result. All I wanted was just…sex and I get this!" I hit his chest but he doesn't move. "You knew!" I yell, beating his chest with my fists while he just looks down at me with pain in his eyes. "This is all we get! This is all we get Tyler, is this moment here with us."

He grabs my wrists. "It doesn't have to be that way Sunny if you just let me fucking help you."

I shake my head as tears begin to stream down my face.

He grabs my face in his hand. "Why won't you let me help you Sunny? Huh? Why are you so fucking scared to feel something? Why are you so scared to allow yourself to love me?"

I do love you. But I am not supposed to.

I swallow hard. "You know what happened to me the last time I loved someone, Tyler."

"I am not fucking Ryan," he seethes. "And you are not the same woman you were just a few months ago."

"I know that," I say. "I know that."

"Then why are you running from me?" He makes me look at him again, even though I close my eyes through the tears, shaking my head like it'll somehow change things. "*Why* are you always running from me?"

Looking up at him through watery eyes, he takes a thumb and wipes the tears. He brings his forehead to mine, and we sit there for a beat, taking in one another.

"Just stay with me, Sunny. Just stay with me," he whispers with his forehead still pressed to mine. His eyes close shut and I feel his breath on my lips. I can taste his anguish and pain. His desire and need.

I'm not even sure who initiates it, but one minute we're sharing breath and the next we're sharing tongues.

It's rushed, it's fervent, it's desire, and need in its deepest form as our hands frantically pull and search and touch. It's teeth hitting and lip biting and faces still wet from tears.

He pulls away, removing himself from me, creating a distance I don't appreciate. But in the same breath he comes back to me, grabbing my face to make me look at him. His eyes frantically search mine for answers I refuse to give him.

"What does this mean, Sunny? What does this mean?"

I just look at him. The words are stuck in my throat, banging with each beat of my heart. *Don't marry her. Don't marry her. Don't marry her. I love you. I love you. I love you.*

His grip tightens. "What does this mean, Sunny?" he pleads each word out slower, as if I didn't understand the first time.

His eyes are panicked now. Hoping I'll say the answer in the heat of the moment so that I won't stop myself from doing the things I want.

"It means that you can't do this with me if you're going to marry her."

I can't give him what he wants. I can't give him a life together, no matter how much I want it. I can, however, give him this. Just not while he is engaged to another.

"But is this all we are going to get?" he asks.

"It's all I can give you."

He removes himself from me. "Fuck, Sunny." He covers his mouth. "I-" He shakes his head. "I'm engaged. I'm engaged because you told me to move forward. And now we are here, doing this."

I look down because I can't meet what's behind his eyes. *I can't.* I know I'm confusing him. I'm confusing myself. He can be with anyone else. *Anyone.* Just not her. Yet my heart whispers *that's a lie.*

If I have to be the thing to pull them apart, I will be. It's selfish. It's confusing. It's a power trip. *I know that.* Of course I know that. But I don't know what else to do.

"I can't let you go, Sunny. My heart is bruised by you pulling away." His voice breaks.

Tears sting my eyes again, because I understand the feeling of a bruised heart. It feels like mine is in that perpetual state until we're together.

He starts pacing again, trying to formulate his thoughts. I still stand against the wall, my hands behind my back as I watch him.

He stops his pacing and looks at me as he runs a hand over his face. His emerald eyes are back to that raging fire.

"We can't." I shake my head.

"Fuck it." He grabs my face in his hands, pressing his lips on mine.

One moment we are two separate beings, the next we are one. His body molds to mine with a deep moan. His need is prevalent through the layers of his suit. My hand falls to where he's pressed against me, creating a friction that drives him wilder into this feral haze.

"Fuck, Sunny," he groans. "It's a good thing no one can hear us down here, because I'm going to have you screaming my name," he says, sliding a hand through my skirt band and into my underwear, pushing his fingers inside me.

I gasp. Or moan. Or both.

All I know is it feels fucking good. I'm soaked for him. My hips immediately start grinding, trying to get him deeper. Peeling his suit jacket off, he removes those god damn fingers from me to help shimmy himself out of that tight suit.

My hands run up the carved muscles of his arms, wrapping around the back of his neck and pulling him back to my lips. And I taste it all as his tongue twines with mine. Love, desperation, need and pain.

If there's anything I know about Tyler, the more contact the better. The less clothing even better.

One hand grips my thigh, bringing it up his hip while the other slowly inches between my spread legs.

"You're so fucking wet for me." He smiles against my lips.

When he pushes his fingers into me again, I lose control as my head rolls back with a loud moan. A gentle kiss is placed on the tender skin of my scar, creating a chain down the plunge of my dress until he's on his knees in front of me.

And damn, is that a sight to see.

"Take them off," he demands, toying with the lacey fabric of my panties. Before I can even help, he's already tugging them down while he licks his lips in anticipation. "These belong to me now." He fists them in his hand and stands to his full height.

Wrapping my arms around his neck, I press my nose in the place between his collar and jaw, taking him in. The intimate part that only I can access as I inhale his scent.

Regardless of my need for him, the desperation to make him tremble under my fingers takes over. I undo his belt, almost freeing him save for his boxer briefs, but he snatches my hand, pinning it against the wall above my head.

"I'm going to show you just how much I want you." His lips slam into mine.

We're so close to crossing the line we have been balancing on for months.

Then we hear the door open.

TYLER

I have big plans for the way I will make her mine. I will explore every line, every mark, every crook, every inch of her skin. I'll watch her face as I push myself into her and make her mine. And as she screams my name, my lips will brand all the places he's ever hurt her as proof that another's love can erase another's abuse.

As soon as I'm convinced I'm going to throw all those plans out the window and make love to her right here, the doors open. Instinctively I cover her, guarding her body with my own, so that whoever chooses to risk coming down here won't see her.

Bracing the wall behind her to cocoon her body in mine, I look over my shoulder to see who our intruder is. "Mace, what the fuck are you doing down here?"

"Oh." Her eyes dart between me and Sunny.

"Macey, what the hell?" I ask again.

"Everyone is looking for you, Tyler." She points a thumb behind her.

When I look at Sunny her face tells me nothing again. The fortress is back up.

Stuck on what to do, I swallow hard, weighing my options. I want to grab her hand and walk out with her, showing all those bastards what's truly mine. What I actually *want*.

Her blue-green irises look up at me. "Go," is all she says.

"Come on, Tyler. Shelby is on a mission trying to find you. And down here will not be good," Macey urges.

"Come with me," I say, looking at Sunny.

She slowly shakes her head—defeat has my hands slide off the wall and hang at my sides.

"Tyler, they are about to make a toast." Macey glances over her shoulder.

I hear another set of footsteps coming down the stairs in congruence to my heart hammering in my chest. I stand here like an idiot in hopes she'll change her mind. I'm ready to set my world on fire for her, burning it all down if it means she'll walk through the flames with me.

"Tyler, come on." Cole grabs me by the shoulders, guiding me out of the cellar. He picks up my coat and shoves it into my chest. "Mitchell has a manhunt for you."

Before I can even say anything else, I'm shoved out into masses of people. It all feels like it's in slow motion as I pull my jacket back on. Realizing Sunny's underwear is still in my hand, I shove them in my coat pocket. She won't be getting them back.

Shelby saunters over to me with two flutes of champagne, preparing for the toasts and speeches. Turning to Cole, I look at my brother frantically.

"I need you to do me a favor."

SUNNY

"What just happened?" Macey asks, rushing next to me against the wall.

My eyes pan over to her, finally admitting the one thing I'd been running from. "I fell in love with him."

"Well, we all knew that."

"What?" I croak.

"You're just now realizing you love him?" She laughs.

"I don't understand. You all knew?"

"Of course we knew! *Oh Sunny.* You've loved him for a while now. You just haven't wanted to admit it." She wraps her arms around my neck in a hug.

Clearly I spent a lot of time running from my feelings that I just came full circle, and smacked into them instead.

"So what's going to happen now?" She eyes me. A hope sets flame behind her eyes. Hope Tyler won't marry Shelby. Hope that this would be a reason for me to stay. But he still went up there with his bride to be, and I still have to leave.

Everything changed. But in the same breath, nothing at all.

"I don't know." I push off the wall. "I'm so confused, Mace."

"Do you think…do you think he will call it off?" she asks, darting her eyes between me and the staircase waiting for us. I don't want to go back up. I don't want to hear the toasts. I don't want to see her hang on his arm like the gloating bride to be.

I shrug without any other words.

"Why can't you just stay, Sunny?"

"Because I can't let him find me."

While the links on my chain to Ryan have grown longer, I'm still shackled by him. I will be forever unless he turns up dead or in prison.

Maybe I underestimate Tyler too much, but if detectives can't even find him, how will he? The longer I stay, the higher the risk Ryan can find me. A false hope of his death was a beacon to a better life. But now, this is what I get. And maybe what I deserve, too.

With a sigh, she loops her arm through mine. "Come on. Let's go back out there."

I hate breaking their hearts. But if there's anything more painful than this, it'd be a life with Ryan. It'd be him finding me, and having to relive the nightmares I finally have a handle on, to come back and haunt me.

I can't. I can't. I can't.

She jerks us back into the crowds of unfamiliar faces.

"Dude, did you two fuck?" Sam joins me and Macey.

"Say it a little louder Sam." I murmur.

"Let them hear!" She throws her hands up.

"No, we didn't," I whisper.

"But they were about to," Macey says.

I shoot a look at her.

"Oh, come on, Sunny. You and I both know that's the truth," she laughs.

"What does this mean?" Sam eyes me.

It's the same answer. "I don't know."

"I mean, he has got to end it, right? There's no way he's going to follow through with this when y'all were literally about to fuck downstairs," she continues "I mean your plan had to work, right?"

In a haze of desperation, my only way to save him was to make him consumed by me. Lead him on in a way that would lead him away from her, even if it meant he didn't get me in the end.

But much like my plan I had for Boston, I don't think this one will work, either.

TYLER

Toasts are made. People clap. Forks clink against glasses as the anticipation of a kiss between me and Shelby looms like a heavy storm in the air. I don't want to do it, but I have to play my part, like I always fucking do.

The taste of Sunny still lingers on my tongue, a sweetness I savor as a reminder of her feelings for me, so deeply on my tongue. Until it's taken away by lip gloss and champagne.

My disappearance is only shown in subtle signs from Shelby, like her red nails clutching my bicep and her persistent presence right next to me. Still, she keeps that barbie doll smile plastered to her face as we greet our guests.

I wonder if she can smell the other woman on me.

We leave the marble interior and trade it for the outdoor view of lush trees and a pond that glistens the reflection of a full moon. The garden is filled with people forming around the string quartet filling the cold night air with music.

"This would make such a gorgeous venue, too. I think the venue our parents secured will be perfect." Shelby says on my arm.

I don't say anything as I scan the area, searching for any way out of this conversation because frankly, I don't fucking care. And where the hell is Sunny?

"Maybe we could hire them for the wedding." Shelby looks up at me.

"Maybe," I say, but my eyes are on my family now.

There she is.

Macey is curled into Cole, her shield from the cold while Anthony talks to them, the grin never leaving his face despite the circumstances.

Sam and Sunny stand together, murmuring things I can't read from this far. The friendship I hoped and prayed for between my sister and the woman I'd maybe one day love. And I got it.

Sam downs her champagne, already grabbing another from a waiter tray. A wind kicks up, blowing Sunny's curls around and making her rub her bare arms against the cold.

Instinct takes over, and I immediately start peeling my jacket off.

"Ugh, thank you. It's so cold out here." Shelby takes it as if it's meant for her. "Such a gentleman." She shrugs it onto her shoulders.

I look across the way, still seeing Sunny fighting off the cold.

My jacket is on the wrong girl.

It's a brief moment, one where her eyes flick to mine, and nothing else exists in the world. Until her already big blue-green eyes round even wider as she looks at Shelby.

It's in slow motion. It's all in slow motion as I look from Sunny to Shelby who stands next to me.

And Shelby pulls her hand out of the pocket of my jacket, holding another woman's underwear in her hands.

CHAPTER FIFTY-NINE

SUNNY

OH SHIT.

Reality sets in as she holds the black lace proof of Tyler's commitment to her. Shelby finds me in the crowd, her warm brown eyes turning cold as they bounce between me and Tyler. I'm still not sorry, and hope she feels a fraction of the pain she's caused him.

Once they meet eyes, it's not long before her red nails are grabbing Tyler's face, pulling him down so hushed words are said between them.

It's a primitive thing, what happens inside me. Something so visceral I can't put a name to. All I know is before I can even realize it, I'm pushing through the people, moving directly towards Tyler and Shelby.

Before I can make it, she is dragging him back into the venue, disappearing into the crowds of people.

"What the hell is going on?" Anthony calls.

Cole and Macey follow my gaze as they step up next to me.

"Oh, hell no." Sam downs her drink.

"I have an idea. I'm about to go find out." I chase after them.

It's stupid. I will only be adding fuel to the fire.

But I'm ready to burn this place to the ground anyways.

TYLER

I'm glad she found those panties. They are only further proof that she will always be an obligation rather than a choice. Her red nails only release their grip once we stand in the cellar, where I received those panties. Shelby shoves me against the same wall I had Sunny pinned to.

Then she slaps me across the face.

"No wonder you couldn't get your dick up, and fuck me like a man, because you were already sticking it in her!" Shelby yells.

I smile and lean into her. "I wish."

She slaps me again.

Leaning down, I say, "You really think I was going to marry you, and not fuck other people?"

She needs to know her place. I'm about to be the one to tell her. Shelby sucks in a breath, as if she's shocked by this news.

"You know what you did to me. What you *took* from me. You may want me, but I do not want you. I'm only doing what I'm supposed to do because the one thing I want, I can't have. So I'm left with you instead," I say blankly.

She doesn't deserve any more of me.

"I gave you the chance that I thought you deserved, and *you* fucked it up. I was willing to try and commit to you, but you broke my trust. So don't expect commitment from me. I only have a commitment to the agreement our parents made. Not you. Not anymore. Our marriage license is a contract for your father. Nothing more. Nothing less. That's all you are. *A contract.*"

She slaps me again. Then she starts taking fists to my body in an attempt to hurt me. And maybe I deserve it. Maybe I deserve all the pain she caused me. All the pain I've been feeling. *I deserve to hurt*. I am not a good person, and this is my punishment.

"It doesn't matter! You will still be stuck with me." She continues to hit me. "You're a whore!"

Then she's pulled from me. My vision fills with Sunny, my little fire, my fucking salvation, yanking Shelby by her blonde hair off of me. Sunny grabs her arm, twisting it behind her back, and slams Shelby against the wall next to me.

It shouldn't turn me on. It shouldn't fucking turn me on but it does. Watching her utilize the skills I have taught her is something that creates a deep pride settling over me.

Shelby tries to maneuver herself, crying out when Sunny holds firm and presses her face into the ragged stone even harder.

"Touch him again and I'll make sure you never have the privilege to do it again," Sunny seethes. She releases Shelby, sending her across the cellar on stumbling feet.

A step forward makes her a barrier between us. A wall of fucking fire ready to burn anything that comes close to me. Her round eyes flick back at me, something unexplainable igniting behind them. A fucking inferno ready to burn this place down and Shelby is the first victim.

For once, someone is saving *me*.

Hair in disarray and dress wrinkled, Shelby turns around with labored breaths, and anger ringing her brown eyes. "You may be his whore, but I'm going to be his *wife*," she seethes.

The words hit a shield, and Sunny stares at her blankly. "I may be his whore, but at least the whore knows what it's like to be loved by him."

The words are a physical blow to Shelby as she takes a staggered step back. It's a fragment of a moment where there's visible evidence the words cause the laceration that is intended.

As quickly as it comes, it leaves all too soon. Gaining her composure, Shelby smooths her dress and hair.

As she walks out of the cellar, she says over her shoulder, "We are moving up the wedding." Then leaves us in the shadows of our sin.

I watch Sunny stare at the empty staircase, the air around us so quiet, but I know her mind is screaming so many things I wish it wouldn't. The doubt is prevalent in her eyes when she turns and looks at me. A few short steps, Sunny closes the distance between us. The echo of her footsteps as loud as my heart thumping against my chest.

Grabbing my hand, her soft skin against my callused, she places her black panties in my palm.

"Keep it as a souvenir for when I'm gone."

TYLER

I'm pulled out of my fitful sleep by my phone vibrating on my nightstand. I roll over in bed, reaching for it, sure after the events of last night it'd be blown up by too many fucking people.

Sunny's words still linger through my head and her panties still sit on my nightstand as a reminder. The bundle of lace as my only souvenir and remembrance of her for when she leaves.

I look at my phone with blurry eyes to see texts from my family chat, but also at least seven text messages from Shelby. Rubbing my eyes, I try to look at the bright screen and see the time. It's only 7:30am, but the thread of messages with Shelby has me sitting up straighter.

> Don't forget we are going to the venue today
> at 10am to pick out linens and other details.

We will talk to the venue about moving up the
wedding. I want it at least this month.

You better be awake soon.

Both our moms are coming to help us out, too.

Tyler, how are you not awake yet?

Probably too tired from sticking your dick in
another woman all night.

The messages go on.

I forgot. And I'm not sure why she expected anything more.

Sleep evaded me with insistent tossing and turning. I rub my
hands over my tired face, recalling the events of the night prior.

The fact of the matter is, it doesn't matter what the fuck I do,
people are going to be mad, people are going to be hurt, so I may
as well take the damn path of least resistance at this rate to
reduce the casualties.

My phone buzzes again, notifying me of a text from my
father.

Keep me posted about the venue. You made
the right choice.

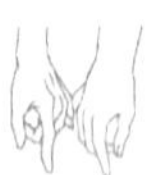

I walk around the venue with my hands in the pocket of my suit,
hearing Shelby talking to the wedding planner a million words a
minute—something about importing plates from Italy. I stopped
listening after the fourth zero.

I stop in front of the massive panoramic windows that over-
look the city and the water. The venue is certainly beautiful, with

hardwood floors and a grand staircase leading up to a lofted second floor. Crystal chandeliers hang from the ceiling, illuminating the grand ballroom.

It's everything Shelby. But absolutely nothing Sunny. I see her in everything.

It's no secret my thoughts about Sunny have gone beyond the confines of the timeline she's given us. A wedding with her would be simple and intimate. Only her parents and our inner circle. Most likely in her hometown on the beach. We'd maybe even elope at the courthouse. Solely the two of us, and then celebrate with our family afterwards.

I know it's crazy to think these things about Sunny. To be in love with her so quickly. To buy a damn engagement ring so quickly. To imagine a wedding with her and what it'd be like. I've only known her for maybe four months, but these things have all been on replay in my mind since the moment I met her. It's easy to envision a life with her.

When you know, you know. I knew the moment I ran into her in the coffee shop. *I've always known.*

"Tyler, this venue is gorgeous," My mother says next to me, taking me out of my thoughts.

Nodding, I stare out the window, watching the water glisten in the sunshine.

"Smile, Tyler. This is a very good thing." She places a hand on my shoulder.

"For you." I look at her.

She frowns at my comment. "You've known Shelby your whole life. It's not like you are strangers being forced to marry."

Her amber eyes look at me with remorse. There's a sadness that mimics my own. Like she somehow understands my pain, without me even having to tell her.

"It's her, isn't it?" She looks out the window.

This is the moment of my downfall. I know Mitchell knows.

Of course he does. Mitchell has me under a microscope. But my mother? I wasn't expecting that.

"It will always be her." I stare out the window.

She sighs. "I understand that. I've felt the way you feel once upon a time."

I look at her, my shock almost snapping my neck in the process. But she's still staring out the window, her mind in a memory I'm not aware of.

"I learned to love your father. And maybe you'll learn to love Shelby, too." She looks at me with a weak smile, but her eyes show everything that isn't happiness.

She'd always been so devoted, so loyal to Mitchell despite everything. But now, I see that devotion is nothing compared to the grief in her eyes.

Just as I'm about to speak again, I'm called by Shelby. "Tyler!" she squeals from across the room. "Come look at these centerpieces!"

Me and Diane's eyes meet. We don't need to share anymore words.

Putting my arm around her shoulders, she slips her arm around my waist, and we walk over to the wedding chaos before us.

CHAPTER SIXTY

SUNNY

Exiting my apartment building, I head towards Martha's for family dinner. The cold January evening is bustling despite the frigid air.

Regardless of my efforts, the engagement still hadn't been called off. To my knowledge, the details had even gone into picking out dishes for the wedding ceremony. It's a loss I've finally succumbed to as I wave my white flag.

I broke you, Tyler.

It's a sickening feeling, knowing what we could have if life played us different cards. We stand so close, yet so far, knowing one another so well but also not at all. Almost, but also never quite even close. A broken girl who no longer understands what being whole feels like.

It's hard to grasp that people like the family I met here have learned to love me—my jagged pieces included. It doesn't matter that these pieces continue to cut them. Every broken part of me loves them.

Ryan spent so much time trying to put my fire out, to contain it. Keep it small so I didn't burn him. Meanwhile, Tyler fuels it, he encourages me to set it free. He will gladly burn in it if it means my freedom.

Without an update on Ryan, it's easy to want to stray from the direction I've been on. They say no news is good news. Though I know with Ryan, his silence is violent.

The constant worry isn't as persistent. Some days it's brief, while others it becomes the very air I breathe. It is suffocating me, despite my labored breaths. On the days where it's not my very essence, the thoughts like to crawl into my mind. All of them asking what if.

What if I stayed?

It's hard to imagine all these small moments that lead me here. From a girl who couldn't even walk out of her apartment without looking over her shoulder to now considering staying in a place she swore she never would.

The words Ryan left me with have somehow embedded themselves into my very skin. It's altered my brain chemistry, and repeats every day as my reminder. Woven so deeply into my ribs that I feel the stab of them with each breath.

If you walk out that door and leave, I promise I will find you.

I approach Martha's, hoping the night is as simple as beers and the football game. While it's only been a few days since the engagement party, I'm hopeful it's enough time for everyone to calm down. Regardless of the fact my own rage is still an inferno inside my veins.

The wind kicks up, stinging my gold hoops against my skin and blowing the curls that escaped my bun. I tug my black coat tighter, trying to cover the spots my oversized sweater hasn't.

As I'm walking through the parking lot, Tyler is getting out of his truck. I don't stop for him though, I just keep walking. He slams his truck door a little too harshly, indicating that he knows I've walked here through the growing night.

I pick up my pace, regardless of the fact I'll see him inside.

But at least it won't be alone. His long legs are a disadvantage to mine as he closes the space between us.

I almost audibly groan. How can a man I'm upset with look so good in jeans, and a long sleeve shirt under a peacoat?

He doesn't say anything as he approaches my side. We just walk a few paces in silence as I side eye him, noting the fatigue in his emeralds.

"Did you walk here?" he finally asks, his breath filtering in front of him due to the cold air. I don't answer him, because it's none of his concern. He has a fiancé to worry about now.

He rolls his eyes at my lack of response. "You're going to give me a heart attack doing this."

"No barbie Shelby tonight?" I offer.

He swallows hard, a muscle flexing in his jaw. He doesn't look at me, he just keeps his gaze straight ahead of us as we walk.

"No." Is all he manages to get out.

I purse my lips followed by a shrug. "Okay."

He stops, grabbing my arm and pulling me back. "Why does it bother you?"

The already gray sky grows deeper as night takes over, illuminating the streetlights in the parking lot. The darkness clings to him. It hovers around him and shadows his face, darkening the emeralds that sometimes seem too bright.

His hand doesn't leave my bicep. I contemplate my words, trying to figure out how I'll angle this. I stare at him, searching his face.

"Answer me," he urges, pulling me closer to him. His body heat stretches out in a cry for my own.

"You know why," I manage to get out. "You deserve someone who makes you happy. And that is not her."

"You bring me happiness, Sunny. *You do.*" His grip tightens.

I want to look everywhere, except for his eyes, because I

know my own will give away everything I'm feeling right now. I'm tired of keeping the fortress up.

I bite my quivering lip, hopeful he will excuse it for the cold and not my emotions. Once I finally meet his gaze, a brokenness that I know doesn't belong to me reflects back.

That isn't *from* me.

"You slept with her," I whisper.

He swallows hard and breaks our gaze, indicating a yes to my revelation as he releases my arm and sets me free. I stumble back, as if his words physically hit me.

"Oh my god," I croak. "Oh my god, Tyler. How could you?"

I don't give him time to respond. Instead, I'm turning on my heel and trying to run away, like I always do. His large hand wraps around my bicep, pulling me back into him again.

With ragged breaths, he looks down at me. Over the sound of my own frantic heart, I can hear his, too. And I'm almost certain I hear it so clearly with each thump.

I'm sorry. I'm sorry. I'm sorry.

But yeah, that's what Ryan used to say too.

TYLER

It's an admission I won't speak, but one that I won't refuse either.

She fights my hold on her, trying to get out of my grasp but I keep her close, unwilling to let her go again.

She will never understand. I cannot stop loving her any more than I can stop breathing. And even then, when my last breath goes, my love for her will still remain.

It doesn't matter, nothing after her matters.

I curse the man before me who destroyed her so harshly that her only means to protect herself is to run.

I spin her around, grabbing her biceps to make her look at me. "You think you can come into my life and do all these things with me just to up and leave? I was doing *fine* before you, Sunny. But then you came, and I realized I wasn't. You gave me light when I was content in living in the darkness."

"You were supposed to find a way out!" She cries, crumpling under my grasp, making my heart ache, pummeling into my chest.

"How do you expect me to find my way out when my light is no longer in my life?" I counter, my voice as weak as I feel.

"That's not fair." She shakes her head, breaking our gaze, trying to remove herself from my grip, but it only makes me hold on tighter.

I'm not willing to lose her again. Her reaction to this has told me everything I need to know.

You love me, Sunny.

"And what about you? How is running an out?" I growl.

"Because I'm running away! I'm not sharing a fucking bed with the enemy. I had the courage to leave and *stay* gone. Where's yours?" she seethes, pushing against my chest.

I clench my jaw, hating that she's fucking right.

Her nostrils flare and brows crease together as she looks up at me with those fiery blue-green eyes. Her body trembles, and I'm not sure if it's from the anger or cold or both. I want to pull her into me and give her all my body heat if it means she will never be cold again.

"Have some goddamn mercy on me, Sunny," I choke. "You don't understand the pressure I live with every day. It was worth it to fight for you. It was worth it to go against the expectations held against me *for you* but now you aren't an option, so it is no longer worth it. So don't fucking make me feel guilty for following my duty and the expectations I always knew would rise up eventually and the pressure that is *suffocating* me."

She bites her quivering bottom lip and looks down at the ground while she sniffles.

"Baby…" I say. "Baby if I didn't do it, I never would've been able to. I can't…" My voice catches because I fucking hate myself for this.

My justification had been so she wouldn't go running to our parents, crying that her betrothed is in love with another woman. Crying because I won't give her children when that's the whole reason we are forced together.

"It's… it's too complicated to explain, Sunny. All I know is I'm disgusted with myself for it."

She shakes her head, refusing to look me in the eyes. I cradle her face, as gently as possible, to brush the tears that streak her cheeks. I want to take her pain away.

"Please, baby," I whisper, but she jerks from my touch.

Her irises meet mine, and an anger that I've never seen sits there, burning in those wide eyes.

She doesn't say anything else as she turns around and walks into Martha's.

Now I know exactly what I need to do next.

CHAPTER SIXTY-ONE
TYLER

I sit in my truck outside the hotel, looking at the camera feed I've hacked on my phone. Needless to say, I don't even have to go inside to get what I need. It's simple enough. Although, the idea of going inside seems almost poetic. Theatrical, honestly.

Patiently, I wait for them to arrive as I watch the live feed on my phone. Cole got the information for me after the engagement party. Now, I actually have a reason to use it.

Governor Matthew Goodman told his wife and daughter that he was catching a red eye flight to California for a campaigning event. The two of them believe he is going to contract with other politicians to ensure votes, showing support for one another, and so on. When in reality, he's here, pulling up with a young woman, ready to fuck her in the penthouse suite of this hotel.

Matthew's car drives up to the valet and hands him the keys. A young woman steps out of his expensive car. She looks a little *too* young. I take a deep breath in, leaning back in the seat because this means I very well may have to do something about this.

My eyes shift back to the feed on my phone, and watch the

two through the cameras. She looks around the grand hotel, wide-eyed, while Matthew checks them in. Repulsion forms like bile in the back of my throat.

While I send off a screenshot of the girl's face for Cole to research, they make their way into the elevators alone. I switch my camera views to follow them.

Matthew swipes his card to give them access to the suite. No one can enter unless they have a card. And sadly for him, one sits in my wallet right now.

He corners the girl in the elevator and fists his hand in her blonde hair, yanking her head back painfully. She cries out as her eyes go wide. My jaw tics at the action, but she doesn't try to stop him.

Matthew and the woman make it up to the penthouse. I made sure to plant cameras there before their arrival. So, I switch to the feed inside that gives me a clear view of every angle. I need no questions asked if I have to use these tapes. There will be no skewing whether this is Matthew or not.

He throws his bag on the floor and wastes no time grabbing the girl, dragging her by a bundle of hair in his fist, and throwing her on the bed.

He pulls out a pair of handcuffs, and secures them on her wrists behind her back. A whip of his belt has it off and smacking across her ass. Her cries do nothing to stop him from rolling her onto her back, crushing her secured hands in the process.

I don't have sound on these cameras, but her head shakes as tears start to stream down her face.

Sitting up straighter, my heart starts to pound. She tries to crawl away from Matthew now, but he drags her back over, making her kick her legs to get him away.

This is no longer consensual.

Immediately I'm getting out of my truck, slamming the door shut and racing into the hotel.

"Mr. Caddell, good evening." The receptionist says at the desk.

I ignore her as I run to the elevators, pushing the button multiple times even though I know it won't make it come faster. I pull up the feed to see Matthew securing her legs to the bed posts.

Fuck.

I hate that this is happening, but now it's the best fucking leverage I have against him.

The elevator doors open, and I swipe the card to get access to the suite. My eyes dart between the switching numbers in the elevator to the feed on my phone. Matthew is now gagging the poor girl.

Fuck, fuck, fuck.

I grab my knife from my jeans pocket and slide it open, putting my phone in my pocket as the adrenaline courses through me. The elevator doors ping open and I rush through, running to the bedroom where Matthew is now naked, and I hear the girl screaming through the gag.

"What the– " His words are cut off by my hand around his throat, slamming him against the wall. I bring my knife to his carotid as I meet his brown eyes.

"No means fucking no, Matthew," I growl. "Why do people in your goddamn family not understand the concept?"

"What the fuck are you doing here?" he snaps as he attempts to shove me off.

"This is what's going to fucking happen, you're going to call off the stupid fucking arrangement you and Mitchell made. If you don't, I will hack every station, every news outlet, every goddamn TV in this city and blast the camera feeds of you almost raping a girl. It will destroy your reputation, your career, your fucking life."

He blinks at me, his brown eyes rounding with fear. "And what do I tell Mitchell?"

I smile. He's listening like a well-trained dog. "You give him whatever the fuck he asks for in exchange."

The girl still tied to the bed whimpers. My eyes pan over to her.

I tighten my grip on his throat, taking more of his air while pushing my knife into his skin. The blood trickles down his neck and over my hand gripping it. I hit his head with the hilt, making more blood trickle down his face.

"If I catch you trying to do this again, I will fucking cut your balls off and gag you with them myself." That's a promise I will actually keep.

I tie Matthew's hands together above his head on the canopy bed posts. He doesn't fight me. He knows that's a losing battle. I approach the young woman in the bed, tears streaking down her face. She tries to move from me. Scared shitless.

"I'm not going to hurt you." I pull my jacket off to cover her exposed body. I unlock the handcuffs, and cut the rope off her ankles with my knife. She rips the tape of her mouth, spitting her gag out.

She secures the jacket around her bare body as cries escape her mouth. I kneel down to level myself with her, being sure to leave a good distance between us. I grab her panties and the duct tape from Matthews bag, shoving them in his mouth and slapping some tape to seal them in.

"Tell me how you like that." I give his face a tap.

Muffled words come from his mouth and he tries to move around the ropes I have him tied to. Humiliation widens his brown eyes as he stands completely naked, barely on his toes.

I look at the girl, hating what I have to say. "I can't kill him. But I promise you, this won't happen with him again."

She nods with tears spilling down her face. I squat down in front of her. "How old are you?"

"Eighteen," she cries.

Rage gets the better of me as a growl forms in my chest and I turn to look at Matthew. I stand and approach him. "Coward. Having to use me and cling to my name, my legacy, my fucking success to build up your own. Because you couldn't do it without pawning off your daughter to the next highest bidder." He starts squirming.

I want to fucking kill him, but I can't. I can't let rage ignite me. If I do, I'll get sloppy. I need to be methodical. I came here for one thing, and I got it and then some.

"My fucking promise still stands," I say, meeting his stare. I run my knife along his chest, creating a nice long gash across his abdomen. Just enough to bleed, but not enough to kill him.

"It will no longer be my job to ensure your family's success," I say, walking away from his groaning body.

I grab his phone, put it to his face to unlock it and text his wife from it, telling her to meet him here so she can see the coward she married.

My phone rings with the information on the woman from Cole.

"Get dressed," I tell her. "I'm taking you home."

CHAPTER SIXTY-TWO

SUNNY

I SETTLE MYSELF INTO THE COUCH, PLACING A HOT BOWL OF ramen between my crossed legs. Considering the night, I hadn't really eaten much. I just wanted to make my appearance at Martha's and leave soon after.

A pounding knock on my door has me jolting.

My brows crease, and my heart thumps a little harder against my chest. It's midnight, and anything at my door at this hour can't mean something good. I untangle myself from my blanket, and stand on trembling legs as I set my ramen down.

The knock happens again, and I swipe my phone to make sure I didn't miss any messages. When the knock happens again, I cautiously make my way to where my gun sits in my night-stand. Before I can make it to the door, the knock occurs again, louder and more aggressive. A familiar voice pierces through the barricade of wood. "Open the door, Sunny."

Tyler is at my door.

Through the peephole, I see him standing there hollow eyed in my hallway, despite the wild threat that sits behind those emeralds. Both hands brace the door frame, his head tilting downward causing his hair to hang over his forehead. If defeat had a physical manifestation, it is this, right here.

I blink, easing from my toes, trying to decide which would be the best move. Open the door or not? The way his chest moves up and down, with ragged breaths, tells me he might kick it in if I don't answer.

"Answer the door, Sunny."

With a deep breath, I open the door. Immediately those kryptonite eyes are on me. "Can I help you, Tyler?"

"We need to talk." He pushes past me.

There's nothing to talk about. We have so many conversations without anything being resolved. I'm leaving in a few months, he will stay here, and marry Shelby shortly after. It's as simple as that. I feel that tug in my chest laugh because it isn't as simple as that.

We are not simple.

"Tyler, we can't do this." I point at the door for him to leave.

"Then when will we?" he places a hand above my head on the door, shutting it closed.

"Okay, calm down, because you're going to disturb the entire apartment building." I grab his arm, dragging him in my apartment.

He starts pacing in the small space of my studio. And I see it, the words trying to formulate, a plan being written in his beautifully, unhinged mind.

"You need to leave."

He stops and looks at me blankly as he tosses his coat over a chair, indicating his refusal for my request. I groan, rubbing my hands over my face in frustration.

"You are ridiculous."

"We have to address this thing between us."

"Tyler…" I grumble.

"Don't even start with me," he cuts me off, raising a hand. "You and I both know that there is this *thing* between us. And that thing, whatever this is, I don't think it's going to go away, Sunny." His voice catches at the end, proof that while he is trying to remain neutral, this is slowly destroying him.

I lick my trembling lips and break our eye contact.

"Little fire," he says gently. "You and I both know that no matter how hard we try to avoid it or try to cut it off it won't fucking go away. It hasn't now. It never will. I understand that you're confused about these feelings and that it's not something you wanted but it's here. It's here, no matter how much you want to fight it off."

To my dismay, tears sting my eyes because yeah, he is right. The day I'd broken my tether to Ryan was the day my heart strings were finally able to tie to Tyler's.

I felt it that day, as I sat in the airport, despite my internal desperate cry, something echoed along that thread between us whispering *come home* with a gentle tug to coax my broken heart.

"Something pulled me into the coffee shop that day. *You* pulled me there." He places a scarred hand over his broad chest. "I…I felt it here. Somehow."

"Me too," It's barely a whisper.

"Nothing that has happened has been a coincidence. Not with meeting Sam or having Macey as your patient, or running into me in the coffee shop with Cole and Anthony. Because with me, comes them."

I convinced myself to believe far bigger lies than trying to talk myself out of the reality of this situation, that seems too magical to exist in our world.

What I feel for him is something that you read about in fiction. And yet, here it is, the most real thing I've felt in my life.

"There's a *reason* it never worked out with anyone else," he says. "It's why when things happened with Ryan and you fled here… Sunny, you were coming to *me*. I knew in that coffee shop that we weren't done. If Boston wasn't going to bring us back together then I would've. And when I saw you that night with Sam, I wasn't surprised at all. I knew we had unfinished business. That was the night that I knew, *I knew* I was going to fall in love with you. I didn't even know your name, but I knew, *I knew* I'd fucking love you. We weren't done then, and we aren't done now."

"You're marrying Shelby, Tyler."

"No I'm not." He takes a step closer to me. I rip my gaze to his. "I called it off." Another cautious step towards me.

"How?"

He swallows hard. "Let's just say I found a way. I found my way out, Sunny. Just like we promised."

"Why?"

"It's *you* Sunny. It'll always be you."

He found a way out. And I don't even fucking care what way that was. All I care is that he *did*.

"I thought after you broke it off with us that you'd be better off anyways. But then, I…I felt you. I felt you through that indescribable thing between us. And while you were telling me one thing, I'd heard your screams on the other end, racing down that thread. *Don't marry her*."

My eyes widen hearing the exact words that played in my head being spoken off his tongue.

"Sunny, I didn't see anything before you. I couldn't see anything in my future before I met you. *I didn't see anything*."

Little Fire. The nickname rings in my head. Because somehow, the sad girl became the light in his life. What once was a dark future all of a sudden had an illumination of possibilities.

"You don't have to say it, Sunny. You don't have to say the words because I've already felt it. I've already felt it as your tongue wrote across mine. The way your fingers trace it over the scars that made me believe it couldn't exist. The way the moment I met you, something told me that I'll love you, and you'll love me, too. And that's all there is to it. I love you, Sunny. *I love you.*"

Breathless, I finally look up at him. In the glow of the string lights that cast an orange hue in my apartment, he looks softer here. The words I'd suppressed far too long spill off my tongue in a desperate attempt for him to understand. No matter how it's said, though, I know he will.

"Something died inside of me the day I left Ryan. I was a stupid, hopeless romantic girl who clung to the first boy who loved her in hopes that maybe, just maybe he could love me the way I loved him," I finally say.

He watches me intently, keeping the silence to make space for my words. Something Ryan had never done for me.

"I was a girl who'd do anything to save what we had. Desperate to make all my firsts my lasts. He knew that. And maybe that's why he did what he did to me."

He ruined me, so nobody else would want me.

"Contemplation had turned to plan. If I wasn't alive, he'd have no reason to go after my family. But something told me to...to just hold on. It was a small whisper over my cries, but I listened. And then I got a call from the recruiter."

He rubs a hand over his mouth. "Yeah," he whispers.

"And it was you. All of you." I realize. That voice was a combination of all of theirs as a beacon through my brokenness telling me to just wait. To hold on. *Wait for us.*

In a time where my own life didn't seem worth it, somehow the whispers of my future pulled through the devastation of my end.

"My eyes, they saw you Tyler. But my soul, it just, it *feels* you," I admit.

He takes another step closer. "Sunny, he may have been your firsts, but I promise you, I will gladly be all your lasts."

He gave me a feeling I didn't think I could ever experience, especially after Ryan. Accepting every shattered part of me, and

I accept every shattered part of him, working those broken pieces together to create a brand-new whole. *And how will we ever be the same again?*

I love you, Tyler. You made me fall in love with you.

"Say something." He takes another step.

I slowly move my eyes from where his feet are, up his body and to that treacherously beautiful face. Thinking about all the things that have led up to this moment. Everything he risked, just to have a chance with me, even if it's only for right now.

I realize that, despite what happened with Ryan, if it hadn't happened, maybe I would've never left. Maybe I would've always felt that little tug in my chest, never truly knowing who was on the other end, and experiencing a life lacking Tyler.

What an empty life that would be.

Love is too weak of a word for what is threaded between us. It is the echo of each beat of my heart. It is the air that fills my lungs. It is the man who was somehow able to whisper to me from across the other end of the country, willing me to hold on when I was ready to end it all.

I'm not sure of anything but two things at this moment.

I am in love with him, and I want every part of him.

Now.

I touch the scar on my neck, the brand of his abuse forever embedded on my skin. My daily reminder. He was my best friend, and that was the worst part.

But how long will I punish myself for someone else's actions?

I flick my eyes to Tyler. "I am broken, Tyler. *I am broken.* But you showed me despite being broken, I'm still capable of being loved. And I'm capable of giving love. I'm in love with you, Tyler. *I love you,*" I finally admit.

Something wild flicks behind his eyes, and no longer are the cautious slow steps, but determined ones as he stalks towards me. Using both hands, he grabs my face and slams his lips into mine.

The momentum has us taking a few stumbling steps back, but he doesn't falter. There it is, him writing the words across my tongue, his declaration forever embedded into me.

I love you. I love you. I love you.

He pulls back from me and presses his forehead against mine, meeting my eyes. "I love you, Sunny. I love you so much. All my love belongs to you. It always has. It always will."

It's me who presses my lips to his now, soaking in the words and storing them away to play over and over.

Keeping his mouth on mine, he grabs my thighs, pulling me onto him. He walks through my apartment and swipes everything off the small table I'm sure isn't capable of withstanding my weight. He lays me on it, gripping my thighs and pulling me towards the edge.

Exploring hands move up my legs, his eyes looking down at me hungrily and admirably.

Without warning, he grabs my face, "I want you, Sunny. I want every part of you."

"Then take it."

CHAPTER SIXTY-THREE

SUNNY

ANTICIPATION BEATS WITH MY HEART. A BUILT UP, VISCERAL need courses through my veins, centering between my legs as his hands diligently explore my body.

"I've imagined this moment in so many ways, so many times," he says, hooking his fingers in the waistband of my sweats. "And now I'm going to make you live the fantasies that have consumed me."

He peels them off and tosses them to the side.

"I'm going to devour you like my own personal feast." He kisses up my bare legs, creating goosebumps in his wake as he falls to his knees. "And I'm not going to stop until you're screaming my name."

Then he's on me.

His hands brace my hips as I roll with his tongue strokes repeatedly until I explode. My moans are practically screams, my hips buck as he continues to ride me with his mouth, enjoying every moment, tasting every bit of me.

He drinks me. Consumes me like a starved man. His tongue knows all the right places to explore as he goes back and forth between biting and sucking to tongue fucking me. Until I finally give way, panting, my legs shaking.

"This is only the beginning, Sunny. We have so much to make up for." He starts placing kisses all over my body. "And I'm going to erase him from your skin, replacing his touch with my own. I'm going to make it where you forget all about him, and all you can think about is me. He may have been your first, but I sure as fuck will be your last. "

And I feel it. I do. I feel it as he presses his lips on my skin. Gently, he kisses the scar in the crook of my neck, taking away a pain I thought would never stop. And he replaces it with words as he traces it with his tongue across the tender skin. *I love you.*

He lifts me from the table, carrying me to my bed. With heavy breaths, he stands tall at the foot of the bed and looks down at me.

"This is it for me, Sunny. *You* are it for me," he declares. "If we go here, and cross this line, I don't think I can ever go back."

"I know," I whisper.

He grips the back of my neck, pressing his lips against mine again. My fingers toy with the hem of his shirt, slowly peeling it off to reveal the canvas of scars across his body. With gentle fingers, I trace the lines that lace through his skin, admiring his beauty.

And he doesn't stop me. Because it doesn't hurt with me. *He* doesn't hurt with me.

He pushes me down onto the bed and grabs my shirt, completely ripping it down the middle to expose my body. A smile quirks my mouth, because it's just another item to add to the list of ruined clothes by him.

When I meet his eyes, the feral look doesn't do anything to scare me, but excite me.

My bare body is on display, and he takes a step back at the foot of the bed to witness it. "Oh Sunny," he breathes, slowly shaking his head.

"Tyler," I groan, the need for him becoming unbearable.

"What is it, Sunny darling?"

"I want you," I moan.

His eyes turn savage at my pleads. "Say it again."

"I need you."

"You didn't think it would be that easy, did you?" He tilts his head. "I want to savor this fucking moment. I want to savor *you*."

My need takes over as I get on my knees, urgently fumbling with the waistband of his jeans. A devilish smile spreads his lips, curving the scar that slices through them. He toys with a curl in his finger while I struggle with his pants, growing my frustration.

A dark chuckle leaves his lips. "Lay down," he commands.

I do as he says, impatiently watching him as he slowly peels his pants off. He starts at my feet, grabbing an ankle and pressing a delicate kiss to my skin. He works his way up, branding words into my skin. *Mine. Mine. Mine.*

I arch my back, the need becoming painful. He smiles against my skin, and I swear I hear a soft chuckle. He gives me a taste of what I want, what I need as he moves between my breasts. One hand toys with a nipple while his tongue works the other. It fuels the fire threatening inside me, igniting that small flame to an inferno of need.

"Tyler, please," I beg again.

"You have no idea how long I've waited for this," he whispers in my ear.

This was so long overdue. *So long overdue.*

He grabs my thighs, spreading me open like a book. A groan leaves his throat and he slowly presses himself at my entrance. A lingering question hangs in the air over us as his emeralds meet my eyes.

Do we use protection?

We won't use a condom. Not for this. The primitive part of

me has a visceral need for *just* him. I don't want barriers between us.

Thank god for IUDs.

I give him a small nod. And with a whispered *yes, finally,* he pushes into me.

"Sunny," he croaks as he pushes another inch. His body crumples over me, pressing his nose into my neck. "Fuck, Sunny."

"More," I whisper into his neck, despite the painful stretch of him inside me.

And he gives me exactly what I want. Sitting up on his knees, he grips my thighs and slowly pushes fully into me. A cry leaves my throat, but he grabs my face to watch the way he makes me come undone.

"Tyler," I cry. "I don't…I don't know if I can…"

"Yes, you can Sunny. Your body was *made* for mine. Open up for me." He slaps my thigh. It hurts. It hurts so fucking good. The undeniable pull between us settles and sings all at once. Grateful that the resistance is no longer present, amplified by this moment between us. Fire and darkness wrapped together.

With slow, measured thrusts, he works himself into me. My nails dig into his back and his body trembles under my touch. It's a powerful feeling. So damn powerful knowing I have this effect on a man like him.

"Jesus fucking Christ, Sunny. You're so tight."

"Don't stop," I plead.

Getting on his knees, he takes each leg of mine onto his shoulders and grabs my hips greedily and starts thrusting again. The intensity of it has my body tensing in all the best ways. Sitting back up, he slaps my thigh again, and I feel myself finally opening up for him. He runs a soothing hand over the stinging skin, rewarding me.

"Yes, Sunny. Just like that. That's my girl." He leans his head back with a hiss.

My back arches as I take him in, the moans escaping me are unlike any I've heard come out of my mouth before. I feel him everywhere, all over my body, inside me, and dowsing my heart.

Our bodies move in congruence, communicating in a way I've never even known existed. This moment says all the things we'd been holding back for the last few months. It's written in the air between us, filling our lungs and traced across our skin with exploring hands. It's said between heavy breaths and moans.

He's devastating as I watch the muscles, scars and emerald eyes make me his. My body submits to his because my trust now belongs to him.

Cradling the back of my neck, he pulls me up to sit in his lap, straddling him. Instinctively I wrap my arms around his neck, his arms curling around my waist to keep us close.

"Show me that fire, baby. Show me how you ignite. How you burn for me," he whispers against my skin.

I tilt my head back, feeling that flame growing bigger in the base of my belly. There is no beginning and there is no end. *Just us*.

"*Sunny*. Look. At. *Me*." He grabs my face.

He kisses my jaw, down my neck and on my collarbone to my scar, whispering along my skin his *I love yous*. And I revel in what it feels like to be loved, even when broken by another person.

"*Sunny*," he growls. "*eyes on me*." He grabs the back of my neck, forcing me to look at him. "I love you," he whispers against my skin.

"I love you too." I lace my fingers in his hair.

"Say it again, Sunny. Say it again. Let me feel you fall in love with me. Let me feel you become mine," he whispers, tracing his thumb along my bottom lip.

"I love you, Tyler."

"Fuck," he breathes. Pressing our foreheads together, he continues to move inside me.

I catch fucking fire. It courses through my body as if fuel ran through my veins, lighting me up and making me burn from the inside out. I scream out, wondering if the flames have licked their way up my throat by the burn I feel with it.

My body seizes and submits to the orgasm burning through me. So long and the most fucking incredible experience. I see stars, filled and surrounded by the night sky. The space I saw in my dream becoming reality as the fiery orange and black night somehow appear around me, sending me off into it.

The ringing in my ears sends his voice as a whisper yet so far away as my nails dig into his skin. I feel him everywhere, all over me.

When I finally open my eyes, a smile is spread across his face as he bears witness to me unraveling before him. What he does to me. I'm still coming undone but he finally catches up to me. Every muscle in his body goes taut as his grip on me tightens.

"Fuck, Sunny, fuck!" he groans.

He falls down the abyss of night and day colliding, taking me down with him again. We are lost somewhere in it. Our moans and screams merely echoes around us as pleasure consumes us.

The flames that erupt inside me lick my skin and crawl through my veins, once again. He releases inside me, completely filling me up to the point he spills all over us.

That bond between us is raging an inferno of silk black night and fiery radiance as we both dive into the pleasure unfolding between us. Solidifying what has been a maybe for far too long.

He grips the back of my neck, keeping our sweaty foreheads together. Panting heavily, he brushes my hair from my face, those kryptonite eyes meeting mine.

And finally, *finally*, all these feelings, everything over these last few weeks, it all makes sense.

He hasn't even removed himself from inside me when I feel him already growing hard again. I haven't even had a chance to come down from this round, to calm the fire that's still coursing through my body as my heart continues to pump it through me.

"*Again*," he growls.

So we do it all over again.

CHAPTER SIXTY-FOUR

TYLER

Laying on my back, with Sunny across my chest, my eyes close as I feel her soft fingers trace the features of my face. I toy with her wild hair, curling a strand on my finger. Both our bare chests press against one another, our breathing rhythmic with our calmed heartbeats.

It honestly feels unreal, making me wonder if I'm dreaming. The way her fingers feel on my skin tells me otherwise. *I love your fingers, Sunny.*

I take them and press each one to my lips, savoring this moment, this woman, this fucking feeling. My reality now surpasses my dreams. I did what I needed to do in order for us to be able to be together.

It is worth it for you, Sunny.

I'll continue what I need to do in order to keep her safe and happy. *To keep us.* I risked the repercussions for a maybe. A possibility.

This is my life now. Sunny everything, everywhere, all the time.

I love her. *I love you, Sunny.* I love her so fucking much. *So, so much.* The time I'd said it before was a desperate admission. This time, though, it's different. *She says it back.*

If anything feels like poetry, it's those words rolling off her lips. I want to kiss them to take it all in.

"*I love you, Tyler,*" she says in my ear as she traces my face, memorizing it.

She begins tracing my lips, gently pressing a kiss to the side of my mouth where my scar is. I crack an eye open and see a crooked smile upon her lips, her forearms braced on my chest, her sunshine hair in disarray from the night. Never had I thought someone would love my scars.

"Say it again, baby," I whisper, lacing my fingers through her hair, showing off that face I've memorized since the moment I saw it. Blonde curls and waves, blue-green irises, and seventeen freckles that cascade across her nose and cheeks in a constellation—just for me.

"I love you, Tyler."

"Fuck," I whisper, trembling at her words and touch, unable to explain the way it makes me feel.

I tighten my grip in her hair, forcing her lips to mine and deepen our kiss. There's a need to absorb those words she lets roll off that sweet tongue. It's like candy, and I'm a sucker for it.

She gives a ragged moan under my urgency, surely surprised for a third go around between us.

I roll us over so she's under the weight of my body, pinning her to the bed so she has nothing to do but take what I'm going to give her.

"What am I, Sunny? Tell me what I fucking am to you," I growl, pulling her head back where I see her pink lips now swollen from my own.

"Mine," Her breath catches, and I can feel her breathing pick up as she feels my hard dick press against her belly.

"That's my girl. And what are you?" I ask.

"Yours," she breathes as those big blue-green eyes search my face.

"Good girl. Do you know what happens to good girls?" I say, using my fingers lacing her hair to tilt her head, allowing access to her scar. "They get rewarded," I whisper against her skin.

I can feel the slow roll of her throat under my touch as her thighs try to clench together to relieve the ache that I know is there.

I brand my silent words against her skin with each press of my lips. *I love you. I love you. I love you.* And no part of her will go without that reminder. I will erase him from her body. I will love all the parts he broke until they are whole.

Sitting up on my knees between her legs, I run a hand along the plane of her stomach, admiring the beautiful body beneath me. She trembles under my touch and bites her bottom lip, trying to hide her need.

"Oh, Sunny," I whisper. "Baby, your body is begging, pleading to be fucked by me." My hand cups a breast, letting my thumb roll the taut pink nipple begging for my tongue.

"Tyler," She breathes my name.

"What did you do, baby? All those nights you denied yourself of me, what did you do to satisfy that craving?" I continue to play with her.

She swallows hard and clenches the sheets in her fists. I widen my legs, making hers spread more where I can see my girl is desperate for me already. I bite back my smile.

"I– " she starts but sucks in a breath when my other hand pushes my fingers in her. *Fuck.* I groan when I feel she's still wet with me. My mouth is watering, desperate to taste us.

"Yes?" I ask, tilting my head, waiting for her answer.

Her nose flares, and my dick is so fucking hard it hurts. She's everything to me, but I'm going to savor her, play with her, make her need me the way I need her. Remind her that if she leaves, no one, not even herself, can satisfy her the way I do.

"Tell me, Sunny," I demand as I circle a thumb over her clit. She lets out a low moan, then bites her lip again.

"I would take care of myself," she admits.

Goddamn. The idea of that pisses me off and turns me on all at once because I'm a possessive prick, wanting to be the only reason for her pleasure. But also *fuck*, knowing she got herself off, because of a deep desire for me, has me reaching a whole new level of feral.

"And did it make you feel better? Did it satisfy you the way I do?" I ask, already knowing the answer.

I pump my finger in her, curving it along the spot that makes her toes curl and my name roll off those pink lips.

She moans, tilting her head as her back arches with it. Smiling, I watch as she slowly unravels beneath me. My little prey is trying to get away from my grasp.

"Tell me, baby," I continue my fingers inside her.

"No," she whimpers.

"Mmmm," I hum. "Good, because I will be the only one to touch you, Little Fire. If I find out anyone else, even you, touches you, then you will be punished." I smile, seeing her dark brows crease together and her breathing pick up.

She just stares at me, heated and so fucking fiery.

Removing my fingers from her, I trace them along her bottom lip. "Taste how good we are together, baby. Taste why I'd do anything to keep us."

She does as she's told, licking her bottom lip where we both glisten. I suck my fingers clean, groaning at taste of her. She watches me, and I love and hate the fact she knows the power she has over me. I want her to abuse it, I want her to know she can bring me to my goddamn knees with one glance of those lethal eyes.

I throw each leg over my shoulder and dive between her thighs, licking my greedy tongue along her. Her hips rock against my face, fucking and riding my mouth like a good fucking needy girl, making me smile against her.

Her moans fill the room just as the lightning and thunder from the incoming storm do. She rides my face the way she rides my cock, chasing her release, using me in all the best ways.

Once she becomes undone in a symphony of moans and gasps, I'm wrapping my arms around her waist, bringing her flush to my body, and rolling us so she's on top of me.

Placing my hands on her hips, I guide her onto my aching dick, slowly, making us both groan and tremble at the union. Her nails dig into my chest while her head rolls back, giving me a view of her on top of me as lightning cracks the sky. Her breasts bounce as she slowly rides me, covering us in her arousal and my cum as she moves.

Gripping her hips, I meet her thrusts with my own, bucking into her to get deeper. A groan leaves me when I see I am so far into her that I can't tell where I end and she begins.

"Look at me, baby. Eyes on me," I tell her, running my hands up her waist and to her jaw.

Pleasure and lust sit heavy in her eyes, making my heart pummel knowing I'm responsible for that desire and heat.

I can feel her already tightening around me, chasing that release firing inside her. Then she catches flame. She ignites in a way that has her body trembling and curling into itself.

Holding her up by her jaw with one hand, I grip her hip with the other to keep our rhythm, to keep her in this moment where we become one. I'm chasing right after her, my balls tightening and the pleasure rattling at the base of my spine, traveling up and throughout my body as I release myself inside her.

Lightning flashes through the apartment as I fill her, giving me a full view of what we do to one another. Blackness and fire fill my vision, and pleasure consumes me the way she does. She's fucking burning for me and I love it.

I've spent months leading us up to these moments I've only

ever imagined, and it's finally fucking here. I finally have my girl.

Spilling into her, I empty myself entirely, giving everything I have to her. I always have, and I always will.

I let go of my grip on her, letting her fall to my chest, where her head nestles in the crook of my neck. Bringing my nose and lips to her hair, I take in her coconut and vanilla scent.

We both try our best to calm our labored breaths, our hearts and breathing falling in sync, the sheen of sweat prevalent on our skin. I caress her back, tracing fingers along her spine, admiring her and the fact this is real.

We haven't even gotten out of bed. The past few hours have been spent with me inside her or curled together in a tangle of limbs as we watched the storm.

I own her now just as much as she owns me, if my fucking cum spilling out of her isn't her reminder enough. She assured me that she's protected with an IUD and that pregnancy isn't possible. Either way, I don't care, we'd cross whatever bridge that came our way.

I trace her stomach, imagining it filled with my baby, growing day by day with a part of her and a part of me. I'd be lying if I said the idea of her with a pregnant belly, with my child, didn't turn me the fuck on.

I would do it with you, Sunny.

Lifting her head up, she looks at me with hazy eyes and a drunken smile. She continues to trace my face, my lips, the bridge of my nose, the arches of my eyebrows. *Memorize me, Sunny.*

I finally see my future and it's with her. I'll do anything to make that a possibility for us.

Before I know it, she's asleep across my chest. Despite my weary eyes, I don't want to sleep. *Not yet.* I want to continue living in this moment, watching her, tracing her face as her eyes flutter during a dream.

I lay on my back with an arm behind my head and my girl on my chest while I look up at the glow-in-the-dark stars on her ceiling I bought for her months ago. I smile at the memory of putting them up with her, talking for hours about everything and anything.

As a child, I had glow-in-the-dark stars in my bedroom, and I continued that trend as an adult. Every night when I was going to bed, I'd pick a star and wish on it, since I couldn't see many in the city.

A smile rises to my lips, because one of my wishes has finally come true. She's right here, curled into me sleeping soundly.

With a snore too loud to belong to her, she rolls over, pressing her face into the pillow. The loss of her is brutal. I reach for her, needing contact, her skin on my skin. I bite my fist, suppressing a laugh at the sounds coming from her.

Watching her sleep, I continue tracing her face and her back. A faint little smile whispers on her lips in response. *That's my girl.* She even recognizes my touch in her dreams.

"Stay with me," I whisper. I press my lips to her forehead and pull the blanket higher onto her so she won't get cold.

I reach over to get my phone because I have to tie up some loose ends. Once I finish up my typing, I place it on her night stand and roll over, curling an arm around her and pulling her back to my chest.

"Rest easy, baby. This is only the beginning." I kiss her lips.

Closing my eyes, I let sleep take me away.

CHAPTER SIXTY-FIVE

SUNNY

The morning sun peers through the curtains that cover my ceiling to floor windows in my apartment. It's warmth kissing my skin, urging me to open my eyes. The first thing I realize is the loss of Tyler from my bed. The second is that he is standing in my kitchen, in his boxers, cooking.

He is making me breakfast.

He turns around, hearing my rustling. As he approaches, my heart races faster. He leans against one of the pillars in my studio and crosses his arms over his chest with a wide grin. He looks more rested, more at peace than I've ever seen him.

I smile. *I did that.*

I stretch my sore body with a yawn. "Good morning."

"Good morning." He looks at me, and something is different in his eyes now. *Don't look at me like that, Tyler. I'll love you more than I already do.* "You know…" He makes his way to my bed, "I had big plans to wake you up in my own ways."

"And what ways might those be?"

He wraps an arm around my waist, pulling me to him as he kisses my nose and lips with a doting admiration I never thought could exist.

Tell me everything.

"How about I just show you?"

Show me everything.

"Won't the food and coffee go cold?" I taunt him, giving him small kisses.

He slowly lowers himself between my thighs and looks up at me from under his brows. "That's okay, it's shitty coffee anyways."

TYLER

After spending the entire morning in bed, making up for lost time, I stand in her kitchen again, remaking food for us. She sits on her counter, wearing my t-shirt, sporting my marks from the night and morning prior.

If this is life with you, I want it all.

Don't get me wrong, I'm a realistic man. I know life won't always look like this every single moment, but that doesn't matter because I want all the moments outside of this with her, too.

While the look on her face and ease in her body tells me she's finally accepted this, I'm not sure where that head of hers is at. I hand her a fresh cup of coffee, and twirl a curl over my finger.

"How's the shitty coffee?"

"You say this coffee is shitty but it's doing the job." She smiles.

"It does get the job done." I smile and go back to cooking breakfast.

I'm still on a high from last night and this morning, but the ever present loom of her leaving is still a dark space in the back of my mind. I'd made it clear once this line was crossed, I couldn't go back, and I meant it.

"We do need to talk about this, Tyler," she says, pulling me from my thoughts.

I don't want to talk about it. But instead I say, "I know."

"Maybe…maybe we just take it day by day?" She gnaws on her lips while she white knuckles the coffee mug.

Yes. I can do day by day. We need day by day.

The dreaded storm of this conversation breaks between the heavy clouds, giving a glimpse of some sunlight. Of some way that this story doesn't have a definitive end. Sunny has tried to write our book with permanent ink, but I'd rip the pages out if it meant it could be changed.

"I can do that."

She smiles back at me. "Good."

Grabbing her chin gently, I make her eyes meet mine. "One day at a time." I place a soft kiss on her coffee lips.

She grips the back of my neck, pulling me in closer. As difficult as it is, I pull away, which elicits a pouty lip at me. I laugh, because this girl has spent weeks denying this undeniable pull between us to now run right into it.

"You need to eat. Build your strength for our afternoon activities." I spoon eggs and sausage on a plate.

"What kind of activities?"

"Guess you'll have to find out."

"Can't wait." She grabs the plate, padding to the little table I threw her on last night. I plan to do it again today.

I grab her wrist, spinning her around, so I can get a perfect view of her in my t-shirt. She laughs as I twirl her around, drinking her up, and then ushering her back towards the table.

God, this woman is going to be the destruction of me.

I don't care. Destroy me, Sunny.

CHAPTER SIXTY-SIX

TYLER

It's been a long day with an early start and a late ending of dinner with my parents. Factor in all the turn and burn business trips I've been making recently, I feel it all catching up to me. I'm exhausted, but knowing Sunny will be waiting for me at home makes the day that much easier.

I get to come home to you.

Browsing Leslie's floral shop, I get to pick out three bouquets instead of two because I'm going to bring one home to Sunny, too.

I get the usual arrangement for my mother, purple flowers for Sam and sunflowers for Sunny because those are her favorite.

Sam walks around the flower shop, observing the numerous colors and types, holding her own bouquet. "Y'all are disgustingly cute." She eyes the second bouquet of flowers in my hand.

I just smile at her comment.

"At least one of us has someone to come home to after a shit dinner with shit parents," she comments.

It's a hard thing to not worry about my sister. Her recklessness is the reason I'll have grey hair next year, but seeing her anything outside of that adds another reason to worry. Cole was a goal, an end game for her. Now that opinion isn't available, I fear she may not have sight of anything else.

"What about Anthony? Have you considered that?" I ask, opening her car door.

Her eyes flick to me, hesitation clearly in them. I lean on the door frame, waiting for a response.

"I'd be lying if I said I didn't," she finally admits.

Smiling, I nod then shut the door and get myself situated in the driver's seat. "Explain."

"Well, it's Anthony. He's sweet, he's kind, he's caring, and he knows me more than most people do. We wouldn't have to go through that awkward stage, I'd hope. He's handsome and talented and all the things a woman would want."

"Anthony is all those things, no doubt."

"But he's also Anthony. One of my best friends, my twin pillar, he matches my energy. We all grew up in diapers together. He's my best friend."

You fight too much Sam.

"You know." I lean an elbow on the car door and start the drive out of the city. "Sunny and I didn't know one another for very long. So, I can't say I relate to that. However, she and I considered ourselves best friends before, well, whatever it is we are."

We still haven't had that talk yet. The time is ticking as I still wait for unanswered questions. I just need more time that I fear I won't get.

"You guys are different, though. You two were made for one another. Soulmates."

We are made for one another.

"How do you know you and Anthony aren't?"

"How did you know you and Sunny are?"

I contemplate on how to explain something that feels so unexplainable. It's something I simply cannot put words to for her to understand its depth.

"It's…" I start, but shake my head because the words die on my tongue. "It's this undeniable, indescribable pull between us. As if there'd been some invisible string tying her to me."

Sam's eyes widen, and she blinks dramatically. "What the hell happened to my brother? Who is this mushy mess of a man now? Hopeless romantic?"

"I told you it's crazy. But in my defense, Cole feels the same way too, about Macey. It was nice to know I wasn't crazy," I laugh.

"It's not crazy, Tyler. It's beautiful. You're so lucky to experience such a thing. You're the epitome of finding your soulmate." She looks down at her flowers.

"You'll find yours too, Sam."

"What are you going to do, Tyler? What are you guys going to do when she leaves? How are you going to just do it?"

It'll destroy me, Sam. I'm working on it.

"We're taking it one day at a time."

"And what happens when those days end?"

"I'm not sure, honestly." I've been doing everything to make sure that doesn't happen.

"I'm surprised you haven't talked to Sunny about it," I say.

"I didn't want to put a damper on her parade. Plus, wouldn't it be weird to talk to my best friend like, what are your intentions with my brother?" Sam laughs.

"What are you going to do? When she leaves?"

Sunny is obviously my soulmate, but she's also my sister's best friend.

"That day is going to fucking suck. She's one of us now. She's my best friend. I'm hoping she'll find her way back to us. I get it, she needs to do what's best for herself."

I take in a deep breath, but my grip on the steering wheel tightens regardless.

"I wish we could fucking catch Ryan. I don't understand how

he hasn't been found," Sam says. "What if we got the lawyers involved? What if we ask for their help?"

"I've already tried to ask her that. She doesn't want us to have anything intervening with the detectives. She wants the justice system to do it their way."

"I just don't understand." She shakes her head.

The thirty minute drive to our parents house feels too short as I pull into the driveway. I just need to get through this, then I can go back home to my little fire.

I get to go home to Sunny.

"Ready?" I ask as I open Sam's car door.

"Never."

Still, we both go inside.

We always go inside.

CHAPTER SIXTY-SEVEN

SUNNY

As I step outside into the cold, I see the car Tyler had sent to pick me up idling in the front.

He sent a car.

Instead of approaching it, I turn the other way and hit the street to walk. The driver may assume I got held up at work, which isn't unusual as a nurse. So I hope it grants me time before I can text Tyler that I'm safely home before suspicions are raised.

Leftover snow crunches under my shoes as I walk up the stairs to his townhome entrance. Before I can open the door, my phone buzzes in my pocket. My brows crease at the unfamiliar number, and I understand why whoever had this one before doesn't anymore. Because the amount of spam calls is absurd.

I slide the screen to answer. "Fuck off and stop calling this number."

"Sunny?" he breathes.

Sheer panic inches over me as I hear the familiar voice. The voice I'll never forget. The one that made a promise that loomed like a rainy storm over my head.

Ryan's voice.

I stop breathing. I *can't* breathe. I try to suck air in, but nothing will fill my lungs. I'm frozen with fear, the phone still against my ear as he speaks again and all my nightmares start coming true all at once with the baritone of his voice.

"Sunny, please. *Please* let me talk to you. Tell me where you are so I can apologize to you in person. Sunny *please*, I'm so sorry. We can work through this."

Fucking think Sunny. Think.

I can't. I'm frozen still, as if the cold winter air finally got the best of me, frosting my bones over, making me immovable.

Hearing my heartbeat in my ears, I feel the blood rushing through my body. My vision starts to go black. Then the flood comes rushing over me, snapping me out of the frozen trance and back into this reality.

How could I have been so careless? So reckless? How did he get my number? Does he know where I am? What if he traces this call?

Feeling the air finally fill into my lungs, I start hyperventilating, sucking in the oxygen my body forgot to give me. I have flashbacks to the night I left, reminding me of all the reasons why I started running in the first place.

I tried Ryan. I tried to help you. To fix you. But you broke me instead.

Rather than hanging up the damn phone, my mind takes me back to the darkness that was that night.

I walked into the door of our apartment to him sitting on the couch, his hands together and knee bouncing. He wouldn't look at me. Not even a *hi* as I walked inside. When before it used to be forehead kisses, bear hugs and dinner cooking so it'd be fresh for me.

He's upset.

"Hey, honey. You got my text right? The night shift nurse didn't show up, so I stayed a little later until they got a cover for the patients." I kicked my shoes off and placed my backpack down on the ground.

I remember every little detail.

I sent him a text, but he never responded, despite the fact it was read. The emergency department was swamped, and they needed help. I was waiting for the nine pm shift to come in for coverage over my patients.

I was just doing my job, Ryan.

He sat on the couch, his fingers drumming, which was always a telltale sign of his anger, and the muscle in his jaw ticking as he ground his teeth together. His brown hair falling in his brown eyes that flicked to me and I saw nothing but anger in them. A look I'd become all too familiar with.

I knew it was going to be a bad night, I just didn't realize it'd be *that* kind of a bad night.

I didn't want to deal with this, not after the fifteen hour day I'd just had. *Not tonight, Ryan.*

"Where were you really?" he ground out.

"What do you mean? I was at work."

After a few years, Ryan had started to become possessive. I'd noticed during nursing school, when he'd question my hours away from home or why I needed to go to the library to study and couldn't do it at home. When I became a nurse, it became worse.

It became easy for Ryan to obsess over a small comment I'd make that I didn't think twice about. My whereabouts always at the forefront of his mind.

"Did you eat? Maybe we can order a pizza?" I tried to change the subject, noting there was no food prepared for dinner as I walked over to him.

I didn't take my stethoscope off.

I didn't take it off.

"No, I didn't eat because you didn't respond to me. Now don't fucking lie to me." He stood up.

I winced at his aggression and he *scoffed* at my reaction. As if, he'd never been close to hitting me before. It was always so close but never actually me. It's how I justified staying with him.

The wall behind my head.

The car dashboard in front of me.

The grip on me leaving bruises, without *actually* hitting me.

But never actually hit me.

Until that night.

"Ryan, I'm not lying to you. I was at work. Where else would I be?" I pleaded. "You have my location."

Something switched in his brown eyes. Something I'd never seen before, and could never unsee again.

"Don't lie to me!" He grabbed my stethoscope with both hands, yanking me towards him.

I reached my hands out, a useless shield between us.

"What? You think I'm going to hurt you?" he laughed.

Don't mock me, Ryan.

"They just needed me. The ED was swamped."

You're scaring me, Ryan.

"Your job isn't that important, Sunny. You work in a small-town hospital. I needed you here tonight! A wife to her husband!"

Originally, Ryan was supportive of my career, but when his parents died and their business was handed to him, he felt like it was my job as a wife to stay home while he made the money. He wanted a traditional wife, but he should've known after years together, I'm anything but traditional. If I'm being honest, I don't think he thought I'd actually follow through with my schooling.

My job is important too, Ryan.

He shoved me off, making me stumble on my feet.

"I hate when you fucking say that Ryan! My job is just as important. Just because I don't make as much as you do doesn't mean it's any less important than yours!" I fought back.

"Why is it so crazy to you for me to just want a partner who will be home? To cook, to clean, to be home when I'm home! You're *my wife*, act like it."

"Okay, you're just saying this because you're hungry and upset." I headed straight for the door, trying to leave so I could cool down and let him get out of this mood before anything else was said that shouldn't be.

Before I could even know what he'd do next, his hands were around my stethoscope and slamming me against the wall.

He started to *choke* me with it.

I could feel my body begging for the oxygen he now restricted. My hands uselessly clawed at him, but he didn't even flinch.

"Ryan!" I wheezed.

This couldn't be happening. It couldn't be fucking happening.

I am now a statistic.

He finally let loose but his anger didn't relent. I was coughing and trying to get my bearings and fell to the ground, crawling towards the door, but I couldn't escape.

"Do you see how crazy you make me?" he yelled and grabbed me, throwing me on the floor.

"Ryan please, we just need to talk about this!" I started to get up, but he kicked me, sending shocks of pain through my ribs, and I fell back down, unable to get the air he'd stolen.

With a cough, blood splattered on the floor and all over me, hanging from my mouth with drool as I tried to suck in air.

Through the haze of black dots taking over my vision, he sank onto his knees and grabbed my hips, pulling me under him. With his knees, he pinned my thighs down. Using one hand, he secured both of mine above my head.

I tried. I tried to put up a fight, but it was pathetic. I was disoriented and weak from the lack of oxygen and a fifteen hour day on my feet.

"I'm going to fucking show you who you belong to," he seethed as he started to undo the belt on his jeans.

The realization dawned on me.

"Ryan, no! Stop, stop, stop, stop!" I pleaded underneath his weight.

Tears cascaded down my face, sobs clawed at my throat as I tried to move anywhere that wasn't underneath him. But his grip was unforgiving, despite *his wife* begging him to stop.

He started pulling my scrub pants down, untying the draw string and ripping them down my hips, exposing me to his anger and intrusion.

His hand was bruising my wrists, fighting against my fight. Refusing to listen to my pleas and cries. They meant nothing to him. *I* meant nothing to him.

I was screaming, but it was like I wasn't even saying anything at all.

"No! Please, Ryan. *Please*," I cried.

The look in his eyes was terrifying. It was vengeance for something I had never even done.

He was so far gone. He could never come back from this. *We could never come back from this.*

Never in my life had I cried the way I did that night. *I was unrecognizable.*

I almost gave up. I almost let him take over my body. Violate it in a way no person should experience. Small cries escaped my mouth as he started to lean over me and pulled my underwear down next.

I tried to clench my thighs together so that he couldn't force himself in me, but he only dug his knees into my thighs harder, making me scream louder.

"You will learn your goddamn lesson about fucking around," He seethed. "I'm going to fuck you so hard no man will ever want you. You will be ruined by me, Sunny. You'll be so ruined that no one will ever love you or want you."

And all in one moment, everything I was desecrated.

A guttural scream clawed up my throat as he simultaneously ripped through my body. How would I ever recover from this? *I wouldn't.* This wound would fester until it killed me.

That's when I summed up any energy I had left, and I knocked my head straight into his. His nose cracked and his head flew back. Blood from his nose splattered my face and he released my hands. I kicked him in the chest, sending him falling back.

I immediately rolled off my back and started pulling my pants back up, crawling away from underneath him.

Ruthless fingers grabbed my hair, picking me off the ground and slamming me against a wall. The thud of my own head smacking the wall was sickening and dizzying. When he finally faced me, his eyes were black with rage.

I don't recognize you.

The force of the blow had me stepping in and out of consciousness. In the times I was aware, I'd blink through the blood that coated my face to try and understand my surroundings.

"You make me so angry, Sunny. You shouldn't lie to me. I love you too much. Tell me the truth." He was shaking me now, awakening me from the brief relief of him.

It'd never been like this. There was no amount of reminiscing on the good times to cure this bad one. This bad one outweighed all the good ones.

We can't come back from this, Ryan. We never will.

I finally blinked away the blackness and blood. His incessant shaking of my body and screaming made it hard to think, but still, the words filtered through in a silent cry. *Get out.*

It was when he started to pull my pants down again, taking advantage of my unconscious state, that the words screamed through the bloody haze.

GET. OUT.

Summing up whatever energy I had left, I swung my fist, clocking him right in the temple and knocking him out. In his fall, he took me down with him. Unwillingly, my body landed on his and instinct had me scrambling of him to see he was unconscious.

A moment for me to get my composure, even with the blood covered eyes and shaking arms. The words whispered desperately in my mind.

Get out, get out, get out.

I ran to our bedroom, grabbed a backpack, and filled it with whatever clothes I could fit in it.

Get out. Get out. Get out.

A moan from the living room had my neck snapping towards that direction, seeing his body twitch. I licked my cracked lips and used shaking hands to swipe *Looking For Alaska* on my nightstand.

Nausea rolled through my stomach as I ran from our bedroom to our living room where he started to stir, murmuring incoherent things. "*Sunny,*" he groaned.

I hadn't removed my eyes from him as I frantically packed. When he reached a shaking arm out for me, doubt filled my mind even as I jumped over his body towards the door. The blood spilling across the floor from a wound on his head told me that in his fall, he hit the corner of our TV stand.

I wished I could say I didn't think twice before opening the door and leaving, but that'd be a lie. Seeing his vulnerable body on the ground as he called my name was something that had me thinking twice.

I *did* think twice and maybe even three times.

It was at that moment a hatred for myself grew fast and deep. I hated myself for thinking twice, three times. I hated myself for pausing on such precious seconds to my safety. Even if for only three seconds at the door. It was the whispers that snapped me out of it.

Get out. Get out. Get out.

Freedom had a short window of opportunity, and here I was, questioning it.

"If you leave, I'm going to fucking find you Sunny. I promise I'll fucking find you," he groaned, rolling on the floor.

Finally, my sanity took over and I opened the door, slamming it shut behind me. Sobs escape my mouth. Sobs that didn't belong to me, yet somehow still came from me.

I don't recognize myself.

My shaking hands dialed 9-1-1 and I got in my truck, driving straight to my parents, whom I called immediately after.

I didn't even remember how I got to their place. All I remember is pulling into their driveway to see both waiting for me on the porch along with the police.

I remember running to them, still bloodied from Ryan and my father running to me, meeting me halfway in the long driveway before I became a crumpling, sobbing mess that collapsed in his arms. I left too much of myself in that apartment, that I barely had anything left in me to hold myself up.

The nausea that'd made a prior appearance came back violently, forcing me to throw up what little food I had in my system. As if I was trying to purge the tarnished and ruined feeling that became my very marrow.

The look on their faces told me everything I needed to know about the damage he had done to me.

All in one night, my soul, my body, my very being was desecrated by the one person who was supposed to love it.

The girl I used to be died that day. I buried her so deeply in the ground, praying no one would ever find out who she was and how she let a man ruin her from the inside out.

As the memory fades, I bring my fingers to the scar on my neck. The brand of his abuse forever embedded into my skin. He was my best friend, and that was the worst part.

"Sunny?" The voice says again.

His voice.

"I'm sorry but you have the wrong number. Please stop calling." I hang up immediately.

The same sobs from that night try to escape me again, clawing up my throat in a desperate attempt to express the pain I thought had started to dull.

I shoot a text to Tyler, but then my rage takes over. Ragged breaths do no justice to cool and calm the fire that floods my veins.

How could I let this happen?

My shaking hands use all force possible as I slam my phone on the ground. I watch the screen go black as it dies, much like how a part of my soul does, too.

He's going to find me.

Which is the whole reason I have an escape plan in case this ever happens.

I need to leave.

Now.

CHAPTER SIXTY-EIGHT

TYLER

Glancing at my watch, I see that it's already seven thirty, which means we'd eat dinner soon. Which means I'm another step closer to going home to Sunny. I smile at the idea of her being there, waiting for me.

I get to go home to Sunny.

Sam's leg bounces as our father talks about the campaign coming up. She clutches her glass like she always does. It makes me wonder if painting gives her the same outlet sparring gives me.

I'm sorry, Sam. I tried to protect you.

He won't shut up about the campaign, because work apparently is the only thing that brings value to his life.

I don't know the details of what happened after the night I left Matthew in the hotel room. And quite frankly I don't care. All I know is no one has bothered me about it, and that's all that matters.

"Everyone is going to be there. It's going to be so spectacular. We're going to feel like celebrities, honestly," My mother chimes in as her eyes light up at the idea.

I try not to roll my eyes. *Celebrities.*

"You two need to be on your best behavior." Mitchell points a finger at us as if we're eight years old again.

Sam rolls her eyes and a smile slowly spreads across my face. Maybe we *are* still eight years old.

My phone buzzes in my pocket, but my reach is interrupted.

"Our agreement was no phones, remember?" Diane eyes me.

"Woman please, he's the heir to our fortune and company, and we have a huge event. It could be work." Mitchell waives a hand.

I stare blankly at them for a moment and then pull my phone out, seeing a text from Sunny waiting for me.

"Well by the looks of that smile, I don't think it's work," Diane scoffs into her drink.

It's that moment I realize I do have a too wide grin pulling my lips. They both still aren't happy about me breaking Shelby's heart a second time, especially my mother.

Moving my eyes back to the screen, my smile quickly fades.

He got my number.

My body tenses as I read the words over and over, refusing for it to be real. *How did I miss this?*

"Tyler? What is it? Is everyone okay?" Sam asks.

"I need to go." I stand up.

"What's the matter, boy?" Mitchell grunts.

"Tyler, you're scaring me," Sam says, standing with me.

"He got her number," I respond, trying to call Sunny. My call won't go through, making the panic rise in my chest.

Sam's eyes turn wide as she grabs her purse, ready to leave.

"You guys!" Diane says sternly. It's honestly the most assertive I've ever seen my mother. "What is going on?"

"Our friend Sunny needs us." Sam grabs her coat out of the closet.

"Sunny? Are you kidding me?" Mitchell spits out.

"Sunny, the girl you brought to our events? Why does that concern you, Tyler?" Diane asks

"Oh, for the love of god, Tyler." Mitchell rolls his eyes, standing up. "Are you fucking her?"

Still having the phone pressed to my ear, Sam hands me my coat, but the call won't go through. I try again. Fucking nothing.

"Fuck," I mutter. "That doesn't concern you," I snap at Mitchell.

"Tyler!" Mitchell yells after me. "We have talked about this how many damn times! What if you get her pregnant? You can't have a bastard child."

I see my mother wince at his aggression but I don't have fucking time for this.

"You have a reputation to hold!" Mitchell yells.

I bring my phone to ear, trying Cole. "Fuck your reputation," I seethe.

Then I slam the door shut behind me.

By the time we make it to my place, I notice none of the lights are on in the house. Which probably means Sunny isn't here. I already called Cole and Anthony, and they're on their way.

Ryan could fucking be here.

"Stay in the truck," I order Sam.

Words are lost on her tongue when she stares at me wide eyed as I pull a gun from the glove box. "What the fuck, Tyler!"

I rack the glock, do a chamber check and then meet her eyes as I shove the extra magazine in my pocket, right next to my knife.

I grip the back of her neck to make her look at me. "I said stay in the fucking truck, Sam."

Running up to the entrance of my home, I find Sunny's cell

phone smashed on the ground. A quick glance around gives me nothing. No Sunny. No Ryan. I take the phone and pocket it.

My mind runs through a series of different possibilities. Panic makes it impossible to think. When headlights break through the dark night, I see Cole and Anthony pull up and get out of the car. It's at this moment I didn't even think to check the cameras. Instinct had me driving here.

What if he has her? Is that why her phone is smashed? Because she fought him?

"Do not go in that house alone!" Cole yells, running up with a gun in his hands.

"What's the plan?" Anthony asks.

Find her. Is all that keeps echoing through my mind.

"Cole, you and I will clear my house, then hers. Then we'll scour the fucking city. Anthony, call every airport, every airline, every fucking hospital to make sure she isn't there. He could be here and have her." The reality dawns on me.

Before, it was Sunny everything, everywhere, all the time. And now it's fucking nothing. She's nowhere. It's fucking dark.

I hear Sam running behind me. "Sam get back in the fucking truck."

"I can go to Martha's?" she breathes, shivering from the cold.

She couldn't have left. She wouldn't do that. Right?

"Tyler, she wouldn't at least leave without a goodbye," Sam assures.

As much as I want to give Sunny the benefit of the doubt, I know it isn't true. Ryan makes her do out of character things. She knows that not only will it compromise her own safety, but all of our friends too. That's why she left her own home to begin with, not just to protect herself, but her family, too. Because at least if Ryan was trailing her, she could lead him away from them. From us.

"Okay, let's get going. Time is of the essence. Anthony take

Sam home. Then call every single place you can think of," I order.

"I'm not going home when she is out there!" she yells as Anthony grabs her by the bicep trying to pull her away.

We were so close, Sunny. We were so close.

Cole looks at me. "You ready?"

It wouldn't be the first time we've had to do this. It won't be our last.

"I'm ready," I say as I unlock the door.

CHAPTER SIXTY-NINE

SUNNY

I BURST THROUGH MY APARTMENT DOOR, FRANTICALLY TRYING TO figure out where to even start. Why did I buy so much shit if I knew I was leaving?

I go to my room and grab a duffle bag I pre-packed sitting in my closet. It has a few outfits, hygienics, all my money and everything I need for my escape.

I just never thought I'd actually have to use it.

I peel my scrubs off and throw them on the floor and put on sweatpants and a big hoodie, hoping it'll cover my face enough so no one can recognize me. I throw a beanie on too and tuck my hair into it.

How could I have been so careless? Did I trust the words of the detectives too much?

Ryan's absence meant a possibility of a future. That if he hadn't shown up by this point, he probably never would. Even though they still have no idea where he is, they said it was enough to move forward until something arose.

But he got my number.

He called me.

Could he trace my number here? I smashed my phone. Would that help prevent him from tracing it?

Grabbing all my things, I rush to the window, knowing the fire escape is my best plan because what if he is outside my door?

I look around this apartment that has been home for the last five months, a place of peace I thought I'd never get. Swallowing hard, I give my mental goodbye and slam the window shut.

CHAPTER SEVENTY

TYLER

Once my home is cleared and secured, Cole and I jump into my truck to take on Sunny's apartment. I was hopeful that maybe she was hiding somewhere, waiting for me to get there.

But she wasn't. Of course she wasn't. I should know better by this point.

My jaw flexes, the pain of my grinding teeth radiating through my temples as we drive to her apartment. My grip tightens on the wheel, a useless attempt at trying to contain my anxiety.

"We're going to find her." Cole looks at me.

I don't say anything because I feel like I'm going to fucking combust. If Ryan had been here, I would've known. *I would've fucking known.*

Cole checks the security footage on his phone. "It looks like she smashed her phone herself. Then she took off." He's still watching the tapes. "I don't see any points of which Ryan was here or anyone else."

Relief fills my chest. I'm not sure if Ryan has someone helping him or if he is a lot smarter than I give him credit for. I really can't credit a man on brains when he lays hands on a woman. But he's doing a pretty damn good job of laying low and flying under the radar.

I'm not sure of the extent of his capabilities. We'd be able to tell if my cameras were hacked, but I made it almost impossible for that to happen. Same with my alarm system and entry system. My home is a fortress only my family can access.

"Okay," I say, still gripping the steering wheel. "Check the cameras at her place."

When I installed her security system, that included cameras. To which I had access too. But of course she will never know that.

Only outside her door and windows where someone could access. Not inside her home. I won't invade her privacy like that, even though I really wanted to. Cole had to be my voice of reason for that decision. Now looking back, I wished I'd just done it.

It needed to be done. It just needed to fucking be done.

"On it." Cole pulls up the feed.

I don't peg Ryan to be able to hack into systems or even know I placed one. But we still have to clear her apartment before we assume anything.

"I don't see any point of entry except for her about a half hour ago. But she doesn't leave. So maybe she is still there," Cole says, watching the tapes. "Let me check the windows to be safe." But before he can, we're pulling up at her complex.

My heart beats frantically in my chest, but I already know she isn't here. I just do. Still, I run up the stairs and kick in the damn door, clearing her studio to see scrubs strewn across the floor.

She was here. And I barely missed her.

"Fuck," I groan, holstering the gun in my waistband.

Cole watches me. "I can start contacting car companies, taxis…" he starts.

"She was supposed to be dropped off by the car company."

"I'll have Anthony hack their system."

I blow out a frustrated breath and pinch the bridge of my nose. *Where the fuck is she?*

Cole watches more of the feed. "I can hack the street cameras to see where she went. Use facial recognition. She was wearing a hoodie when she left though. She went through the window to leave, I guess. Maybe she knew we had a camera at the door?"

My phone rings. "Sam?" I answer.

"She isn't at Betty's Beans, the studio or Martha's," she says over music and people.

"Sam, I told you to go home."

I know a man on a mission would do anything to anyone to find her. Because now I'm that man. But so is Ryan.

"You really think I'm just going to sit my ass at home while my best friend is missing?"

"Okay, well you have done your part now. So please, *go home*," I push.

"Yeah, yeah. Keep me posted. I love you."

"I love you too." Then I hang up.

"I'll start making some calls. I can try and hack the street cameras from my phone. See where she went. If she used a car service," Cole says, tapping away on his phone. "She climbed out the damn window down the fire escape."

I start pacing her apartment, trying to control all the panicked thoughts haunting my mind. It's barely been an hour and I'm fucking losing it.

"She always talks about the plan. What if she had an escape plan in case he made his appearance here?" I place my hands on my hips.

"So maybe the airports." He meets my stare.

Then my phone rings again. "It's Anthony." I answer. "Anything?"

"I found her."

"Bring her home." I hang up.

I pull her shattered phone out of my pocket and hand it to Cole.

"You know what to do."

CHAPTER SEVENTY-ONE
SUNNY

I sit at the gate, clutching my boarding pass, knee bouncing with each second that passes until boarding time.

I know it'll hurt them to not say goodbye. But it'll hurt them more if he finds me. Finds them.

If Ryan is anything, he's vengeful. And he'd hurt all the people around me first to taunt and torment me. To hurt me.

I have enough cash to purchase a new phone and spend some nights in a hotel. I've always wanted to go to Colorado, anyways. It was the earliest flight I could catch getting out of here.

Leaving them is just as hard as it was leaving my parents. But it's something that needs to be done, whether it's now or when my contract ends. I've been here too long.

People rush all around me, bustling to get to their flights. I pull my hood in tighter, scared to look anywhere and see Ryan's face.

Despite my efforts, there is a presence that demands my attention. A pull that forces me to look up and meet golden eyes and warm skin.

Someone familiar. Someone who feels like home.

Anthony.

He stands still in the motion of people. A pillar to the family that has somehow accepted me, regardless of my broken pieces that keep cutting them.

A small smile pulls his lips and he places his hands in his pockets with a shrug.

Tears sting my eyes, my pain a physical manifestation as my heart breaks all over again. Neither of us move. We are still among the chaos.

That's what they've all been to me.

I don't even think before I get up and run into his arms. He wraps them around me tightly as I bury my head in the chest of his button up.

"You've got a lot of people worried about you," he murmurs as he places his cheek atop my head.

A choked sob leaves my lips because tonight may not be the night, but it's coming no matter what. I have to leave. Tonight proved that.

"Come home, Sunny. Just come home. Finish out your contract. Just come home and we'll figure out the rest. Day by day, okay?" He squeezes me tighter.

"I don't know what to do," I admit.

"Just come home. That's all you can do. Come home and give yourself the next four weeks like you promised yourself, us, your work. Give yourself those four weeks to prepare for the next stop after here. But don't leave like this. Not like this, Sunny." He rubs his hand up and down my back.

My lip quivers trying to hold back the sobs.

I have a family here. A family who loves me so much they were scouring the city for me. A family who is begging for just a little more time with me. A family who doesn't want to say goodbye to me.

"Okay," I whisper. "Okay."

Approaching my apartment door, Anthony pauses, giving me a brief glance over his shoulder. "Do you need a minute?"

I contemplate. "I think I'm okay."

"Alright." He opens the door, moving aside to let me through.

I walk in to see Tyler sitting on my couch, elbows on knees and hands pressed together at his mouth. Those eyes flick up to me from under his brows, no emotion behind them.

Cole leans against the counter in my kitchen behind him, arms crossed over his chest, feet crossed over one another.

They don't move. They just watch.

I swallow down the thickness in my throat and blink back the stupid fucking tears that seem to not want to subside, no matter my efforts.

Tyler's words from months ago echo through my head. *They will protect you on instinct.*

Anthony places my duffle on the ground and presses a kiss to the top of my head. With a nod to Tyler, he exits the apartment.

Cole follows, giving Tyler a pat on the shoulder and a murmured, "She's safe."

With a muscled arm, he wraps it around my head and places a kiss in my curls and exits the apartment right behind Anthony with a click of the door.

Few words were even said. Yet somehow, they knew Tyler's command.

I shift on my feet, refusing to meet the piercing emeralds I know are focused on me. Nervously, I toy with the beanie in my hands but soon enough my eyes betray me, and I feel that undeniable pull lifting my gaze to Tyler's.

He stands to his full height, boots thudding against the wood floors as he makes his way to me. No words are said as he wraps his arms around me and presses my head to his chest.

"Tell me everything," he murmurs in my hair.

My body trembles as I fight another sob clawing up my throat. He leans down, gently cradling my face and wiping my tears with his thumbs.

I'm not okay, Tyler.

"I've been getting these spam calls but..." My voice catches. "it was him."

He doesn't say anything, he simply watches me while stroking his thumbs along my wet cheeks. The predator, analyzing every detail I'm giving him.

"He begged for me to tell him where I am, and I was too fucking stunned that I kept him on the phone for too long and he's probably going to be able to trace the call to the location." I back out of Tyler's embrace and place my hands on top of my head as my frantic cries escape me. My heart beats violently in my chest, making it thunder in my ears and amplifying my spiraling thoughts.

"Baby..." He reaches for me.

I can't stop it. My brakes have gone out on this steep downward spiral.

"I won't let that happen." He takes a step forward.

I step back. "How do you know?"

Shaking my head slowly, I shove past him and run back into my bedroom, placing the duffle bag on the bed where me and Tyler first were together.

The bed where you knew you loved me.

"Sunny, you can't leave. You still have a month left."

I ignore him, going through my things, deciding what to give and what to just leave behind. Maybe I'll donate it. Maybe I'll just trash it. I don't care. I just need to stop being the fucking problem in people's lives.

I am the problem.

"Sunny stop, please!" He grabs my wrists.

I rip myself from his grip, looking him directly in the eyes despite the fact I know my face is breaking just like my heart.

"I. Am. The. Problem," I say in a broken, choked sob.

And finally, the predator breaks, and through the cracks, I see the human, hurting for me in a way that no one has.

I have secrets, Tyler. I have dark places no one should see.

"Baby," he chokes, stepping towards me.

I hold a hand up, halting him as I try to compose the tears running down my face. I'm broken, and maybe he will finally see that.

He has been desperately trying to piece me back together, cutting himself along the way, but maybe finally he will realize I'll simply never be able to be put back together.

"I was a stupid, hopeless romantic girl who clung to the first boy who loved me in hopes of a future filled with promises he couldn't keep. In hopes that, maybe, just maybe, he could love me the way I loved him. A girl who'd do anything to save what we had, desperate to make all my firsts my lasts too. And he knew that. *He knew that.* And he used it. He used *me*," I cry.

"You are not the problem, Ryan is," he growls out. "None of this is your fault. You think my life was problem free before you? That is the absolute opposite. The farthest thing from the truth. You belong here, Sunny. Even if you feel like you have to run, you belong here. With *our* family."

I run my fingers through my hair, clutching the curls in frustration as another anger filled sob releases from me. I hate that I let myself do this again. To plant roots. To feel what I feel. To feel at all. *I hate myself for loving you all.*

But it's too late. I feel it. And now I'm here. My soulmate is standing before me, begging to help me.

No one can help me, Tyler.

"He took so much that I'm not sure I have anything else left to give," I say.

"Baby, can we just take tonight to breathe?" he finally asks. "Just stay at my place for now, please. You'll be safe. I have security cameras everywhere. I can't–" he cuts himself off. "I'm not leaving you like this. So it's either here or there, but there has cameras and a security system and I can have some of my guys stand post outside all hours," he assures me, grabbing my duffle now filled with god knows what.

I lick my chapped lips. "Okay."

"I just need to text Sam and Mace and let them know you're safe." He pulls his phone out.

They love me. And I have to leave them.

I'm not only going to break Tyler's heart, but all of theirs, too.

CHAPTER SEVENTY-TWO

TYLER

I UNLOCK THE FRONT DOOR USING THE APP ON MY PHONE AS WE make our way up the shirt steps. Moving to the side, I open the door to let her in first and follow after.

Useless is an understatement of how I feel right now. As she walks by me, I can still see her red ringed eyes and sniffling nose. It's a visceral blow to my heart.

I place her duffle and keys on the kitchen island and run a hand through my hair with an audible sigh.

"I'm bad at love, Tyler." I hear her say.

I turn to her. "What?"

"I said I'm bad at love."

"Stop." I shake my head.

"Look at me! Look at where I am. How I keep running. I am bad at love, and you deserve so much better –"

Before she can even finish the sentence my hand is around her neck, bringing her inches to my face. Tight enough so that she stops saying those stupid words, but soft enough so I don't take her air.

"You aren't bad at love, Sunny. *He is*. And I'm going to show you just how much better I am at it," I growl.

Her eyes widen, but they're challenging me, wanting to see just how far I'll go to prove it to her. I feel the slow roll of her throat as she swallows in my hold, her pulse quickening under my grasp.

If only she knew…

"Bite me," she says through clenched teeth.

My little fire. All that anger is finally coming to the surface now that it's blazed and burned through the panic and fear.

"Don't challenge me. I will gladly sink my teeth into you." I throw her over my shoulder, taking her upstairs.

Nothing will scare me away from her. Nothing in this world scares me more than myself. I don't care how broken she is, I will gladly cut myself on all those jagged pieces and bleed for her if it means a life with her.

"Tyler, what are you doing?!" she yells as she tries to fight me. Luckily this time, she actually utilizes some of her training moves I've taught her. And she actually gets a good hit to my face, causing blood to trickle out of my nose.

I wipe the blood, looking at it on my fingers, and my fucking cock grows rock solid in my pants because her fire is incredible.

"You're going to learn your lesson about trying to run away from me, Sunny darling."

"I'm not in the mood."

"Oh, but you will be." I toss her onto the bed. "But first, you will sleep because you need rest."

She gives me a scowl as I stand at the edge of the bed, watching her challenge me. I smile with a tilt of my head. I'm going to worship that body while simultaneously punishing it.

Fatigue is prevalent in dark circles around her bloodshot eyes. She's fighting sleep her body is begging for. So punishment for now will be forcing her to submit to it.

I crawl over her, hooking a piece of hair behind her ear and brush my lips against hers. Her eyes flutter closed as she turns into satin submission underneath me.

Pulling back, I sit on my knees and grab the bottom of her oversized hoodie, which is actually *my* hoodie, and pull it off her. Underneath hides a small tank top that I also peel off, bearing her breasts that fit perfectly in my hands. I shake my head slowly, admiring the love I almost just lost.

Splaying a hand on her chest, I gently push her down and hook my fingers in the waistband of her sweats and peel them off. "Stay," I order her, walking over to the dresser and pulling out clothes from the drawer she's claimed since she's claimed my heart.

Simple black panties and one of my shirts. My absolute favorite look on her.

I walk over to her sitting shyly on the bed, nibbling on her lower lip as she watches me. She looks as exhausted as I feel. I pull the shirt over her head and loop her arms through it then put the panties around her ankles.

"Tyler you don't…" she starts.

"Stand," I tell her. She does as she's told and pulls the panties up. She's not used to someone so diligently taking care of her, and I'm going to show her what that's like.

"That's my girl," I praise her, grabbing her chin and giving her a light kiss as her reward. "Now let's go brush our teeth and get ready for bed,"

"You saying I have bad breath?" She gives me a small smile.

I chuckle. "You will if you don't brush those teeth." I grab her hand and lead her into the bathroom.

We brush our teeth side by side like we do every night, and I watch as she completes her skincare routine. We both crawl into bed, our bodies and hearts exhausted from the day. I hook an arm around her, bringing her front flush to my own. My fingers her hair from her face and start tracing those features I've had memorized since the moment I laid eyes on her.

I kiss her nose and say, "Sleep."

It doesn't take long before she's softly breathing, her body going slack against my own, and I'm counting each and every breath of hers, thankful that they even exist in rhythm with my own.

SUNNY

Citrus and salt fills my nose as my mind starts to crawl out of the deep, dark sleep I was in. Warm, callused hands are trailing my body, rubbing up and down my back gently and soothingly. I smile at his touch, knowing I'm safe in his bed.

My body is exhausted as well as my mind, but I feel a lot better after a few hours of sleep, even if I didn't want to originally. Is it morning already?

I'm on my stomach, one leg hooked up while my face is buried deep into my pillow. His hand pushes up the t-shirt of his I'm wearing, revealing my bare back. Soon enough, those full lips are gracing soft kisses along my spine.

"Tyler," I mumble, rousing from my sleep. I blink away the blurriness, my eyes adjusting to the still dark room. The bed is warm, and I don't want to get out of it. I'd rather we stay in it together all day.

"Time to wake up," he says, rubbing his hand gently up and down my back.

"What time is it?" I groan, nuzzling myself into him, melting under his touch. My stomach already has a low ache forming just by his touch alone.

His hand grazes my ass, and then slaps the skin there hard enough for me to jolt and my eyes open wide.

"Time for you to learn your lesson about running from me."

CHAPTER SEVENTY-THREE
TYLER

"You want to run from me?" I ask. "I'm going to make you too tired to even think about it."

I grab her ankles, pulling her towards me at the end of the bed and hook my fingers in her waistband of her underwear, shoving them down her legs.

Lifting her from her lying position, I rip the shirt down the middle, exposing her body to me. Her nipples are already hard, and goosebumps cascade her bare skin. Frustrated breaths bounce her chest up and down as she looks up at me under creased brows.

Fuck, I love her so much.

I grab one of those nipples that's calling my name in my lips and suck hard, then slap her breast. She lets out a mix of a hiss and a moan.

Pushing her back down on the bed, I grab a wrist, pulling it across the opposite side of her body, securing it to the restraints I have on each corner of my bed. I take the other wrist and pull that across her body on the opposite end, tightly.

"Tyler," she breathes.

"Yes, baby?" I ask, kneeling between her legs, pushing them open with my knees.

I take one of her feet in my hand, press a gentle kiss to her ankle and work my way up her leg. I feel her shudder under my touch and then I take that leg and secure it to the corner of the bed. I do the same with the other.

"You know the drill, Sunny. You say the word. And I'll stop." I glance at her as I round the bed to go to my nightstand. She glares at me and doesn't say anything, and her chest heaves up and down with her arms across it.

I smile. "That's what I thought, little fire."

"Keep that attitude up and I'm going to show you a fire," she bites back.

"Who's the one tied up again?" I say as I lazily trace a finger down her bare chest and stomach, stopping right above her aching clit. Her hips rise with the touch.

Little does she know, she's going to be begging for me to stop because she can't take it anymore.

I trace my finger back up to that flat stomach of hers. "Imagine what this belly would look like filled with my baby." I meet her eyes.

"Tyler," she warns me.

I want her to think about a future with me. I'm done playing the day-by-day game. Especially when a future with her is all I can think about.

I kiss her bare stomach, working my way to her breasts. "It would be beautiful," I whisper on her skin.

It's taking everything in me to not devour her right now. Flicking my tongue over her hardened nipples, she lets out a small moan.

I sink my teeth into her breast and she groans. I move my mouth to do the same on the other. Sitting up, I look at my art, seeing perfect teeth marks around each breast, her hardened nipples centered.

"What the fuck, Tyler?" she growls.

"You said bite you, baby. And I always obey your command." A wicked smile pulls my lips.

With a breath of frustration, her nostrils flare as she looks up at me.

I chuckle, pressing kisses up the column of her neck as she arches her head back. One hand massages and toys with her tender breast and nipple while the other finds its place between her legs. My mouth is salivating at the wetness I find there.

Taking her arousal, I circle her clit slowly. Her breath hitches and her hips arch up.

"You'll learn you can never run from me, Sunny. Now tell me, how many times have you cum in one day?"

I already know the answer because I'm the one responsible behind the number. But tonight, we're going to set a personal record.

"I, I don't know," she breathes as I push my fingers inside her. She's so fucking wet for me.

"Well, I guess tonight we'll learn your limit." I start working my fingers fast in her. A moan escapes her mouth, and I crush my lips to hers to take it in. Her hips start rocking as my fingers continue working.

"For every orgasm, I'll take a piece of clothing off."

Her eyes run over my fully clothed body. I've got layers, lots of them due to the cold. This is going to be *fun*.

She starts clamping around my fingers. "Just like that, baby. Keep going."

She's pulling against the restraints as the climax starts to engulf her body.

She ignites.

Her body tenses and trembles as the orgasm rips through her. Her moans are muffled by my lips on hers, taking in what I've created. She finally goes limp as her body exhausts from the high. This is only the beginning.

Sitting up on my knees between her legs, I peel my jacket off and toss it to the side. Her eyes run over my still covered chest, and she bites her lip knowing this is going to be a long process.

I pull a marker from my side table and pop the lid off, writing a tally on her bare stomach.

"One," I say, tossing it to the side and bring my lips to her bare skin.

"What— " She tries to look at her stomach.

I grab her face in my hand. "Again," I say as I lower myself between her legs. I can't fucking wait to taste her.

I slack the ropes on her legs, pushing her knees bent and wide for me to write all the words I could never say with my tongue between her legs. I pin her rolling hips down, practically lapping between her legs like a desperate man. The headboard rattles in a symphony with her moans as her body moves in waves.

She tries to bring those legs back up and I slap her thigh hard this time, leaving a red welt where my hand made contact. She lets out a growl from deep in her chest that turns to moans. Soon enough, her body tires again as she pants hard before going still. I fucking consume this orgasm I made.

Bringing my face to hers, I grab the marker, writing a second tally on her stomach. "Two."

I whip my belt off, tossing it to the side. I'm not going to make this easy for her. And she has the power to put it to a stop whenever she wants. But my girl is fiery. She sees the challenge and she's going to fucking take it.

I grab her chin and meet her eyes. "You're doing so good, baby," She rips her chin from my grip and I give a dark chuckle at that.

She's gone about six times in one day. But not back-to-back like this. Usually there's time to recover between each. But not tonight. She wants to run? I'm going to make her too exhausted to even think about it again.

I glide my hands up her smooth, naked skin that now has a sheen of sweat. I kiss from her tallied stomach, the curve of each breast and then back down her legs. They're already shaking, and I smile against her skin.

I pull a vibrator out from the drawer. I wanted her already sensitive from the other few before I brought this into the mix.

Turning it on, her eyes go wide. I place it on her now swollen clit and her body immediately tries to curl and move away at the sensation.

I tongue her hard nipples as I straddle her small waist. Sitting up to my full height, I watch her crumple in on herself.

"Eyes on me," I say, tilting her chin so she's looking up at me. Her breathing gets faster and I can feel her body starting to tense as the orgasm takes over. "That's it, baby. Just like that," I encourage her.

She explodes again. Ignites as I keep my firm grip on her face, watching that fire rage to an inferno as she climaxes. Moans turn into screams and I smile as I watch her burn for me.

It's taking a lot of fucking will power to not take her right now. But that's for the grand finale.

I grab the marker and place a third tally on her stomach. "Three," I say.

Then I go right back to worshiping my girl.

CHAPTER SEVENTY-FOUR

SUNNY

I didn't know pain could feel good. Yet here I am.

Sweat sheens my body, my labored breaths make it hard to get any air at all. A burning sensation between my legs licks up my spine and slowly courses throughout my body.

If I say the word, he'll stop. But I refuse to let him win this one.

Tyler sits between my thighs on his knees, wearing only his boxers now, watching what he's doing to me. An animalistic scream comes out of my mouth as my body burns with the orgasm coursing through it.

He pops the lid off the marker to write another tally on my stomach. "Nine." He smirks too proudly.

The headboard rattles as my body trembles, making my already sore wrists and ankles worse from the unintentional tugging.

This version of Tyler is one that I knew but only got small glimpses of. A man who borders the line of dangerous and adventurous in bed.

And I fucking love it.

Jealousy pools my chest thinking he's probably done similar things with other people before me. Which is another reason why I didn't tell him to stop.

He stands to his full height, slowly peeling off the boxer briefs to free his hard dick. Even though my body is so exhausted, I want him so badly.

"Take them off," I say, tugging on my bound wrists.

I don't even have to ask twice because he's already unraveling my restraints. As soon as I'm free, my arms wrap around the back of his neck, slamming my lips to his. He moans and grabs the back of my neck to keep me close. As I straddle his hips, I slowly slide myself onto him.

A groan reverberates through his chest, and he grabs my hips to guide me along him. I wrap my legs around his waist as he sits back on his knees.

"Fuck, baby," he murmurs against my lips. He fists his hand in my curls. "Ten. Give me number ten."

"I don't know if I can," I admit.

"You will."

A press of his lips on my scar and a thrust deeper into me has me digging my nails into his back. He hisses, tilting his head back and pushes deeper and harder into me.

And somehow, there it is. That fire is like a small kindle in the base of my belly, licking tortuous flames across my body as it continues to grow with each thrust of his hips.

Somehow, number ten comes.

An inky black sky and fiery sunset takes over my vision. All I can hear are animalistic sounds that come from both of us. And once my body relents to number ten, I go limp across his chest, my arms hanging over his shoulders, and my nose pressed to the warm skin of his neck.

He follows immediately after me, his dick pulsing and filling me so much I have no other choice but to accept.

Falling onto his back, he keeps me pressed to his chest. A smile pulls that scar on his lips and he brushes my sweaty hair from my face. He grabs the marker sitting next to us and rolls me onto my back to expose the tallies on my stomach.

"Ten," he says, writing it and pressing a soft kiss to my lips.

CHAPTER SEVENTY-FIVE

SUNNY

Since the night Ryan called me, Tyler has been at work or here at home with me and nothing in between. Late nights seem to be a consistency, only biting at my ever growing anxiety since the call.

Despite the book that sits in my lap, my thoughts fester as the clock on his wall ticks another minute that goes by without an answered text or call from Tyler.

I toy with the corner of the book, one that he wanted me to read, while the one I wanted him to read sits on the coffee table, almost finished.

He's normally home no later than 7:30 if it's a longer day, but the clock shows it's already 10:30 and not a word has been communicated to me.

It's a dark place that my mind instantly goes to.

What if something happened to him? Was it Mitchell? A bitter person who put a hit on him? Ryan…? He got my number, what if he got my location, too?

Just as my brain is about to hold me hostage in a trauma I hoped was forgotten, my phone buzzes with Tyler's name across the screen.

I'm so sorry, Sunny. I'll be home soon.

He gives me nothing in that text message but my chest decompresses with relief.

A grueling twenty minutes later I hear the front door unlock and Tyler walks through, holding his usual gym bag he brings to work.

I stand from the couch. "Hey."

"Hey, baby." He sets his things down.

The weak smile he gives me does nothing to mask the fatigue that circles his eyes. He looks like he has been on the hunt for hours.

"Are you okay?" I ask, noticing the disheveled clothing.

He runs his hand through his hair. "Yeah, I'm so sorry I didn't text you sooner. I got so caught up and I…well I wasn't able to reach my phone." He swallows hard.

Which only means that my suspicions were right. "When was the first time you killed someone?"

He blinks at me and licks his lips. "Fifteen." He doesn't hesitate to answer.

I try not to react, but the wince that takes over my face is undeniable, even in the shadows of the fireplace.

So young. He was so young.

"What was the reason?" I ask.

He takes a few cautious steps towards me, afraid this honesty will send me running. But I'm the one asking questions.

"Mitchell." I'm not surprised. "It's a dirty game, the world we live in. We are too heavily tied into politics and government and basically the world around us to allow anything to slip through the cracks. Mitchell, he doesn't do the dirty work. I am the reason any threat to our family or our company gets taken down."

I remain silent, waiting for the rest of the story.

"A mole was found in our company, and it was my job to

figure out who else was involved. Which meant...*questioning.*" He blows out a breath and sits on his couch. "He made me torture the guy until every last drop of blood left his body. If I didn't do it, the risk would outweigh the nightmares it gave me."

"What was the risk?" I push.

"Anthony's life." He meets my stare. "It was the traitor's life or Anthony's. So the choice was easy. He said that's how it would always be. That if I didn't take the traitor out, then they'd take away the people I love. That we couldn't let people who cross us walk free or else they'd do it again and again. Taking more each time. And I knew if the traitor didn't hold true to the promise of taking away the people I love, Mitchell would. It's why I'm bound to this company. So I did it. I made the bastard pay. Wishing it was Mitchell instead." He watches the crackling fire. The flames dance in his emerald eyes, just like the haunted memories do.

"Later that night, I sat in Sam's bathroom, crying as she washed the blood off my hands." He rests his elbows on his knees. "I cried because I took a life. I cried because I also enjoyed it, imagining it was Mitchell. I was so angry at him. No matter how awful these people I kill are, it's still taking a life. The night he put me in the hospital when I was eight was when he created a monster inside me. A predator that refused to be the prey again. So that's what I became, and I'm okay with that."

"Does he still try to use that against you?"

I notice he doesn't have sadness, not even anger really, in his eyes. It's like he said before, he is okay with it now. He somehow made peace with this part of himself. A comfort amidst the chaos. And I realize I made peace with it, too.

"He tries." He smirks. "But Mitchell knows not to fuck with the things I love most now. I still don't like to take the chances, regardless."

"And have you...tried? Or if not, why haven't you?"

"Because if it's one thing I know about Mitchell, he is much like me, he will fucking fight. And I'm not in the business of the war of my life. I'm content with the way things are. Once he gives the company to me, I'll do things the way they should've always been done. But if I kill him, that'll create a lot of complications and a lot of pissed off people. And my empire will crumble fast."

I nod. It makes sense. I don't blame him for doing what he needs to do to keep the peace.

It's a conflicting thing, knowing what I know about Tyler. A portion of him that maybe even Sam doesn't quite know or understand. It's hard to discern whether he is a good man who does bad things, or a bad man who does good things. But one thing I know is that he will never hurt me.

His phone buzzes, and with a sigh he grabs it and runs a hand through his hair. "I'm sorry baby, I have to go back out."

I look at the clock on the wall. "It's already eleven though."

He quirks a humorless smile. "I know, but I have a business meeting at..." He swallows hard. "It's a strip club but it's business only, baby."

He goes on to tell me about Barton's Babe's and all the details that go into the club. But he mentions the small detail that nags at the back of his mind. How he knows, occasionally, they slip a girl or two in there against their will to groom them and auction them off, whether Barton, the owner, knows it or not.

"One day, I'll burn as many of those places down as I can," he says, staring into the fire.

I trust him, and understand he has to do a lot of things he doesn't like for the sake of business. I don't blame him for wanting to take down seedy places that strip women of their choice and dignity.

"Don't wait up for me. I still have a lot of things to do tonight." He hooks a curl behind my ear. "Sleep, and I'll come join you when I get back."

"Okay."

CHAPTER SEVENTY-SIX

SUNNY

I RUSTLE IN MY SLEEP, TRYING TO IGNORE THE TOO FAMILIAR feeling of someone watching me. It's only heightened since the phone call, revamping the paranoia I thought I had kept somewhat at bay.

I reach a hand out, realizing Tyler still isn't in his place in bed. I've had to have been asleep for a few hours. Where is he?

Taking a deep breath in, I roll over and grab my phone to see it's 3:34 am. I sit up, trying to clear my blurry eyes and send him a text when I'm met with a shadow of darkness in the corner of the room.

Gasping, my phone flings from my hands as panic blooms my chest but settles just as quickly when I'm met with emerald eyes. He sits in the corner with his face painted like a skull, just like Halloween, twirling his knife in his hand effortlessly.

He doesn't even react to me.

"Tyler," I whisper, shuffling out of the bed.

He cocks his head to the side but doesn't say anything to me as he continues twirling his knife, eyes gleaming brighter when surrounded by the hollowness of the black paint.

He mentioned the masquerade theme for Barton's Babes, so

the face paint makes sense. To keep the identity of all the higher ups masked in a place like that one. A secret no one else outside their circle can know or use against them.

"Little fire, you're the bravest person I know because you face me daily. I'm probably the scariest thing you will come across in your life, Sunny. I'm fucking scarier than Ryan, yet you don't run from me. I'm a far worse person." He gets up from the chair and takes slow deliberate steps towards me. With his face inches from mine he asks, "Why?"

He grabs my face in his hand and uses his other forearm to pin me against the wall. He pins his hips against mine, the hard length of him pressing into my stomach.

"Because you don't have a choice." It's breathless.

"Everyone has a choice."

The glint of his knife catches my attention, ripping my gaze from his hollowed eyes. He runs the cold, sharp tip along my jawline. But it doesn't scare me, if anything it has me squeezing my thighs together in a desperate attempt to stop whatever it is this does to me.

And maybe he's right, maybe I have already met my most dangerous predator, yet I can't get enough of him.

He drags the cool metal along my thigh, then uses it to slap my skin. "Open," he growls.

I do as he says and part my legs. Maybe we all are fucked up in our own ways, but this feels freeing in a sense for me, because I know that no matter what he does, I will always have the control with one simple word.

Something I never had with Ryan.

He glides the tip of the knife along the sensitive skin inside my thighs. The tip of the knife lifts his t-shirt I'm wearing, tracing along my bare stomach. His eyes flick to where his knife and my skin meet then to my now hardened nipples that peak through the shirt. He drops the knife and his t-shirt drops with it, covering up the skin that now has goosebumps all over.

"Answer me. Why aren't you scared of me?"

I know what he's trying to do. He's trying to test me. He's trying to see how far I'm willing to let him take it before my limits are reached. The thing is, I trust him completely. I know he will stop the minute I feel uncomfortable. He wants to make sure I'm well familiar with all these dark and depraved parts of him, that way I can love him with no surprises. That way I can love him fully.

But little does he know, I already do.

"Because I trust you," I say, swallowing hard under his grip on my throat.

"The power will always be yours. Do with it what you will, but don't think for one minute I won't bleed for you and not enjoy it. You say the word, and I will stop. But first, the power is yours. It always has been and always will be." He flips the knife so the sharp edge is in his palm, facing the handle towards me, waiting for me to grab it.

I stare at it. "What do I do?"

"Whatever you want." A smirk pulls his lips. "You can create scars on me. Scars I'll look at and love." He steps back from me, putting his arms out exposing his bare chest. "Brand me, baby."

I can see what he's doing. He's scared that I have the knowledge of who he is and what he's done. He thinks he is losing control, losing me. This is his way to give me a power he thinks I've somehow lost by our earlier conversation.

"I don't know…" I stutter.

"Why is that? Because you're scared this will make you cum instead of bleed?" He grabs the knife by the blade again, snatching it from my hand.

Blood starts to trickle from his palm, but he doesn't react. Instead, he flips it and grabs the handle, pressing the knife to my neck. The tip of the blade is pressed under my chin, making me look up at him into those lethal eyes.

"Lay down." His pupils dilate and flare.

I do as he says and watch as he sits on his knees between my thighs, knocking them open. Tilting his head, he brings the knife to the t-shirt I'm wearing and flicks it up, exposing my belly that is now filled with a kindling flame.

"Any marks I leave on your body will always be for pleasure, never for pain." He removes the knife.

I nod, letting him know I understand.

"That's my girl," he says, fisting my shirt and slices the knife down it. He hooks a finger in my panties and slices those, too. And I'm convinced I'll never have a wardrobe without Tyler ruining it. Maybe it's his plan all along.

He removes himself from me to take off his jeans and boxers. "Open my legs." He taps the blade against my thigh, urging me to let my bent knees fall open.

He shakes his head as his eyes fall between my thighs. "Baby, you're already so wet." He licks his lips, aching to taste me.

He runs the blade down my burning skin again, starting at my neck all the way down between my legs. I swallow hard, feeling the cool metal press against my heated flesh. It's when he flips the knife so the blade is in his hand and the hilt toys at my entrance that my breath catches. Yet, I don't want him to stop.

He pauses and his emeralds meet my stare, waiting for me to give him the command. And I fucking nod.

A gentle push and the hilt is inside me, making my head roll back in a mix between a moan and a cry.

"Beautiful," he breathes as his bloody hand grips my hip, covering me in his blood.

My hips start to ride the rhythm he creates with the knife, inching deeper inside me. I test the waters by reaching for my breast, but his bloody hand snatches my wrist before I can make it halfway.

"You know the rules." He presses his lips to my wrist as he picks up the pace with the knife.

My head rolls back as I feel the handle hit the aching spot inside me. And when I look down, I see his bloody handprint on my hip, and it does something wild inside of me.

"Cum on my fucking knife." He grabs my face with his bloodied hand, forcing me to look at him, pushing my cheeks deliciously painfully together.

He brings his face inches to mine. I'm so close, but not quite there. He doesn't stop the rhythm of the handle inside me.

"I said *cum*," he says through clenched teeth.

And my body submits to his command. The fire in my core kindles throughout my body, rattling me as I clamp down around the hilt.

Tyler sits back up to his knees while he continues moving the handle inside me, prolonging the pleasure he creates in me with a fucking knife.

My back arches and my head rolls back as the pleasure seizes me. I grip the blankets, trying to contain the convulsing my body is doing. I feel his large, bloodied hand run over my possessed body, admiring the pleasure that takes it over.

He grabs my thigh, yanking me closer to him, pushing that handle so deep in me, I scream from the delectable pain.

My instinct is to grab his hand to stop it, even though I don't want to. He snatches that wrist too quickly and pins it above my head as his face gets inches from mine. I'm pretty sure I have tears streaking my face, but it feels so fucking good.

"You will take my knife the way you take me."

He lets up, pulling out only slightly so I can regain myself through my labored breaths.

When I look up from my body covered in his blood, I meet those emerald eyes and say so confidently, "Recreate my scar."

He pauses. "What?"

"Make it yours with that knife. Your lips have done a good job. But make it permanent." I didn't even realize how much I needed this until now.

I want him to make that scar his. Officially. With his own knife. So that way it can no longer belong to Ryan, but to Tyler. That way the only scar on my body was by a man who only brings me pleasure, never pain. By a man who loves me.

"Sunny…" he starts.

"Please, baby. Please. Make it yours." I give him pleading eyes.

Slowly he removes the knife from me. My arousal coats the hilt, and I watch as he glides his tongue along it with a deep groan when he tastes me.

He grabs my jaw, tilting my head to the side so he exposes the scar on my neck. Cool metal is pressed against the sensitive skin.

"This is what you want?" he asks, pressing the knife a little harder as a prelude for what's to come.

I nod with a breathy, "Yes."

"If you're going to bleed, then I will too." He flips the knife so I can take it.

"Where?" I ask.

"Exactly where yours is." He kisses along my jaw, the column of my neck. Clearly this idea seems great to him by the way his hard dick is pressing against me.

I grab the hilt of the blade and arch my hips, begging for him to push inside me. A dark chuckle reverberates through his chest as he grabs my hips and does just that.

"I want you to brand me," he whispers.

He tilts his head back, exposing his neck for me. So selflessly wanting to feel my pain and make it his own.

When I don't move, he chuckles again as he takes a nipple in his mouth, making me moan and arch into him. I drag the tip of the blade down the lines of muscles that build his back, noting the way he trembles with it.

"Again," he demands when he sits up, still inside me,

guiding my hand with the blade down his chest and abs. He hisses, even though I haven't even drawn blood yet.

"Good girl. Keep going." He cascades kisses along my body as I continue. "Make me bleed."

Once I've finally grown comfortable with the blade in my hand and feel myself about to jump off the edge he's been pushing me towards, he wraps his hand around mine on the hilt. Anticipation lights in his eyes when he guides our hands to the crook of his neck.

"Just a little pressure, baby," he encourages me.

I push the knife into his skin, but it isn't as fragile as mine, so I have to give more pressure. Then his skin pierces, and I see the crimson blood start to trickle onto his tanned skin.

"Fuck, yes just like that." His hips start to thrust wildly.

The power completely obliterates me.

Of all the times I was convinced that small flame turned into an inferno, I was wrong. This moment is proof of that. The flood of power becomes everything inside of me. From the way my heart beats to the air filling my lungs to the very way my mind is wired.

It burns so deliciously that I'm arching myself in any way I can as screams rip through my throat. Pleasure that I didn't know could exist floods my veins in fiery tendrils of power.

The knife drops from where I have it pressed against his neck, but Tyler snatches it before it hits the bed. Soon enough it's pressed to my neck, exactly where I want it to be.

When I finally come through the smoke of the fire that set flame, I look up at him to see his blood trickling from his neck and onto my body.

Hesitation is clear in his body. From the slow roll of his throat to the way his eyes bounce between the knife and my face. Still he moves inside me, making my labored breaths do nothing to bring me down from the high of adrenaline and power.

"Do it," I tell him. "Fucking do it."

His jaw flexes and then he pushes the knife into my scar. He makes it a point to continue moving in me, trying to tread that line of pleasure and pain.

And somehow, I love the pain. I love it so much that I find myself chasing that release again. Fire licks through my veins, filling every part of my body as it engulfs me. The world explodes and I'm met with a night sky clashing with a fiery sunset. I can feel the warm blood trickle down my neck and wet the sheets below us.

Our now matching scars are bleeding together.

We bleed together.

Because his pain is my pain. And my pain is his.

Finally, what was once a brand of abuse is now a brand of love. This scar is filled with begging for more, not begging for less. This is no one else's but mine and his.

I *chose* this scar.

"Mine, Sunny," he murmurs, taking a tongue to the stinging cut on my neck. "Your pain will always be my own," he says, using his bloody hand to grab my face, making me look at him.

Despite our labored breathing, he presses a gentle kiss to my lips where I can taste my own blood on his tongue.

And somehow, I feel a little more free.

CHAPTER SEVENTY-SEVEN

SUNNY

I walk through my door ready to strip my clothes off. The grime of the work day makes me very ready for a shower. I'm stopped in my trek by a large white box with a single sunflower placed on it. Picking it up, I see a note accompanied with the present.

Can't wait to see you in this. Thank my sister. See you tonight. Love, Tyler.

I sigh, because the idea of backing out of being Tyler's date at the campaign sounds more and more appealing. But he wants to make a statement by bringing me as his date. For some reason, I agreed. I like the idea of him showing me off. Especially in front of Shelby and Mitchell. It's the only thing that's kept me from backing out entirely.

Glancing at my watch, I see I'm in a time crunch since he'll be picking me up soon. He spent last night in another city on a business trip. A quick turnaround but he said he'd be coming straight from it to pick me up.

He's been doing a lot of those lately, and I can see the exhaustion prevalent on his face, even when he tries to hide it. Every week seems like he is in a different city.

To cut my shower short, I decide to salvage my hair that I have and refresh my curls as best I can. Tyler likes it messy anyways. It's his favorite look on me.

I pull the dress out of the box, the black satin material pooling on the floor. Different than what I'd choose to wear, but appropriate for the night. Sam not only knows how to dress well, but she knows how to do it comfortably, too.

When I put the dress on, I notice the slits on the sides that go too far up for me to even wear panties without them being exposed. *Only Sam would.* The v line plunge down my torso does nothing but reveal more skin, and I wonder if Tyler even has a clue on how his sister decided to dress me tonight.

I fumble with the strappy black heels that go with it, tripping over the dress while the straps hang loose since I'll need Tyler's help to fix it. I toss the shoes aside and continue my makeup at the mirror with my spot on the floor while I wait for his arrival.

It's going to be a big night. And while it's one thing for his friends to make appearances at his events, it's another for someone to show up as his date.

It's been a week since my phone call with Ryan. I hadn't even thought about my phone until Tyler gave it back to me the next day to give to the local PD to try and trace the call. But unfortunately, the whole thing was too broken to recover.

With much deliberation, I decided to commit myself to my remaining time here. It's not much longer anyways. And Tyler and I will just have to enjoy the time we are given. It's all we can do. I just haven't told *him* yet.

A knock sounds on my door, rising me from my spot on the floor and seeing Tyler standing casually through the peephole.

But nothing about him is casual.

He's devastating in his tuxedo that's tailored to him. That lethal body packed full of muscles easily seen through the layers of material. His face is clean shaved and his hair is groomed back neatly, showing off all the sharp lines of his jaw and nose.

He holds a sunflower in his hand, twisting it around and staring at it while he patiently waits for me to answer.

I open the door and his eyes flick up to me. His full lips part, and his face softens as he drinks me up. Those damn eyes roll over me, taking in every inch. He takes a fist to his mouth and bites it as if he has to hold back any urges he feels right now.

"Oh, Sunny," he breathes. "Fuck."

A smile plays on my lips. I look down to the floor and hook a piece of hair behind my ear. I never had a man look at me with so much love and admiration. If he keeps doing that, this dress isn't going to stay on much longer.

"I need some help zipping up."

A smile curves at the corner of his mouth. "I can certainly help with that."

His hand finds the small of my back, guiding me towards my bedroom area. I'm worried if we go there, we'll end up not coming out. With him looking like that, it's hard to want to go anywhere.

He hands me the sunflower. "For you," he gestures. "Now turn around."

I swallow hard at the tone. It's breathy. It's low. It's hungry.

Turning around, I hear him rubbing his hands together to warm them up so I won't feel the cold from outside on his skin.

Considerate Tyler.

He grabs my hair and brushes it over my shoulder, so it falls over my chest. His calloused fingertips trace the back of my exposed arms leaving a trail of fire in their wake on my skin. I take in a deep breath, trying to keep my composure.

His hand finds the small of my back again while the other tugs at the zipper, pulling it up to secure the dress I so desperately want to be on the floor instead.

He grabs my hair and moves it back to its rightful spot down my back. His breath in the crook of my neck is a prelude to the way his lips tenderly kiss the column of my neck where my scar sits. The scar that matches his. They're both still freshly pink in their healing process. And a part of me hopes people notice the brand we have on one another.

"Let me see all of you." He spins me around, giving him a full view and then I'm facing him. He thumbs my glossed lips. "Can't ruin this masterpiece right now, baby. But believe me, I have big plans once I show you off to everyone."

My skin betrays me as it releases goosebumps all over just by his words alone. Once I get my heels on, he leans back into the dresser and motions for my foot so he can secure the heels.

I place a heel right over his hard cock. I love that I do that to him. He bites his lower lip, rolling his eyes at the contact. He pushes my dress up, exposing my whole leg. His fingers delicately tie the strings in place, securing my foot. He takes those lips and presses them to my ankle and slowly starts making his way up my leg. My breath hitches and I want to clench my thighs to give myself relief from the pulsing between my legs.

"Now the other." He motions.

I bring my leg down, replacing it with the other with a little more aggression against his hard cock. A smile grows on his face as he lets out a small chuckle and shakes his head.

"You're going to make this painful for me, aren't you, little fire?" He starts securing my heel.

"It doesn't have to be."

"Well then what fun is that?" he whispers against the skin of my leg.

My body betrays me once more as my head tilts back at the feel. And I even let out a breathy moan. I feel him drop my leg and grab the back of my neck with his strong hand, making me look up at him.

"Soon," he promises as his eyes search my face. "I need you looking your best so I can show them all the reason why this heart beats in my chest." His hand guides mine over his chest. He takes a step back and observes me again. "A masterpiece."

"You keep talking like that we won't make it out of this apartment," I taunt.

Shaking his head, he places his hands in his pockets and steps into me. "Keep that smart mouth up I'm going to have to find a way to shut it."

"I'd like to see you try," I challenge.

His grin widens and I bring my hands to his face, cupping his jaw between them and place a soft kiss on his lips. He lets out a soft groan and brings his hand to cradle my face.

This man may be powerful, lethal even, but he melts under my touch.

"Come on, Sunny. Let's go piss off a lot of people."

CHAPTER SEVENTY-EIGHT
TYLER

Walking into the venue, I notice heads turn while we make our entrance. Then hands slap other's shoulders so their attention will be brought to us.

My statement is being made, and I can't help but let a too wide grin pull my lips. I see the looks on people's faces, curious about her. The one girl Tyler Michael Caddell finally brought to an event, and at one of his biggest investments of his career yet.

I place my hand on the low of her back, guiding my girl through the staring faces to make my greetings to the governor. Her eyes dart around as she nervously nibbles on her lower lip. I try my best to ease her by lacing my fingers through hers. Still she holds her head high, despite the staring eyes.

People surround tables sprawled with cards, money, and alcohol. Slot machines line some walls of the venue where people cheer and groan at their earnings and losses. It's a good show up tonight, and a percentage of all winnings get put towards Governor Goodman's campaign. The people want him to win again, so they will do whatever it takes to make it happen. They want to feel important, and being here gives them just that.

The look on Matthews face is probably the best damn part of my night outside of having Sunny on my arm.

"Governor Goodman," I say, reaching a hand out with a fucking smile on my face.

"Tyler Caddell. Tonight's event is already going better than anticipated. I have your team to thank." He takes my hand but his face remains tight.

Of course it did. I'm good at what I do. And I'm going to prove my point even further by making this the best damn event he's had without the contract of a marriage with his daughter.

"And who is this fine young lady here?" Governor Goodman's eyes roll over Sunny. It makes me want to gouge his eyes out. The audacity he has to run his eyes over her after our little encounter has me questioning if I should've just killed him then.

I take a step in front of her, wrapping a secure arm around her waist. "This is Sunny. She is my date for tonight. And the rest of my life if she'll have me."

She gives that knee buckling smile and reaches a hand out for him to kiss.

My fucking girl.

Governor Goodman takes her hand and presses his lips to her skin. It makes me want to wire his lips shut. But if he did anything less for her, I'd have him on his knees begging forgiveness.

I pull her closer into me so he knows to back the fuck off.

"We wouldn't have been able to do it without Tyler here. He has a sway that I don't." Goodman releases her hand as he sees my warning stare on him. "Well, if you'll excuse me, I better be finding my wife. I'll find you later, Tyler," Goodman gives a fake strained smile and takes off into the crowds.

"One down, a whole lot more to go," I whisper in Sunny's ear.

SUNNY

Tyler plays a role tonight, one that I'm not used to as we walk around the venue, greeting all the people here and diving into business and political conversations.

He's significantly younger than the majority of the people here, yet he holds them like little puppets attached to strings he controls.

I watch as they follow his mannerisms, leave space for his voice, and make room for him whenever he approaches a conversation.

They know who he is, what he can do, the way he and his father hold the secrets, the livelihoods, everything of these people. One misstep from them, and Tyler can have their world come crashing down. His value goes beyond the money in his pockets.

We answer the same questions over and over about who I am, how we met, and soon enough my name is rolling off tongues of people I didn't even meet.

"Who is she?" A woman whispers to another behind us.

Tyler turns around looking at them. "The best damn part of my day."

The look on Shelby's face was priceless when Tyler and I made our appearance. The look on Governor Goodman's and Mitchell's were even better.

Standing by his side, I don't feel like the rest of the women here. Just as he promised. Not a wife. Not a mistress. Not just a date. No. I'm his partner. His equal. If anything, the matching scars on our necks prove that.

The venue is massive, and the amount of people filling it will keep us on our feet all night by the way Tyler's attention is pulled in every direction. Chandeliers create a low light in the vicinity, adding to the ambiance of the music the band in the corner plays by one of the marble pillars. It's unlike anywhere I've been.

Once my body got over the jitteriness of it all, it settles back into the state I was feeling in my apartment before we made it here. Tyler's touches feel extra tonight. Maybe it's because he's making it known to everyone who I am to him. But each touch sets fire to my skin.

The way his hand grips my waist.

The way he lazily traces fingers down my arms, on my shoulders.

The way he leans down and whispers in my ear.

Something about making ourselves known to the public sends a frenzy in me. And seeing the power he holds and knowing mine over him is so much stronger, is something I'm completely drunk on.

I know this isn't the place or the time. But that makes it even *better*.

I can't help it, Tyler. Not with you.

Amidst conversation, I roam my hands up his arm, staring up at him dotingly. His jaw flexes when he glances at me and returns his gaze to the people he's talking with. Then a smile curves his mouth.

He laughs at something the person says. He's good at this. That's when I realize Tyler is not only the best predator physically, but psychologically too. He's easily likable. And he knows how to morph himself to appease the people around him.

"If you'll excuse us." He grabs my hand and sets his drink down on a waiter's tray, leading me out into a grand hallway that has numerous doors. "Follow me."

My heels sound against the marble floor as we run down the hallway. The only other noise echoing the empty hallway are our laughs.

"Where are you taking me?" I laugh.

He opens a door to find a dark, smaller dining room. It's pretty, but definitely not as grand as the rest of the venue we're in.

It's dark save for the windows that have lights from outside shining inside, creating just enough light for me to see the shadowed features on Tyler's face.

"To do what we've both been thinking about all night." A feline smile widens as he closes the door and locks it behind him.

"Tyler we can't here."

But of course I want to.

"What fun is that?" He slowly closes the space between us and traces his fingers up my arms, gripping the back of my neck to make me look up at him.

I wrap my arms around his neck and pull him in for a kiss. The bourbon on his tongue makes me melt deeply into him.

He slips his jacket off and sets it on a chair, bringing his hands to my face again. There it is, anytime his lips press to mine, I feel it every damn time. The words written across my tongue. *I love you.*

He lifts me by my thighs and places me on one of the tables, never removing his lips from mine. *I love you. I love you. I love you.*

I have to leave you.

He pulls away and watches me as his hand explores down between my legs to where it's so evidently clear how much I want this.

I need you now.

Slowly, he presses two fingers inside me easily by the wetness he finds. He knows exactly what to do for me.

"Tsk tsk," he says, kissing down my neck. He circles his thumb around my clit, still moving his fingers inside me, eliciting an even louder moan. "Shhh. They'll hear us." He covers my mouth with his.

He works his fingers faster, stroking like a match to light a flame. It's just so easy with him. Our bodies just know one another.

"Just like that, baby," he praises me.

"Oh my god," I groan.

"Not god. *Tyler*. My name is the only one that will leave those lips like this. Now cum."

I submit to his command.

And I come.

Hard.

It's a series of muffled moans and Tyler's murmured *good girl*'s against my lips. Once I'm able to come down from the high and cool the flames that heat my skin, I reach at his belt buckle, trying to set him free.

A smile curves his lips as he lets me fumble with his pants. He brushes the hair from my face, and whispers kisses on my lips.

Once he's free, he pushes the satin material of my dress up my legs and steps between them. The tip of his cock teases me, treacherously inching in and then out. I let out a small whimper, tightening my legs around him to try and push him deeper.

"Fuck," he murmurs. "So wet, baby. That's my girl."

He pushes completely inside me and his body trembles at the sensation. The power of causing that creates a high I can't resist. It only gets stronger and stronger when I see those emeralds flick up at me, a predator so dangerous and yet submits to *me*.

I press my forehead against his and wrap my arms around the back of his neck, reveling in the high. It's something he gives me that Ryan never did.

"Yes!" I breathe out. "Don't stop."

I can feel his desire heavy in each thrust of his hips. In the way his hands lock into my hair. In the way his lips press so desperately into mine.

And even through the haze of the high, I still hear the echoing pain that comes with every heartbeat.

A reminder.

And it makes me wonder how we will ever say goodbye.

CHAPTER SEVENTY-NINE
TYLER

My body is occupied by a bunch of business men while my attention is stuck on my girl sitting at the bar with Mace and Sam. Cole and Anthony stand as pillars of protection on either side of them.

Her hair is a little wilder than earlier, subtle proof of my fingers through it. I smile as I take a sip of my bourbon, but it's soon gone when I feel a presence next to me.

I knew I'd run into her tonight, considering it's her father's campaign, after all. I haven't seen her since I called off the engagement. Well, since I forced her father to. I still wonder what Matthew gave Mitchell for it.

"Hey," she mutters, looking at me.

I don't look at her. Rather, my gaze is still pulled by Sunny, looking devastating as ever. They all see tonight that she's my partner. My equal. She's not some accessory to hang on my arm like all the other women here.

Without her, I'm not complete.

Without her, I'm nothing.

"Shelby."

She doesn't hold the aura of confidence she normally does.

She looks more timid tonight, more sad. As if seeing me bring Sunny here told her everything she needed to know about her future with me.

She follows my gaze. They're all laughing at something Sam said.

My family.

"My father told me about the contract you made."

I'm unaware of said contract. Eventually I'll find out what that is. Something tells me it was a cop out for her father so his infidelity doesn't get leaked.

I finally look at her. "And?"

She's wearing a burnt orange gown with her hair clipped up on one side. She's pretty. But she's no Sunny.

"I just…" she exhales a waivered breath. "Is that truly what you want?" Her brown eyes spark with hope I'd say no.

"It's always what I wanted. It was just a matter of the push I needed to make it happen."

"I'm sorry, Tyler. For the things I did. I know it's probably too late for that, but I feel like I still owe it to you." She places her hand on mine.

I flick my eyes to where our bodies meet. I almost smile. She's sorry because it means she no longer has me. And she never will.

"I know you are."

She's watching Sunny now. "Was that push because of me? Is it because of me? The things I did?"

And I wish I yelled *yes, of course it was*. Bingo. Right on the fucking mark. But the truth comes out instead.

"No. It's because of her." I look at the love of my life. The one who changed it all for me.

My initial breaking up with Shelby was me showing her she couldn't fuck around. I knew eventually my obligations would rise again and I'd do what I needed to do to fulfill them.

But then Sunny came, and she changed everything. Absolutely everything. My little fire set flame to a world I hated and burnt it to a crisp, freeing me of it in a way.

"I knew the night of the Hernandez campaign," Shelby whispers. "I saw the way you looked at her. Because it was the way I always hoped you'd look at me. The way you tried to protect her from your parents. The way you touched her." She swallows hard. "You were never like that with me. Never so in love."

"I knew, too. I knew way before then." I look at Shelby.

She gives me a weak smile and nods. "It'll always be her, won't it? There will never be room for anyone else."

I nod. "It will always be her."

And in that moment, I feel the door finally close on us.

"I hope you get all the happiness you deserve, Tyler. You really do deserve it. I can see what you guys have and I hope one day I can experience that too." She places a kiss on my cheek and then walks away back into the crowds.

SUNNY

"So, you're a nurse?" The lady with a diamond necklace asks me as she takes a sip of her cocktail.

My eyes flick from her necklace that looks like a collar around her neck to her light blue eyes that match and nod. "That's correct. I'm a travel nurse. I'm here on a six month assignment."

I feel Mitchell come up next to me, his eyes bore into me. His salt and pepper hair is styled back in a way that reveals all the fine lines that frame his face. While I hate him, I have to attribute his role in Tyler's good looks.

"Wow! Do you know where your next assignment will be? Sounds so spontaneous." Her eyes gleam.

Maybe she always wanted a life of travel but never got it. That's another reason I made the promise to myself to do this. I never want to go to my grave filled with regrets of the things I should've done.

I already wasted so much time letting Ryan do that to me.

"I actually do," I say, eyeing Tyler who stands a few people down. I watch his head slowly turn towards me as the words dawn on him, indicating he is always listening, always aware of my surroundings even when I think he isn't.

I haven't told him yet. I haven't told anyone.

As my contract here is nearing to an end, my recruiter called me a week ago with a twelve week assignment in Colorado. In the heat of desperation to flee from Ryan, I said yes.

How could I say no after that fucking phone call?

It always comes in waves now. One minute I'm content, happy, and almost forgetting why I came here in the first place. Then the next wave I'm in sheer panic, wanting to run the first chance I get. Unfortunately, the recruiter got me in one of those frenzied waves.

Tyler looks at me as I admit this secret I've clutched onto and his mask of authority crumples to confusion and hurt when he realizes what I'm saying.

The almighty powerful front he had all night gone within seconds by me. Because this hits the nail on the coffin of the potential for me to stay, burying any hope he had deep into the ground due to its inevitable death.

"And how does your *husband* feel about that? Ryan it is, right? Ryan Crawford? He must miss his wife very much with you being gone for so long." Mitchell watches me intently now as he takes a sip of his drink, spilling the one thing I didn't want anyone to know.

Especially Tyler.

Because I know that if he's already on the edge of breaking his promise to me, this would have him jumping off ready to immerse himself into shattering it entirely. And I refuse to have him do that. I will not be like his father.

The world pauses, and the only thing I can hear is my frantic heartbeat in my ears and slamming against my chest. It begs for an out, for something other than this part of myself that is now being revealed to a bunch of strangers.

I am married.

I've been running from my husband this whole time. Not boyfriend. *Husband.* Legally bound to one another.

My head snaps to Mitchell as my drink simultaneously falls from my hand and shatters on the floor. Glass and champagne splatter all over the front of my dress. That's when the nausea settles deep in my belly, making me clutch it in fear of throwing up everywhere.

Mitchell looks down at it unphased. Then he looks back up at me, and I swear there's a ghost of a smile hovering on his lips.

He knows what he just did.

He knows what he did.

Tyler stares blankly at the mess by my feet. His eyes slowly move up and meet mine, and I know there's no hiding the truth that's all over my face.

"Sunny?" he breathes.

"Oh, didn't you know, Tyler? I figured if you two are sharing scars, you'd at least share a first name basis. I guess I'm wrong. Her name hasn't always been Sunny. Isn't that right, Lauren Sunshine Crawford?"

The panic rises in my chest as I search for the right words to say. I need to say something. Something to crack the silence that sits before me. To stop all the stares burning into me as everyone waits for me to explain myself. Explain that I'm a wife to another man. Explain that I'm not who I said I am.

I shake my head and do the one thing I can think of; ignore the whole thing. I bend down to start cleaning the mess I made. Literally and hypothetically. The champagne sticking to my hands, the glass making me bleed.

"I'm so sorry," I murmur as the wait staff surround me, trying to clean it up.

I know I can't clean up the mess around me, so I try to focus on the one I *can* clean. Even as the pieces of champagne covered class cut my hands and make them bloody, I'd take that over the confusion and pain that sits in Tyler's eyes right now.

The secret I clung to so fiercely ever since I left my hometown is now aired out to people I don't even know and to the one person I didn't want to know.

Mitchell did this on purpose. He did it to make me crack. To not only make me look bad, but make this whole scene look bad.

He knew Tyler would put me on a pedestal tonight to look like his equal. His partner. A woman who will help make decisions rather than submit to his own. But this, this makes me look like a cheater. A whore. A woman who is a mere mistress. A liar.

Not his equal.

Not his partner.

And he knew that would make Tyler damn near crack, too. He's been trying to break Tyler. And I'm scared this may have worked.

"Sunny. Sunny." I hear his voice above me. A calm in this mess of chaos.

Sunny has always been my name. Since the moment my parents took me home. They called me that as soon as they realized I was not a Lauren. It just was never legally changed until I left Ryan. Because I felt like that name, Lauren Sunshine, died with the person I was the day I left him. She needed to be left in the past, which is why I finally legally changed my name to Sunny Mason. I reclaimed myself. And I changed my name in hopes people wouldn't find a past behind it.

Masoner is my maiden name. I needed something different. Something of my own. Something that he wouldn't be able to track down. But something that still remained close to my heart without letting him strip me of everything.

I feel Tyler's hands gently grab underneath my arms to pull me up from the ground. He uses a napkin to staunch my bleeding hands.

"Funny how that works," Mitchell laughs in his glass and walks away from the mess he created.

Before I can even think, I'm chasing after him, ready to fight him. The anger fills me to the point where it blinds me. I feel Tyler's hands on me again, curling around my waist, stopping me in my desperate attempt to give Mitchell all the pay back he deserves for all the wrong he's done in his life.

"*Sunny*." Tyler's shaking his head. "It's not worth it. Don't let him have that hold on you. Now, we need to talk."

I slowly swallow down my anger which now turns to pure nausea at Tyler's words and tone.

I'm going to be sick.

CHAPTER EIGHTY

SUNNY

I think I'm having a panic attack. One I'm not sure I can climb out of. It doesn't relent when Tyler's hand is around my bicep. Or when he drags me outside and I'm hit with the cold night air.

How did Mitchell find this out about me? And why does he care so much about me and my past? It's just another glimpse into the power this family holds. And I wonder how much access Tyler is willing to give himself to it.

He releases my arm but doesn't look at me. A hand is pressed over his mouth while he paces back and forth in front of me in the long drive.

I don't know what to say. My eyes just follow him. His brows crease as he contemplates what he'll say next. His labored breathing tells me he's somewhere between angry and panicked.

Taking a contract elsewhere solidifies my leaving. But the information about me being married and having a whole different name changes things. It gives him information he didn't originally have.

I knew it'd make him become even more protective. More possessive. Because I'm legally bound to a man I'm running from. It connects Ryan and I in a way Tyler wasn't aware of before. In a way Tyler and I aren't. It means Ryan has rights that weren't there before knowing this information.

"You are married, Sunny. Oh my god." He runs a hand over his face. "How did I fucking miss that?"

This has been my secret I was hoping I'd take to the grave. But Mitchell found out and spilled it in a way to make me look awful. A girl who so willingly slept with his son while legally bound to another man.

A wife to another man.

But maybe I am awful for it. For sleeping with Tyler and being with him while simultaneously still being married to another man. Even if he is a man I'm desperately running from.

"Why didn't you tell me? Why won't you let me help you? Why did you hide this when you knew I could help you get out of it? To be divorced from him. I know fucking judges, Sunny!"

His patience is slowly disintegrating. And who can blame him? It's a rare thing to see him unravel, and I fear this isn't the kind of power I chose to have over him.

I hate myself for being young, dumb and in love and thinking binding myself to Ryan was a smart decision.

I looked into divorcing him without knowing where he is. It's possible, but a long process and very costly. So my only plan is to keep moving so that he can't find me.

And so far, it's working. I had a hiccup, but I'm leaving for Colorado in a few weeks. Just a few more weeks and I'd be in a new spot and have a new number again. A new license. Possibly a new name again after this.

"Okay and? Then what, Tyler? You'd be just like your father, abusing your power for selfish reasons. I will not be the person to make that happen. I will not be the reason you exploit your-self. This is *my* problem. No one else. I have a plan, and I'm sticking to it."

"You wouldn't be responsible for that, Sunny! Jesus." He

shakes his head. "I've already done bad things, Sunny. I'm not some knight in shining armor. *I have done bad things.* Why do you act like me doing this would be the first? And this would be for good reason. It's for your safety. *Your freedom.* For you. How do you not see that? Sunny, we could end it all. You wouldn't have to keep running. We could end this all. Then we could..." he chokes out.

"And then we could what, Tyler? Live happily ever after? You don't know Ryan. He said he'd find me, and he will if I stop running. It's as simple and as complicated as that."

"It's simple for me, Sunny! It's simple for me! You give me the word and I can make him go away. I can do it with my own fucking hands."

"See and that is exactly why. This is *my* life Tyler. This is for me to handle. Not you. You're right. You're not a knight in shining armor so stop fucking acting like it!" I yell.

He places his hands on his hips. "Oh yeah? And how's that plan working out for you, Sunny? He already got your number!"

I hate that he's right. What I'm doing isn't a permanent solution. But it's *my* solution for now. It's working for the most part. I just spent too long here.

"Sunny, I don't care that you're married. I care that you didn't tell me. It changes things. It changes things because we can use this. We can use this to help you." He takes a step towards me.

I take a step back. "No. You made me a promise. You made me a promise and you better stick to it."

I see his jaw harden and flex as he takes in my words. He looks away and then back at me, shaking his head. "This isn't fair. This isn't fair and you know it. You're so fucking confusing Sunny. Why won't you just stay with me? I stopped it all and pissed off a lot of fucking people for *you*." He points at me. "You won't stay with me. You won't let me help you. You won't give me anything on this man so I can find him. Why is it so hard for you to stay with me? Fuck, even if you don't. Go live your life Sunny but do it in freedom. Let me find him so that you are no longer shackled by fear. Let me give you a life where you know you are free. Even if it isn't with me."

I don't know, Tyler. I guess I have gotten so used to running.

I admire Tyler, being able to face his abuser daily while I constantly run from mine. And maybe that's where we're different. Where we can't meet eye to eye.

He faces reality.

I run from it.

But maybe that's just it too. He could take the revenge he so desperately sought out and channel it into a pursuit to Ryan to compensate for the fact he can't to his father. He said that's why it's become easier for him to complete his hits, because he always imagines it as Mitchell.

Or maybe, maybe it's simply because he's a man in love, ready to tear the world apart for the girl he loves. The girl he bled for, and she for him.

"I couldn't sit back and watch you give your life away to Shelby like that! Tyler, you act like you didn't know what this would end up in. I told you. I *warned* you. You know I'm leaving. Why are you acting like you haven't known? Why is it so hard to just enjoy the now?"

"Because I love you! I...I love you so much, Sunny. My heart belongs to you. Even if it means it will be broken into a million pieces, it was only ever yours to break anyways. But maybe that's just the thing, maybe I will always love you more than you love me. So you will never understand. Love is such an understatement, Sunny. It is such an understatement for the way I feel about you. I can't watch you give your life away to Ryan like this. It's *killing* me," he chokes. "Absolutely killing me knowing a fucking monster like that is still out there, walking around, hunting you down. And you won't let me do anything about it. Just because I knew you're leaving doesn't make it any less painful. Nothing will make it any less painful. God, we just need more time…I just, I don't get how I fucking missed this." He pinches the bridge of his nose and walks away from me.

"What the hell does that mean, Tyler? More time? I've spent too long here already."

"Every time you and I get close, just so close to where we're supposed to be… whenever we get in a spot that's comfortable and is *us*, you shut me out. Sunny, I just…I need to go find Cole. I need a minute. I have things I need to do here." He walks away.

I don't go after him.

Something tells me I'm not the only one keeping secrets between us.

CHAPTER EIGHTY-ONE
TYLER

How can I be okay with a man walking this earth who hurt the one thing I care about most in this world? The answer is easy.

I can't.

Amidst my conversation with Cole, Sam approaches with a bottle of champagne in one hand and the skirt of her purple dress clutched in the other.

"What's up? Where's Sunny?" She leans on the railing with me, taking a swig of her champagne and hands it to me.

"Didn't you hear? She's fucking married." I take a long drink from the bottle.

I can't believe I let that slip under my nose. I can't believe Mitchell found out before me. "Oh, and apparently her previous legal name was Mrs. Lauren Sunshine fucking Crawford. Or prior to that, Lauren Sunshine Masoner."

"I mean, that doesn't surprise me." She looks blankly over the balcony.

"How come?" I hand the bottle back.

She shrugs. "It just makes sense. She never called him her ex-boyfriend or life partner or whatever. She never put a label on him. And I mean yeah, when you're on the run, trying to hide from someone, the smartest option is to change your name."

I realize that, too. Sunny never put a label on him. Ryan. She'd let his name slip. And I wasn't going to give her any inclination that I'd picked up on it. She was careful, but I was observant.

"What do you know about him?" I ask.

"Probably as much as you do. He beat her. She took off and he did too."

"Mitchell was the one who aired it out. In front of a lot of people," I say, looking over the balcony.

I search the crowds for blonde curls but find nothing. If she ran off again, I'm going to lose my fucking mind.

"That doesn't surprise me, either. They'll do anything to make you get back with Shelby," she says, looking at me. "Listen, can you blame her? I mean, she went through hell. She's trying to leave that part of her life in the past. So who could blame her for not telling us."

"If she would just let me help her," I say, toying with a callus on my hand.

"Believe it or not Tyler, it's not your job to save everyone. And also believe it or not, not everyone wants to be saved." Sam hands me back the champagne. "You knew what was going to happen when you started things with her. So stop acting surprised that she isn't changing her plans for you."

I don't like what she's saying, but I know it's true.

"You okay?" I ask as I pull my phone out to my private thread with Sunny.

"Yeah, I'm fine. You going to go find her?"

I nod. "I'll come find you after." I kiss my sister on the cheek then walk away.

"At least someone is going to get fucked tonight," she murmurs.

SUNNY

After I stole a bottle of champagne from the bar, I made my way back to a quiet, dark dining room. I lean back in a chair and prop my feet up on the table where Tyler fucked me earlier. As I stare at the spot while I down the champagne, my attention is pulled to my new phone lighting up with a text from Tyler.

> Where are you, little fire?

He's been gone for maybe thirty minutes. I understand. He needs time to process. But I'd be lying if I said I was expecting more in that text than just that.

I decide to play petty. The champagne is making me bolder than usual.

> In the room where you fucked me before you left me.

> Stay there.

Setting the champagne down on the table, I stand from my seat. He's coming and I need to prepare for another intense conversation. Tyler's obsession has ignited after the details of tonight, and it's time for me to put that out once again.

Pacing the room, I tap my phone in my hands until I hear the door open. I whip my head to see Tyler standing in the doorway, taking up so much space despite the fact it's double doors.

It's a brief pause, and then he is stalking towards me in long strides.

"Tyler..." I try to start but his hand is grabbing my jaw, forcing me to look at him while his other hand braces my hip, pushing me against the wall and pinning me there.

"Don't ever hide anything from me again," he says with lethal calm.

I nod and fucking squeeze my thighs together.

"Is there anything else I need to know?" He searches my face for a semblance of a lie.

"No."

"Why Lauren? You are *not* a Lauren at all," he says, a glimmer of amusement passes his eyes.

I let a small laugh out. "Parental pressure. My grandparents insisted I deserved a regular name. Pressured my parents into making my first name Lauren instead of Sunshine. But as soon as they brought me home, they said fuck that, she's Sunny. They never got around to legally changing it. So, when I left Ryan, I did. I've always been Sunny, but Lauren Sunshine Crawford just didn't exist at all anymore, anyways." I shrug. "Sunny Mason feels right."

"You will never hold another man's last name again but mine," he says.

And before I can argue, he's pressing his lips against mine. It isn't the tender, passionate kisses from earlier. These are rushed, needy, possessive.

He throws his coat off, tossing it into the dark room and slides my dress straps down to reveal my breasts. He takes a pink peak between his teeth, biting and pulling a little too hard that has my head tilting back in a hiss.

He reaches a hand between my thighs where I'm soaked with both of us. The remnants of what we did earlier in here is physical evidence as he pulls a glistening finger from between my legs.

"Open," he demands.

And I do.

He slides his finger along my tongue. "You taste that, little fire? That's *us*. Taste how fucking perfect we are together. Taste how we belong together." He pops his finger from my mouth.

The wild look in his eyes and labored breaths that rise and fall from his chest all tell me one thing.

"Are you…jealous?" I ask.

"*Yes*," he says. "I will always be jealous for you."

Tyler is jealous.

That just might be his very downfall.

CHAPTER EIGHTY-TWO
TYLER

I know what Mitchell was doing when he told me I needed to go on a trip with him. It's a business trip, but more importantly it's to get me away from my final days with Sunny.

I send a text to Sunny letting her know we're taking off, hoping it'll be a quick turnaround. I'm sure Mitchell will try to do anything to keep me gone as long as possible. He knows Sunny's days are being etched off rapidly. He's trying to distract me. And he knows exactly what he is trying to distract me from.

We're meeting with a group of men, planning a way to release them of their obligations of another company so they can partner with ours and become new board members in our California location. It'll most likely end up in a hit.

These trips always come with surprises for me. It's like Mitchell tries to keep me on my toes, make sure my skills stay sharp.

Sunny is leaving in just two weeks, and now I'm most likely going to have a week taken from us.

My phone buzzes in my lap as I watch the private jet start to take off. Looking at my phone, my smile widens when I read her text.

Just get home soon and safely.

I'll try my best, Sunny.

We landed in Los Angeles within a few hours. I hate this place. From the smog to the people.

The McAllisters secured us their best rooms for the trip, as they always do. Business with them was one of our best investments yet, considering we always have a place to stay with the advantage of being able to do whatever we want during those stays. The perks of having lifelong friends in the hotel business with empires across the world.

We all traveled from around the country to be here for this meeting. They will meet with our team here. This is where these guys' other investors are located.

We'll spend the week examining their contracts, the company, the owner. Learn his ways, learn the company ways, then take it down from the inside. It's a simple task, and I'm ready to get it over with so I can go back home to my girl.

A couple hours later, I find myself sitting in a business office of the hotel reserved just for people like us. The room is filled with six other men. All around the same age as Mitchell except for one. He's maybe in his forties.

They all wear expensive suits and hold expensive cigars in their hands with glasses of expensive bourbon sitting next to them.

The decanter sits in the middle of the circular table as they pass it around, talking shit about their wives, their mistresses, their children, their companies.

I never get involved. I just observe.

I don't really drink, and I sure as shit don't smoke. Anything can happen in a meeting like this. Especially in a room full of men on a power trip.

They're all discussing avenues and ways to get the man to release them of their contracts so they can join our company.

"We could steal his bitch," Daniel, the CEO of an insurance company chimes in.

"No," I say coldly.

They all look at me, because it's the first word I've said.

"Well, you've been so silent over there, Tyler. Why chime in now?" he asks, leaning back in his seat, taking a drag from his third cigar.

"We don't involve innocent people." I meet his stare with a lethal calm. "It's simple, we find a loophole in your contracts, if we can't see an out there, we force him to make one. And I'll be glad to do it." If it means getting me back to Boston with Sunny, then so be it.

Mitchell's eyes pan over to me. I can't tell what he's thinking, but I at least know it isn't disappointment.

"I mean, if you're offering," Nixon, the owner of a finance firm quips.

"I just want to get this done." I cross my arms over my chest.

"Why? You don't enjoy the thrill? The power? The hunt?" Daniel asks.

"Tell me what to do and I'll do it. Have a goodnight, gentlemen," I say, standing from my seat.

Walking out, I hear the men mumbling, but I honestly don't have the patience or care to listen to what they say. I have a job to do, and I just want to get it done so I can go back home to the things I actually care about. I'm too distracted here already.

I pull my phone out to see a text from Sunny. God I fucking miss her, and it's only my second day away.

Wearing your t-shirt and only that t-shirt.

The things I would do to be home with you
right now. The things I would do to you if I
were home right now.

I respond.

I'm missing out on valuable time with her. I pull my suit jacket off, unbutton my shirt, and peel it off. I pull off the under-shirt, readying myself for a shower while I think about my girl at home, in bed, wearing my t-shirt and nothing else. My phone buzzes on the table while I continue undressing.

Too bad you aren't home. Guess I'll have to
take matters into my own hands.

Absolutely the fuck not.

You know the rules, Sunny. If you break them,
you'll be punished.

Just the idea of doing that gets me going. She's *mine*. All fucking mine.

And what might that punishment entail?

Oh, I can think of a few ways, little fire.

Sitting on the bed, my thoughts and text are interrupted by a knock on the door. I place my phone back on the nightstand and pull a gun from the drawer.

I look through the peephole to see a woman with bleach blonde hair wearing something that's hardly considered a dress. Her heels are so tall I'm surprised she's able to stand at all. Her eyes are heavy, like she's either been drinking or taking drugs.

Is there a fucking escort at my door?

I open the door. "Can I help you?"

"I was sent here by Mr. Caddell. He says you have some stress I need to ease." She traces a finger over my bare chest.

I immediately grab that wrist, stopping the contact. I may have to participate in the fucking game this society plays, but there's one thing I will always be honest about in who I am. I'll never, absolutely never, participate in the skin trade. I'll never hurt a woman. I'll never take advantage of a woman. Mitchell knows that.

Her eyes are glazed, and she stumbles into me. I grab her by the chin to make her look at me. "Who did this to you?"

"What are you talking about?"

"Who did this to you?" I growl.

"Mr. Caddell and all those other men. They called our service and made us take something to assist us in your needs." She meets my eyes.

Fuck.

I don't want to have to deal with this. I just want to go in and out of this trip. But clearly there is an ulterior motive to this escort at my door, and I need to figure out why.

It's a test, an assignment, and I'm going to fail. What is he trying to accomplish right now? Is this girl someone important? Or is someone she works with important? There's a fucking reason he sent her specifically to *my* door. And I'm going to find out why. There is always a reason behind his actions.

"Get inside." I grab her by the upper arm and drag her in my room, setting her in the seat at the table. She looks up at me with wide eyes.

"How many others are here?" I ask, kneeling in front of her.

"Seven," she breathes.

Fuck. Seven others I have to go hunt down.

"Do you want out?" I ask her. There's no point in saving someone who doesn't want to be saved. No point in wasting my resources, time, and energy and taking it away from other important things I have if she will go crawling back to this lifestyle.

"What?"

"It's not a trick question. Do you want out of this life?"

I watch the slow roll of her throat as she contemplates.

"Listen, I am not like those bastards. I'm offering you an out. I need you to want it and give me the okay if you do."

Her lip quivers with a nod as a small sob escapes her. "But not without the others."

"Okay." I nod. "Now tell me where the others are."

CHAPTER EIGHTY-THREE

TYLER

She doesn't know where the rest are, which means it's up to me to figure out. However, I do know where Mitchell is. And we're about to have some fucking words.

He's trying to test me. Because with a little coaxing and research, she gave me her full name, to which I researched and learned she's the daughter of the man we are trying to sever these bastards from.

His name is Adam Lannister, owner of Lannister Land Investing.

She was kidnapped and sold into the skin trade. And now, Mitchell had her at my door. She's his token. His prize for a trade. We give her back to Adam, he gives us these men we're trying to contract. It's vile. It's wrong. But fuck, he's good.

Marching down the hall with the woman, who I learned is named Katerina Lannister, I kick in Mitchell's door. The rage inside me is blinding.

"This is what you fucking do? This is what you do on your goddamn business trips?" I yell as I hold the woman by her upper arm. She's stumbling over her own feet.

Mitchell takes a sip of his bourbon as he eyes Katerina with

514

no remorse. Not even a reaction comes from him as I burst into his room.

"And?" he asks.

"You're participating in the sex and skin trade. These are people, Mitchell, fucking people," I say, sitting the drugged woman down. "You know who she is and you're using her instead of saving her."

"Do you tell yourself that when you complete your hits, Tyler? Did you tell yourself that when you killed the four men who tried to drug your sister? When you do your own hits based on personal vengeance? When you do things for the woman you claim to love but didn't even know her previous legal name?"

I remain silent. How the fuck he knew that, about Sam's predators, I have no clue. About Sunny…

"Don't act holier than thou, Tyler. You may not do what I do, but you still do fucked up shit. We are not that different. Just enjoy the girl. Then return her to her father. Your girl is leaving anyway." He sets his glass down.

"We are not the same. I'd never hurt a woman. I am not *you*," I growl. "Do fucking better, Mitchell. Do better!" I grab Katerina by the arm to bring her back to my room. I need to book a few rooms for her and the rest so they can sober up.

"Where are the rest?" I demand.

God knows who those other girls may be with. Women of higher status can become higher targets. People will pay big money for them to be able to connect bloodlines. It makes me think about those men who tried to drug Sam and take advantage of her.

My gut drops thinking about if Sunny were one of these girls. Sam… Mace..

"Guess you'll have to find out. Happy hunting." Mitchell turns his back to me.

I hate myself. I hate that I care. I hate that I've created these morals to live by. I hate that I couldn't finish my texting session with Sunny. I hate that I've been too busy to even check the cameras in my home and make sure she's safe.

I now sit in my hotel room, trying to hack the hotel system so I can find what rooms these men are in. I also booked rooms for the girls, too.

Katerina is now in the room next to mine so I can keep close watch with my men standing outside her door. Mitchell always has a purpose behind everything he does. And I learned that shit quickly tonight. All my life, really. But little does he know where he has purpose, I have a plan.

My phone buzzes with Cole on the other end.

"Anything?" I ask him upon answering. But then I pull up the information of the rooms each bastard is in. "Wait, I got it."

"Okay, I was going to say facial recognition picked up their faces in the hotel. So you got the rooms?" Cole asks.

"Yes, I do," I say, typing on my computer, writing down each room. "How is Sunny?"

She's staying at my place while I'm gone. It makes me feel safer since I have cameras in every corner imaginable in my home.

"Sleeping soundly in your bed," Cole says.

My heart pummels in my chest. Knowing she fell asleep without so much as a response from me, but my hands are quite literally full right now.

Now that I know the purpose of this trip, I can get it done and move on. Any time away is less time for me to focus on her.

"Okay, you let me know when to send our guys to the rooms. Send me the information as soon as you can," Cole says.

"I will. How the hell am I going to do this without pissing off all these guys? They're supposed to be contracted with us." I rub a hand over my face. "I mean, sure, Katerina is the key to the contracts, but I can't just let the other girls stay. And she refuses to leave without them."

"We will figure it out. It just shows them they can't fuck with the Caddell Company."

"Okay, I just emailed you the rooms."

"Alright, on your command, boss."

"Send them over," I tell him.

"They should be there in ten minutes."

"Perfect. I'll be waiting."

Then our call goes dead. I pull my phone to the thread of messages where Sunny's text is left unanswered.

You better have listened to me. No one touches what's mine except for me. Not even you. Sleep well, little fire. I love you.

CHAPTER EIGHTY-FOUR

TYLER

CHECKING MY PHONE TO SEE SHE HASN'T TEXTED BACK, I PULL up the feed and see her passed out in our bed.

She's on her back, curls sprawled across the pillow, arms above her head. And I'm pretty sure I even see a little drool on the side of her chin.

I fucking *love* that girl.

When I go to check the cameras at her apartment, I'm alerted by Cole's text that the guys are here.

I make my way to the hallway, gun in hand, walking down with the guys behind me, assigning them to each room, guiding them and giving commands.

They all kick in the doors, and I watch on the feed, the cameras going back and forth to each room in different parts of the hotel. The chaos unravels as girls scream and men yell unhappily.

My men drag the girls out of the rooms to the ones I have booked for them. Some of them are half naked. Some of them are almost completely knocked out. It makes something flip in my stomach and rage burns me from the inside out.

They finally bring all the girls to the room I have for them.

Half are shaking scared while the other half are barely coherent from the drugs.

I run a hand over my tired face. It's three in the morning and I need sleep.

"Okay, you have two choices. Get out and go home or stay. I want you to know the option for freedom is here. You need to decide. You have until tomorrow morning to make your choice so I can get you all out of here before someone comes looking for you." They all look at me like deer in the headlights.

How did I get myself into this shit?

"The choice is yours. My guys will be here all night to make sure you are safe. Get some sleep. Think about it. Then let us know. You each already have a new name and life assigned to you if you choose to leave this one. Katerina, you're staying. I'll be returning you to your father in the morning."

"Kitty is leaving?" A girl asks.

"She doesn't get the choice," I affirm.

I start to walk out of the room when stopped in my tracks by a soft voice. "Thank you," I hear Katerina say.

I've probably stuck my head in places I shouldn't have too many times. I've probably taken on too many jobs doing this just to tell myself I'm somehow doing some good despite the man I work under. Despite the bad that I have done. But either way, it all makes up for it when I know I've at least made someone safe.

I could've said no to her. I could've told her she had no choice. I could've handcuffed her to the bed until I could return her to her father without batting an eye for the others.

But no. I had to do *this*.

Going to my room, I strip my clothes off from my body and lay in my bed. I pull up the feed of my cameras in my bedroom that gives me a side view as if I'd be lying right next to my girl.

She's sleeping on her side and stomach, arms under the pillow, face buried in it. A smile curves my mouth despite the ache that wraps around my ribs.

I place the phone propped up as if she's lying next to me and imagine myself in bed with her. One night, I can't even go one night without her. How the hell am I supposed to watch her leave?

I take a deep breath in. Within hours, the previous identities of the girls are wiped off the face of existence and replaced with new ones. All on their consent.

That's why I can't do it with Sunny. Because she has a life she intends to live. And I can't take that from her, not when Ryan has already done it once. I won't be that man.

"I love you, Sunny," I say as I close my eyes and go to sleep, wishing it's right next to her.

By the morning, five out of the seven women decide to take our offer and move on with a new life, leaving behind everything and everyone they know. Another decides to continue her life, but out of this lifestyle of being a high-end escort. The other went back to this life.

I won't judge. I don't know her life. All I know is she was given an out, and this life seems more secure than that for her.

I end up being summoned by Mitchell to meet in the conference room again. When I walk in, I'm greeted by all six other men sitting around the table, stewing in the aroma of cigars and bourbon. Scowls are present on their faces as their eyes narrow on me.

Good.

"Nice of you to join us, Tyler." Mitchell stands with a glass of bourbon in his hand.

"What can I do for you gentlemen?" I place my hands in my pockets.

"You interfered with my night away, Caddell," Nixon says as he takes a drag from his cigar.

I turn my head to him, giving him nothing. "And I'd gladly do it again. I'm sure your wife will appreciate the favor."

"Easy, guys." Mitchell takes a seat, motioning for me to sit down.

"I'd rather stand."

"You all only got a glimpse of what my Tyler can do." Mitchell starts. "*My boy*." Mitchell grins. "We are in a kill or be killed world. And he, gentlemen, is a trained killer. You have a hit you want done, my boy here will get it done for you. You want a system breached, he will hack it within minutes. Anything you want can be done through us. The Caddell Company."

There it is. The ulterior motive has finally been revealed. The puppeteer tugged at my strings he stitched in my skin and I fucking moved on his command.

Rage pricks at my skin and wraps around my ribs. With an exhale, I rub a hand down my face to try and blow off the smoke of the flames kindling inside me. He used helpless women for a power trip.

"He just proved to you all a *fraction* of his capabilities. His split-second decisions, the way he so easily hacked the hotel system and cameras, got men here, and saved those girls to then give them completely new identities so they can go about their merry fucking lives." He shakes his head with a sadistic smile. "A saint, a savior, but a fucking lethal predator. He's trained for this. Which means he's trained to make these things happen for you, too. Imagine, he did that all in a span of a few hours. On a split-second decision. Think about what he can accomplish with detailed planning and precision *for you*."

They all look to one another, then to me, contemplating in silent communication as Mitchell goes on selling me like a fucking prize to win if they join our company.

"So, you see now what he can do for nobodies. Let's see what he can do for somebodies. He will not only protect our empire, but yours too. You each can give me one hit you want to complete. We will get it done."

We. Meaning me.

Feeling my jaw clench, I roll my neck to try and workout the tension. He's always a fucking step ahead.

"Not only that, but I have you out of Lannister's grasp. See, the girl sent to Tyler's door is Lannister's daughter. She was kidnapped and trafficked. And my boy Tyler here saved her and is ready to serve her up on a silver platter to Lannister in exchange for you to be free of your contracts. The rest, well, he was just showing off. Showing you what he can do for you when you become a part of us." He shrugs as he puffs his cigar.

"Well played, Mitchell. I have to give it to you, that was a good plan." Another one of the men says, Greg, who's a Judge.

"And this will work?" Daniel asks skeptically.

"It always works. If it doesn't, we will find another way. But how can Lannister say no when we have his baby girl." Mitchell shrugs, as if he'll be the one putting in the hours of work it will take.

As if Katerina is a fucking piece to be tossed around.

All the men shake hands with me and Mitchell and exit the room to let me get to work.

"You fucking used me. Used my skills and knowledge as leverage. The skills and knowledge I had to learn to survive this world you forced me into. You used a vulnerable girl," I growl.

"Oh please, Tyler. Don't act like you aren't using it to your advantage, either. It's what you do. It's why we have all the investments and contracts we do. You know the job. It isn't always pretty. Sometimes all it is, is a contract. Sometimes it's someone's head on a platter to secure that contract. I cleaned up the mess you made. You pissed off each of those men and I had to find a way to morph it to work out in our favor and I did. You should be thanking me."

I let out a snarl, angry at the fact there is truth in his words.

"That's what I thought." He takes the bourbon decanter and pours another glass.

"And those women?" I ask.

"A bunch of whores. See, I did a good thing. They have better lives now because of this whole plan." He sits down, looking smug.

I shake my head. "Why didn't you just give me the assignment like normal instead of all this bullshit?"

"Because they needed to see you caught off guard and doing your best work to gain their trust. I'm asking all of them to sever their loyalty to a huge company. They needed raw, real proof of your capabilities."

No other words are shared between us when I exit the room. After hours of working out severing their contracts, I have our guys bring Katerina home safely.

I spend the next few hours creating our own contracts for these bastards, damning myself for even creating ties with men like this in the first place.

We'll spend one more night here to celebrate and solidify our win with each of the men. Making sure there are absolutely no loopholes for them to leave without crumbling their own empires. That's all this is. Modern day kingdoms run by stupid foolish kings in suits.

After I do research on their hit requests, I finally make it back to my room and lay on my bed, finally looking at the thread with Sunny. And I wonder if that's what it'll be like when she leaves. If she will even let me live in this thread with her or shut me out entirely.

It feels weird being apart.

The words make me smile. Because it means she's realizing how empty a life apart will be. Maybe it will make her realize she needs to stay.

Just stay with me, Sunny.

> It is, isn't it? I'll be home tomorrow. I don't think I can handle another day apart.

I shoot my text to her.

That's when I realize, I don't want to spend another minute away from her. I send Mitchell a text, telling him I'll finalize the contracts from Boston and email them to him to have the men sign.

I don't care if it pisses them off. I'm going home to my girl. I don't want more time stolen from us.

CHAPTER EIGHTY-FIVE

SUNNY

After a long shift, I walk from the doors of the hospital, through the dark parking garage to Tyler's truck. He's been letting me use it to get to and from work while he's been gone over the last few days.

A cold feeling creeps up my spine. I pause in the dark lot and turn around, plagued by a sense of impending doom. Goosebumps crawl my skin, like I somehow have eyes on me.

I've been feeling this way for a while now. And I can only blame being apart from Tyler along with the phone call just a few weeks prior. Ever since then, I've been really on edge, making Tyler resistant to leaving me at all for his trip.

I shake the feeling off and get into his truck. Turning it on, I check the back seat and all the mirrors and blow out a breath of relief.

I'm getting so into my head. In less than two weeks I'll be leaving, and I can feel myself getting antsy as each day etches off.

As soon as I pull up to Tyler's home, I rush to the door and lock it, putting the alarm system back on. I do have to say,

Tyler's home is a fortress that is not easy to break into. Staying here has made me feel safer.

I kick my shoes off and my eyes peer over to his office door. I've been here hundreds of times and have never been there. But the only reason it piques my interest now is because he *locked* it while he's away and I'm here. It makes me wonder what he has in there that he doesn't want me to see.

Waltzing to the door, I jiggle the handle as if it'd magically unlock on its own. There isn't even a key fob for a key to go into, making me think he has an app to lock and unlock it.

Maybe I'll ask him about it when he comes home.

I go to the bathroom and turn the faucet for the shower where we spent probably one too many times naked together.

Then I hear the front door open and close.

The alarm doesn't go off.

Feeling my heart sink, I grab the gun that sits in his night-stand drawer and slowly make my way downstairs. No one is supposed to come over tonight, and my phone didn't have any messages from the family.

Slowly, I make my way down the stairs, gripping the gun in my trembling hands. Thoughts fester over and over how I should've trusted my instinct.

More sounds rustle around the downstairs, making my heart lurch in my chest. Nausea rolls through me, but I steel my spine and hold the gun up to the shadow that is standing in the living room. My heart thrums in my ears as it beats frantically against my sternum.

"Woah," Tyler says, holding his hands up and turning around. "Looks like all that training paid off."

"Jesus Christ, Tyler! I thought you weren't coming home until tomorrow?" I set the gun down and run to him.

Relief washes over each tense muscle of my body. My hands are still trembling, but it slowly disappears when his smile widens as he brings his surrendering arms down and wraps them around me while I jump into him.

I'm engulfed in his citrusy scent, feeling his warm body press against mine, his heart thrumming in his chest against my own. Each inhale of him makes my heart slow to a calm.

"I just couldn't stay away any longer," he murmurs in my hair, taking in a big inhale of me.

He pulls away and cradles my face with both his hands. When I meet his gaze, I can see exhaustion ring his dark emeralds. He presses his forehead to mine and we sit there for a few breaths. Then he finally presses his lips against mine.

"I missed you."

"I missed you too," I reply. "Wanna take a shower with me?"

A feline smile spreads across his face. "Absolutely."

I'm going to miss you so much, Tyler.

CHAPTER EIGHTY-SIX

SUNNY

I sit on Sam's couch, knowing the times left for moments like these are dwindling down to practically nothing. It's our last bach night, and honestly, I still don't feel ready to leave.

I thought as the time reduced and I got closer to my departure, I'd feel ready the way I did before coming to Boston. But I just don't. If anything, I can't shake that sense of impending doom. That string between me and Tyler seems to protest anytime I think about leaving. Like it's tugging at me, and he whispers *but just stay*, along it.

"It's not going to be the same without you, Sunny." Macey plops down next to me, handing me a bowl of pasta.

"Seriously. I know you said we could facetime but who is going to help us finish off the wine? My ass has gone lightweight having to share." Sam sits on the other side of me.

"Please Sam, we both know you can finish a bottle and not feel a thing." Macey takes a bite of her pasta.

Sam shoots Macey a look without her seeing. There is a hardness in her amber eyes that didn't exist there before New Years Eve. An unspoken tension that lingers between the two despite the make-up they had that night.

Trying to brush off the tension, I just chuckle and look at my sisters. But with the way both their eyes turn wide, I know they see what I wished they didn't in my face.

"Spill it." Sam places her bowl on the coffee table.

Macey pauses the TV. The two wait patiently for me to admit the truth I've kept locked for a while now.

"I don't know…I just…I don't feel ready."

"I fucking knew it!" Sam jumps up giddily.

"Calm down, princess."

"Have you told Tyler?" Macey asks wide eyed.

"Of course not. You guys know he wouldn't even hear the words I say. His brain would just translate it to *Sunny stays*. Ugh, I just, I guess I started to question…"

"Question what? Question what?" Sam says too excitedly.

"Just, what if? You know? What if I could have normal? What if I could stay here? What if he never tries to find me? What if it worked out between me and Tyler? What if it all just worked out? But that's the reckless part of me," I counter. "The rational part tells me how I did that once upon a time. I let myself get too comfortable. How can I stray from this plan I've held strong to for this long? Do I just get attached too easily? I have to stick to my plan, right? I have to stick to my plan. Not just because of the promise Ryan made to me, but to myself too."

The two look at me with stupid fucking grins on their faces.

"Stop," I warn.

"You know we can help…" Sam starts.

I shake my head. "I know you can, but at what cost? Tyler already takes enough heat from Mitchell. This is nobody's job but mine to handle. And I can't trust myself, not after what happened. My judgment has clearly not been good in the past, why should I trust it now?"

"You were a different person then, Sunny. You are not who you were even just six months ago. You're stronger. You're better. You're even happier," Macey says.

"Sunny, involving a lawyer won't cross any boundaries. It won't have Tyler doing anything illegal. It's just some options and different avenues on how you can navigate this. You can navigate it instead of running like hell from it," Sam offers.

"This can be handled however you want it to be handled. We've all got your back. No matter what you end up choosing, we will all support you. We always have, we always will." Macey gives me a weak smile.

"Fuck that shit, Sunny stay! Just stay! Talk to Tyler about it. See what our lawyers can do. Weigh out all the options before you fucking run. We need you here. We want you here. If you leave, I'm gonna be so mad." Sam grabs my hands.

"I love you both so much."

"Okay, so then stay." Sam smiles.

A weak smile pulls my lips. I know what I'm going to say is going to cause more chaos than the last six months. And I can't even believe I'm considering this.

"I'll talk to him," I finally say.

Squeals that I didn't know could exist ring through my two sisters. They jump up and down and pull me up with them.

"Okay, okay calm down. It doesn't mean I'm staying. It's simply weighing all my options and seeing which is the best," I clarify, even though I know it didn't go through their happy ridden heads.

"Bach nights don't end here!" Sam hugs me.

"Maybe, maybe they won't."

"It doesn't matter. Even if you leave, even if you stay, we will always be sisters. No matter when, no matter where, no matter what," Macey says.

"Oh my god we need to get that tattooed," Sam says.

"What?" Both Macey and I question.

"On our wrists. Friendship tattoos."

That's exactly what we end up doing.

Written across each right wrist of ours, we get the words inked into our skin.

Macey with *No Matter When.*

Sam with *No Matter What.*

And mine with *No Matter Where.*

Because that's how it is. No matter all those things, they will always be my sisters.

CHAPTER EIGHTY-SEVEN

SUNNY

I walk into the warmth of Tyler's home and shut the door behind me. Leaning back on it, I huff out a slow breath trying to steady my nerves.

My whole body is shaking as the nervousness coils around my ribs, making each labored breath difficult.

The idea of staying and maybe, just maybe building a life here has been slowly plaguing my mind. But as the days on my calendar get less and less, the thoughts consume me. Along with the unsettling feelings that come with either option.

Ever since the phone call, my entire being has been split in two moods; the need to run and the need to stay. I cling to both desperately, unsure of which to let go of.

Nothing about my leaving feels right. I chalk it up to nerves. And I have to admit that, while I'm so fucking nervous, a small sense of relief blooms in my chest at the possibility of staying. Of talking with their lawyers, having Tyler promise to do this the right, legal way. Living a life that no longer has limits, rules, or a plan.

If we can do that, then maybe I can stay. Build a life in this place that has somehow become home. It creates options that never would've existed otherwise.

Before, I didn't think I had a choice. Maybe because I didn't believe I deserved to have one. But now, I know I do. I have a choice. And I choose to stay.

"Tyler?" I call shakily as I remove myself from the door. I place the keys and my phone down on the kitchen island.

"I'll be down in a minute, little fire." I hear him call, the shower shutting off.

I shift on my feet, glancing around the townhome that has somehow become my home, too.

Watching the fire in his black marble fireplace, my gaze is pulled to his office, noticing the door is ajar. I sit for a beat, then immediately walk over to the beckoning door. Like something in there is summoning me to it.

I peek my head inside the dark room. Four massive computer screens light up a mess of paperwork on his desk.

I chuckle because Tyler is the farthest thing from messy. Seeing those scattered papers is foreign.

A wall is lined with books like a library while the other is decorated in fancy weapons, each having their own light to display them.

A keypad sits on that wall to open what I'd assume to be a safe filled with other weapons. Disguised as a painting to lead to the safe, which makes sense why it's locked when he's gone.

The wall behind his desk is all ceiling to floor windows giving off a view of the city. It's warm and looks like your typical office, but something echoes eerie and deadly, too.

The computer screen saver switches pictures. First a picture of Sam and Tyler as kids on the beach in Cape Cod. The next a selfie of me and Tyler. I smile at it. It's sweet he has me as a part of his screen saver.

It clicks to a picture of all of us at Martha's, sitting in our usual booth. One Tyler took of all of us. And I smile at that too, because maybe, just maybe we can all have more nights like that.

The idea of staying sounds more freeing than running.

But then the screen shines down on the paperwork on his desk, bringing light to a familiar name across one of the papers. *My name*. Then I notice my name on *all* the papers.

The air is lost from my lungs and I'm convinced my heart stops beating entirely. While my mind is telling me, screaming at me to turn around and walk out, I rush to the desk.

I look at all the pages on his desk, filled with my previous name, current name, Ryan's name, his parents, their car accident that killed them.

Both of our entire lives, scattered across Tyler's desk. I move his mouse on his screen to see just more details of my entire life spread on the screen.

I can't stop looking, regardless of the fact I already know what this all is. Regardless of the fact that fiery rage is fueled with each violation of my privacy I see.

Every single bill in our names, all the places we lived, GPA's, jobs, sports, criminal records, travel, our marriage license, ways to get it annulled, divorced, emails with judges, lawyers, bounties, investigators, his security, every location Ryan has been to since the moment he left our hometown. Which happens to be every single city *Tyler* has gone to on his *business* trips.

I bring a shaky hand to my mouth, trying to stifle the screams I want to unleash. He's been his own personal investigator, a bounty hunter, a predator tracking down his fucking ultimate prey.

He promised and he *broke* it.

He shattered every sliver of trust I've gained in him since the moment we met. The pieces of my broken heart that somehow got sewed together by that thread connecting us starts to unravel, releasing all my jagged edges that causes internal bleeding to my soul.

How can I possibly stay and expect him to make a promise when he can't even keep all the others he made to me?

He broke his fucking promise.

Sucking in a breath, I take steps back, realizing the violation of my life in front of me. This whole time, this whole time he's not only been lying to me but *investigating* me. Investigating Ryan. Mapping out all the ways to find him and kill him. Even when he promised not to.

Everything you could know about my life sits on this desk.

I was ready….I was ready to *try*.

For him.

For me.

For us.

Ready to stay. But he broke his promise to me. It wasn't the first, and it clearly won't be the last. How can I derail my plan, put myself at risk for someone so willing to betray me? And who will most likely continue to.

I see the medical records and police reports of that night, the pictures of the face I wished I didn't have to see again. The face of a broken, battered girl. The face of the girl who died that day. My whole life, right here.

A sob escapes my throat as I hold up the pictures of my injuries from that night. The photos I wished no one else would ever see. The bruise along my cheek bone, the gashes all over my face. The bruises on my thighs from his knees pinning me down. The handprints on my hips and the bruises on my ribs. The busted lips. The blood coating my face. The scar on my neck from when he strangled me with my own stethoscope.

The hollowness and death that sat in those eyes I don't even recognize.

I don't recognize that girl.

That's not me. That girl, she died that night. And I wanted her to be left there. Yet somehow, Tyler resurrected her.

I know he will say he did this because he loves me, but that's what Ryan said, too. And just because someone does something in the name of love doesn't make it right.

It doesn't make it hurt less.

"Sunny." I hear his voice. It's breathy. It's panicked. It's fearful.

As he should be.

He stands in the doorway, his chest moving up and down rapidly as he holds a hand up in surrender. His wet hair slicked back as if he ran his hands through it. Wearing a white t-shirt and gray sweatpants, looking as devastating as I feel.

I drop the picture back onto the desk and meet his stare.

We don't say anything.

We don't move.

The silence looms over us. He's too scared to do anything in fear I'll run for the hills.

That's exactly what I do, I fucking run.

CHAPTER EIGHTY-EIGHT

TYLER

She bolts past me before I can even think to grab her.

"Sunny!" I yell out for her. But I can't run fast enough. Panic, sheer panic courses through me.

I was going to tell her.

I was going to tell her.

"Sunny!" I yell again. She doesn't even look at me.

She grabs her things off the kitchen island, frantically looking around the living room. Grabbing all her things she's acquired here over the last few months.

Her half-read book on the coffee table.

Her sweater slung across a barstool.

Her stethoscope sitting on the island.

Her water bottle I always have to remind her to drink from.

Her favorite mug sitting by the coffee station.

She's going to leave.

"Sunny, *please*!" I beg as I run to her. I grab her shoulders, trying to spin her to face me. She keeps her eyes closed and her shoulders move up and down with each cry.

I remove the items from her arms and set them on the island and cup her face, trying to make her look at me.

"Sunny please. No, no, no. I was going to tell you, okay? Don't leave. Just don't leave. This is such unchartered territory for me. These feelings I have they're just too big. How can I say goodbye to you, Sunny? How can I say goodbye to you?" I realize tears are coming from my own fucking eyes, and my words are a mix of sobs and pain.

Her freckled nose scrunches with each sniffle as she stares at her feet, refusing to look at me again.

"You lied," she seethes and her heated eyes meet mine. "You lied to me and you broke every fucking promise you made!"

Something in my chest cracks at her words. This wasn't the way I planned on telling her. But here we are. And now I have to cling to that bond between us in hopes she will understand why I did everything I did.

I broke my promise.

I broke it and didn't tell her.

I broke it and it's been broken for a while.

It was broken before I even made it. I shattered it like a fucking piece of glass. Of course I broke that promise. How could she expect me to keep it?

I broke it because *I* broke.

The night she finally accepted us, I sent an email to Cole to start our hunt. Because I knew that we couldn't let something that I could easily take care of stand in our way. Because if two people can't stay away from one another the way we couldn't, then maybe we aren't meant to be apart at all.

I found him. With only a first name to guide me. I fucking found him.

When Sunny shattered her phone, I had Cole take it apart and analyze everything we could there. I traced the number to a burner in Washington. My plane ticket was booked in the same hour, telling Sunny it was a work trip instead. Cole and my security team scoured every store, every hotel, trying to find him. It ended up being a dead end, but I gave it everything I had.

Somehow, I'm still a step behind him, following his trail like a mad man. I let an average man somehow get out of my grasp. Soon enough, I'll catch up and have him in my palm, squirming and begging for the freedom he will never get.

I called in a favor to Lannister, asking him to have his men watch over Sunny's parents. He owed me for saving his daughter, anyways.

How can you blame me? Love made me fucking crazy. I'll do anything to protect the ones I love. Sunny should've known that by now.

I'm usually able to find even the hardest of hunts in a matter of weeks. Yet I've spent months trying to find him, and I'm always somehow a step behind him. I didn't give him the credit he deserves. I underestimated him. He doesn't seem to have a rhythm or rhyme to his travels. It's all sporadic chaos. There's no pattern for me to follow. Nothing to track and get answers to.

The last known location I had on him was on the opposite end of the country. I'm trying to keep up while managing my life here. It was hard keeping this from her, but it needed to be done.

How could she expect me to not hunt down the one thing that was keeping us from being together? The one thing threatening her safety.

Her life.

It'd be the only promise I'd ever break to her. But it needed to be done because her safety is my priority, even if it means she'd hate me forever. Even if it means that we won't be together. Even if she still left and lived a life that isn't here, with me, with us.

At least she could still live a life free of her abuser. Free from him. And I'd be okay with that. I would have to be.

I won't stop looking even after she leaves. Of course I fucking won't.

I hoped, *I hoped* we'd find him before she left. Then she could stay. And yes, I felt awful for breaking my promise to her.

But I'd feel even worse knowing I sat back and did absolutely nothing.

"Yes, okay?! I broke my promise. I broke it because I broke, Sunny. *I fucking broke*," I yell.

My voice doesn't even sound like my own. This is the sound of a man crumpling. A man so desperate to cling to the one thing that's finally made me feel alive. The one thing that gave me light and life in death and darkness.

Just as the moon cannot glow without the sun, I cannot live without her. She is my sun. And I am the moon, so desperate to keep her light I didn't think existed, shining through my darkness.

"So this whole time." She shakes her head as tears stream down her face. "It was all a lie. The promise was broken before it was even made. The way you reacted at the campaign was… fake because you already knew. You already knew the real parts of me, while I clearly knew nothing about you." Her anger rises through her words.

"You've hid things too, Sunny. Let the campaign be clear of that," I remind her.

"Because that version of me, she was dead, Tyler! She was dead!"

My hands tighten on her face. "I can't do this, Sunny. I can't say goodbye. How can I let go of this beautiful, wonderful thing that has come into my life?" I choke, grappling onto this in desperate hope. "That has made it so much better. That gave me light in a time when darkness was all that consumed me? How can you expect me to just let you go while he is still out there? How do you expect me to let you go at all?"

Her shoulders shudder with her cries. She won't look at me. That's when I see it. The woman I'll never stop loving is falling out of love with me.

I feel her fucking slipping. I had all of her and now I'm about to have none of her. Losing her is losing a part of me. I had a life before her, and I had a life with her, but I can't ever imagine a life after her.

It wouldn't be living at all.

"Just stay with me, okay? Just stay with me. You know now, you know and we can use all of this. We can go to my lawyers, we can do whatever you want, baby. I'll stop my hunt. I'll stop it if it means you'll take their help. Whatever you ask I can make it happen for you. We can give you a life, Sunny, a life here."

I'm not sorry. I won't deny her right to be angry, either. I'd broken a promise to a girl who barely had any trust left after someone else had broken it.

But there would not be a world where I'd let her live in fear when there was something I could do about it.

Even if it meant losing her in the process.

CHAPTER EIGHTY-NINE

SUNNY

I can't keep watching this. Watching him *beg* like this. Watching that small sliver of hope hang between us. Watching a predator crumble at my feet. Watch a man shatter from the inside out.

I need to bring the anger back.

"You did this, Tyler, you did this!" I remove myself from him. "Why is it so hard to just ask you to be a good person? Just for this? You say you'll handle it my way but you haven't this whole time! I actually thought you respected me enough to stay true to your promises. *You can't.* That's reason enough for me to leave. I was a stupid fucking girl to think I could derail it for a guy. I've never questioned you or what you do or who you are. I was never afraid of you. But now I'm starting to think I should be."

I run up the stairs and hear his footsteps chasing after me. I search the home for all the shit I left here.

He grabs the back of my neck, yanking me to him and forces me to look at him, a low growl forming in his chest.

"I'm not a good person, Sunny. I never have been, never will be. You all claim me to have a hero-savior complex when in reality I am the fucking *villain*," he seethes. "A hero, a savior, will sacrifice you for the world, but a villain will sacrifice the world for you. And that's exactly what I'll do. I will sacrifice everything for you. I will break every law, every moral, every fucking promise if it means that I can be with you. I don't plan to change that anytime soon. Not for anyone, and not for you. Because at the end of the day, if I have to break your trust, break *us* in order to keep you safe, I fucking will. You fell in love with me knowing all the dark, twisted, depraved parts of me. That was the whole fucking point, Sunny. To make sure you knew every part of me and could love all those parts. And guess what? *You do*. And I fell in love with you knowing those broken pieces of yours would cut me bleeding. And I still love you."

I try to shove him off but he grabs me by my bicep.

"Sunny, don't." He looks at me, face solemn, tone demanding. "Don't leave yet. We can't. We can't leave like this. We can't let this one moment change all the memories we have together. We need to talk through this."

"There is *nothing* to talk about. You already know every detail of my life. Are you able to read my goddamn mind too? Plant a tracking device in me while I was sleeping? Put cameras in my home?!" I yell.

And he winces. This grown, lethal, predator winces at *me*.

"Anything I've ever done has been to ensure your safety," he growls.

I step back. He didn't deny any of those things. What else has he done behind my back that I don't know of?

"Tell me everything," I say firmly.

"Sunny…"

"*Everything*."

He blows out a shaky breath. "I started researching after the night you told me everything. I made you the promise, and I stopped. But then, I fell in love with you. *I fell in love with you, Sunny*. And I spiraled from there. The night…the night…" The words die on his tongue. "I texted Cole and told him the hunt was back on, even though it'd never really ended. We crossed that line and I fell more in love with you when I didn't even think it was possible. We made love and I knew there was no going back. I told you that, Sunny. I've been searching this whole time. That's why I said the promise was broken before it was ever even made."

"Why did you even make it to begin with?"

"Because you were spiraling, and I didn't know how else to bring you back."

"You know, I actually considered staying. I actually fucking considered throwing my plans out the window for a life here with you. With them. But it's not worth it, not when we keep doing this. This just reaffirms I have to leave because I can't trust anything, not you, not even myself. Life will go on, after this, after us, Tyler. It may not be the same. But it will go on. And one day, you will get the love you so deserve. The way you should be loved, and you won't have to fight for it, to save it. You won't have to break promises to try and keep it. Keep her."

Because even while my body courses with rage for him right now, my love for him echoes with each beat of my heart, each breath I take.

Clearly I am not capable of matching his love, and he deserves that. All my broken pieces keep cutting him, and this is prevalent. Yet he still wants me to stay, and that's just something I can't do.

I can't give that to you Tyler.

He shakes his head. "Fuck, Sunny! *You* are what I want. *You* are who I love. It won't change. My love for you won't change. Just stay, baby. Just stay until we figure this out." He presses our foreheads together.

I pull away, leaving the look on his face empty. "No, Tyler. I can't. I can't. I can't. I can't." I run my hands through my hair. "I had a plan! Okay, I had a plan and you ruined it. You made me fall in love with you and now we have to do this! It hurts! It fucking hurts so much!" I sob, bringing a shaking hand to my mouth.

"Then love me, Sunny! Love me and stop fucking running. Love me and let me fucking love you!"

"It's not that simple." I shake my head. "You can't try and write over this ending that has been written in ink on paper for us."

"Then I will rip out the pages and write an entirely different one." He steps into me.

"You knew," I seethe. "You knew my plan. You knew I was leaving, and you still made me love you!"

We never really fought before. Not like this.

Never like this.

There's no point. There's absolutely no point in this because we are going in circles.

"We can't keep going back and forth like this, Tyler. You are right. We fell in love. We knew the end. It's here, Tyler. The end is here, and we just have to accept it."

I feel my stomach churn at our words. At the look on his face. The desperation that hangs in the air between us. The devastation slowly coming about to wreck both of us.

"There is nowhere you can go in this life or any other that I won't find you, little fire. Go ahead and run, but remember that somehow, you will always come full circle and smack right back into me," he growls, stepping into me, polluting my space with him. "because this isn't what you want."

"There is a difference between want and need," I snap back as I turn around towards the closet and grab my clothes.

"Tell me, Sunny. Tell me there is a way this works. Tell me there is a version where there is nothing standing in our way. Tell me there is me and you somehow finding a way to find a place to put all this fucking want. Tell me there is a way for us to build a life together. Tell me there is a way I can change your mind," he chokes.

I spin around to face him, so filled with anger. "Nothing would ever change my mind." Then I turn back around, walking into the closet.

I feel his hand grip the back of my neck again, yanking me to him and making me face those heated, lethal emeralds.

"Then I will change your mind," he says, crushing me to his lips.

CHAPTER NINETY

SUNNY

I PUSH HIM BACK AND SLAP HIM ACROSS THE FACE, BUT something primal switches in him. Within seconds, our bodies are molded to one another again. It's hard to know who even initiated it, but all I know is there's something in our DNA that refuses to let us stop this cycle.

That kindles the fire within my soul and lights up his darkness. That's all we've been. He is the darkness, me the fire, and our only existence is to enhance one another.

He lets out a groan as he curls an arm around my waist, hoisting me onto him and lifting me off the ground. My legs wrap around him, and I press into the hardness filling his pants.

With a shudder, he slams my back against the wall and places me on the shelf of the closet. One moment my shirt is on and the next it's off.

"Tyler–" I breathe.

"Don't speak, just do." He peels his shirt off, exposing the artwork of scars across his body.

Everything is fervent and rushed. From the way he rips my pants off to the way my fumbling hands pull his sweats down.

Then all at once, we're both completely naked in this closet, somehow. We both know we shouldn't, yet we don't stop.

I almost second guess this decision, but he doesn't give me much time to decide because he wraps his arm around my waist again, lifting me onto him as he slides inside me.

I bury my face in the crook of his neck as he enters me. Admiring the scent that I can only get so close, savoring it one last time.

"Tyler…I don't know–"

He grabs my face, "Yes, you do, Sunny. Your body knows mine."

Frustration has me digging my nails into his back, and biting his lip so hard it bruises.

He gives my thigh a slap while his other arm tightens around me. "Open up for me, baby."

Leaning my head back against the wall behind me, he kisses the column on my neck and tongues the scar there, the one we will share forever.

Nothing about this is gentle. Each of his thrusts grows wilder and deeper, making items fall from the shelf above us. As much as I know I should stop this, I fear we are already too late.

So, I divulge.

"Tyler…Tyler, don't stop. Don't stop," I say, already feeling myself crescendo to the edge with a series of moans and claw marks across his back.

"Fuck, baby, I'd never dream of it."

Something about my words drives him unhinged. With my back against the wall and him leaning into me, there is nowhere to go and nothing to do, but take everything he's giving me. His arm tightens around me, the other slapping against the wall to steady himself. Nips, bites, bruised lips, and claw marks.

There is no beginning or end. We're one as we become a tangle of fire and darkness.

Sweat sheens across both our skin, giving me all the best

angles of his perfectly carved muscles that work in congruence to please me. He removes a hand from the wall and grabs my thigh, unlocking my legs so I'm open for him.

Through the chaos, his hand grips the back of my neck, pressing our foreheads together.

This is sweaty, possessive, angry, but fuck, *it's so good.*

I can feel the orgasm kindling. A fucking inferno ready to be raged inside me. My moans turn to screams as the fire engulfs inside my body. Roaring from my core and coursing through my veins, seizing me entirely.

Together, his groans and my moans become one in the air around us. He doesn't stop as he continues wildly in me, prolonging the already consuming pleasure that devastatingly holds me captive.

"There it is. Don't stop, Sunny. Keep going. Fucking ignite," he demands. His hand slams against the wall behind my head as some primal sound erupts from him.

I can't tell if this is one grand prolonged orgasm or a series of multiple ones. All I know is I'm consumed.

"Fuck, Sunny, fuck!" he yells. Both hands slam against the wall on either side of my head. His body tenses and seizes as his dick pulses inside me, filling me up and making me whole all at once.

We're both panting heavily as we come down from the flames. Our foreheads press together and our eyes meet when we realize what we've done.

He hooks my hair behind my ear and out of my face while his eyes search my face for an answer to the question that lingers between us.

What does this mean?

He cradles my face and brings his lips to mine. This kiss is gentle unlike the chaos that just unfolded between us. Unlike the raging inferno we created, this is a small flame, creating an aura of peace rather than a fire ready to consume the world.

He thumbs the lips he just ever so gently kissed, savoring this moment. Because just as quickly and frantically as it came, it'll leave, too.

Because we absolutely cannot do it again.

TYLER

I watch as the steam from the shower trails from the bathroom, wondering how I somehow convinced her to stay. To shower and sleep off our argument and discuss everything tomorrow with clear minds.

She didn't seem sure, but at least she hasn't left.

Yet.

Just as I think everything is okay, that we somehow made up through closet sex and words that have been waiting to be said, I hear small sobs come from her in the bathroom.

My own heart fucking cracks in my chest, bearing itself to the world if it means it'll take her pain.

I did this to her. I am the reason behind those tears. It doesn't matter how much I tried to explain my reasoning to her. She still sees it as a betrayal. And I don't fucking blame her.

Bringing my face to my hands, I sit on the edge of our bed. I hurt her when I told myself I'd do anything to protect her. But I couldn't protect her from *me*.

I glance over at the pile of clothes and belongings of hers that sits in the corner of our room. She was going to stay. Or at least consider it. But then she saw my best kept secret. Her whole life reduced down to paper and computer screens.

I won't apologize for doing what I'm doing. I sure as hell will spend the rest of my time trying to make it up to her. She has a few days left. A few days for me to rally up my lawyers and do this the way she wants to do it.

The shower shuts off and my heart pummels in my chest. We didn't say anything after our moment in the closet. It was fast, it was heated, it was what I thought was making up. But something tells me it might've been something different to her.

After a few grueling minutes, she steps out of the bathroom wearing baggy sweatpants and an oversized t-shirt. She towels her wet, wild hair.

We stare at one another for a beat, both still not knowing what to do next. We've never really fought. Not like this, at least.

It somehow feels like the end, even though we both desperately don't want it to be.

I stand and step into her, cradling her face and brushing her wet hair back. "Can we just take the night to let our emotions calm down and talk about everything tomorrow with clear minds?"

Her gaze is elsewhere, but then her eyes flick up to me and she nods.

"Okay." I feel my chest decompress just a little bit.

It's a step. A baby one, but a step, nonetheless. If there's anything I learned about Sunny over these last few months is I need to give her room for that and take what she gives me. Then give it back to her double. Patience has become my new best friend as I've navigated these last few months with her.

I nod and kiss her forehead. "Just sleep, baby. Just sleep here." I grab her hand to lead her to our bed. Because it's *our* bed. There is no place for anyone else but her in it.

She doesn't say anything as she crawls under the covers and snuggles herself up to me. I curl my arm around her and hold on for dear fucking life because I am not ready to let my girl go.

I never have been, I never will be.

I wake up in full panic, sweat coating my body, my heart beating wildly in my chest, that tug in my soul yanking me awake.

I haven't had a nightmare in a while, but after the night we had, it doesn't surprise me. It regurgitated a lot from both of us.

My eyes open and my hand searches the bed for Sunny. Feeling the emptiness where she normally lays, my eyes open wide as I try to adjust to the darkness in the room and rid the sleep from my mind.

"Sunny?" I ask into what I realize is an empty room. A room where I only exist right now.

"No," I choke as I fumble from the bed.

She's gone.

Her pile of belongings are gone from the corner of our room. I run to the closet to see all her clothes that once hung there are also gone, and all that remains are empty hangers. I look in the bathroom to see her toothbrush no longer sits next to mine.

My chest heaves up and down as I bring a hand to my mouth to try and stop the sounds that want to escape it.

I thought she was going to stay. I thought we were going to work this out. I thought that maybe, just maybe she could see why I did what I did. I thought things were going right instead of so wrong.

What once was a full heart becomes a void. Frantically it beats in my chest as it loses a part of itself, leaving a hollow, jagged mess. The lack of her so ever present, and that string now screaming as she slips from me.

That soul bridge now seems so long, her too far, that no matter how loud I yell, no matter how much my heart calls her name, she will never hear, and she will never come back.

I turn back into my bedroom and pick up my phone off the nightstand. I have one single text from her.

> I took the night to think, and I know what I need to do.

CHAPTER NINETY-ONE
TYLER

Before I know it, I'm unlocking the door to Sam's apartment with shaky hands, struggling to open it through blurred tear-filled eyes.

I didn't even think before getting in my truck and driving here in the middle of the night.

As soon as Sunny walked out the door, leaving me in bed oblivious to the hollowness I'd wake up to, it's like something inside me snapped, waking me to realize my new reality.

A life without her.

I spent every free minute I had tracking Ryan down and I still don't know where he is. All my efforts and exhaustion have led to the one thing I didn't want it to lead to.

Sunny walking out the door.

Defeat. That's what this unfamiliar feeling is. It grips my chest like a vice, making everything I am feel worthless. Failure courses my veins and fills my chest in place of her.

My entire purpose is her. My heart is so filled with her, I can't even call it my own anymore. Yet somehow, it has been wasted, failed, and defeated because I can't even protect or save the one reason for my existence.

It isn't something I'm familiar with, and I'm not happy about this introduction to one another. It's like a fucking sucker punch to my gut, leaving a hallow void where my girl once filled me.

I wanted to know the parts of her that died and came back to life. I wanted to know the things that haunt her as she tries to find rest from her long days. I wanted to know why her home was full of ghosts and why she swore to never go back. I wanted to know the strings inside her that kept her together since mine were so deeply woven there, to. And for how long they'd last until they snapped. I wanted to know why she refused to tell anyone about her past and why she left scarred and wrecked, refusing to let anyone help her.

It made me angry and useless, not being able to understand these things. Even after six months of feeling like I knew every part of her, it made me realize I still barely know who she is.

And I hate it because despite the fact I have the knowledge of her entire life in my hands, on my computer, scattered across my desk, despite the fact I spent the last six months exploring her body and soul, I simply don't know her at all.

And I hate it because while my mind screams at me to say she is the absolute worst person in the world for shattering my heart, it also tells me she's the best. Because even at her hands, my broken heart will still undeniably beat for her.

I curse and praise the man who came before me for not giving her exactly what she needed but leading her to me. But fuck him for making her so broken she can't even understand a love that expects nothing in return.

She's gone now. And I'll never be whole again.

I won't stop searching. Not then, not now. The damage is done. And she made it clear what she wants to do. Because of what I did to her. Am I no better than Ryan?

This won't be one of those things where my heart was so broken and shattered that I won't believe in love or that it doesn't exist. Because it does.

It exists in her.

In me.

In us.

I only ever thought there were two kinds of love. The kind you'd kill for and the kind you'd die for. But she, she is the kind of love I want to fucking *live* for.

Sam emerges from her loft with a bat in her hand, ready to fight me as the intruder. I didn't even call, I didn't warn her and probably scared her.

"Tyler?" She flips the lights on. "Oh, Tyler." She places a hand over her mouth.

"She left." I look at my sister through tear blurred eyes. "She left. She fucking left. I don't know why I didn't think she would. But she left," I sob, as if all the pain in my life is finally coming to the surface, and I can't stop it.

I can't breathe. *I can't fucking breathe.*

The pain, the fucking pain consumes me the way she did. It takes her place. It's like I have smoke inhalation in the wake of the fire inside her that devoured me and has now been put out. And yet I still desperately want to follow the smoke trail, hoping it will lead me back to her.

Falling to my knees in my sister's apartment, the sobs take over. I don't even recognize the sounds coming from my own mouth. *I don't recognize myself.*

Sam is immediately on her knees, hugging me as I cry into her neck. "I know, Tyler. I know. I think we all clung to a little bit of hope that she felt safe enough to stay with us."

I know now that you truly lose a part of yourself when you lose someone you love. And I know that the only thing stronger than my love for Sunny is the pain that comes with missing her. The only thing stronger than that is my need to protect her.

"It's okay. It's okay," she continues.

But it's not okay. Call me obsessive, call me delusional, call me pathetic. I don't care. I love that girl. That won't ever change.

"I thought she changed her mind? I thought she was going to talk to you about meeting with our lawyers?" She cups my face, searching for answers.

"I fucked up. I broke a promise to her. And I hurt her," I admit.

"What did you do?"

"I've been tracking Ryan."

She stills, nipping at her lip as she contemplates her answer. "I don't blame you one bit."

I finally gain my composure, swallow hard and nod.

"Did you find him?" she asks.

"No." I shake my head. "Not yet."

"Find him, Tyler. Don't stop. Find him so our girl can be free."

I nod because I never planned on stopping.

I know that I'd do his life all over again, if it meant that I could experience these last six months with Sunny again. Even if it had the same ending. I'd go through this pain over and over if it meant I got what we had each time.

Not everyone is as lucky as we are to experience a love like this.

She isn't just a chapter. No, she's the whole fucking story.

CHAPTER NINETY-TWO

SUNNY

The clock ticked out and the days on my calendar were etched off. And suddenly, I am out of time. My world here in Boston has come to an end.

Saying my goodbyes was more painful than I care to describe.

So I won't.

All I can say is it was filled with a lot of tears. And my heart broke apart, leaving a big portion behind with each of them.

This family taught me how to love after loss. I didn't just learn how to love romantically again. I learned that love is so much more than that.

It's with each of them.

Love and healing isn't just a boy and a girl, man and woman who find one another. It's friendship turned into family. It's coffee at Betty's Beans. Nights in one another apartments, cooking dinner, picking out bad movies, laughing around a table as we share a meal.

It's pool tournaments at Martha's and dancing even when you don't feel like it. It's painting in the art studio and sparring in the gym.

It's walking along the harbor, watching the city as the sun shines down on my skin to a paint class that I didn't realize would alter my entire life.

It's exploring Boston at midnight, running wild around the city, finally feeling some semblance of recklessness and freedom as the rain hits my skin after an almost kiss.

It's a couch that was once empty, but somehow overflowed with people who were strangers mere months ago but are now the closest thing I have to family, and the ones making me question any plans I've had for months.

It's finding home when you have to leave yours behind.

But Tyler and I's love…

Our love is late night kisses. Foreheads pressed together. Watching one another from across the room, staring at the other, only to catch the other staring, too.

It's a hand on a thigh. A finger tracing our features. It's a place between comfort and chaos. Safety and danger. His nose in my hair, mine in his neck. It's matching scars because my pain is his and his is mine.

It's a reminder you're living. It moves and exists with each breath we take. Echoes each heartbeat.

It's the little infinity we somehow sit in together in our minds where the night sky and fiery daylight meet. It's endless. It has no beginning, no end. It simply exists.

And it's ours.

It's something that will find us through our lifetimes, timelines, dimensions, worlds. Just as it did here, just as I'm sure it has before. Even if only for a glimmer of a moment. Not a lifetime, but a moment that I will remember for my entire life.

Maybe we won't get this entire life, but I know damn sure we have before, and we will again. We will find one another again. We always do. We always will.

And I try to make peace and comfort in that, even if everything in me tries to tell me otherwise.

I walked home in the dead of the night, silently crying the pain out, hoping it would make it easier.

It didn't.

But we fell in love. No matter how or when, we still did. That's more than most people ever get.

Over and over my mind screams the same thing; this is not what I want. *This is not what I want.* But life grabs me by the neck, suffocating the hope I once had and says, *but this is what you need.*

I spent the rest of the day finishing the packing and loading up the U-Haul I rented to drive to Colorado.

I'm grateful I chose this route. I'm even more grateful Sam let me rent it in her name to avoid anything else Ryan could track, despite my name being legally changed. The extra precaution makes me feel better.

The drive will give me time to process everything that happened over the course of the last six months. It'll give me time to grieve and try to move on. *Move forward.*

He broke his promise, and it snapped me out of my irrational thinking and back into logic. Back into my original plan – running.

There were instincts I thought I'd built up over the years of working in healthcare. But after Ryan, it was hard to accept the fact I'd been wrong about the one person who was part of the foundation of my life. And I'd been so foolish to let it happen again.

I kept the couch.

It's my reminder that even on the days it's empty, it was once filled with people I love. It's my reminder that nothing is forever, and change is ever present.

I walk into my kitchen that is now scattered with boxes, glancing around the growing empty space. I'm going to miss this apartment. This city. It's healed me in ways I never expected it too, and clearly it gave me a life and friends I never anticipated

I'd have.

I let it serve as proof that I'm capable of starting over again.

If I could have such a great experience here, I can have it wherever I go next, too.

I sip my coffee, looking around my almost empty apartment, imagining the day I'd picked it out, so scared, thinking life is so unfair.

Some things don't change.

Because that's life.

So fucking unfair.

CHAPTER NINETY-THREE
SUNNY

I tape box after box, lost in my own thoughts. It's all hitting me at once as I stand alone in my almost empty apartment, wrapping up my final moments here.

It's becoming too real. *I am leaving.*

Clearly I'm not good at the leaving thing. I spent my whole life living in one place. Moving around will take adjustment like anything else, but it's something I have to do. Or at least, that's what I try to convince myself.

Tomorrow morning is my target departure considering my tired body desperately needs a night's rest. So I lay on my mattress, looking through my emails to confirm the start date of my next job. I sit up, realizing Ryan and I's anniversary is coming up.

Once upon a time, the thought made me giddy. I loved tallying those months that turned to years. I was proud of the ever-growing number.

Then I realize…

I count the years on my hand and gasp as the realization dawns on me.

My fucking IUD expired.

Panicked gasps leave my lips as I stare at the number on my trembling hand. My heart beating a litany of screams as to how I could let this slip.

I'd gotten an IUD around the time we started dating so we could be safe. Five years comes and passes so easily. I changed my number so I didn't receive my reminder texts and calls from my doctor's office back home.

I clutch the phone in my trembling hand, trying to back track to when it expired. I'd gotten it a few months before our actual anniversary date so my body would adjust... when we'd started talking. Which means it expired *at least* two months ago.

Fuck.

TYLER

"We can just bail," Sam says while we both sit in her jeep outside of our parents' house.

I look at the red brick and marble pillars, wondering how I still come back when once upon a time I'd tallied the days until I was able to get out.

I spent the remainder of the night and day at Sam's place. We watched TV and ordered food until we had to leave for our obligatory dinner with our parents. It's the last place I want to be, but where else would I go? I'm convinced these dinners are the one thing that keeps my mother hanging on.

I shake my head and check my phone one last time. "No, it's okay."

"I don't think she is going to text you," Sam says with a broken look.

"That's not what I'm worried about." I grab the flowers from the back seat. "Come on. Let's get this over with."

After thirty minutes of cocktails and tension, I sit with my hands in my lap and stare at the expensive food in front of me while my parents chat together about things I don't care about.

Lamb chops.

We are eating fucking lambchops for dinner and Sunny is leaving. There's too many forks and spoons to choose from, and despite the fact I grew up learning those types of manners, I've completely forgotten the purpose behind each.

I toy with the smallest spoon, the voices of my parents and sister background to the thoughts in my own mind.

Defeat is crushing. It's suffocating. For some reason, I can't pull myself from the rubble of it.

I feel my phone vibrate in my pocket, but I don't look at it to save an argument from my mother. She only gets a numbered, scheduled time with us, so I'll let it be unbothered if I can.

"Tyler?" She interrupts my thoughts. I look at her concern with furrowed brows. "Are you okay, honey?"

I don't think I'll ever be okay again.

I don't even know what to say, but before I can even think of it, my father speaks. And I'm about ready to make him wish he hadn't. I'm so close to stapling his fucking mouth shut.

"He is just pouting because that little blonde girl, who, by the way, lied about herself, is leaving."

My eyes flick to my father. *I love her, Mitchell. Do you even know what love feels like?*

Another vibration in my pocket.

He doesn't miss a beat, doesn't even wait for a reaction from me, because he knows he won't get one. I don't have the goddamn energy anyways.

A part of me is gone with you now, Sunny.

Then my phone rings again.

SUNNY

I sprint to the pharmacy to grab a test.

Not just one, but five.

A shadow of eeriness radiates down my spine as I frantically rummage through the pharmacy. The ever present feeling of someone watching me persists despite my unrelated panic.

I pee on every single one of the tests, laying them all out upside down in the pharmacy bathroom because I couldn't wait to go home.

I sit on the bathroom floor, foot tapping as I count the minutes until I can look at the tests.

All at once that broken heart of mine slams against my sternum, the pain of it lacing through my bones just as the panic does while it shreds apart my chest.

I clasp my shaking hands and curl into myself as the time to look approaches. Yet I can't bring myself to. But then it's all I want to do. The chances still have to be low, right? It's only a few months expired.

Finally, I sum up the courage and grab a test that sits before me with shaky hands, waiting to find out my fate.

I keep my eyes closed and take a deep breath.

As I flip the test over, and I'm greeted by two dark pink lines staring back at me.

The panic rises like bile in my throat. Or maybe it *is* bile.

I flip over the next, two more pink lines stare back at me.

I flip over the two digitals that read *Pregnant,* like it's mocking me for even thinking it wasn't a possibility.

My body tremors so profoundly my bones shake and some of the tests fall to the floor.

Leaning back against the wall, I slide down to the floor as a painful sob claws up my throat.

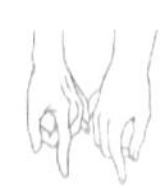

I pick up all the scattered tests and shove them in my bag, rummaging through it to find my phone, but it isn't there. I must've left it on the bed. I pause, trying to steady my breathing.

"Get your fucking self together, Sunny," I mutter before I step out of the bathroom.

I try to gain my composure but the panic still shows as a shaky hand reaches for the doorknob of the bathroom. That lingering impending doom storm cloud is a torrential downpour on me now.

Walking home in the glow of the dusky sky, it's quiet outside, and there isn't a lot of activity on the streets. I swipe at my runny nose as I glance around me.

I'm supposed to leave *tomorrow*.

I thought I was panicking before, but I'm fucking panicking now. I have no clue what to do. *This changes everything.*

Feeling the nausea hit again, I know it isn't caused by nerves. No, it's something much bigger, more terrifying than ever. It's a part of me, and a part of Tyler inside me. I'm taking a part of him with me. And I have to tell him, right?

We're over. But I also know, me and Tyler will never truly be over, because of that damn string, that connection between us, yanking us together.

And now…. Something else ties us together and could potentially connect us *forever*.

The guilt overwhelms me. I'm leaving and now with this heavy secret I haven't told anyone. And I think back to Sam's words when she found out she was pregnant with Cole's baby.

I wish I had told him as soon as I found out.

Taking a deep breath, I know what I have to do.

CHAPTER NINETY-FOUR

TYLER

Cole's name flashes across my screen, making me crease my brows as I stand from the dining table. "I need to take this. It's Cole. Could be about work."

"Go on," Mitchell says.

I don't need his fucking permission. So without another word, I walk into the living room where I look at all the antiques my mother has acquired over the years.

I tap the answer button. "Cole –" I'm cut off by my frantic brother.

"Ryan is in the city, Tyler!" he yells, the sheer panic ripping through each word. A car door slams, indicating he is leaving wherever he was. I'm almost certain my heart stops beating.

Everything I've done since I knew what she was running from led me to this moment.

To find Ryan.

So I can kill him.

It's a brief moment where I stand without a reaction, trying to piece together the words on the other end of the phone. And once they formulate the one thing I've been trying to bring together myself, I snap into action.

"Where?" I growl, running to the coat closet to find my keys.

"Her apartment complex! He's outside her apartment, Tyler! I back tracked her feed and he was there when you were gone. He's been here for a fucking week. We know what that means. He's waiting for his moment."

Of course, *of course* I know what that means. Because I'd done it myself when I was given hits on people. You follow your target around. You learn their routines so you can know when the best time to strike is. You know every little detail about what they do, who they do it with and who they are so you can take their weaknesses and use it against them. *Of course* I fucking know.

"Where is she?" My panic rips through my calm.

"She's not there. I don't know where she is," he blows a breath. "I didn't have time to hack the city cameras, I just left Macey's parents house on instinct. I don't want to miss him, he's been stalking her. Fucking stalking her."

"I'm leaving my parents right now." I finally get my keys from my coat.

We finally found him. But somehow, we are too late. We are always too fucking late.

"Tyler, where are you going?" Sam walks in, our parents following along.

"Ryan's here. I need to get Sunny. You need to stay here." I kiss her on the forehead.

"What? How do you know?" she asks, pulling her phone from her purse.

"Cole saw him on our camera feed outside Sunny's apartment." I scroll through all the fucking alerts I'd missed in my dinner with my parents. There he is, hovering outside her apartment complex like a ghost.

"He's probably been following her since he's been here for a week already. Sam, I need you to call her and text her. Blow up her phone. She probably won't answer me, but I'll keep trying.

Tell her not to return to her apartment under any circumstances. Don't stop, okay? Leave her texts. Leave her voicemails. I need to go. You don't fucking leave this house. I love you." I exit the house.

"Tyler?" I hear my mother call out now.

"Tyler Caddell, what the hell do you think you're doing?" I hear Mitchell.

But it all feels like background noise as I anxiously wait for Sunny to answer her phone. "Come on Sunny. *Come on.*" The rings continue until I hit her voicemail. "Sunny, please answer the phone. Ryan is here, he's outside your apartment. Don't under any circumstance go home. Go to our home, baby and stay there. Stay there and don't leave. I'm coming, Sunny. I'm coming." I hang it up to only call again. I 'm greeted by her voicemail again. "God dammit!" I hit the steering wheel.

I can only hope she left the city already.

That's when I realize I never placed my gun back in my glove compartment.

I'm coming, little fire.

CHAPTER NINETY-FIVE

SUNNY

My heart rate finally calms down to a reasonable, functional rate and my breathing has slowed from hyperventilating, but my panic is still very much alive.

The sun starts to slowly set, making the night air cool down rapidly. A shiver goes across my body as I make my way back to my apartment.

How do I even initiate a conversation after leaving him in the dead of night? After the argument we had?

The thoughts reignite the anxiety, my battered heart pumping the panic through my veins, singeing what little calm I'd managed to gather.

I stop in my walk, realizing he'll be at his parents' dinner. Maybe I should wait at his place for him? I turn around, taking a few steps in that direction but quickly realize I need my phone to access the house anyways since I left it there and the key he'd given me I'd left on his kitchen island in my departure.

When I reach my apartment, I glance around, unable to shake the feeling of being watched. No one is around, so I walk up the stairs on shaky legs and open the door to my empty apartment.

My phone still sits on my mattress, lighting up in the dark with Tyler's name on it as it flashes across the screen.

I only make it a few steps before I stop, seeing the light from my phone screen illuminate a figure standing in the corner of my apartment. The glint of my gun brings my eyes where he holds it in his hand.

I stumble back when a familiar sadistic smile spreads across those lips I'd memorized. Unhinged brown eyes meet mine from the few feet that separate us.

Instinct takes over, and I turn to the door but am immediately stopped when the safety of the gun clicks off.

I was so fucking close.

I feel a scream build in my throat, desperately clawing its way out but nothing comes out as I make eye contact with the ghost of my past standing before me.

His round brown eyes go wild with shock, as if he wasn't expecting to see me, just as much as I wasn't expecting to see him here.

The same man that I left six months ago stands here tonight. I realize the switch never turned off because the person I once saw in his eyes is long gone now.

If there's anything I know is that you don't have to be anyone important to destroy another person's life. Because he has destroyed mine. *Over and over again.*

Ryan's voice echoes through my apartment, wrapping around my neck the way his hands did the night I left him, as he raises the gun at me.

"I finally fucking found you."

TO BE CONTINUED....

ACKNOWLEDGMENTS

What started as a dream that morphed into a pestering idea awoke the writer in me from years of slumber. On nights when I should've been studying, I found myself immersed in this story, unable to stop until they finally got their voices. Years of growth, effort, hours and ideas have led to this moment—my book in your hands. Thank you for not only giving my work the time, but Tyler and Sunny's voices the space to be heard. They are my babies, the first story I'd been brave enough to complete in adulthood. Because of them, I now have a series of completed books, waiting for their moment once Tyler and Sunny have theirs. I can't wait for you all to see what has become, because of the two above.

To the Indie Forge team, thank you so much for taking a chance on my story and being the leading voice throughout this process. Had it not been for your company, I probably wouldn't have taken the leap to publishing. So thank you so much for bringing my story to life and believing in me and Tyler and Sunny.

To my betas, the friends who stood with me through the chaos of getting this book published and celebrating all the wins and navigating all the lows—thank you for continuously being my voice of reason through it all.

To my husband, for always supporting my goals and dreams, even if they seem delusional or irrational. For being one of the very first people to read all the scenes that became the bricks to build this book.

Lastly, to my readers and author friends—thank you for taking the time to read this book, go on the journey with Tyler and Sunny and support my work in all faucets. Without you, there is no version of me as an author.